16.95

Cen

Blood on the Holly

*an anthology of Christmas crime
featuring members of Crime Writers of Canada
and their friends*

edited by Caro Soles

MYS
BLOOD

Baskerville Books

Toronto, Canada

HUNTINGTON BEACH PUBLIC LIBRARY
7111 Talbert Avenue
Huntington Beach, CA 92648

Blood on the Holly © 2007 by Caro Soles
All stories are copyright by their individual authors.

All rights reserved. The use of any part of this publication, reproduced, transmitted in any form or by any means, electronic, mechanical, photo copying, recording, or otherwise, or stored in a retrieval system, without the prior written consent of the publisher – or, in the case of photocopying or other reprographic copying, a license from the Canadian Copyright Licensing Agency – is an infringement of the copyright law.

"A Bigfoot Christmas" by James Powell appeared in *Ellery Queen Mystery Magazine*, 2005
"A Christmas Bauble" by Therese Greenwood appeared in the *Kingston Whig Standard*, 2003
"Blue Christmas" by Peter Robinson appeared in *Best British Mysteries IV*, Allison and Busby, 2006

Library and Archives Canada Cataloguing in Publication

Blood on the holly : stories / by Ed Hoch ... [et al.] ; edited by Caro Soles.

ISBN 978-0-9686776-7-4

    1. Detective and mystery stories, Canadian (English)
I. Hoch, Edward D., 1930- II. Soles, Caro

PS8323.D4B45 2007   C813'.087208   C2007-905045-X

ISBN: 978-0-9686776-7-4

Cover design by Caro Soles

Published by:
Baskerville Books
Box 19, 3561 Sheppard Avenue East
Toronto, Ontario, Canada M1T 3K8

www.baskervillebooks.com

Acknowledgments

This book would not be in your hands without the work of three special people: Cheryl Freedman, ever ready with sage advice on a surprising number of subjects; Jane Burfield, always an email away with her enthusiasm and support; and Madeleine Harris-Callway, who kept me organized. And of course, thanks to all the writers, well-known and otherwise, who handed me such great material. Most of these stories are original works, written for this anthology. I hope you, the reader, will enjoy them with your eggnog. It might, however, be wise to test any festive food or drink on your cat first.

Table of Contents

Chestnut Roasting

❦

Lyn Hamilton

*L*ittle Jimmy Malone figured it would take him eleven minutes—tops—before he'd be back drinking beer at Roxy's with the man whose house he'd just burgled. It would have, too, if some *eejit* hadn't moved the damn Christmas tree.

Up until this moment, it had all gone smoothly, if not totally according to plan: prominent announcement that he was going for a piss and a smoke, leaving his half-finished beer on the bar to prove he'd be back in a jiff; a two-and-a-half minute drive in his '95 Dodge Ram over to Canterbury Lane where the rich people lived. All that was required was a quick entrance into the kitchen, eight steps and a left turn, then thirteen steps across the marble floor into the bright yellow drawing room. He savoured that expression "drawing room," let it roll around in his mind. He'd taken to calling the room in which he lived "the drawing room." It made his girl, Casey Bell, laugh, a sound he liked to hear. How he loved that girl!

Jimmy knew about the thirteen steps and the marble floor and the yellow room because two days earlier, he'd cased the joint, pretending to look for termites. He didn't know if they had termites in these parts, at least he'd never seen one, didn't even have a clue what they looked like. But that was hardly the point. He'd been dressed in the plain blue coveralls he'd acquired a few years back for that very purpose, and had carried the only thing he could find that seemed appropriate: a plastic bottle with hose and applicator actually used to spray dandelions. He'd borrowed this whatchamacallit from his former job with the landscaping company

1

and had forgotten to return it. Or something like that. He'd proved himself quite adept at landscaping, a trade he'd learned in the slammer, except for the part about sucking up to the boss, that particular deficiency of his leading to regular periods of unemployment. Some day soon, he was going to have his own company, it not having escaped his attention that while the workers in landscaping companies are paid shit, the owner does just fine, thank you. He was going to call his company "James Malone, Exterior Design," or maybe even "James Michael Malone, Exterior Design." That had a classy ring to it and kind of distinguished him from the old geezer he'd once worked for. He was going to set up his business in the Big Smoke, too, not the rat's ass of a little town in which Casey and he currently found themselves. Casey would answer the phone.

The house looked absolutely empty, as it should. The lady of the house was having a little pre-Christmas get-together with her mother in Minneapolis and wouldn't be back until the next afternoon, the maid was enjoying her evening off, and the kids weren't coming home from college until Christmas Eve. Best of all, the snow had turned to hard ice, so there'd be no footprints as Jimmy sidled his way around the side of the house or in the unlikely event that he should have to make a speedy getaway out the back. There was nobody out strolling along the freezing pavement of Canterbury Lane, either.

The kitchen door slowed him down some, taking him longer than it should have to get in, even though it was one of those silly sliding jobs that a baby could open—and certainly no match for Jimmy Malone. They wouldn't even know it had been tampered with. The alarm system started beeping its warning as soon as he set foot in the kitchen, but he made it to the control panel near the front door and entered the code in time. The master of the house—the guy who was still sitting at the bar, making like he was just one of the boys in his jeans and plaid shirt, and buying rounds of drinks from time to time—had been just a teensy bit careless when they'd left the house together after Jimmy's inspection, and Jimmy had had no trouble seeing the code. It was "1–2–3–4," which hardly taxed his memory any and just proved that rich people aren't as smart as they like you to think they are.

Now all he had to do was take three packages from under the Christmas tree: one that he knew contained an iPod, the second a very nice laptop with all the bells and whistles, and the third a diamond necklace and earrings. He'd tear the wrapping paper off a couple more packages, bust a few tree ornaments, and scatter some paper around to make it all look good, but those three packages alone would make this one merry little Christmas for Jimmy Malone, all right.

But the frigging Christmas tree wasn't in the fancy drawing room where it had been on his previous visit, all decked out as it was in black and silver—what, Jimmy wondered, was the matter with red and green?—a turn of events that constituted something of a problem. He should have known this would happen. Casey had read him his horoscope that morning; it said if he was planning some big project, today was not the day to start it. Still, he couldn't see telling his employer that he'd blown the job because his stars weren't aligned right, and anyways, James Michael Malone wasn't one to back away from a challenge.

Like it or not, he was going to have to go searching for the blinking thing, which meant more opportunity to spread around some fingerprints and DNA. He wasn't sure what DNA was exactly, but he knew he shouldn't spit. As to fingerprints, let's just say his were to be found in a computer. Luckily, he'd worn gloves. First door he opened was to the dining room. It looked pretty fancy, with twelve chairs around this honking big table and lots of little thingies in some glass cabinet on the side, caught in the quick sweep of his flashlight. But no Christmas tree. Next stop the bloody library, what the rest of the world would call a den: walls of books that he'd bet real money the guy had never read, but again, no tree. That meant he was going to have to go upstairs, although why anybody'd have a Christmas tree in their bedroom was beyond him.

The first room he entered upstairs turned out to be the biggest closet he'd ever seen, one that even had room for a table with a mirror with lights all around it and lots of little bottles of goo lying about. He'd never seen so many clothes in his life, either: two walls of dresses and racks and racks of shoes before you even got to the bathroom beyond. The lady who lived there could open a store. He'd love to take a fancy dress or two for Casey, but it looked like the woman of the house was a skinny broad, not luscious like his girl. They'd have looked real good on his mum, though—rest her soul—even if she'd have been mad at him for stealing them.

The bathroom, when he was able to tear himself away from all the dresses, was like something from Mars. It was bigger than his room—maybe bigger than his whole rooming house!—with some gadget in it that he had never seen before, but which he decided, after some inspection and thought, was probably used for washing your feet. This inspection of the bathroom made him regret the three—make that three-and-a-half—beers he'd had at Roxy's before heading out on the job. He'd have liked to avail himself of the facilities, but he had a bad feeling that the DNA business applied here, same as it did to spit.

On the other side of this bathroom was a door to a second enormous closet. There were no windows in this one, so he closed the doors at either end of it carefully and switched on the light. This one belonged to the man of the house, the lord of the manor. This guy had as many shoes as his wife—if you can believe it—maybe more. Nice shoes, too. There was one whole rack of them: soft, soft leather—Jimmy knew the real thing when he felt it—with tassels. He'd never heard of this Gucci guy, but whoever he was, he sure knew how to make a fine pair of shoes. Size eleven, too. Jimmy took off his trainers, enjoyed for a minute the feel of the rather plush carpet under his stocking feet, and then slipped on the shoes. Man, they were nice. Jimmy did a little dance just to try them out, then counted the number of shoes with tassels. Twenty-two pairs! What did a guy need with twenty-two pairs of tasselled loafers? If he moved them all just a titch, the guy wouldn't notice for a long time that he had only twenty-one pairs, now would he?

He tied his trainers together and hung them around his neck, turned off the light, and slipped back across the bathroom and into the lady's dressing room again. There he chose a pair of black shiny shoes with bows—Ferragamo, whatever that meant—also nice. Size seven and a half. Casey was a seven, but maybe with a little padding in the toes, they'd do. After all, it wouldn't be exactly smart to take a pair for himself and nothing for his girl.

By this time, at least fifteen minutes had gone by, a rather long time for a piss and a smoke, so Jimmy figured he'd better pick up the pace a little. He'd have to string some tale when he got back, about how he'd met an old pal while he was out for a smoke and they'd been chewing the fat for awhile. Everybody would assume it was a fellow ex-con, but that he'd have to live with. It'd help if the rich guy who owned all these shoes would stand him to another beer.

Just off the bathroom was yet another door—like a guy could get lost just trying to get out of the can!—that led to a bedroom. The room was really dark, and it took a minute for Jimmy's eyes to adjust. It was then he had a terrible fright. There was someone in the bed! He stood stock still for a minute to two, listening as hard as he could. He could hear no quiet snore, no rustle of sheets, no breathing. At last, he turned on his flashlight.

The woman lay on her back, a strand of light hair across her face, one arm pinned behind her. A pool of blood soaked the bedding and the carpet beside the bed; a knife protruded from her chest. Jimmy pressed his ear to her nostrils and realized she was dead. She'd been pretty when she'd been alive, he decided, pretty and also kind. She looked sort of familiar, and he had this idea she'd been one of those ladies who'd served him Christmas dinner at the community hall last year—turkey with all the trimmings—after his mum had died and he'd had to go there for a decent meal. She was quite possibly the woman who'd smiled at him and slipped him a twenty when she left. He backed away and stood there, trying to steady his breathing, which was starting to sound like he was the one doing the dying.

Jimmy decided it was time to do a little contemplating. He didn't much like contemplating—did as little of it as he possibly could—but he figured when he had to, he could contemplate with the best of them, even if he had something of a reputation as a guy maybe lacking in brains. That asshole Garth Rainey had referred to Jimmy as the dumbest crook he'd ever had the pleasure of arresting, a taunt Jimmy considered unfair. Just because he'd parked his truck illegally and got a citation, a citation that placed him at the crime scene at the moment the theft of some stereo equipment had taken place, and had further compounded the problem by forgetting to pay said fine, thus bringing himself and his truck to the attention of Rainey within seventy-two hours, didn't mean he was dumb. He'd a lot on his mind at the time. His mum was sick and all. He wasn't as smart as that guy Einstein maybe, or the other one, the one in the wheelchair, Hawking it was, or something like that, who tried to explain black holes to people. If the structure of a black hole wasn't as useless a piece of information for everyday life as you could possibly get, Jimmy didn't know what was, and it sure wasn't going to help him out of this mess.

It was the tree that bothered him the most. He knew where it was now, of course. It was standing in front of the window in the room with the dead woman. A short burst from the flashlight revealed the packages he was looking for: the big one with the laptop, the small one with the iPod, and the squarish one with the necklace and earrings.

He decided he'd better go back to the beginning of this sorry affair, the moment when the rich guy had approached him. He'd felt kind of sorry for the guy, really. He'd never have agreed to help if he hadn't. He'd promised his mum on her deathbed that he'd give up the life of crime. If he were to be perfectly honest, though, feeling sorry for the guy was one thing. The five thousand dollars didn't hurt either.

This guy had gone all the way to the Big Smoke to buy a necklace and earrings for his little piece on the side. The wife had found the package before he'd been able to present it to the girlfriend and had assumed it was a Christmas present for her. He'd told the wife she couldn't have it until Christmas. The guy wanted someone to break into his house, steal the jewellery, make it look like a real robbery, and then bring him the package so he could give it to the girlfriend, while he commiserated with the wife about her gift being stolen. The rich guy'd hold up the bar as his alibi and would provide Jimmy with one, too. Jimmy had been straight for eight months now, ever since he'd met Casey, but the five thousand dollars, plus the iPod and the laptop he'd been told he could keep just to make the whole deal look authentic, was going to make a pretty good start for James Michael Malone, Exterior Design. In fact, he hadn't a hope in hell of starting the business without it.

The guy had shown him around the house—Jimmy in his blue coveralls with the dandelion whatchamacallit—while the maid was out shopping and the wife was at her art class. He'd promised Jimmy the kitchen door would be unlocked and the alarm system off, and had handed him an envelope with a thousand in cash as a down payment, the rest to follow when Jimmy handed over the bling.

Now that he was doing all this contemplating, though, Jimmy had to wonder why the guy didn't just buy some other jewellery for the girlfriend. For sure, he could afford it. Not only would it be a whole lot less trouble, but the wife would think he was a hero, and so would the mistress. That sounded like a pretty ideal situation, really. Mr. Lord of the Manor had said that the jewellery wasn't worth that much, that it had more sentimental value, really, than anything else. That might explain it, but Jimmy didn't think so. He ripped the wrapping paper off the blue velvet box and had a look. Jimmy'd worked with a jewellery thief, studied with the best, and these little baubles had to be worth maybe thirty thou. He could get downright sentimental about that kind of money, too, now that he thought about it.

The kitchen door had been locked, no problem for someone like Jimmy, but there was also the matter of the alarm system. It was supposed to be turned off, but it wasn't. If he hadn't been lightning fast with the "1–2–3–4," he'd be sitting in a cell, watching Garth Rainey on the other side of the bars laughing his ugly face off by now. And the tree, that—now what was

6

the word Casey had taught him the other day, the one that meant wandering? Peripatetic, that was it—that peripatetic tree: What the hell was that all about?

All this contemplation was giving Jimmy a headache, but the inescapable conclusion had been reached, and it was this: He'd been set up. He supposed it could have been the mistress who'd decided she wanted to be the lady of the manor and believed that divorce was not only too slow, but almost certain to cut into her future husband's income. But no, the kitchen door had been locked, the alarm had been left on, and the tree had been moved. He, Jimmy Malone, reformed burglar who was just trying to do a guy a favour, was supposed to dash all over the frigging house, leaving his spit and fingerprints everywhere while he looked for the tree, a search that would lead him right to the scene of the crime while the silent alarm summoned the cops. The story would be that the lady of the house had come upon him as he was stealing Christmas presents, and he'd killed her. While he was standing there like an eejit, the rich pervert was waiting at Roxy's for the police to arrive to tell him the terrible news. He was probably wondering what was taking so long. Jimmy could just see the jerk tearing up when he heard the grisly details, the look of pathetic gratitude when he was informed the perp had been caught.

Now what? The way out was hard to figure until Jimmy looked down at his feet. He was standing in the poor woman's blood at the side of the bed. Suddenly, he smiled. "You were real nice to me last Christmas and I'm truly sorry what happened to you, ma'am," he whispered. "Now, don't you worry. You did right by Jimmy Malone, and Jimmy Malone will do right by you." Three minutes later, he walked out the front door.

They were half way to Saskatchewan when the announcer on the Dodge Ram's radio, quoting one Officer Garth Rainey, said that wealthy businessman Jason Chestnut had been arrested for the murder of his wife, Jeannine. Acting on a tip from a concerned citizen, police had found Mrs. Chestnut's body on the second floor of their Canterbury Lane residence. The house's alarm system was armed but not tripped, and there was no sign of forced entry or evidence of a robbery. An expensive laptop and an iPod had not been taken, as good an indication as any that the murder had been committed by someone on the inside. More damning still, a trail of bloody footprints led from the body. A search of the property revealed Mr. Chestnut's shoes—tasselled loafers with traces of blood on the soles—in a plastic bag hidden in a hedge. Mr. Chestnut had been apprehended at a bar just two-and-a-half minutes from his home.

Casey fingered the diamond earrings and smiled at Jimmy as Garth Rainey's voice came over the airwaves. She was wearing the shiny black shoes with the bows made by that Ferragamo fellow, and they looked like they belonged there on her lovely feet. She'd put some tissue paper in the toes, just like he'd told her. Jimmy had made it clear they'd have to sell the necklace to get enough money to start the Exterior Design business, but that the shoes and earrings were hers to keep forever. In fact, Jimmy had told her everything. Casey leaned over to give him a quick kiss on the cheek as she switched stations on the radio and Bing Crosby's voice filled the Dodge. "Chestnuts roasting on an open fire," Casey sang along with Bing. Jimmy Malone decided, right then and there, that this was his best Christmas ever.

Lyn Hamilton *is the author of a successful series of archaeological mysteries published by Berkley Prime Crime in New York. The series features Toronto antique dealer Lara McClintoch, who travels the world in search of the rare and beautiful for her shop, finding more than a little murder and mayhem along the way. Each book in the series is set in a different and exotic location and calls upon the past in an unusual way. The first book,* The Xibalba Murders, *was nominated in 1998 for an Arthur Ellis Award for Best First Novel, and the eighth,* The Magyar Venus, *was nominated in 2005 for an Arthur Ellis Award for Best Novel. Book four,* The Celtic Riddle, *formed the basis for the 2003* Murder, She Wrote *made-for-TV movie, starring Angela Lansbury.*

Blue Christmas
an Inspector Banks Story

Peter Robinson

A *three-day holiday.* Banks sat down at the breakfast table and made some notes on a lined pad. If he was doomed to spend Christmas alone this year, he was going to do it in style. For Christmas Eve: Alastair Sim's *A Christmas Carol*, black-and-white version, of course. For Christmas Day: *Love, Actually.* Mostly it was a load of crap—no doubt about that—but it was worth it for Bill Nighy, and Keira Knightley was always worth watching. For Boxing Day: *David Copperfield,* the one with the Harry Potter actor in it, because it had helped him through a nasty hangover one Boxing Day a few years ago, and thus are traditions born.

Music was more problematic. Bach's *Christmas Oratorio* and Handel's *Messiah*, naturally. Both were on his iPod and could be played through his main sound system. But some years ago, he had made a Christmas compilation tape of all his favourite songs: from Bing's "White Christmas" to Elvis's "Santa Claus is Back in Town" and "Blue Christmas," The Pretenders' "2000 Miles," and Roland Kirk's "We Free Kings." Unfortunately, that had gone up in flames along with the rest of his music collection. Which meant a quick trip to HMV in Eastvale that afternoon to pick up a few seasonal CDs, so he could make a playlist. He had to go to Marks and Spencer, anyway, for his frozen turkey dinner, so he might as well drop in at HMV while he was in the Swainsdale Centre. As for wine, he still had a more than decent selection from his brother's cellar— including some fine Amarone, Chianti Classico, Clarets, and Burgundies—which would certainly get him through the next three days without any pain. Luckily, he had bought and given out all his Christmas presents earlier—what few there were: money for Tracy, a Fairport Convention boxed set for Brian, chocolates and magazine subscriptions for his parents, and a silver-and-jet bracelet for Annie Cabbot.

Banks put his writing pad aside and reached for his coffee mug. Beside it sat a pristine copy of Sebastian Faulks's *Human Traces*, which he fully intended to read over the holidays. There should be plenty of peace and quiet. Brian was with his band in Europe and wouldn't be able to get home in time. Tracy was spending Christmas with her mother, Sandra; stepdad, Sean; and their baby, Sinead; and Annie was heading home to the artists' colony in St. Ives, where they would all no doubt be having a good weep over *A Junkie's Christmas*, which Annie had told him was a Christmas staple among her father's crowd. He had seen it once himself, and he had to it admit that it wasn't bad, but it hadn't become a tradition with him.

All in all, then, this Christmas was beginning to feel like something to be got through with liberal doses of wine and music. Even the weather was refusing to cooperate. The white Christmas everyone had been hoping for since a tentative sprinkle in late November had not materialized, though the optimists at the meteorological centre were keeping their options open. At the moment, though, it was uniformly grey and wet in Yorkshire. The only good thing that could be said for it was that it wasn't cold. Far from it. Down south, people were sitting outside at Soho cafés and playing golf in the suburbs. Banks wondered if he should have gone away, taken a holiday. Paris. Rome. Madrid. A stranger in a strange city. Even London would have been better than this. Maybe he could still catch a last-minute flight.

But he knew he wasn't going anywhere. He sipped some strong coffee and told himself not to be so maudlin. Christmas was a notoriously dangerous time of year. It was when people got depressed and gave in to their deepest fears, when all their failures, regrets, and disappointments came back to haunt them. Was he going to let himself give in to that, become a statistic?

He decided to go into town now and get his last-minute shopping over with before it got really busy. Just before he left, though, his phone rang. Banks picked up the receiver.

"Sir? It's DC Jackman."

"Yes, Winsome. What's the problem?"

"I'm really sorry to disturb you at home, sir, but we've got a bit of a problem."

"What is it?" Banks asked. Despite having to spend Christmas alone, he had been looking forward to a few days away from Western Area Headquarters, if only to relax and unwind after a particularly difficult year. But perhaps that wasn't to be.

"Missing person, sir."

"Can't someone else handle it?"

"It needs someone senior, sir, and DI Cabbot's on her way to Cornwall."

"Who's missing?"

"A woman by the name of Brenda Mercer. Forty-two years old."

"How long?"

"Overnight."

"Any reason to think there's been foul play?"

"Not really."

"Who reported her missing?"

"The husband."

"Why did he leave it until this morning?"

"He didn't. He reported it at six o'clock yesterday evening. We've been looking into it. But you know how it is with missing persons, sir, unless it's a kid. It was very early days. Usually they turn up, or you find a simple explanation quickly enough."

"But not in this case?"

"No, sir. The husband's getting frantic. Difficult. Demanding to see someone higher up. And he's got the daughter and her husband in tow now. They're not making life any easier. I've only just managed to get rid of them by promising I'd get someone in authority to come and talk to them."

"All right," Banks said, with a sigh. "Hang on. I'll be right in."

Major Crimes and CID personnel were thin on the ground at Western Area Headquarters that Christmas Eve, and DC Winsome Jackman was one who had drawn the short straw. She didn't mind, though. She couldn't afford to visit her parents in Jamaica, and she had politely passed up a Christmas dinner invitation from a fellow member of the potholing club who had been pursuing her for some time now, so she had no real plans for the holidays. She hadn't expected it to be particularly busy in Major Crimes. Most Christmas incidents were domestic, and as such, they were dealt with by the officers on patrol. Even criminals, it seemed, took a bit of time off for turkey and Christmas pud. But a missing-person case could turn nasty very quickly, especially if she had been missing for two days now.

While she was waiting for Banks, Winsome went through the paperwork again. There wasn't much, other than the husband's report and statement, but that gave her the basics.

When David Mercer got home from work on December 23 at around six o'clock, he was surprised to find his wife not home. Surprised because she was always home and always had his dinner waiting for him. He worked in the administration offices of the Swainsdale Shopping Centre, and his hours were fairly regular. A neighbour had seen Mrs. Mercer walking down the street where she lived on the Leaside Estate at about a quarter past four that afternoon. She was alone and was wearing a beige overcoat and carrying a scuffed brown leather bag, the kind with a shoulder-strap. She was heading in the direction of the main road, and the neighbour assumed she was going to catch a bus. She knew that Mrs. Mercer didn't drive. She said hello, but said that Mrs. Mercer hadn't seemed to hear her, had seemed a bit "lost in her own world."

Police had questioned the bus drivers on the route, but none of them recalled seeing anyone matching the description. Uniformed officers also questioned taxi drivers and got the same response. All Mrs. Mercer's relatives had been contacted, and none had any idea where she was. Winsome was beginning to think it was possible, then, that someone had picked Mrs. Mercer up on the main road, possibly by arrangement, and that she didn't want to be found. The alternative—that she had been somehow abducted—didn't bear thinking about, at least not until all other possible avenues had been exhausted.

Winsome had not been especially impressed by David Mercer—he was the sort of pushy, aggressive white male she had seen far too much of over the past few years, puffed up with self-importance, acting as if everyone else were a mere lackey to meet his demands, especially if she happened to be black and female. But she tried not to let personal impressions interfere with her reasoning. Even so, there was something about Mercer's tone, something that didn't quite ring true. She made a note to mention it to Banks.

❧

The house was a modern Georgian-style semi with a bay window, stone cladding, and neatly kept garden, and when Banks rang the doorbell,

Winsome beside him, David Mercer opened it so quickly he might have been standing right behind it. He led Banks and Winsome into a cluttered but clean front room, where a young woman sat on the sofa wringing her hands and a whippet-thin man in an expensive, out-of-date suit paced the floor. A tall Christmas tree stood in one corner, covered with ornaments and lights. On the floor were a number of brightly wrapped presents and one ornament, a tiny pair of ice skates, which seemed to have fallen off. The radio was playing Christmas music faintly in the background.

"Have you heard anything?" David Mercer asked.

"Nothing yet," Banks answered. "But if I may, I'd like to ask you a few more questions."

"We've already told everything to her," he said, gesturing in Winsome's direction.

"I know," said Banks. "And DC Jackman has discussed it with me. But I still have a few questions."

"Don't you think you should be out there on the streets searching for her?" said the whippet-thin man, who was also turning prematurely bald.

Banks turned slowly to face him. "And you are?"

He puffed out what little chest he had. "Claude Mainwaring, solicitor. I'm Mr. Mercer's son-in-law."

"Well, Mr. Mainwaring," said Banks, "it's not normally my job, as a detective chief inspector, to get out on the streets looking for people. In fact, it's not even my job to pay house calls asking questions, but as it's nearly Christmas, and as Mr. Mercer here is worried about his wife, I thought I might bend the rules just a little. And believe me, there are already more than enough people out there trying to find Mrs. Mercer."

Mainwaring grunted as if unsatisfied with the answer; then he sat down next to his wife. Banks turned to David Mercer, who finally bade him and Winsome to sit, too. "Mr. Mercer," Banks asked, thinking of the doubts that Winsome had voiced on their way over, "can you think of anywhere your wife might have gone?"

"Nowhere," said Mercer. "That's why I called you lot."

"Was there any reason why your wife might have gone away?"

"None at all," said Mercer, just a beat too quickly for Banks's liking.

"She wasn't unhappy about anything?"

"Not that I know of, no."

"Everything was fine between the two of you?"

"Now, look here!" Mainwaring got to his feet.

"Sit down and be quiet, Mr. Mainwaring," Banks said as gently as he could. "You're not in court now, and you're not helping. I'll get to you later." He turned back to Mercer and ignored the slighted solicitor. "Had you noticed any difference in her behaviour before she left, any changes of mood or anything?"

"No," said Mercer. "Like I said, everything was quite normal. May I ask what you're getting at?"

"I'm not getting at anything," Banks said. "These are all questions that have to be asked in cases such as these."

"Cases such as these?"

"Missing persons."

"Oh God," cried the daughter. "I can't believe it. Mother: a missing person."

She used the same tone as she might have used to say "homeless person," Banks thought, as if she were somehow embarrassed by her mother's going missing. He quickly chided himself for being so uncharitable. It was Christmas, after all, and no matter how self-important and self-obsessed these people seemed to be, they *were* worried about Brenda Mercer. He could only do his best to help them. He just wished they would stop getting in his way.

"Has she ever done anything like this before?" Banks asked.

"Never," said David Mercer. "Brenda is one of the most stable and reliable people you could ever wish to meet."

"Does she have any close friends?"

"The family means everything to her."

"Might she have met someone? Someone she could confide in?"

Mercer seemed puzzled. "I don't know what you mean. Confide? What would Brenda have to confide? And if she did, why would she confide in someone else rather than in me? No, it doesn't make sense."

"People do, you know, sometimes."

"Not Brenda."

This was going nowhere fast, Banks thought, seeing what Winsome had meant. "Do you have any theories about where she might have gone?"

"Something's happened to her. Someone's abducted her, obviously. I can't see any other explanation."

"Why do you say that?"

"It stands to reason, doesn't it? She'd never do anything so irresponsible and selfish as to mess up all our Christmas plans and cause us so much fuss and worry."

14

"But these things—abductions and the like—are much rarer than you imagine," said Banks. "In most cases, missing persons are found healthy and safe."

Mainwaring snorted in the background. "And the longer you take to find her, the less likely she is to be healthy and safe," he said.

Banks ignored him and carried on talking to David Mercer. "Did you and your wife have any arguments recently?" he asked.

"Arguments? No, not really."

"Anything that might upset her, cause her to want to disappear?"

"No."

"Do you know if she has any male friends?" Banks knew he was treading on dangerous ground now, but he had to ask.

"If you're insinuating that she's run off with someone," Mercer said, "then you're barking up the wrong tree. Brenda would never do that to me. Or to Janet," he added, glancing over at the daughter.

Banks had never expected his wife, Sandra, to run off with another man, either, but she had done. No sense in labouring the point, though. If anything like that had happened, the Mercers would be the last people to tell him, assuming that they even knew themselves. But if Brenda had no close friends, then there was no one else he could question who might be able to tell him more about her. All in all, it was beginning to seem like a tougher job than he had imagined.

"We'll keep you posted," he said, and then he and Winsome headed back to the station.

Unfortunately, most people were far too absorbed in their Christmas plans—meals, family visits, last-minute shopping, church events, and what have you—to pay as much attention to local news stories as they did the rest of the time, and even that wasn't much. As Banks and Winsome whiled away the afternoon at Western Area Headquarters, uniformed police officers went from house to house asking questions and searched the wintry Dales landscape in an ever-widening circle, but nothing came to light.

Banks remembered, just before the shops closed, that he had things to buy, so he dashed over to the Swainsdale Centre. Of course, by closing time on Christmas Eve, it was bedlam, and everyone was impatient and bad-tempered. He queued to pay for his turkey dinner because he would have had nothing else to eat otherwise, but just one glance at the crowds in HMV made him decide to forgo the Christmas music for this year, relying on what he had already and what he could catch on the radio.

By six o'clock, he was back at home, and the men and women on duty at the police station had strict instructions to ring him if anything concerning Brenda Mercer came up.

But nothing did.

Banks warmed his leftover lamb curry and washed it down with a cold beer. After he finished the dishes, he made a start on *Human Traces*, then opened a bottle of claret and took it with him into the TV room. There, he slid the shiny DVD of *A Christmas Carol* into the player, poured himself a healthy glass, and settled back. He always enjoyed spotting the bit where you could see the cameraman reflected in the mirror when Scrooge examines himself on Christmas morning, and he found Alastair Sims's over-the-top excitement at seeing the world anew as infectious and uplifting as ever. Even so, as he took himself up to bed around midnight, he still had a thought to spare for Brenda Mercer, and it kept him awake far longer than he would have liked.

The first possible lead came early on Christmas morning when Banks was eating a soft-boiled egg for breakfast and listening to a King's College Choir concert on the radio. Winsome rang to tell him that someone had seen a woman resembling Mrs. Mercer in a rather dazed state wandering through the village of Swainshead shortly after dawn. The description matched, down to the coat and shoulder-bag, so Banks finished his breakfast and headed out.

The sky was still like iron, but the temperature had dropped overnight, and Banks thought he sniffed a hint of snow in the air. As he drove down the dale, he glanced at the hillsides, all in shades of grey, their peaks obscured by low-lying cloud. Here and there, a silver stream meandered down the slope, glittering in the weak light. Whatever was wrong with Brenda Mercer, Banks thought, she must be freezing if she had been sleeping rough for two nights now.

Before he got to Swainshead, he received another call on his mobile, again from Winsome. This time she told him that a local train driver had seen a woman walking aimlessly along the tracks over the Swainshead

Viaduct. When Banks arrived there, Winsome was already waiting on the western side along with a couple of uniformed officers in their patrol cars, engines running so they could stay warm. The huge viaduct stretched for about a quarter of a mile across the broad valley, carrying the main line up to Carlisle and beyond into Scotland, and its twenty or more great arches framed picture-postcard views of the hills beyond.

"She's up there, sir," said Winsome, pointing as Banks got out of the car. Way above him, more than a hundred feet up, a tiny figure in brown perched on the edge of the viaduct wall.

"Jesus Christ," said Banks. "Has anyone called to stop the trains? Anything roaring by her right now could give her the fright of her life, and it's a long way down."

"It's been done," said Winsome.

"Right," said Banks. "At the risk of stating the obvious, I think we'd better get someone who knows about these things to go up there and talk to her."

"It'll be difficult to get a professional, sir, on Christmas Day."

"Well, what do you...? No. I can read your expression, Winsome. Don't look at me like that. The answer's no."

"But you know you're the best person for the job, sir. You're good with people. You listen to them. They trust you."

"But I wouldn't know where to begin."

"I don't think there are any set rules."

"I'm hardly the sort to convince someone that life is full of the joys of spring."

"I don't really think that's what's called for."

"But what if she jumps?"

Winsome shrugged. "She'll either jump or fall if someone doesn't go up there soon and find out what's going on."

Banks glanced up again and swallowed. He thought he felt the soft, chill touch of a snowflake melt on his eyeball. Winsome was right. He couldn't send up one of the uniformed lads—they were far too inexperienced for this sort of thing—and time was of the essence.

"Look," he said, turning to Winsome. "See if you can raise some sort of counsellor or negotiator, will you? In the meantime, I'll go up and see what I can do."

"Right you are, sir." Winsome smiled. Banks got back in his car. The quickest way to reach the woman was drive up to Swainshead station, just before the viaduct, and walk along the tracks. At least that way, he wouldn't have to climb any hills. The thought didn't comfort him much, though, when he looked up again and saw the woman's legs dangling over the side of the wall.

❧

"Stop right there," she said. "Who are you?"

Banks stopped. He was about four or five yards away from her. The wind was howling more than he had expected—whistling around his ears, making it difficult to hear properly—and it seemed colder up there, too. He wished he was wearing something warmer than his leather jacket. The hills stretched away to the west, some still streaked with November's snow. In the distance, Banks thought he could make out the huge rounded mountains of the Lake District.

"My name's Banks," he said. "I'm a policeman."

"I thought you'd find me eventually," she said. "It's too late, though."

From where Banks was standing, he could only see her in profile. The ground was a long way below. Banks had no particular fear of heights, but even so, her precarious position on the wall unnerved him. "Are you sure you don't want to come back from the edge and talk?" he said.

"I'm sure. Do you think it was easy getting here in the first place?"

"It's a long walk from Eastvale."

She cast him a sidelong glance. "I didn't mean that."

"Sorry. It just looks a bit dangerous there. You could slip and fall off."

"What makes you think that wouldn't be a blessing?"

"Whatever it is," said Banks, "it can't be worth this. Come on, Brenda, you've got a husband who loves you, a daughter who needs—"

"My husband doesn't love me, and my daughter doesn't need me. Do you think I don't know? David's been shagging his secretary for two years. Can you imagine such a cliché? He thinks I don't know. And as for my daughter, I'm just an embarrassment to her and that awful husband of hers. I'm the shop-girl who married up, and now I'm just a skivvy for the lot of them. That's all I've been for years."

"But things can change."

She stared at him with pity and shook her head. "No, they can't," she said and gazed off into the distance. "Do you know why I'm here? I mean, do you know what set me off? I've put up with it all for years—the coldness, the infidelity—just for the sake of order, not rocking the boat, not causing a scene. But do you know what it was?"

"No," said Banks, anxious to keep her talking. "Tell me." He edged a little closer so he could hear her voice above the wind. She didn't tell him to stop. Snowflakes started to swirl around them.

"People say it's smell that sparks memory the most, but it wasn't, not this time. It was a Christmas ornament. I was putting a few last-minute decorations on the tree before Janet and Claude arrived, and I found myself holding these tiny, perfect ice skates I hadn't seen for years. They sent me right back to a particular day when I was a child. It's funny because it didn't seem like just a memory. I felt as if I was *really* there. My father took me skating on a pond somewhere in the country; I don't remember where. But it was just getting dark, and there were red and green and white Christmas lights and music playing—carols like "Silent Night" and "Away in a Manger"—and someone was roasting chestnuts on a brazier. The air was full of the smell. I was… My father died last year."

She paused and brushed tears or melted snowflakes from her eyes with the back of her hand. "I kept falling down. It must have been my first time on ice. But my father would just pick me up, tell me I was doing fine, and set me going again. I don't know what it was about that day, but I was so happy, the happiest I can ever remember. Everything seemed perfect, and I felt I could do anything. I wished it would never end. I didn't even feel the cold. I was just all warm inside and full of love. Did you ever feel like that?"

Banks couldn't remember, but he was sure he must have. Best to agree, anyway. Stay on her wavelength. "Yes," he said. "I know what you mean." It wasn't exactly a lie.

"And it made me feel worthless," she said. "The memory made me feel that my whole life was a sham, a complete waste of time of any potential I once might have had. And it just seemed that there was no point in carrying on." She shifted on the wall.

"Don't!" Banks cried, moving forward.

She looked at him. He thought he could make out a faint smile. She appeared tired and drawn, but her face was a pretty one, he noticed. A slightly pointed chin and small mouth, but beautiful hazel eyes. "It's all right," she said. "I was just changing position. The wall's hard. I just wanted to get more comfortable."

She was concerned about comfort. Banks took that as a good sign. He was within two yards of her now, but he still wasn't close enough to make a grab. At least she didn't tell him to move back. "Just be careful," he said. "It's dangerous. You might slip."

"You seem to be forgetting that's what I'm here for."

"The memory," said Banks. "That day at the pond. It's something to cherish, surely, to live for?"

"No. It just suddenly made me feel that my life's all wrong. Has been for years. I don't feel like *me* any more. I don't feel anything. Do you know what I mean?"

"I know," said Banks. "But this isn't the answer."

"I don't know," Brenda said, shaking her head. "I just feel so sad and so lost."

"So do I," said Banks, edging a little closer. "Every Christmas since my wife left me for someone else and the kids grew up and moved away from home. But it does mean that you feel something. You said before that you felt nothing, but you do, even if it is only sadness."

"So how do you cope?"

"Me? With what?"

"Being alone. Being abandoned and betrayed."

"I don't know," said Banks. He was desperate for a cigarette, but remembered that he had stopped smoking ages ago. He put his hands in his pockets. The snow was really falling now, obscuring the view. He couldn't even see the ground below.

"Did you love her?" Brenda asked.

The question surprised Banks. He had been quizzing her, but all of a sudden, she was asking about him. He took that as another good sign. "Yes."

"What happened?"

"I suppose I neglected her," said Banks. "My job…the hours…I don't know. She's a pretty independent person. I thought things were okay, but they weren't."

"I'm sure David thinks everything is fine as long as no one ruffles the surface of his comfortable little world. Were you unfaithful?"

"No. But she was. I don't suppose I blame her now. I did at the time. When she had a baby with him, that really hurt. It seemed…I don't know… the ultimate betrayal, the final gesture."

"She had a baby with another man?"

"Yes. I mean, we were divorced, and they got married and everything. My daughter's spending Christmas with them."

"And you?"

Was she starting to feel sorry for him? If she did, then perhaps it would help to make her see that she wasn't the only one suffering, that suffering was a part of life and you just had to put up with it and get on with things. "By myself," he said. "My son's abroad. He's in a rock group. The Blue Lamps. They're doing really well. You might even have heard of them."

"David doesn't like pop music."

"Well…they're really good."

"The proud father. My daughter's a stuck-up, social-climbing bitch who's ashamed of her mother."

Banks remembered Janet Mainwaring's reaction to the description of her mother as missing: an embarrassment. "People can be cruel," he said.

"But how do you cope?"

Banks found that he had edged closer to her now, within a yard or so. It was almost grabbing range. That was a last resort, though. If he wasn't quick enough, she might flinch and fall off as he reached for her. "I don't know," he said. "Christmas is a difficult time for all sorts of people. On the surface, it's all peace and happiness and giving and family and love, but underneath… You see it a lot in my job. People reach breaking point. There's so much stress."

"But how do *you* cope with it alone? Surely it must all come back and make you feel terrible?"

"Me? I suppose I seek distractions. *A Christmas Carol. Love, Actually*—for Bill Nighy and Keira Knightley—and *David Copperfield*, the one with the Harry Potter actor. I probably drink too much as well."

"Daniel Radcliffe. That's his name. The Harry Potter actor."

"Yes."

"And I'd watch *Love, Actually* for Colin Firth." She shook her head. "But I don't know if it would work for me."

"I recommend it," said Banks. "The perfect antidote to spending Christmas alone and miserable."

"But I wouldn't be alone and miserable, would I? That's the problem. I'd be with my family and miserable."

"You don't have to be."

"What are you suggesting?"

"I told you. Things can change. You can change things." Banks leaned his hip against the wall. He was so close to her now that he could have put his arms around her and pulled her back, but he didn't think he was going to need to. "Do it for yourself," he said. "Not for them. If you think your husband doesn't love you, leave him and live for yourself."

"Leave David? But where would I go? How would I manage? David has been my life. David and Janet."

"There's always a choice," Banks went on. "There are people who can help you. People who know about these things. Counsellors, social services. Other people have been where you are now. You can get a job, a flat. A new life. I did."

"But where would I go?"

"You'd find somewhere. There are plenty of flats available in Eastvale, for a start."

"I don't know if I can do that. I'm not as strong as you." Banks noticed that she managed a small smile. "And I think if I did, I would have to go far away."

"That's possible, too." Banks reached out his hand. "Let me help you." The snow was coming down heavily now, and the area had become very slippery. She looked at his hand, shaking her head and biting her lip.

"*A Christmas Carol*?" she said.

"Yes."

"I always preferred *It's a Wonderful Life.*"

Banks laughed. "That'll do nicely, too." She took hold of his hand, and he felt her grip tightening as she climbed off the wall and stood up. "Be careful now," he said. "The ground's quite treacherous."

"Isn't it just?" she said, and moved towards him.

Peter Robinson is the author of the Inspector Banks novels. His books have won or been short-listed for numerous awards, including the prestigious John Creasy Award (U.K.), the Edgar Award (U.S.), the Martin Beck Award (Sweden), and the Arthur Ellis Award (Canada). Peter is also known for his treatment of music in the series. "Blue Christmas" is a reprint of a little-known story, starring Inspector Banks. Peter lives in Toronto, Ontario, but takes numerous trips to catch up with things in Yorkshire.

Swiped:

a Zack Walker Story

Linwood Barclay

Every December, as Christmas approaches, I think back to that year when I ended up with the dead elf in my trunk.

It's not exactly a nostalgic recollection. We haven't turned the incident into a family tradition or anything. My wife, Sarah, does not, for example, say to me a couple of Saturdays before the twenty-fifth, "You know what we should do, Zack? We should go out, cut down a tree, maybe keep our eyes open for a dead elf along the side of the road." There's a thought. Elf roadkill.

The fact is, the dead-elf-in-the-trunk incident rarely comes up in conversation. I don't like to talk about elves. Not even live ones. I'm willing to tolerate the subject long enough, however, to tell what happened.

This was three years ago, and it was, in fact, a couple of Saturdays before Christmas. Sarah wanted to hit the mall, the massive one downtown that takes up a couple of entire city blocks, to look for, among other things, a bracelet for our seventeen-year-old daughter Angie. I was recruited for this mission because we were seeking, for Angie's fifteen-year-old brother Paul, accessories for the latest generation of some ridiculous video game system, and Sarah was under the impression that I was more knowledgeable about these things, even though I haven't been able to figure out the buttons on an electronic game since Pong.

We'd tried to get some Christmas shopping out of the way in the evenings, but Sarah had been working some extra shifts on the city desk at the *Metropolitan*, and even though I, as a stay-at-home writer of largely unsuccessful science fiction novels (published under my own name, Zack Walker), had time through the day to get errands of this type done, I was not trusted to tackle them alone.

Blood on the Holly

By the time I realized everyone in the world was driving downtown to shop this particular Saturday, it was too late to abort the mission and opt for the subway. I normally try to find a spot on the street, figuring that if Sarah knows she's up against a meter due to expire, she'll move things along a bit, but there was no chance of that. We were destined for the parking garage, which, at this particular mall, is down near the centre of the earth where, once you've parked and are headed for the elevator, you're likely to run into a Jules Verne expedition.

A large garage door rose up as we turned onto the parking ramp. I was expecting an attendant in a booth to hand us a ticket, but instead, there was a machine with instructions for me to swipe a credit card, which I would also have to swipe to get out. I dug my wallet out of my back pocket, pried out my VISA, powered down the window, swiped the card into the machine, powered the window back up, slid the card back into my wallet, put my wallet back…

Honk!

Sarah said, "I think you're holding things up."

I glanced in the mirror at the car behind me. "Dickwad," I said.

The ramp down into the parking garage was so steep I had my foot on the brake the whole time. We were descending in spiral fashion, the ramp a corkscrew into a subterranean world. By the time we came out onto the actual parking area, Sarah and I were both feeling woozy.

But we had our footing back by the time we stepped off the elevator into the heart of the mall. The place was so packed with shoppers Sarah and I could barely walk shoulder to shoulder, one of us always having to drop back to make way for people coming the other way.

We came upon the electronics store before the jewellery outlet, so we popped in to look for an extra controller and some other doodads for Paul's gaming system. There was already a line-up at the cash, so Sarah grabbed something at random, joined the line, and waited while I picked up the items we actually wanted, which included a controller, a game carrying-case, and a book filled with secret codes. I handed them over to Sarah just as we reached the head of the line, and I put back on the shelf the item she'd grabbed to hold her place. A short woman in line behind Sarah, who was struggling to hold onto a boxed DVD player and seemed to have irritation lines etched permanently into her face, gave us both a death stare.

Sarah handed over her credit card. The clerk swiped it once, swiped it again, swiped it a third time, unable to get the machine to read it. The short lady with the DVD player let out an audible sigh, rolled her eyes. I gave her my best insincere smile. "Merry Christmas," I said.

"Bite me," she said.

The clerk meticulously folded a piece of paper over the card, swiped it very slowly once again, and bingo, the sale went through.

"You might want to get a new card," the short lady said huffily.

"Thank you," I said. Nodding at the DVD player, I said, "Something for the special Ewok in your life?"

She gave me a look that suggested she suspected she'd been insulted but wasn't sure exactly how, so she opted against a comeback. Not a Star Wars fan, I figured.

I told Sarah I'd wait for her by the front of the store and take in the passing parade of panicked shoppers. I found a spot where I wasn't in the way and watched the hordes go by. Hundreds if not thousands of people, their faces contorted in countless variations of stress, rushing to find just the right things for the people on their lists with the little time they had left, wishing to God that this whole horrible holiday season would be over.

Then I spotted Santa with two of his elves.

They were working their way leisurely through the crowds, forcing people to manoeuvre around them, Santa doing his *Ho Ho Ho!* thing while Elf One and Elf Two handed candy canes to kids. (I was immediately able to distinguish them because Elf One had the eyebrow piercing. Things, evidently, had loosened up a bit at the North Pole.)

I thought a mall as upscale as this one could have hired better. They were a motley crew, this Santa and his two elves, definitely down-market. Santa, a slender, short, anaemic-looking guy, was decked out in a faded red suit several sizes too large. One hand was clutching a chequered blue sack that looked more like something that would hold laundry, and the other was hitching up his loose pants every few seconds. The sack, far from being stuffed with goodies, hung straight down from Santa's hand and seemed to hold only a couple of small, heavy items. His scraggly white beard appeared to be not much more than a collection of cotton balls and did a poor job of covering his actual unshaven face.

Either one of the elves might have been better cast in the role of Santa: both overweight, both stuffed into their red and green outfits. I wasn't sure, but it looked as though the costume rental agency might have substituted leprechaun outfits. They'd painted their faces green, for starters, and were tossing candy canes from small, plastic, golden pots.

I wasn't sure whether they were aware that about twenty paces behind them, a mall security guard was watching them, matching them step for step. Without taking his eyes off them, the security guy reached for his radio and said something into it that couldn't be heard amidst the mall hubbub.

"Okay," Sarah said, suddenly next to me. "Now let's see if we can get a bracelet for Angie."

"Sure," I said, looking away from Santa and his helpers. "Lead the way."

At the jewellery store, Sarah quickly got distracted from her mission to find Angie's present when she gazed into the glass display cases filled with dazzling diamond rings and earrings and watches.

"If you haven't figured out what to get me yet," Sarah said, pointing to a pair of earrings with a $1500 price tag next to them, "these are tasteful."

"If only you'd spoken up sooner," I said. "Just yesterday I got you some slippers."

I managed to move her away from that display case and over to the bracelets, most of which had price tags less likely to bring about cardiac arrest. Sarah's price range for Angie was around $100. "Just what does Angie want?" I asked. "A charm bracelet?"

Sarah gave me a look. "How old are you?"

"What?" I said. "Aren't charm bracelets still a thing?"

"Your ignorance on the subject of jewellery and your aversion to purchasing same has not gone unnoticed all these years," Sarah said.

"Did I mention the slippers look like bunnies?" I said.

It was becoming clear Sarah did not need my assistance in choosing a bracelet for our daughter, so I wandered around the rest of the store, looking at things, pretending to be interested.

Out in the mall, I heard a distant *Ho Ho Ho.* Not very deep—and not particularly jolly.

A few minutes later, I happened to glance over and saw Sarah with her purse on the counter. She had settled on something and was in the process of paying for it.

I wandered over. "Find something?"

Sarah said yes. The woman who'd helped Sarah make her selection was swiping her credit card in the machine. There were a couple of customers waiting behind Sarah, one of whom, incredibly, was the short lady from the electronics store.

She couldn't believe it when she saw who was holding her up. When I approached and caught her eye, I said, "What are the odds?"

After several failed swipes, the sales clerk said to Sarah, "Some of these cards, I swear."

"I just had trouble with it at the other place," Sarah said apologetically.

"Tell me about it," said the short woman.

The clerk tried again with a piece of paper folded over the card, the same trick they'd used successfully at the electronics store. This time, however, it was not a go.

"Here," I said, handing my own card over the counter to her.

"Oh, thank you," she said and handed back Sarah's card.

"Ho Ho Ho!"

I stepped around Sarah and saw that Santa and his elves were making their way into the jewellery store. The clerk glanced up, frowned, and said, "What do they think they're doing?"

Then, as they say, all hell broke loose. Fast.

Elf One and Elf Two suddenly had guns in their hands. I didn't know whether they'd pulled them out of their green tights, their golden plastic pots, or out from under their red and green striped toques, but I guess it didn't much matter where they'd come from. They were using them, not only to scare the shit out of the customers and staff in the jewellery store, but were using the butts of them to smash the glass of the display cases.

Santa, meanwhile, had produced a gun and a hammer from his sack, waving the weapon around with his right hand while taking the hammer to the cases with his left.

"Everybody, down!" Santa shouted.

I guess most of us in the store, collectively, either didn't believe what he was saying or were having a hard time grasping the reality of what was happening. It wasn't until Santa waved the gun some more and shouted "Down!" at the top of his lungs that we finally got the message.

We went down.

I grabbed Sarah and pulled her to the floor with me on my left. On my right was the short woman, who'd positioned the box containing her DVD player on its side ahead of her head, turning it into a small shield.

So while she couldn't watch Santa and his elves, I could. All three of them had on gloves to protect them from the shattered glass as they reached into the cases and came up with fistfuls of necklaces and watches and earrings, which they dumped into their pots and Santa's sack. Clearly, they'd scouted things ahead of time. They knew exactly where the expensive merchandise was.

I just wanted them to grab what they wanted and get out. So far, no one had gotten hurt, and I really wanted to see things stay that way. But I seem to have a history of being involved in situations that go from bad to worse, and this particular day was not going to prove to be any exception.

I reached that conclusion a couple of seconds after I heard someone yell, "Freeze!" It was the security guard, the one I'd spotted earlier trailing these clowns. He had his weapon drawn and was pointing it at Elf One, who was half turned toward the guard and had the best chance to get off a shot.

But it was Elf Two who got off the first shot.

He whirled around, plastic pot in one hand, gun in the other. He caught the guard in the right shoulder. The guard spun around and hit the wall, but not before getting off a shot in return. It was, to the best of my recollection, the first time I ever saw an elf get half his face blown off.

Elf Two hit the floor. I'm not exactly an expert in these things, but I'd say he was dead halfway down. People continued screaming. Santa shouted, "Shit!"

The guard had slid down the wall and now was on his side on the floor of the jewellery store, still moving but writhing in pain. The gun had slipped from his fingers, but no one else felt like running over and grabbing it, not while Elf One and Santa were still armed.

"We gotta go!" Elf One shouted.

Santa slung the sack of treasures over his shoulder and started to join his remaining elf in bolting from the store, then stopped suddenly and shouted "Shit!" a second time.

"He's got the keys!" Santa said. He knelt down next to Elf Two, recoiling at the blood that was, in only a few seconds, everywhere. He patted the pockets of Elf Two's elf pants. "Where are the goddamn keys?"

"We gotta go!" Elf One shouted.

Santa had screwed up his courage to dig into the dead man's pockets. I wasn't sure, but I thought I saw a set of car keys on the floor a few feet away, just beyond the edge of the display counter. Maybe when Elf Two hit the deck, his keys had fallen and slid in that direction.

"We need a car!" Santa shouted to all of us on the floor.

I had my arm over Sarah, who had her face pressed to the floor. On the other side of me, the short lady tried to hide behind the DVD box.

I guess it was the box that attracted Santa, who walked over, kicked it out of the way, and said to the woman, "You. Come on. You're driving us out of here."

She looked up, screamed. "I don't have a car! I don't! Honest!" She glanced at me, the guy who'd made the Ewok comment, and must have figured that she had an opportunity, not only to save her own life, but to get even. "He does! I bet he has a car!"

Before I could say anything, Santa reached down, grabbed me by the collar of my jacket, and dragged me to my feet.

"Zack!" Sarah screamed.

Santa pitched me toward the crowded mall area. "Listen," I said, "I'm really not your best guy to drive a getaway—"

Santa pointed his gun at my head. "Where's your car?"

"Basement," I said.

And we were off. Santa, Elf One, and I, running through the mall, heading for the bank of elevators that led down to the parking facilities, Santa's gun poking me in the back, Elf One's waving at everybody else to get out of the way. It was pure pandemonium. People screaming, shouting, diving for cover.

As we reached the elevators, one opened, revealing a young couple with a toddler in a stroller. The woman screamed as she saw the armed St. Nick and his associate. Santa ordered them off, threw me in, and punched one of the parking level buttons even before he knew where my car was.

The doors closed, and for a brief moment, it was almost peaceful. Okay, I was still the hostage of Santa and Elf One, but at least there wasn't as much screaming.

"What floor?" Santa said.

"Uh…" I said, struggling to remember. "P2."

Santa had already punched P1, but now lit up another button with his index finger.

"Jesus Christ," Elf One said. "Did you see Roy? His goddamn face came off."

"Watch him," Santa said to his surviving elf, and started stripping off his outfit. The jacket came off, the oversized pants and hat. He kicked everything into the corner of the elevator. Underneath, he was wearing jeans and a sweatshirt. He started picking at the cotton stuck to his face, getting about half of it off before he realized we'd nearly reached our floor.

"What do you drive?" Elf One asked me.

What? If he found out I drove foreign instead of domestic, would he decide to walk?

"A Virtue," I said.

Elf One cocked his head to one side. "That one of those hybrid things?"

I said yes.

He nodded approvingly. "That's good, doing something for the environment. Stop global warming."

"I suppose that's a worry where you're from," I said.

Elf One just looked at me.

"North Pole, moron," Santa told him.

"Why do you care what kind of car I've got?" I asked.

"Roy had one of those vans, the sides are all covered up," the elf said. "Now, in your car, people are going to see my green face when we drive out of here."

"Not if you're in the goddamn trunk," Santa said, picking away at more beard bits as the doors opened. "Let's go."

With the gun poking into my back again, I led them through the garage, so rattled it was taking a moment for me to remember where Sarah and I had parked. I stopped for a moment, getting my bearings.

"Don't you have a thing on your key?" said Santa, who now did not look very much like a Santa, even with wisps of beard on his face.

I said, "Huh?"

"An alarm button?"

I got out my keys, hit the red button, and off to the left, a car alarm began to whoop and flash its lights. I hit the button again, shutting the alarm down. A moment later, the three of us were standing at the back of the car.

"Pop the trunk," Santa said.

"Aww, come on," Elf One said.

"Cops are going to be looking for Santa and a guy all green who looks like you," Santa said. "So you can hide back here until we get where we're going."

"Where's that?" I asked. How far was I going to have to drive these two?

Santa said, "Shut up."

Elf One crawled into the trunk, which, for an economy car, wasn't too bad. He scrunched in as Santa lowered the lid and pressed down on it until it clicked. "Get behind the wheel," he told me.

I did. Once Santa was in next to me, I turned the key and backed out of the spot.

"Just take it easy," he said, looking into the rear view mirror to pull off the last shreds of beard. He didn't look, now, anything like the traditional character who'd pulled off the jewellery heist.

By this time, I figured, there had to be police cars swarming the mall. The question was whether they'd be there before we exited at the top of the spiralling ramp. Sarah, no doubt, would have told the police by now what kind of car the bad guys—and her husband—would be making their getaway in.

"I'm getting dizzy," said Santa as the car continued to turn hard left as we made our ascent up the ramp, going round and round and round. From behind the back seats, we both heard a muffled, "I think I'm gonna puke."

"He'll be fine," Santa said.

Finally, the ramp straightened out, and there was the huge garage door ahead of us. I pulled the car up to the machine and powered down my window. Once I'd paid, a gate barring our path would rise, followed by the door.

"Move it," Santa said.

"If I don't pay for the parking, the door's not going to open," I pointed out.

I got my wallet out, opened it, looked for the credit card I'd used to enter the garage.

"Where the hell—" I said.

"Come on!" Santa shouted.

There were a couple of credit cards there, but not the one I needed. And then I realized where it was: I'd given it to Sarah to pay for the bracelet at the jewellery store when her own card wouldn't scan.

"Uh…" I said. "We have a problem."

Behind us, someone honked.

"What kind of problem?" Santa asked.

"I don't have the right credit card to get us out of here. It's back in the store."

"Try one of your other ones."

"They won't work," I told him. "It has to be—"

"Do it!"

So I put a card I knew wouldn't work in the machine. Then I put another card I knew wouldn't work in the machine.

Behind us, someone honked again. Santa, so frustrated his cheeks were actually starting to look a bit jolly, slammed his gun so hard on the dashboard I was afraid he'd trigger the air bags. "Goddamn it!" he said. He kept looking back and forth between the machine and the garage door that separated him from freedom.

"Lean back," he said.

"What?"

But I could see what he was planning to do, and did as he asked. He fired through the car and out the window and into the parking machine. The blast inside the Virtue was deafening, and it's a wonder the bullet didn't ricochet off the machine and lodge itself somewhere inside my brain.

Now the guy behind us was leaning on the horn. Maybe he thought the car in front of him had backfired. Surely no one in his right mind would start honking at someone who'd just tried to kill a parking machine.

Santa turned in his seat and pointed the gun behind us, preparing to shoot out the back window of the Virtue and, with any luck, nail the driver behind us. I had to admit, there'd been a few times when I'd wanted to kill someone behind me who was leaning on the horn, but I didn't think in this instance that this particular person was deserving of a death sentence.

So as Santa pulled the trigger, I shouted "No!" and grabbed hold of his arm, forcing it down. He still got off a shot, but instead of going through the rear window, the bullet buried itself in the car's rear seat.

From the trunk, we heard an *Uh*.

No scream. No shriek. Just... *Uh*.

Santa said, "Oh shit."

"Santa," I said. "I think you just offed your elf."

Then, suddenly, there was a rumble of noise from the other direction. We both whirled around to see the garage door slowly opening. Even before it had come to a stop, we could see that about half the police cars in the city were out there, several dozen cops crouched behind fenders, weapons drawn.

"Shit," Santa said one last time.

Anyway, this particular Santa didn't turn me off Santas in general, but the whole experience did turn me off elves. I don't like elves. I hate elves.

But not nearly as much as shopping.

Linwood Barclay, a staff columnist for The Toronto Star, *started his journalism career at* The Peterborough Examiner *in 1977. He joined the* Star *in 1981, where he worked in a variety of editing positions before becoming a columnist in 1993. He's had seven books published to date, including four Zack Walker mysteries so far plus* Last Resort, *a memoir. His third Zack Walker book,* Lone Wolf, *was nominated in 2007 for an Arthur Ellis Award for Best Novel. His new thriller,* No Time for Goodbye, *came out in the fall of 2007. Linwood lives in Burlington, Ontario, with his wife, Neetha, and children, Spencer and Paige.*

Christmas Crossing

Edward D. Hoch

*T*he middle-aged Englishman had been staying at Beaver Island's only hotel for two days before Matos asked his name. It was not something a bartender usually asked a customer, but he sensed they might have something in common. "You've been here a couple of days," he said casually as he served the man his vodka and tonic. "Are you waiting to cross to the States?"

The Englishman half turned on his stool, gazing off down the street toward the dock where the ferry came in. "Yes," he acknowledged. "In time, I will cross. Perhaps on Christmas Day."

"The ferry has a limited schedule on Christmas. Be sure to check with them."

"It doesn't really matter: Christmas or the day after."

"That's Boxing Day here in Canada, but I suppose you know that."

The man nodded and took a sip of his drink. "Same as in England."

"My name is Matos." He offered his hand across the bar. "What's yours?"

"Conrad. Philip Conrad."

"You're a long way from home."

The Englishman smiled slightly. "I hope to be back soon."

"I studied in England for a time. It's a fine country. I see you in here the last couple of days and I think you are waiting for someone. There's not much activity on Beaver Island in the winter. Do you have a travelling companion?"

"No. I am alone."

The man named Conrad said no more that night, and as usual, he left the bar after his second drink. He didn't appear during the day, and Matos suspected he might remain in his room to avoid being seen. Still, Beaver

33

Island was an odd place to choose for entry into the United States. One of the larger of the St. Lawrence River's Thousand Islands, it was served by ferries from both the Canadian and American sides. The small hotel in which Matos's bar was located attracted many guests in the summer but was nearly deserted in winter when the St. Lawrence was frozen. The hotel owner, Russ Ruez, usually closed it by mid-December, but he'd kept it open till after Christmas this year. Then it would close until spring when the St. Lawrence Seaway reopened. The weather was only now starting to turn cold, with a chance of snow predicted for Christmas.

It was the perfect place for someone who didn't want to be found.

In the morning Matos did not think about the Englishman. The weather was still chilly and Christmas was only two days away. He was sweeping the cobblestone sidewalk in front of the bar. In the summer, he usually put out two small tables with chairs for those wishing to drink outdoors, but even a sunny day wasn't warm enough for that in late December.

He'd just finished his sweeping when the morning ferry pulled in from Kingston on the Canadian mainland. That was when he saw a woman leave the boat and start up the street toward the hotel. There was something in the jaunty way she moved—purse tucked under her shoulder, head back and long trousered legs moving like pistons—that reminded him of…

Yes, there could be no doubt. It was Monica Lowell, a woman from his past. Monica was an Australian and he was a Croatian who'd been educated in England, but somehow, they'd hooked up in Germany shortly after the fall of the Berlin Wall. It had been three months of bliss that he still remembered after fifteen years.

"Monica!" he called out, waving to her.

She paused at the sound of her name and lifted her stylish sunglasses for a better view of him. "Who…? Matos? Can that be you?"

"It's me," he said with a grin.

"What are you doing in this place?" She pushed the glasses up on her brown hair, its lighter streaks still glistening in the December sun just as he remembered from fifteen years ago.

"I could ask you the same thing. Come into the bar and I'll buy you a drink."

She followed him inside, and he was suddenly aware of the shabby interior with its worn stools and peeling plaster. When he stepped behind the bar, she seemed surprised. "Do you work here, Matos?"

He laughed. "I own the place, such as it is. I won it from the hotel owner in a poker game."

"Russ Ruez? I know him. I have a room booked at the hotel until Christmas."

"You're spending two nights on Beaver Island?"

"Well, it depends," she answered vaguely. "How did you end up here in the first place?" She frowned as she brushed off one of the bar stools and sat down.

He held up a bottle of Bombay. "You still drink gin?"

"Sure, but not in the morning. Give me a Corona."

"I've got a few cans of Tusker if your tastes run to African."

"Corona will be fine. Now tell me your story."

He opened two bottles and poured one in a glass for her. "After Berlin, I did some interpreting for the World Court in The Hague. That lasted about eight years. I decided I needed a change of scene, so I came over here to Canada. I got a job bartending here two years ago and ended up owning the place."

"Russ Ruez is not one to take defeat easily. Didn't he try to win the bar back from you?"

"It was never a money-maker. He was happy to get it off his hands. So I settled down here."

"Does that mean married?" She gave him a sly look.

"Not so you'd notice. What about you?"

"Still single. I have a consulting business in London."

"I can't believe we both ended up here after all these years," he said. "You still haven't told me what you're doing here."

She grinned. "If I told you, I'd have to kill you."

"Do I have to guess? Does it have anything to do with Christmas?"

Monica took a sip of her beer. "I'm meeting the three wise men."

"I suppose that's as good an answer as any. Where are you going next? South to the States?"

"Maybe. Do you have a house on the island or do you stay at the hotel?"

"The hotel. I was never too much on settling down. I go to Florida after the New Year, till the place reopens in the spring."

She finished her beer and slid off the stool. "I'd better check in at the lobby. They were taking my bag up from the ferry."

"Maybe I'll see you later."

She paused at the door. "In another fifteen years?"

"Lots sooner than that."

It was toward evening when a bearded German entered the bar from the adjoining hotel lobby. Matos knew he had just checked in because he still had his room key in his hand.

"You sell meals here?" he asked with a thick accent.

"We serve light meals," Matos explained, showing him the menu.

"Good! I will wash up and return."

The man's name was Bruno Belsen, and he told Matos later that he was a buyer for a chain of German gift shops. Matos guessed him to be in his mid-forties, a bit older than himself, and his carriage seemed to be that of a military man. Business was slow that evening, as it usually was during Christmas week.

"Where are all your customers?" Belsen asked.

"The locals are with their families or over on the mainland. Actually, it's surprising for the hotel to have as many guests as it does. Mr. Ruez, the owner, was thinking of closing early this year until some last-minute reservations came in."

Matos served him a plate of food, and the two drifted into a casual conversation about his days in Berlin. That was how Philip Conrad found them when he entered the bar shortly after eight o'clock and sat alone at a table. The Englishman was still wearing the suit he'd arrived in, and Belsen immediately asked who he was.

Matos shrugged. "English, name of Conrad. That's all I know."

"On his way to the States?"

"I guess so." He went on polishing some glasses behind the bar.

Belsen finished his food and said he was going for a walk. Once he'd left, the Englishman came over to the bar. "Was he asking about me?"

"Not really. Just wondering about the other guests."

"He arrived today, didn't he?"

Matos nodded. "This afternoon."

"Can you find out if anyone else checked in today? It's worth a tip for the information."

The man seemed so nervous that Matos agreed to the request. There were no other customers at the moment and he slipped out the door to the lobby. Russ Ruez himself was behind the desk. This late in the season, he'd already laid off most of the regular employees. "You've had a lot of check-ins today," he said casually."

Ruez nodded, scratching his bald head. "Three, so far. And the Englishman a few days ago. They all had reservations. I'm not expecting anyone else, though."

"Unusual for Christmas week. I've seen the woman, the Englishman, and the German. Who else is there?"

"A Chinaman in Room 23. He came about an hour ago. I told him you served food, but he said he was going right to bed."

"What's his name?"

"Tommy Yin. He's young, travelling on an American passport."

Matos went back and reported to the Englishman. "A Chinese-American? Did you see him?"

"No, he's sleeping."

He rubbed a hand over his face. "What is he doing here?"

"Perhaps waiting to cross, like you and the others. There's also the German you just saw, and an Australian woman named Monica Lowell."

His eyes shot up to Matos's face. "Did I tell you I was waiting to cross?"

"You said maybe Christmas Day or the day after."

The Englishman merely shook his head and asked for another drink.

Monica Lowell was waiting for him when he closed the bar that night. She came to his room and showed him some of the things she'd bought at the local shops. "This would make a nice wall hanging," she said, holding up a colourful woven sunset. "The folks on this island are very talented."

"I buy a few things myself," he admitted. "These little wooden animals are all hand-carved by one of the local ladies."

She picked up a carved polar bear and examined it. "These are good. We have gift shops back home that would buy any of these things."

He poured them both gin-and-tonics and sat down beside her. "Funny. There's a German here who claims he's a buyer for gift shops."

"What's his name?"

"Belsen. Bruno Belsen. He was in the bar earlier."

"I don't know him."

Matos rested his hand on her knee.

"Don't touch me unless you love me," she said. It was one of her favourite lines from their days in Berlin.

"I did at one time, long ago."

"I don't know if we want to start that again, Matos."

"Neither do I, but I've missed you."

In the morning while she was fixing them breakfast in his little kitchenette, she said, "You've put on weight."

"Middle-aged spread. It happens to the best of us." He sipped his coffee and asked, "What are you doing here, Monica? Really."

"I thought I told you."

"You said you were meeting the three wise men. They're all here now: an Englishman, a German, and a Chinese-American. But they don't seem to know each other."

"Matos—"

"Is it so difficult to tell me the truth? We were close once."

She pushed back her hair. "Nothing is like it was, Matos. We were different people then. Sometimes I think about it and wonder how I got from there to here. At least, you've got an answer. You won it in a card game."

"This is what I won: a seedy bar on an island in the middle of the St. Lawrence River. A border crossing."

"Why don't you cross it? Cross it with me when I leave here on Christmas."

"Those three men—"

"Forget about them. I've said too much already."

"They came here to meet you, didn't they?"

"It's a business arrangement."

"But they don't know each other."

"It's best that way. I can't explain any more."

He glanced out at the sun-streaked sky. "It's Christmas Eve. Let me show you around the island. I don't open the bar for a few hours yet."

"Does it ever snow up here?"

"Oh yes. When the lake effect kicks in from the southwest, we can get buried in no time at all. We had a touch of it last week before it warmed up."

They went down to the lobby together, and almost at once, a young Chinese man approached. In one hand, he held a cell phone, which he quickly closed.

"Yin? Tommy Yin?" Monica asked.

"Yes," he admitted.

"Did you just take our picture with your cell phone?"

"I took no pictures," he said in perfect English.

Matos grabbed the cell phone from his hand and brought up a photo on the viewing screen. It showed them coming down the stairs a moment earlier. "Here's the picture you took."

Tommy Yin lowered his eyes. "I take a picture of the pretty lady. That is all."

"Can you delete it?" Monica asked.

Matos deleted the picture and handed the phone back to the Chinese man, who hurried away, seemingly embarrassed by the entire incident. "Just another of your admirers," Matos told her.

"Perhaps." She seemed troubled by the incident and fell silent for a time. When he asked what was troubling her, she replied, "He could have transmitted that picture to someone immediately—before you deleted it."

"Why should that worry you?"

She shrugged. "Because it shows us together."

"We're old friends from Berlin. Nothing strange about that."

"I don't want you involved in this, Matos. It could be dangerous."

"What are you—a spy or something?"

She laughed. "Nothing as simple as that."

He didn't see Monica that evening. She told him she had business to conduct, and he had to accept that. Russ Ruez came into the bar early, looking around.

"Where is that woman, Monica Lowell?" he asked Matos.

"I have no idea. She hasn't been in here."

Later that night, Philip Conrad came in and sat at the bar with a few local shopkeepers who made up the bulk of their business at holiday time. "Just one drink," the Englishman said. "I need to get some sleep. I have to get out of here tomorrow."

"On Christmas Day? Why don't you stay a day longer?"

"Can't do it. I have to get back. I didn't expect to stay this long. And I think that Chinese chap took my picture today."

"Tommy Yin? He's taking everyone's picture. He took mine, too."

"He's an American, probably FBI or even CIA."

"What interest would they have in you?"

He sighed. "It's a long story. You don't want to hear it."

"Give me the condensed version. Is Monica Lowell involved?"

"I can't go into details," he said, downing the rest of his drink.

"But something was important enough to bring you here during Christmas week. It's the same thing that brought Monica Lowell and that German Belsen and Tommy Yin."

The Englishman snorted. "I was told Beaver Island was about the most remote place imaginable, yet linked to both Canada and the U.S. by ferries. No one else would be here except the island's few residents. I didn't expect snoopers with cell phone cameras."

Monica hadn't appeared by the time Matos closed the place shortly before midnight. It had been a quiet Christmas Eve, and the local residents were gathering for midnight church services. He went up to his room, feeling confident that she would join him there. Almost at once, there was a knock at the door and he opened it.

"I must have a word with you," Tommy Yin said. "It's important."

Matos concealed his surprise and invited the American in. "Sorry I was a bit abrupt with you earlier," he said. "The lady doesn't like having her picture taken."

Yin glanced around the little room and chose a chair that faced the closed bathroom door. "Is there anyone else here?"

Matos smiled and swung the door open. "I'm alone. If you're concerned about the lady—"

"I'm concerned about Conrad, the Englishman. Your apparent friendship with him could mean trouble."

"He told me people were after him. I thought he might be paranoid."

"How much has he told you?"

"Wait a minute!" Matos held up his hand. "First, you'd better tell me who you are."

Tommy Yin smiled. "That needn't concern you just yet."

"What about Belsen? Is he involved, too?"

"We're all here for the same purpose. You don't need to know anything else."

Monica arrived an hour later, well after the American had left. Matos didn't mention his visit. "I came to wish you a Merry Christmas," she said.

"I'm leaving today," she told him over breakfast. "My work here is finished."

"And what would that be? Is this about drugs? Are you buying or selling?"

"No drugs. This is bigger than drugs."

"Are you going to tell me?"

"I can't, Matos."

There was a sudden pounding on his door, and he went to answer it. Bruno Belsen was standing there, wearing trousers and an undershirt. "He's dead!" the German exclaimed, barely able to control himself. "That American, Yin, is dead, and his room has been ransacked!"

Monica rushed to the door. "What are you talking about?"

"I...I went to his room after I learned he'd won the bidding. The door was ajar, and I found him on the floor, dead."

"Come on!" Monica told Matos. "His room is right down the hall."

It was as the German had said. Matos knelt by the body and saw the blood still trickling from a head wound. A pillow with powder burns and loose feathers lay nearby. "It looks as if he was shot. A pillow was used to muffle the sound." He stared up at Monica. "What did he have that cost him his life?"

"Nothing!" she insisted. "He had nothing."

"We have to report this." He used a handkerchief to pick up the phone and call the desk, telling Russ Ruez what had happened. "You'd better call over to Kingston and get the police." When he'd hung up, he explained, "We only have a couple of police officers here. There's no one on the island who can handle a murder. The RCMP investigators will be here on the afternoon ferry."

"I have to get out of here," Belsen told them.

41

"We'd better check on the Englishman," Monica said.

Conrad wasn't in his room, and they found him downstairs, eating breakfast. "What's the matter?" he asked as they approached his table.

"Yin is dead," Monica told him. "He's been murdered."

"Does that mean—?"

"It means nothing!" she snapped, cutting him off. "It means nothing happened here and nothing is going to happen."

Ruez had left the desk and come over to join them. "What is this? A dead man in my hotel?"

"That's it," Monica confirmed.

No one had heard a shot during the night. Ruez confirmed that the hotel's front door remained unlocked all night, and a thief might have entered to loot the rooms. "But we've never had anything like that," he insisted. "There is no serious crime on Beaver Island."

The island's police officers arrived and sealed the victim's room to await the mainland police. After the investigators conducted some preliminary questioning, Matos was allowed to open his bar. He made a detour on the way, taking the duplicate key to Monica's room from behind the desk and hurrying upstairs. He knew they'd still be questioning her and he slipped into the empty room with ease. Her old-fashioned hard-sided suitcase was open and mostly packed, ready for her planned departure. There was nothing that gave any hint of the reason for her visit, although a pad by the telephone bore some scratched-out figures. And the German had mentioned an auction.

He looked around the room, lifting the mattress and checking the toilet tank without finding anything. The drawers were empty, and even a half-used box of face powder yielded no secrets. What was it: drugs, diamonds?

No, nothing like that would bring bidders from three different nations. This had to be a one-of-a-kind.

His thought process was interrupted by the opening of the door. Monica stood there, key in hand. "What in hell do you think you're doing?"

"Looking for it."

"For what?"

"Let's not play games, Monica. Bruno Belsen mentioned an auction. Tommy Yin bid highest and got the prize, whatever it is. Then someone killed him and stole it."

She shook her head. "Nobody stole it."

"Then where is it? You must have it here. People aren't bidding large sums on something they haven't seen."

"I'm holding it until the bidder's money is deposited in a numbered Swiss account. Unfortunately, that can't happen on Christmas Day."

"Then how can you leave today?"

"I planned to take the ferry to the States with Tommy Yin. As soon as I received confirmation of the wire transfer, I would hand over the object to him."

"Let's see it. I'm through playing around."

"Matos—"

"Didn't these last two nights mean anything to you?"

"Of course, they did. It was like Berlin and I was young and innocent."

"You're still young."

"But not so innocent. Want to know what I do for a living, Matos? I auction off stolen art treasures to the highest bidder. Thieves contact me, and I contact some of the wealthiest men in the world for bids. They send their representatives to inspect the merchandise and then they bid on it."

"That's what Yin and Belsen and Conrad are? Representatives?"

"Exactly."

"And the treasure is—?"

"A painting by Vincent van Gogh, stolen from the Hermitage Museum in St. Petersburg a year ago. It's called *Landscape with House and Ploughman*. It measures just thirteen by sixteen inches and fits quite nicely into the lining of my suitcase."

She walked over to the hard-shelled plastic case and carefully undid the inner satin lining. Matos caught his breath as he saw the painting, protected by a tough plastic envelope. "They couldn't hope to sell that anywhere."

"Of course not. Wealthy men buy these for their personal collections, just to look at, to know they own one of the world's great art treasures."

"You said if you told me you'd have to kill me."

She smiled. "I guess I changed my mind. With Tommy Yin dead, I want you to accompany me to the States. When the killer didn't find the painting in Yin's room, he'll be after me."

"Do you know who it is?"

"Belsen or Conrad. I don't know which."

Matos shook his head. "It couldn't be either of them because they knew you wouldn't surrender the painting till the money was transferred. They'd have come after you, not Yin."

"Who else is there?"

"Only one possibility: Russ Ruez. You said you knew him. You'd used Beaver Island before as your meeting place, hadn't you? Only this time, he decided to cut himself in. You took the bids over the telephone and he listened in at the switchboard. He heard that Yin was high bidder and went to his room early this morning. He killed him, but the painting wasn't there." Matos heard the faint click of the room's door opening. He whirled to face a pistol in Ruez's hand. "Be very quiet, both of you. I just want the painting."

"Are you insane?" Monica stormed. "Where'd you get that gun?"

"From Tommy Yin. He was an Interpol agent, but not very good at handling firearms. He made a high bid to keep the painting out of the others' hands. He caught me searching his room and tried to hold me for the police, so I had to kill him."

"Now you'll kill us, too?" she asked.

"If I have to. I want that painting."

She sighed. "Very well. You can have it."

Matos watched her return to the suitcase and open it. When she turned she held a tiny .22 automatic, which she fired without aiming. Ruez dropped the pistol with a gasp of pain and fell to the floor.

"Grab my suitcase and let's get out of here," she told Matos. "It's now or never."

"What about him?"

She kicked Ruez's gun across the room. "They'll find him if he groans loud enough, and the murder weapon has his prints on it. With that bullet in him, he's not going anywhere."

Matos led the way downstairs and through the door to his bar. He emptied the cash from his safe and took his passport as well. The few hundred dollars would buy him clothes to replace the ones he was leaving behind. He took a fur-lined jacket from its hook behind the door. There were flurries in the air outside.

A few people coming from Christmas morning church services had paused by the police car parked in front of the hotel. One of them asked Matos what was going on, but he shrugged and kept walking. "The ferry to the States leaves in ten minutes," Monica told him. "We'll just make it."

"Then what?"

"Then I'll get us some money for this painting, even if I have to sell it back to the insurance company."

He grinned, suddenly feeling good about it. "You think of everything."

"This is an easy customs crossing. They won't check us."

The ferry blew its whistle just as they boarded. Then they stood at the railing together and watching Beaver Island receding into the distance. "Merry Christmas," she said, and kissed him.

"To Berlin...again."

"To Berlin."

When they landed at Cape Vincent, she took the suitcase and headed off the ferry. He was a few steps behind, allowing an elderly couple to go first. When she reached the customs station, he saw the agent on duty gaze intently at his computer screen, and suddenly he remembered the cellphone photo Tommy Yin had taken of them both.

Another agent appeared and took the suitcase, leading Monica into the customs shed. A sharp western wind had come up, blowing the snow against Matos's face. He turned and went back on board, paying his fare for the return trip to Beaver Island.

Edward D. Hoch is a past president of Mystery Writers of America and winner in 1968 of its Edgar Award for Best Short Story. He received the MWA's Grand Master Award in 2001. He has been guest of honour at Bouchercon, a two-time winner of its Anthony Award, and the recipient of its Lifetime Achievement Award. As well, he has won lifetime achievement awards from the Private Eye Writers of America and the Short Mystery Fiction Society. Author of more than 900 published stories, he has appeared in every issue of Ellery Queen's Mystery Magazine since 1973. Hoch resides with his wife, Patricia, in Rochester, New York.

Water Like a Stone

an Ellis Portal Story

Rosemary Aubert

*T*here are some people to whom it's almost impossible to say no, and my wife, Queenie, is one of them.

It was the Sunday before Christmas. Outside the window of our apartment, snow fell softly into the fading afternoon light. Already the trees in the river valley were burdened with white, and the Don, after five days of bitter cold, was frozen solid.

"Not much in the newspaper today," I said.

Queenie nodded. "Guess not."

She took a sip of sherry. Well, not real sherry. Neither of us drinks any more. What passes for sherry in our home is a distilled juice of yellow apple and white grape, steeped with clove, cinnamon, and essence of fig—our wassail.

"Except it looks like somebody got murdered down the street…"

Though the sight of Queenie reading by the light of our fireplace was one of the chief delights of my winter evenings, I didn't look up.

"Yep," she said, "it looks real bad."

I turned a page of the book review section of the Sunday *Daily World*. There was a lengthy piece on Christmas reading. Glossy coffee-table items. A few biographies of prominent Canadian figures. I didn't see any judges among them.

"Blood all over the place." Queenie shook her head, whether in sorrow or disgust I couldn't tell, glancing up at her for only an instant.

"Some people have everything," she said, "and then they throw it all away."

I knew by the tone of Queenie's voice that she was about to ask me to do something. Something I'd clearly told her I was not about to do again— ever. I gave the book review section a little shake so that the paper would rustle and she'd get my point, which was: *I'm reading and I'm not interested in solving any more murder mysteries.*

Putting her section of the paper aside, Queenie stood up. For a moment, she gazed through the window where the fat flakes danced in the white air. She moved to the stereo and put on a disc. The sweet sound of a choir filled the room, singing an old favourite of ours, "In the Bleak Midwinter."

The words of Christina Rosetti distracted me from the book reviews, and I put the paper down.

In the bleak midwinter
Frosty wind made moan.
Earth stood hard as iron,
Water like a stone…

Queenie picked up her section of the paper but didn't resume her seat by the fire. Instead, she came and sat beside me. I reached out to touch her hand. Truth was, I'd do anything for her. Even if I'd sworn not to.

"So," I said, giving her hand a gentle squeeze, "who's this poor unfortunate who threw everything away?"

Knowing my wife as well as I do, I could tell just by the motion of her hand as she slipped it from my fingers and held up the newspaper that she was excited at my interest.

"It's like this," she said. "Just a bit south of here, at the foot of the Scarborough Bluffs on the edge of the lake, there's a place where a lot of houseboats moor for the winter—"

I nodded. "Yes. I know the place."

"Most of the owners of those boats are really rich," Queenie said, "but not everybody. Some people don't have anything *except* the boats. Those are the ones that live down there all year long, no matter how cold it gets. I guess they put all their money into getting one: you know, a sort of pearl-of-great-price thing. Sell all you have—"

"Yes." Despite the fact that I was now retired from the bench, I still had the judge's impatience at a witness who dragged out evidence by extrapolating on what it all meant philosophically. "So…"

Queenie smiled. "So, Your Honour, I guess you want to hear more after all."

"Keep it brief and to the point."

She leaned over and kissed me on the cheek. "Sure."

I put down the newspaper and gave her my full attention.

"Last night, the cops got a 911 call from a distraught guy. He said he came home from Christmas shopping at Eglinton Square just a few blocks from here."

"What time of day?"

Without consulting the paper, Queenie supplied the details. "He said he left the mall at about four o'clock. He drove south on Pharmacy to Kingston Road, then over to Brimley and down that road that winds to the lakeshore where the boats are—"

"They mentioned his exact route in the paper?" I asked. "Doesn't that seem unusual?"

"No," Queenie answered, "because he told the police he was trying to figure out the exact time he got to the houseboat."

"Yesterday was the last Saturday before Christmas—probably the busiest shopping day of the year," I observed.

"Busiest except for the Feast of Stephen," Queenie said, "Boxing Day, the twenty-sixth, when all the sales are."

"Yes. Anyway, that trip would usually take, what, about fifteen minutes? So if he left at four o'clock, would it still be daylight when he got to the boat?"

Queenie reached across me and grabbed yet another section of the *World.* "Yesterday, December twenty-second, was the solstice, the shortest day. And the sun set...," she ran her finger along a column of figures, "at exactly 4:43 p.m. That means that if the guy left at four o'clock, he would hardly have any time at all to see anything outside."

"What did he claim to see?" I asked her.

"I don't know, but there's a picture in the paper. Looks like the victim is just inside the open door of the houseboat. She's got on a jacket, like maybe she was just going out—"

"Or just coming in," I said.

"You can't see it in the picture, but the reporter says there were footprints in blood all around the boat."

I thought about that for a minute. As a piece of evidence, it was pretty much the ultimate cliché. "And the footprints led to a smoking gun in the hands of a butler?"

"Okay, forget it. I got better things to do with my time…" She stood abruptly, sending the pages of the paper sliding to the floor.

I reached out and pulled her back down beside me. For a few seconds, she glared at me, but I could see the soft light in her eyes. I brushed her lips with my finger. "Lose the frown and keep talking," I told her. "For starters, tell me about this guy."

"It doesn't say too much about him except that he is a 'well-known area merchant,' but I sort of recognize the name. I think he's the man that runs that antique shop on Queen Street that sells old letters and manuscripts."

"Oh, really?" I'd been in the store once or twice. It was dusty and smelled vaguely of pipe tobacco and oranges. Not unpleasant, but not to everyone's taste. "I don't know how many customers he gets," I told Queenie. "His prices are high and most of what he sells is pretty arcane."

"What?"

"Rare autographs of obscure people."

"Yeah. But worth a mint to collectors, I guess."

"I wonder if the police think robbery was a motive," I said.

"All the police say is that the victim was the guy's wife and that she died from stab wounds."

"Stabbed with…?"

"That's the thing," Queenie said. "The reporter found out that there wasn't any weapon left at the scene. Anyway…" She took a slow sip of her drink and eyed me over the rim of the glass.

"Anyway, I'm the one who's supposed to figure this out?"

She smiled.

"I don't suppose you expect me to get on my parka and go down there and look around?"

She seemed genuinely surprised at this suggestion. I was surprised at her surprise. What exactly *did* she want?

"A long time ago," she said, "when you were helping me to read some of the books you like so much, we read a story about that guy that solved mysteries just sitting in a chair."

I cast my mind back to the hours we'd once spent pouring over books together. "Mycroft Holmes?" I finally said. "Sherlock's brother?"

"Yeah. That's the one."

"So you want me to solve this murder the way Mycroft would?"

Queenie nodded.

I stood up and stretched, gazing out at the gathering darkness and the thickening snow.

When I turned back toward the room, Queenie was looking up at me with an irresistible air of expectation.

"Okay," I said. "A man goes Christmas shopping and returns at dusk. He finds bloody footprints and a wife stabbed. He calls the police. They arrive and find the scene as he described it, but there's no weapon. Also, no motive is immediately apparent, though robbery is a possibility since the man has access to valuable documents and is widely known as a person likely to possess such things."

"Right."

"The man and the victim live in a houseboat. All year long?"

"Yes," Queenie answered. I neglected to ask her how she knew this.

"So the two of them live in a confined space. It's Christmas, a difficult time of the year, especially if money is tight because you run a shop with a very limited clientele and what you sell isn't exactly giftware."

"Yeah."

I kept silent for a moment, considering various possibilities. "Okay," I said. "Let's say you're a thief. You live in the neighbourhood either of the store or of the houseboats or both."

"And?"

"Both of those places—Queen Street, where the store is, and the Scarborough Bluffs, where the boats are—both of those places are mixed neighbourhoods, aren't they?"

"Mixed? You mean rich people and people who aren't rich live there together?"

"Yes. But it's a little more complicated than that. As you yourself pointed out, in some neighbourhoods in the city, people who are genuinely rich and people who only appear to be rich live side by side."

"Yeah. So?"

"So there's tension—economic conflict, of course. But also the conflict of keeping up appearances."

"Well," Queenie said, "that could sure cause somebody to want to rob somebody else."

"True. But the need to save face leads to other problems as well."

"Like what?"

Queenie was a person who'd risen from a life on the streets to a position of prominence in our community as a tireless defender and servant of the poor, but she had as much pretension as a cabbage. Which was one of a million things I loved about her. I, however, had often been accused of having a high idea of myself. I knew a lot about saving face.

"It takes money to pretend you have money," I answered. "That means there could be arguments between a husband and wife if they disagreed about how their limited funds should be spent."

"All show and no go," Queenie commented. She loved the pithy sayings of the street people she served.

"Something like that."

"So you don't think this was a robbery?"

"Queenie," I said, coming back to sit beside her, "the fact that no weapon was found means nothing. If the killer was a robber, he might have fled, taking the weapon with him. He might have tossed it."

"The lake was frozen. Even down by the boats. We saw it ourselves the other day. And it's been real cold ever since."

"He didn't need to toss it in water. He could have tossed it into a trash can, into the woods, even onto the road. There's so much slush from the ice and the salt—"

"Or the weapon could be something else," she said quietly.

"Something else?"

She picked up the paper and studied the photo. I leaned over and studied it, too. It was grainy. You could see the body, and beside where it lay, you could see what looked like a little pile of ice, as though it had been chipped away from a window—or a path.

"If the killer was a robber," Queenie said, "he picked a stupid time."

"Broad daylight on a Saturday afternoon."

She shook her head. "It doesn't make sense. If the robber thought the couple had money or something else valuable and kept it in the boat, why wouldn't he come at a time when nobody was home? He could see that a person was there if it was broad daylight, don't you think?"

"Yes," I answered. "And if the robber thought valuables were held at the store, why would he—or she—come to the boat?"

"There's another thing," Queenie said. "This guy, he didn't have anybody working with him in the store, did he?"

"I can't say. I was only there two or three times. Maybe he hired somebody for Christmas."

"That's just it," Queenie said. "The middle of the last Saturday before Christmas is a dumb time for a store to be left unattended by 'a well-known area merchant'!" She wrinkled her face in a gesture of disbelieving contempt.

Our fireside "investigation" ground to a halt. On the stereo, one disc ended and another fell into place. Queenie seemed to have an endless supply of carol renditions. The choir was replaced by a smooth-voiced tenor crooning "Silent Night." Outside our window, it had suddenly become night, all traces of snow erased by the warm reflection of our home in the depths of the cold window glass.

I thought about that little pile of chipped ice beside the body.

And then I understood.

I had no idea what had really happened to the manuscript merchant's wife.

But I knew what Queenie thought had happened. And I knew why she cared so much.

"They sold everything they owned for the pearl-of-great-price: that boat," I said, keeping my eyes on the fire. "Maybe they were both excited by the idea, at least at first. They took ownership of the boat in the spring when the trees on the bluffs were just beginning to come back to life after a long winter of being covered with ice: the frozen mists off the lake. The two of them worked together to set up their new home. It didn't matter that that was all they had because they loved it. As spring turned to summer, the birds returned. The white gulls soared in freedom over the water. The Canada geese spread their wide returning *vees* over the beaches.

"It wasn't hard in summer to look like you had as much money as anybody else because who down by the bluffs dresses in anything but deck clothes in the summer? Besides, summer is the time a merchant is most likely to sell arcane wares to tourists on a street like Queen East."

Queenie said nothing. I took a sip from my glass and went on.

"But when autumn comes, things begin to change. A person—a couple—begins to need to spend most of their time inside. No more barbecues on the deck. Fewer walks along the beach. If you entertain often, as the rich do, you entertain at good restaurants. Or better, at your private club. If you accept an invitation, you also accept the obligation to reciprocate.

"It becomes harder and harder to hide the fact that the money is running out."

I looked around our own home: the marble fireplace with its brass accoutrements, the mahogany bookcases, the paintings… We were blessed in that our finances were secure. But that had not always been the case. Not by a long shot. So both Queenie and I understood what it meant to be poor. The additional burden of having to pretend otherwise must have proven excruciating for that couple on the boat.

I continued my narrative, my speculation.

"Tensions mount. Ironically, the poorer the couple becomes, the more time they have to spend together in the cramped confines of their boat. Under such circumstances, many unpleasant things become clear, such as, for example, the inevitable accusation—"

"'This was all *your* big idea,'" Queenie offered.

I smiled, despite the grimness of the tale. "Right. Sooner or later, the husband or the wife comes to the conclusion that all of their troubles result from some decision, some desire, on the part of the other."

"And then there's a fight."

"A man comes home when he should be working. Or a woman is spending time doing things like scraping ice instead of having a job," I said. "Whatever the words exchanged, there's an escalation."

"And there's a weapon. A kitchen knife or something?" Queenie asked.

"No." I pointed to the photo. I could see understanding dawn on her face.

"'Water like a stone...'"

"He picks up a heavy shard of ice. The lake has been frozen solid for a long time. He stabs her. Again and again. Then he goes into the kitchen and washes the weapon down the sink..."

The horror of the idea penetrated the peace of the afternoon and stunned us into a silence interrupted only by a sudden fall of embers in the fireplace.

"But you knew that, Queenie."+

"What? I didn't know about that ice part."

"No. But you figured out that he was the one who killed her and you figured out why."

She didn't look at me. "How do you know that?" she asked softly.

"The pearl-of-great-price? The fact that somebody 'threw everything away.'"

She nodded.

I took her hand and held it close to my chest. "Queenie," I asked, "why did you put me through my paces? Did you need to prove I still have what it takes?"

Now she did look at me. I could see the love in her eyes, "You'll always have what it takes, Your Honour," she said. "But…"

"But what?"

"But maybe I won't always have what it takes. I'm not young anymore or brilliant or—"

"Queenie," I said, "what we have here—our home—it's not based on a lie or a wish we can't fulfill or a drama we have to act out. Our home is based on our love."

"But anybody can have a disagreement."

"Of course."

"And anybody can have a fight."

"Right again."

"But…" She lifted our entwined hands, turned them over, and softly kissed my palm. "But *we* would never…"

I could have answered that we never angered each other in the least. I could have told her that I loved her more than I loved myself. I could have observed that in my long career as a judge I'd come to the conclusion that domestic violence is not merely the result of a sudden change of fortune.

But all I needed to say—did say—was "No."

Rosemary Aubert is the author of the Ellis Portal mystery series, set in Toronto, Ontario. The series features a once-esteemed judge who became homeless but climbed his way back into society, solving crimes on the way back up. The second book in the series, The Feast of Stephen, *won the Arthur Ellis Award for Best Novel in 2000. Rosemary is also a writing teacher, lecturer, and a retired judge's deputy from the Ontario Superior Court of Justice.*

Turning on the Christmas Blights
a Camilla Macphee Story

Mary Jane Maffini

"The trouble with humbug, if you ask me, is that it doesn't go far enough." Not that my opinion of the Christmas season and all the twaddle surrounding it meant a dog's dropping to Alvin Ferguson. He ignored me and sailed across the tide of rush-hour traffic on Wellington Street—beaky nose high, long ponytail flowing in the winter wind. As Alvin is a human tsunami of seasonal enthusiasm, I found myself swept after him. Not without a certain amount of resentment.

"You can't cross on a red," I shouted as a westbound STO bus narrowly missed my butt.

"Rules," Alvin shouted back over his bony shoulder, "are made to be broken."

His plan was to join the thousands of frost-bitten citizens gathered on Parliament Hill to watch the annual Christmas Lights Across Canada ceremony. It was a good plan if you like lights or Christmas or ice-cold feet. And Alvin would be lucky if his seven visible earrings didn't contribute to frostbite on a grand scale.

The overcast December night combined with an icy mist made it hard to see even at this early hour. Even so, I couldn't pretend to lose Alvin. Not with that scarf. His recent knitting binge had yielded a six-foot-long red and green number, which was wrapped four times around his neck. In case red and green was a tad too subtle, he had thoughtfully woven gold LED Christmas lights into the final product. Or Christmas blights, as I thought of them. I assumed there was a small battery pack attached somehow, too. Of course, I wouldn't have given a flying fig what he was wearing if he hadn't made me the twin scarf. He claimed it was an early Christmas gift.

Besides being way too noticeable from a mile away, it was also pretty scratchy on the neck. I took mine off and stuffed it into the pocket of my parka. We'd been getting way too many stares.

Alvin sniffed. "What are you doing that for? If you don't like your gift, I'll take it back."

"It's not that, Alvin..." But he had already snatched the scarf out of my pocket and stomped off ahead. Why is everyone I know such a drama queen? And why are people with more stuff than they need obsessed with heaping gifts on other people who are drowning in possessions? Alvin wasn't alone in this. I'd already had my annual snarl at my friend Merv about that. Merv, the morose Mountie, is crabby and miserable all year long, which is part of what I like about him. Up until this December, he's been worse than usual, something to do with one year left before retiring from the RCMP and still on Hill patrol on the long winter nights. But come December and he gets all misty-eyed. Gift swap, indeed. I just said no to that. What was he thinking?

I puffed up the hill and tried to catch up to Alvin, who had joined a jumbled line going somewhere. "Too bad you didn't knit Christmas socks instead. It's minus seventeen and dropping by the minute." I stamped my feet to keep warm. "Let's just get it over with."

"The lights don't come on for another forty-five minutes, Camilla."

"Forty-five minutes? I'll be dead by then. Do we have to keep standing in this line-up?"

"We're getting hot chocolate. Traditional. And even better—free," Alvin snapped. "Lighten up, Camilla."

Yeah right. "Why are those people grinning? What's wrong with them? New teeth?"

Alvin reached for his hot chocolate. "They're volunteers, Camilla. Happy to be out here, meeting members of the community and getting in the spirit of the season."

"I guess," I said, accepting a cup of steaming hot chocolate from a frighteningly happy fellow.

"Trust me," Alvin said.

"It's too dark and I can't see over all these people," I grumbled as we headed back to battle the crowds.

Alvin said, "Let's not get separated."

I wouldn't want you to think I kowtow to the world's most irritating office assistant, code name Alvin, but the truth was I'd lost a bet with him over who would win the Liberal leadership race. For payback, I had to be dragged along to the ceremony and make nice.

"Come on, Camilla, we need torches."

This will teach me to gamble on something as futile as politics, I reminded myself as I followed him to a tent staffed with still more smiling volunteers. Where did they find these people?

"Great scarf," the volunteer said to Alvin as she handed each of us a candle stuck in a plastic glass. My glass was red and Alvin's was green. "Very twinkly."

Alvin said, "Take it, Camilla. You use the bottom of the candle as a holder and the plastic keeps the flame from going out. Cool, isn't it?"

"If you say so." It was actually very cool, and the sight of thousands of bobbing little lanterns made for a pretty sight on the frigid, dark Hill.

"You can humph all you want, Camilla. This is fun. Let's find a bonfire."

Around us, hundreds of cheerful families prattled on in English and French, jostling for places in the hot chocolate line-up or a space near the many bonfires.

"Toasted marshmallows," Alvin said, elbowing his way through past a couple of guys in Sens sweaters.

"Watch out," I said as a young man in a puffy maroon ski jacket jostled my arm. Hot chocolate spilled down the front of my old brown parka.

He said, "Excuse me, ma'am. Let me help with that."

"Back off," I said.

His eyes widened, with surprise at first, then a flicker of recognition. "Sorry," he said, turning away.

I tapped him on the shoulder. "Hey, not so fast. I know you."

He turned and said in low voice, "Maybe not, because what you don't know won't hurt you."

"Don't you threaten me."

I stepped forward but he was gone, melted into the crowd of happy families, hand-holding lovers, cocoa-swilling babies, and gleeful volunteers. The maroon jacket was dark enough to blend with the night. I staggered after him, waving my little candle torch like a deranged tree decoration.

"Rollie!" I called.

Perhaps he'd dodged behind the beaver-tails hut? I checked, but except for a few people trying to have a quiet smoke, it was deserted.

Maybe he'd scurried toward the front where we'd soon be hearing

Christmas carols by local choirs and seasonal drivel from politicians. Was he lurking behind one of the dozens of Christmas trees that had sprung from the snow on the hill? Wherever he was, I intended to find him.

Alvin yelled in my ear. "Do you want your toasted marshmallow or not? I only have two hands."

I whirled. "I just saw Rollie the Roach."

"Did you say 'Rollie the Roach'? Who's that? Can you take this thing?" Alvin thrust the marshmallow at me. "It's not like I'm your mother, you know."

"Rollie is the slickest little pickpocket this town has even known. Pulling the old distraction game: Bump into some poor mark, spill something on them, wipe it off, and pick their pockets. That little creep makes more than a bank robber on a good day."

"What? That guy you were just talking to? A pickpocket? Here? Where? Let me at him."

"He got away. That must be obvious, Alvin, even to you. Damn. He could lift dozens of wallets here."

"But," Alvin sputtered, "it's Christmas!

"Of course, it's Christmas. Best time of year for these guys. Bonanza. Fat wallets. Credit cards he can use or sell to scammers. He'll make a fortune. Then, if he's not too exhausted from all this pickpocketing, he'll break into people's homes while they are at midnight Mass and steal the kids' gifts."

"Someone has to stop him!"

"Not much chance of that."

"How do you even know this guy, Camilla?"

"I was his legal-aid lawyer on more than one occasion. For my sins. But mostly for his."

"Really?"

"Eventually, I had to fire him as a client."

"Why?"

"Long story. Client privilege while it lasted. Do you know the little rat told me what I didn't know wouldn't hurt me?"

Alvin scowled. "That's pretty bold. And he didn't even look like a crook. That jacket probably cost like five hundred plus. Even that cap was more than I can afford."

"Pickpockets usually look pretty well-dressed. Less suspicious. Clothes are the tools of the trade. He probably ripped it off a retailer or maybe some poor devil who's standing around tonight shivering. Do you think you can recognize him?"

"Pretty distinctive jacket."

"Was it? I'm not too much into that snowboarder style. And if we don't find him fast, he'll probably slip into something else. Would you recognize him if he was wearing different clothing?"

Alvin frowned in concentration. "I think so. I'm good at faces and I got a clear look at his. You made him nervous, that's for sure. But we have to stop him!"

"Well, I know that, Alvin. But I can't see him anymore. The thing is he's probably not working alone. He likes company. He likes to vary the approach. They'll play all the old scams, distraction, compassion. One minute, he'll jostle some unsuspecting mark, the next he'll... Oh, hold on."

I dashed around a couple of kids and grabbed the collar of a young man who was just apologizing to a sweet-faced, white-haired lady in a beaver coat. He turned pale at the sight of me. His hand dropped.

"Bunny," I said. "How could you?"

Bunny Mayhew stared at his feet and fidgeted. He'd probably stolen that baby-blue jacket because it went with his eyes.

I cleared my throat.

He bent down, stood up again, and said to the woman in the fur coat, "Sorry, ma'am. You seemed to have dropped this."

She took the wallet from his hand. Her face lit up like one of our candle torches. "Why, thank you."

"Better check the clasp on your purse, ma'am," he said.

"Bless you. You're too kind," she said, fishing out a twenty and pressing it into Bunny's hand. "Merry Christmas."

At least, he had the grace to look sheepish. As soon as she'd turned away, I snatched the twenty from his larcenous fingers. "This is going right in the first Salvation Army kettle I see. Or have you already plundered that, too?"

Bunny protested. "What do you think I am, Camilla? You think that I'd steal from the Sally Ann?"

"I know you're a thief, Bunny. But I believed you confined your habit to works of art. And furthermore, I thought you'd promised to settle down and straighten up. What's Tonya going to say?"

"It's not my fault."

I rolled my eyes. "Trust me, she won't be saying that."

"No, it's really not, Camilla. I got arrested and held at Regional Detention Centre. There was a problem with my bail. It was all a big misunderstanding. But then Christmas was coming, and I wanted to get Trace and the baby something special. She works so hard at the salon and—"

"And you're such a screw-up. So now you're working this crowd with Rollie the Roach? Don't bother to lie. You're lousy at it, and I can tell by your face that I'm right. What is the matter with you, teaming up with Rollie? He is the epitome of sleaze. He would steal from dying children. You're going down the tubes, Bunny. I can't believe you would let everyone down like this."

"I got no choice, Camilla. He's got something on me."

"Oh, come on. Who doesn't?"

"This is kind of serious. This would get me hard time. Two years plus a day, and I'll be in Kingston. I might need you to help me on that one."

I held up my hand. "Don't prejudice me. I don't want to talk about it. Just tell me about Rollie before he wipes out every wallet on the Hill."

"Well, he needed a partner for here tonight. We just got separated in the crowd. There's a lot of people, eh? Tonya wanted to come, but I told her it was too cold for the baby. If she saw me with Rollie, she'd go ballistic."

"I'm going ballistic myself. Rollie's going to get arrested tonight. You can be a partner with him for that."

Bunny blanched. "No. No no no. If he sees us talking, he'll think I ratted him out and he'll roll over on me for that other thing that we're not talking about. They don't call him Rollie for nothing. I never should have talked to him at the RDC. We were just waiting by the pay phone and got to shooting the shit. He seemed harmless. You'd think you could trust a fellow prisoner."

"You might think that. Where are you meeting him?"

"Oh no. I'm not going to—"

"Oh yes, you are, Bunny."

"But you're a legal-aid lawyer. You can't turn on him."

"What are you talking about? I can turn on both of you."

"Are you sure, Camilla? What about client privilege?"

"Don't make me laugh. How many wallets did you get?"

"That was my first."

"Take it from the top, Bunny." The good thing about having represented

Bunny on one too many occasions was that I can always tell if he's lying.

Bunny tried the truth. "Just that one. It felt kind of creepy: that old lady, and then she gave me the twenty. I should really stick to art. I don't have the heart to do this."

"Or you could even just get a job and try to keep it. Crazy idea, I know, but…" I felt so hot under the collar during this conversation that I forgot the temperature was dropping.

Bunny grabbed my arm and pleaded, "I won't be able to get a job if I'm in the pen. Rollie will—"

"Get arrested. I'm calling the cops."

"I think, Camilla, if you check the code of ethics, you'll see that you can't really do that to a client. You could be reported to the Law Society of Upper Canada."

"Are you on crack? Because that's just plain insane."

"No, it isn't. I had a lot of time to read in the RDC. They got a library and law books, too. Up-to-date criminal code and digests. Everything."

"Digest this." I snapped open my phone. "I'm calling my brother-in-law."

"He's with the Ottawa force. Ottawa doesn't have jurisdiction here. It's RCMP on the Hill. Federal."

"I'm impressed, Bunny, that you know so much about my family circumstances and about police jurisdictions. Obviously, imprisonment has been good for you. Think of how much more you can learn in Kingston."

Bunny paled and swayed. Of course, I couldn't imagine how long he'd last doing hard time. And he was my favourite client ever.

"I can't go back. I'll die, Camilla. And think about Tonya and the baby. Think about—"

"Why don't you think about how you got yourself in this situation?"

"It's not my fault. You don't know how easy it is when you're with some people to get pulled over to the dark side. Like Rollie."

"The dark side? Oh Bunny, you're such a poet."

"But I don't want to be there. I'm going straight now. This is a lesson to me, for sure." Bunny stopped and blinked. "Except Rollie has got me stuck. I'm trapped. You know?"

I snapped the phone closed. "Here's a deal. Where are you meeting him? Tell me right now."

Behind Bunny, Alvin stood listening to the entire conversation with his mouth hanging open. Luckily, it was too cold for flies.

Bunny gulped. "Behind the Centre Block. By the edge of the Hill, near where the stray cats are. We're supposed to connect and sort everything out, plan the next step. He tosses the stuff over the fence into the bushes; in case he gets made, he won't have much on him. He can climb up from the bike path and pick it up after. But if you show up, he'll know I ratted him out. He probably saw me talking to you."

That was true enough.

And Rollie was more than just a small-time crook. He was a vicious and unpredictable small-time crook. Bunny knew that, and so did I.

Alvin headed away from us, striding purposefully. That's never good.

"Come back here, Alvin," I yelled. "I may need your assistance with this situation." But I was too late. He, too, had melted into the crowd. It's so hard to get good help these days.

Bunny shuffled from foot to foot, a pathetic vision of anxiety. Of course, he was Bunny and still good-looking. Any woman but me would have taken pity on him. I glanced around looking for an RCMP vehicle. Of course, it was too dark and they were too far away.

Twenty minutes later, the politicians were still droning, and I was still lecturing Bunny. Blah blah blah.

Up in front of the Centre Block, choirs launched into Christmas carols, and politicians took the mike and made muffled comments. Small children began to cry. Alvin moved forward, seeking political guidance or something. The light show was in full flow, with the purple against the front face of the Centre Block and the Peace Tower changing to blue, then to snow flake patterns.

"Promise me, Bunny, that you mean it this time."

"I promise. Anything."

At that moment, with the choirs in the background, a hundred thousand lights bloomed, cutting the dark, raising spirits. A sea of bodies parted, and Alvin emerged. As scary as that was, I thought it might be good news. He was wearing a triumphant grin, but no scarf. I couldn't see a bulge in his pocket either, indicating that my scarf was gone, too. He did have an expensive maroon jacket slung over his arm.

Alvin leaned over and whispered in my ear, "Rollie would love to apologize for his threat, but I'm afraid he's tied up at the moment."

"Really?" I said, feeling a smile break out. "Did he put up a fight?"

Bunny turned white.

I said, "Did he recognize you?"

Alvin shook his head.

"Ah. But he knows it wasn't Bunny who, um...?"

"Pretty sure."

"Where's your scarf, Alvin?"

"What you don't know won't hurt you, Camilla. Isn't that what Rollie told you?"

"Hmm. Remind me not to ask where my scarf is, too."

"The lights are on, and Rollie's nowhere near home."

I flicked open my cell phone and keyed in a number. "I've changed my mind about that Christmas gift exchange, Merv," I said. "You'll find a thoughtful present in back of the Parliament Buildings in the bushes. And Merv? You better hurry before your gift gets cold."

I snapped the phone closed. "Time you were home yourself, Bunny," I said.

As Bunny skittered off through the crowd, I said, "You know, sometimes I can really understand going over to the dark side."

"There is a certain appeal," Alvin said.

"Welcome back, Alvin."

"You, too. Do you think they'll be able to convict Rollie on anything?"

"Not a chance. Get him on parole violation maybe. Or revoke his bail if he's on bail. Cramp his style this year."

"Better than nothing," Alvin said. "I feel bad about the scarf. I'll make you another one."

"Don't worry about it, Alvin," I blurted.

"Maybe with neon this time. You want me to drop off this jacket to the Snowsuit Fund?"

Sometimes the Christmas spirit just warms the soul.

"Great idea. Happy holidays, Alvin."

"And to you, Camilla."

Blood on the Holly

Alvin's Christmas Scarf

Six skeins each red and green wool, DK weight (or any other colour combo that gets you in the Christmas spirit). Knit holding both yarns together as if one strand.

Cast on 21 stitches on No. 9 needles.

First row: Knit.

Second row: Purl.

Continue these two rows until scarf measures six feet or longer. Make a fringe at each end. Sew on Christmassy decorations like angels, or weave small, battery-activated LED Christmas lights through here and there to suit your taste.

Repeat as necessary.

Mary Jane Maffini is the author of the Camilla MacPhee and the Fiona Silk mysteries (both RendezVous). Her third series features professional organizer Charlotte Adams in Organize Your Corpses *(Berkley). She's won two Arthur Ellis awards (in 1996 and 2002) for her short stories, was nominated for best first novel award in 2000 for* Speak Ill of the Dead *and for best novel in 2004 for* Lament for a Lounge Lizard. *In 2006, she received the CWC's Derrick Murdoch Award and was the Canadian guest of honour at the Bloody Words Mystery Conference that same year. She is a former CWC president and a member of the Ladies Killing Circle. She lives in Ottawa, Ontario, with her long-suffering husband and two princessy miniature dachshunds.*

Christmas in Alice

Madeleine Harris-Callway

From the moment she sent her reply to Eileen's email, Margaret fretted that she'd made a mistake. She brought up the subject over breakfast, interrupting Brian's sacrosanct morning ritual: his hunt through the pages of the Sydney Morning Herald for the latest sin committed by Australia's prime minister.

"Eileen Grady?" he asked, the reading glasses slipping down his nose as he lowered the paper. "You mean your peculiar friend from graduate school in Vancouver?"

"For heaven's sake, Brian, that was thirty years ago. People change."

"Not that one."

But we've all changed, Margaret thought. She was no longer the slim cross-country runner Brian had married. She hated the soggy wads of fat around her middle. "Eileen's lived, as we all have," she said. "We have no idea what direction her life has taken, what she's accomplished, what's happened to her." She leaned forward, teasing his paper with her forefinger. "Admit it. You'd love catching up on old scandals in my chemistry lab."

"Spare me." Brian glared at the editorial as though his outrage could restore the moral centre of Oz's political system. "That bloody Internet. Just leads to 'googling' ancient friends for fun and profit. How convenient that Eileen's tour dumps her in Sydney."

She watched him turn a page. "Brian, it's not right to leave her on her own for Christmas."

"I was looking forward to being on our own, now that our daughter has buggered off." Brian threw her his naughty-boy look. "Enjoying the surf on Bondi Beach with the wife on Christmas Day, that's what I want. I've had enough obligations for a lifetime. As have you."

She launched her final volley. "I've haven't been back to Canada since we were married. Not once. Eileen's my chance to reconnect."

"The past is gone. I never think about it." But he sighed and closed the paper, signalling capitulation. "You're too damn nice, that's your problem."

No further emails from Eileen appeared. Margaret assumed she'd simply call on Christmas Eve, summoning them to pick her up. Eileen had never been adept at communication—she acted as though others should sense what she wanted and grew petulant when they didn't respond.

On reflection, this was probably why the other graduate students avoided her. At the time, Margaret attributed their attitude to academic snobbery. She and her friends worked for a "name" professor whose lab sprawled over the top floor of the chemistry building, but close to the stairwell lurked the small, dark lab of a minor researcher. She'd often noticed Eileen there, sealing up fluids in glass tubes for analysis. She wasn't sure what led her to befriend the pale, sharp-nosed girl. Was it because so few women ventured into chemistry? Perhaps, but she also felt protective of Eileen as though she could entice her out of her social awkwardness and transform her into someone more confident and attractive. Or, to be honest, more socially acceptable.

Initially, Eileen had been cool to Margaret's efforts at friendship. But one day, she surfaced next to Margaret's bench, brown-bag lunch in hand. From then on, they had lunch together nearly every day.

"She fancies you," Brian had taunted her.

"Don't be ridiculous. You don't like her because she's nerdy."

"Face it, you only hang about that white-coated ninny to showcase your own good looks."

Looks that had pretty much faded now, Margaret thought, catching a glimpse of herself in the hall mirror.

In anticipation of Eileen's visit, she tidied their multi-level house—one of Brian's early designs—and unearthed the Christmas decorations she'd shoved to the back of the storage room because Alison wouldn't be home for the holidays. She was surprised how sad she felt when she uncurled the branches of their artificial tree and popped on the ornaments. No point celebrating Christmas without Alison.

They spent Christmas Eve at home, waiting. Brian did his usual twenty lengths in the pool while she read a paperback novel in the shade, admiring the hard muscles she knew hid under the soft layer of his freckled skin. When they still had no word by late afternoon, she cooked their favourite meal of lamb cutlets and garlic mashed potatoes. No Christmas presents Brian had decided, but he cracked open a bottle of bubbly. Best to start the holidays off with a bang while they still had privacy, he teased her as it grew dark, coaxing her down under the tree, the sparkling ornaments twirling in a breath of wind through the French windows.

She woke to the penetrating cry of the telephone. She sat up in the night, not knowing where she was. Brian mumbled something beside her; they'd fallen asleep under the tree. The phone kept ringing. Alison, she thought, stumbling over the sheepskin rug, fumbling for the receiver.

The voice was unfamiliar, authoritative. "This is Constable Owen of the Alice Springs Police Force. Am I speaking to Mrs. Margaret Dennis?"

The police, oh God, it's Alison. Blood hammered in her ears.

"Do you know an Eileen Grady?" The woman repeated the question with more than a hint of impatience. "She put you down as her contact in Australia. There's been an accident."

"You don't have to go," Brian said later at the airport while she checked her boarding pass. Only one seat left on the night flight to Alice Springs this Christmas Eve. "She isn't hurt."

"She's in shock. We can't just leave her," Margaret said.

"Trust Eileen—histrionic to the last."

"That's not fair. The police don't know what happened."

"Yes, and when you're talking to the police, make sure you tell them about Laura."

Margaret stared him. "What possible good would that do?"

"Payback for buggering our Christmas." His resentful face haunted her as she passed through security and boarded the plane.

The flight to Alice Springs headed west into the dark. Margaret huddled under the thin airline blanket, wishing she'd brought a sweater. It was always so cold on planes.

Laura. She hadn't thought about that poor girl in years. In that way, she was no better than Brian, avoiding unpleasantness by dismissing the past. She stared out the window, imagining Sydney's red tile roofs and turquoise lozenges of swimming pools passing below. The green of the coast would quickly give way to the cracked tan of the desert.

When Alison was five, Brian had hired a Land Rover to drive from Darwin to Adelaide during the holidays. But they hadn't counted on the vast empty distances and the liquid pressure of the heat. Alison grew restless, constantly fighting Margaret's rules about wandering into the wild with its venomous snakes and spiders. Not even a visit to a camel farm with a tame dingo settled her down. And the flies, everywhere the flies. Landing on their food, crawling on their bare arms and faces whenever they left the car, hovering in a hissing black fog over a forlorn kangaroo carcass, a victim of the road trains that hurtled down the highway.

Australia's ancient mountains, once higher than the Himalayas, had dwindled to thousand-foot nubs. All rivers flowed to the deep-set heart of the continent and vanished underground, feeding a strange, otherworldly nature—the Garden of Eden designed by Hieronymus Bosch. Flowers sprouted from tree trunks, not the tips of branches. Incongruous black oak trees split in half when their roots struck artesian water. And ghost gum trees reared up like forked white lightning in their headlights, nearly forcing them off the road.

Their journey had ended oddly enough in Alice Springs.

The plane landed in a rain storm. Fifteen years before, Alice's legendary reservoir had nearly run dry, but now dark drops hammered the windows of the shuttle bus into town.

"Unusual to get rain on Christmas Day," the driver told her. "Hope you're not travelling into the outback. Most roads are flooded out."

Of course, Margaret thought, the parched earth absorbed no more water than a stone. People could drown in the desert.

"Got to take the long way round. Can't use the bridge," he went on. "Todd River is near to setting a record."

Margaret shivered. The police officer had found Eileen near that bridge. She remembered the Todd, a dry river bed thick with straw grass and punctured by black oaks. With the rains, water would rage through it, a torrent metres deep

The driver dropped her off at the police station, a low concrete building near the centre of town. In the dusky pre-dawn, the waiting room rested in church-like silence. No one there except an elderly woman lying on a bench by the wall and a police officer sitting at the reception desk in a pool of light.

"I'll tell Constable Owen you're here," he said when Margaret told him her name. He stood up, straightening his khaki short-sleeved shirt and shorts.

A soft noise made Margaret take a closer look at the old woman. Her heart raced. It couldn't be. "Eileen?" she ventured.

"Yes, Margaret, it's me." The words came out in a whisper. Margaret knelt down beside her and took her hand. It was icy cold.

The woman's stone grey eyes scanned Margaret's face and figure. "You look the same," she said.

Margaret struggled to return the false compliment. She tried to detect traces of the young Eileen buried under the clay of age.

"I see you've found each other," said a woman's deep voice.

Margaret looked up at an indigenous Australian of Brobdingnagian proportions.

"We spoke on the phone. Might I have a word, Mrs. Dennis?"

Constable Owen showed Margaret into an interview room and closed the door. "I need you to get your friend to tell us what happened," she said.

"But you already know." The close air hurt Margaret's throat. "You said she's in shock."

"No, I said she's not talking. That's different. The paramedics with the flying doctor service looked her over. She's okay."

"She's on her own. In a strange place."

"No worries. Oz is a strange place. Full of strange people." Owen smiled, not without irony.

"Eileen doesn't do well in nature," Margaret said. "Something happened back in university."

One weekend, she had talked Eileen into coming along on a hike. Most graduate students, even architecture students like Brian, embraced outdoor sports as an antidote to academia. Camping expeditions doubled as parties. But Margaret hadn't understood how excruciating climbing the slopes of Diamond Head Mountain could be for someone unfit. Red-faced and wheezing, Eileen fell half a mile behind the others. Brian had to carry her pack after she sat down on the trail, too tired and stubborn to budge. He had to put up her tent, as well. Worse, she'd forgotten to bring food, so she had to get by on what Margaret and Brian could spare and on the grudging donations of the others.

"Bad idea to bring her, love. She's an epic disaster," Brian said later when he crawled into Margaret's tent. But the full catastrophe was yet to come.

At midnight, they woke to shrill cries of animal terror. People raced out of their tents into the moonless night. In the dark confusion of hurtling bodies, Eileen's tent got knocked over. Only at daybreak did they realize that she had disappeared.

"So where was she?" Owen asked.

"The Mounties—the rescuers—found her in the woods below the campsite. She was pretty banged up. No one knows what happened."

"Really. She didn't tell you?"

"I felt responsible. She was off work for weeks. When she came back to the lab, I never pressed her about it."

"So what do you think happened?"

Margaret swallowed, remembering the heat and the dirt, the flies and mosquitoes. "Well, hiking's tough if you're not used to it. I think she woke up in the dark and panicked."

"But Alice is civilized—at least we locals like to think so. And it's only a short walk from Eileen's hotel to Old Todd."

Margaret had a sudden vivid memory of the indigenous people wandering through the Todd's dry riverbed, so silent and sad they seemed to be walking through another dimension. "Why all the questions?" she asked. "You found her. She's okay."

"Right you are. It's Eileen's friend I'm worried about."

"Isn't she back at the hotel?"

Owen's shrewd dark eyes took her in. "I told you about Mrs. Redding when I called."

Margaret glanced down at her hands. "I...I'm sorry. When you phoned, I thought it was about my daughter, Alison. She and her boyfriend are camping in the Northern Territory this Christmas, you see. Once I realized she was safe, I simply didn't take in much more."

"No worries." Owen checked her note book. "Eileen and Phyllis Redding took a stroll yesterday evening. When they didn't turn up for their group's farewell supper, the tour director called us. Apparently Phyllis said she was keen on photographing the Henley Boat Races on Old Todd. Bit odd. I found Eileen okay, but…" She spread a large palm.

"Phyllis is missing."

"Right you are. The two ladies were sharing accommodation to save on the single supplement fee. The tour company set it up." She smiled again. "I'm told it wasn't a love match."

No, room mates don't work out for Eileen, Margaret thought.

"Let's hope my mates find Phyllis wandering about, just a bit damp," Owen said. "Hate finding bodies after a flood. Nasty, especially after the dingoes and insects have had a go. You all right, Mrs. Dennis?"

"Is…is Eileen under arrest?" Margaret stammered.

Owen snapped her notebook shut. "No, she's free to go. But no buggering off to Canada till I get a statement."

Owen drove them to the hotel in her Land Rover. A cold galaxy of faint blue lights wreathed the resort's entrance way. Margaret recognized it as the place where she, Brian, and Alison had stayed fifteen years before and said so.

"What brought you to Alice?" Owen asked.

"My daughter got ill—appendicitis. We spent Christmas here after she left hospital," Margaret said.

They entered the lobby. The lively family-run hotel she remembered had been much expanded and renovated, and hardened into a standardized resort. The tacky plastic Santa Claus that had cheered up Alison was long gone, replaced by a spiky white artificial tree.

"Imogen will look after you," Owen said, indicating the blond girl behind the reception desk. "Do your best to have a Merry Christmas." She touched the brim of her straw hat and left them.

Imogen sported a spotless safari suit and a brass name tag. Stepping away from the desk, she explained that she'd put them together in a new room.

"I want my room," Eileen said in a loud, clear voice, startling them.

The girl hesitated. "I'm sorry. Constable Owen asked us to secure it until Mrs. Redding's son arrives from Florida. We'll do our best to look after you."

"Imogen won't lift a finger," Eileen said, once they were settled. She slumped down on the end of one of the twin beds. "I want my things."

Margaret dropped her overnight bag beside the writing desk. "Do you want me to call anyone?" she asked.

Eileen shook her head.

Margaret watched Eileen kick off her clumsy walking shoes. "It's been a long time," she began, not knowing what else to say. "What have you been doing with yourself?"

"Don't act like you don't know."

"Be fair, Eileen. We lost touch after I moved to Australia." She thought for a moment. "Don't tell me you stayed with the chemistry department?"

Eileen shrugged. Her mouth curved up in a strange, sly smile.

"After everything that happened," Margaret couldn't help saying. "My God, why didn't you move on?"

"Nobody gave me a job off campus. And now..." Her fists twisted the limp fabric of her khaki trousers. "The department let me go. Nobody wants technicians over fifty."

"I'm sorry. I didn't know."

"I always wanted to visit Australia." Eileen's slack features bunched up. "The tour company lied to me. All they did was march me through gift stores. They took all my money. And they made me share a room with that stupid, plastic woman."

Margaret let out a breath. "Look, you've been through a lot. Why don't we get cleaned up? You shower first. I need to call Brian."

"You're still with him."

"Yes, of course, I am." The years peeled away. She'd forgotten how much Eileen's words could sting. "And we have a daughter, Alison. She's twenty."

"Everyone else in your lab got divorced."

"What about you? Do you have family?"

"Don't be ridiculous." Eileen vanished into the bathroom. A heartbeat later, the shower roared to life.

Alone now, Margaret phoned home. She counted the rings, thumbing through the postcards thoughtfully provided by the resort—for a small fee, of course. Images of kangaroos, Aboriginal dot paintings, and a strange foot race held in the dry Todd River basin. Thirty rings—where was Brian? He wouldn't have gone to the pub. He promised her he wouldn't. The frigid air conditioning made her tremble.

The bathroom door flew open, nearly making her drop the phone. Eileen emerged, dressed in a white terry-cloth robe belonging to the hotel.

She dumped her clothes on the floor and got into bed. When Margaret suggested breakfast, she flopped down on her side, her back a ridge of ice.

Slowly, mechanically, Margaret replaced the receiver and picked up the unruly heap of clothes. She draped them over a chair: a thin navy cardigan, a stained white T-shirt, and the shapeless khakis. A small silver object thudded to the carpet. A digital camera.

She bent down and quietly slipped it into her purse. Exhausted, but desperate for fresh air, she let herself out of the room.

Outside, the rain had stopped, but even under the dull overcast, the desert heat seared her skin. Enormous ghost gum trees edged the hotel driveway. She followed their chalk-white trunks out to the main road, fragments of their brittle bark crunching under her sandals. Immediately, the flies sprang upon her, invading her mouth and nostrils.

Beating them off, she hurried down the main road, the incongruous roar of a river filling her ears. She spotted the bridge over Old Todd a short distance away, just as Constable Owen had said.

A rickety metal barrier prevented her from crossing over, but from where she stood on the road, she had a clear view. A foaming brown torrent sluiced under the bridge. Branches and debris tore past. Black oaks leaned like charred match sticks into the flood. No one could survive a fall into those waters, not even a giant like Constable Owen.

Several police officers were searching along the far bank close to the raging river. She recognized Owen who looked up and waved to her. Margaret half-raised her hand in reply. The flies settled on her again. She turned and walked swiftly back to the hotel.

"Cheer up," Imogen said when Margaret returned. "Grab some tucker from the breakfast buffet. Christmas present from me to you. Do you good."

Perhaps coffee would help, Margaret thought, and thanked her. She joined the crush of guests charging the buffet tables set up in the dining room, but her appetite was gone. She filled two bowls of fruit salad—one for herself, one for Eileen—and found a table.

Alone in the crowd, she pulled the digital camera from her purse and switched it on. An image of Uluru in the rain popped up on the screen, the rock's blood-red surface laced with streams of water. She flicked through dozens of photos of gaudily dressed tourists who were hugging koalas, brandishing gift store souvenirs, or raiding dinner buffets. A cheerful, heavy-set woman centred in a lot of them. Eileen appeared only once, standing next to the white Christmas tree in the lobby, her narrow face barred with shadow.

The last image was black.

"Fine little camera, that." Imogen had appeared at her table. "Lots of you Americans like it."

Margaret slipped it back into her purse.

"Can I ask you something?" Imogen took the chair opposite her. "Have the police found Phyllis?"

Margaret shook her head.

"It's stupid to hope, I know." The girl's face crumpled. "I should have stopped them. Eileen couldn't possibly have meant the Henley Boat Races. I mean, that's stupid. But Phyllis was so keen. She wanted to see every last thing in her guidebook. She was such a lot of fun, such a nice lady. Everybody liked her."

Everybody liked her. That's what they'd said about Laura, too.

"Her son gave her the trip," Imogen went on. "He's flying in tomorrow. He'll never feel the same about Christmas now, will he?"

Back in the room, Eileen was sitting up in bed, hands splayed on the sheets. She snatched the bowl of fruit salad from Margaret and stared into it. "Why do they always put in cantaloupe?" she grumbled.

"Eileen, we need to talk," Margaret said, setting her purse down on the writing desk. "About Phyllis Redding." She watched Eileen chew the pieces of woody melon. "Her son will want to know what happened to his mother."

Eileen lifted a bony shoulder. "Nothing happened to her."

"Don't be like that."

Eileen shoved more salad into her mouth.

"If you say nothing, people will think the worst. No one can blame you for an accident."

"Don't treat me like an idiot." Eileen's bowl tipped over, the dregs of syrup staining the sheet.

"I want to help, but I can't if you continue this way."

"Okay, fine." Eileen was getting loud. "We were on the bridge. She walked down into the dark."

"What do you mean?"

"I guess she wanted to take a closer look at the river."

Margaret sat down. "Why didn't you stop her?"

"Why should I? She never listened. All she did was talk. Talk, talk, talk. Everything was always so wonderful—like fucking Disneyland."

For an instant, something primal flashed into Eileen's face, the way it had in graduate school when she smashed the glass tubes of her failed experiments into the sink, one after the other.

Rage melted into a craftier look. "Since you like asking questions," she said, "why don't you ask me what happened on Diamond Head Mountain?"

"That was thirty years ago."

"And you're dying to find out."

"No, I'm not," Margaret said. In spite of the air conditioning, her dress felt wet and sticky. "But if you want to tell me, I'll listen."

"I was raped."

"That can't be." Margaret's heart beat like a bird's. The dark suspicion she'd never admitted even to herself now had voice. "We were a dozen students camping together. Everyone was safe."

"Oh, come on. A single woman alone in a tent—why, that's begging for it. A dried-up virgin needs a hard shag to set her straight."

"You had a dream. A nasty, vivid dream."

"The cops took me to hospital. That wasn't dreaming."

"Did the doctors examine you?"

Eileen turned her face away.

"You didn't tell them." Margaret pressed her arms over her chest, willing her heart to slow down. "Why didn't you say something?"

"I was an ugly nerd. They'd just say I was lucky someone bothered to throw me a fuck." She seized the salad bowl. With shocking violence, she shattered it against the wall next to her bed.

After a time, Margaret stood up. She reached out a hand, not quite daring to touch Eileen's shoulder. "I would have believed you," she said.

Eileen stared at the mess on her bed in rigid silence.

"Let's clean this up," Margaret said, pulling on the bed covers. "You'll cut yourself."

"Aren't you going to ask who raped me?" The sly look was back on Eileen's face.

Margaret swallowed. "All right, who did it?"

"Brian."

"You're lying!" The words exploded from Margaret's throat. "Brian would never do that to a woman. And he was with me the whole night."

"Sure about that? He didn't sneak to the outhouse, not even once?"

"No, not even once." Margaret stumbled back to the writing desk and grabbed her purse. "Why did you come to Australia? Why did you look me up? You hated the tour. And you obviously hate Brian and me. I don't understand you. I don't think I ever did."

Unable to look at her, she bolted from the room.

Imogen loaned Margaret her office. Closing the door, Margaret dialled home. This time, Brian answered.

"Oh, it's you," he said.

In his voice, she detected the lingering blur of alcohol. "Are you all right?" she asked.

"Of course, I am."

"You were right, I shouldn't have come. I'm leaving Alice. We'll have a proper Christmas."

"Forget Christmas. By the way, your daughter called."

"Alison." Some of the tenseness left her body. "Thank heavens. How is she?"

"That gormless boyfriend dumped her. She was all teary and sentimental about Christmas. She wanted to come home."

"And you told her to come at once. To have a family Christmas with us. You did tell her that, didn't you, Brian? Brian?"

After a pause, he said, "No, I didn't. Christmas is over and you're not here. What would be the point?"

"Point? She's our only child." Tears burned her eyes. "I want my daughter."

"For God's sake, I can't deal with you crying."

"Did you tell her that I'm here in Alice?"

"Yes, yes, I told her. She'll be fine. Just come home."

"I need to ask you something." She gripped the receiver so tightly she thought it would crack. "Eileen said a strange thing."

"Predictable. All right, out with it."

"You remember our camping trip on Diamond Head Mountain? She said someone attacked her."

"He probably thought her tent was the outhouse."

"That isn't funny! She claims she was raped." When Brian didn't reply, she pressed on, desperate to fill the silence: "It would explain why she screamed so horribly. Why she ran off into the woods. Why she wouldn't talk about it after. But she must have got it wrong. Please tell me that she's off her head."

"I don't know," Brian said finally. "I heard the lads talking. Later, a long time after."

"What did they…what did they say?"

"They were having a laugh. Something about chasing a pig through the woods."

"So it's true!" She remembered laughing at the crude humour of Brian's friends, refusing to take it seriously. "You knew. You knew and you did nothing. You should have told the police."

"They were my mates! What would you have me do? Ruin their lives? And you know Eileen's a bloody liar. In the end, no one got hurt."

"Now who's the liar?"

"Margaret, for God's sake—"

She slammed down the receiver, smothering his voice. She stared down at the desk, feeling that she'd fallen into a vacuum where she could hear and see nothing.

After a time, her eyes focussed on a framed photo. It showed Imogen and her friends in an absurd boat, holding it at waist height, their legs poking through its empty bottom. They weren't rowing—they were running like a large, pale-legged insect across the dry Todd river bottom. Printed across the top of the photo, she read: The Henley Boat Races.

No wonder Imogen hadn't believed what she'd overheard Eileen say. Margaret stood up, left the office, and headed back outside.

By now, the overcast had burned off. The sun was white-hot in a sky of hard ceramic blue. She felt its mad carcinogenic rays beating against her bare skin. Her underarms flooded with sweat. Beating back the flies, she fought her way into town.

By the time she arrived at the police station, she was so dizzy she could barely stand. White spots danced in her vision. A policeman summoned Constable Owen who brought her a plastic bottle of cool water, ordering her to drink it down.

"You're this close to heat stroke, Mrs. Dennis," Owen said, pressing her thick thumb and forefinger together. "You need four litres a day in Alice. Me, I need twice that."

Margaret couldn't laugh. "I have to tell you something," she whispered.

Owen settled her in the same interview room where they'd been earlier that morning. "All right, I'm listening."

"Eileen had a roommate back in university," Margaret began. "Laura was so nice. Everybody liked her." How trite to be echoing Imogen's words about Phyllis Redding, she thought. "Laura worked as a secretary for the chemistry department. She was a very pretty girl. The male students paid her a lot of attention. They didn't find her threatening, the way they did us female grad students."

"Foolish lot, men are," Owen grinned. "Laura and Eileen sound like a strange couple."

"Everyone thought that. Laura took Eileen in after that, well, trouble on Diamond Head Mountain. They did everything together: movies, pubs, shopping. Laura even persuaded Eileen to join the university's hiking club. Got her out into nature again. But then Laura found a boyfriend."

"I'll bet that threw a toad into the pudding."

Margaret rubbed her forehead. "They stopped chumming around. Everyone in the department noticed and made mean jokes about it, especially after Laura asked Eileen to move out. That weekend, the hiking club scheduled a walk up the coast. In spite of everything, Eileen insisted on coming along. Somehow, she and Laura got separated from the others and took a short-cut over the reservoir. The footpath over the dam is very narrow with a railing on one side. And a fifty-foot drop on the other."

Owen opened her notebook.

Margaret closed her eyes. "Eileen said that they were halfway across the dam when Laura lost her balance. The waterfall and the current are so strong it took the searchers six weeks to find her body."

"And you see a pattern."

"I don't know. The coroner and the police said it was an accident, but Laura's parents never accepted it. They hounded Eileen for years. Ruined her life." Margaret wiped her cheeks. "I understand them now. Laura was their only child. I've always believed Eileen, defended her, but after Phyllis Redding, I, well, I don't know what to think any more."

"Right." Owen closed her notebook. "Thanks for coming in."

"You don't believe me."

"No, I didn't say that. But you just told me that the Canadian authorities decided Laura had an accident."

"Just like Phyllis Redding."

Owen spread her hands. "We're still looking for evidence, Mrs. Dennis."

"I found this in Eileen's pant pocket." Margaret set the silver camera down between them on the table. "It's not hers."

"No worries. I'll ask Phyllis Redding's son about it when he comes in." Owen pulled an evidence bag from the voluminous back pocket of her shorts and sealed the camera inside. "Find any interesting photos?"

"The last picture is black. No light." Margaret licked her lips. "I don't think Phyllis took it."

"I see." Owen studied her for a moment. "Look here, Mrs. Dennis. Why don't you ask Imogen for your own room back at the hotel? And catch the first flight home to Sydney."

Imogen was happy to rent her a room far removed from Eileen's. Dead tired, Margaret sank down on her bed, rubbing her sun-burned arms. No point rushing back to Sydney. She couldn't face Brian. Not yet. She needed time to think. About him and their marriage. For she hadn't told Owen that she knew he was Laura's lover.

Thirty years ago, open relationships were the rage. You weren't supposed to be jealous. At least women weren't supposed to be jealous. And Brian's pubs and women had continued for much of their married life, only easing off when he took early retirement. She'd determinedly ignored that aspect of him to preserve the precious illusion of their family life. But now, all she could hear was the silent din of her carefully constructed myth collapsing around her.

Alison, she thought. All I have left is Alison. Perhaps she's on her way to find me here in Alice. I can always hope. She looked round for her suitcase and realized that she'd left it behind in Eileen's room.

Her old key still worked. When she swung open the door, she started. Eileen stood in the centre of the room wringing out her white T-shirt, wearing only a bra and the khaki trousers.

"You took something that belongs to me," Eileen said. "I want my camera."

"Stop it," Margaret said, pushing her way in. She spotted her bag next to the writing desk just inside. "We both know that camera isn't yours."

A flash of white. The T-shirt flared out and smacked her wetly on the cheek. "You hit me!"

The wet shirt flew at her again. She caught it and pulled, wrenching Eileen off balance. She seized Eileen's wiry wrists. Pushed with all she had. Eileen crashed onto the bed.

And, with surprising agility, sprang back up.

"Stay where you are," Margaret panted. "I know why you came to Australia."

Eileen's hard grey eyes narrowed.

"You've always fancied Brian. That's why you acted so helpless on Diamond Head, getting him to carry your things and put up your tent. You were hoping he'd crawl into your tent instead of mine, and when he didn't, you staged a scene. But your drama backfired because of his poisonous mates."

"Fuck you."

"Then he took up with Laura. How you must have hated her. And now, when you're at loose ends after getting fired, you travel to Australia, hoping we're divorced. You're pathetic. And Brian's not worth it."

Eileen leapt, knocking her into the writing desk. Her purplish hands grasped the wet shirt like a rope. Margaret tried to fend her off, but Eileen was too strong. An instant later, she felt a crushing force across her throat. Her cry for help became a croak.

She scrabbled madly for Eileen's hair. Scraped her nails over bare flesh. A shriek of outraged pain. She smashed her knee into Eileen's soft belly.

Air rasped back into her lungs. Eileen sprawled on the carpet, legs splayed. Margaret seized her suitcase, clasping it to her chest like a shield. Eileen rolled onto all fours, still holding the wet shirt.

"Don't try it," Margaret coughed. "I'm stronger than you. I always was."

A rap on the door. Enough to distract Eileen for a moment. Margaret scrabbled for the door handle and staggered out into the hall.

A bewildered elderly couple stared at her, saying that they'd heard loud voices. Margaret managed to shake her head. She turned and fled to the safety of her room.

She threw the bolt lock, leaning against her door until her breathing slowed. She must call Constable Owen, tell her what happened. But would Owen believe her? She hadn't believed her about Laura. In fact, she'd told her to bugger off back to Sydney like a good girl.

I'll wait, she thought. Get clean, and decide what to do.

She stripped off her rancid clothes and stepped under the shower. She scrubbed herself madly to tear away every speck of the horrid Christmas Day. Still wrapped in the bath towel, she stretched out on the bed, too tired to dress.

The telephone on the bedside table shrilled. What if it was Brian?

Or Eileen?

She let it ring. Finally, it stopped.

I can't just lie here, she thought after a time. She dried off, dressed in the shorts and shirt she'd brought, and tossed the rest of her belongings into her bag. A sudden bang on the door made her jump with fear.

She crept over to it in her bare feet and peered through the spy hole. Recognized Imogen in her safari suit. She undid the lock and let her in.

"Heavens, you scared me," Imogen said. "I was leaving you a note. Your daughter's here. She's looking for you. I phoned your room, but you didn't answer."

"Alison! Where is she?"

"I saw your friend in the lobby. She said you'd gone for a walk. They went out looking for you."

"When?" Margaret seized the girl's shoulders. "When did they leave?"

"Not five minutes ago. Mrs. Dennis, please, you're hurting me."

"Call the police!"

Margaret tore down the hall. An intense pain crushed her chest, squeezing her heart. Her lungs had no air.

She reached the lobby. Ran out and down the driveway, oblivious to the bursts of pain in her bare feet. Down the road to the bridge. Saw no one. She bent over, sides heaving.

On the far bank, a flicker of movement. She shouted Alison's name, but who would hear her over the roar of the water? Summoning the agility she'd once had as a runner, she leapt over the metal barrier. Caught her foot and fell heavily.

Her face and hands throbbed with pain. Blood flowed from her knee. She staggered up and hobbled across the bridge. Oh please, God, let there be two people, she prayed. Let there be two. She rolled over the second barrier and screamed in agony as her knee struck the pavement.

In the dim twilight, she spotted two figures by the river's edge. A tall, slender girl with auburn hair and a shorter figure wearing khaki pants.

"Alison!" she cried in pure terror.

The rushing river drowned out her voice. She saw Eileen bend down and pick up a large stone.

"Alison!" She screamed with all her passion as a mother.

Instinct made Alison turn at that moment. The blow from Eileen's rock missed her head but struck her shoulder, knocking her down. Young and agile, she rolled away from the water. Eileen seized the girl's shirt.

Margaret leapt down into the dark. The world slowed. She did not hear the roar of Old Todd or the shouts of Constable Owen and Imogen behind her. She saw only Alison's pale terrified face and the murky torrent boiling past as she tore her child free of those murderous claws.

And hurled Eileen into the river.

M. Harris-Callway is a former management consultant who now writes full time. She is an award-winning mystery short story writer and a longstanding member of Crime Writers of Canada. Her stories have appeared in both print and electronic media. When not acting as "helper monkeys" on their film-maker daughter's movie sets, she and her husband share their Victorian home with two spoiled cats.

A Christmas Bauble

Therese Greenwood

*D*an Tuttle would not have spent Christmas Eve with a shotgun pointed at his head if the woman he adored did her gift shopping on time. But asking Case Doyle to do her shopping on time—to do anything on time—was asking for a Christmas miracle.

Case was a perfect specimen of what the Saturday magazines called "a flapper," and she stood out in December-grey Kingston like a rose on a casket. Her hair and her skirts were too short, her laugh too full. She danced even when her feet weren't moving and she wanted flying lesson for Christmas. She liked aeroplanes, gin, masked parties, the Charleston, and apparently, Elliot "Sammy" Sampsen, the too-charming son of a director of the railway. By all rights, it should have been the well-bred Sammy staring down the shotgun barrel. But if Dan had learned anything in the Great War, it was that the Dans of this world stared down the barrel, while the Sammys had Christmas brunch with pretty, laughing girls.

Case laughed as she and Dan dashed out the front door of the newspaper office where they worked, although with Case, "work" was a word to be used loosely. It had been snowing since before dawn, and King Street was blanketed a foot thick. Dan would never have guessed a weapon existed in this clean, white city. It was five years since the Armistice and he still thought of death as muddy and wet and reeking.

"Bright and crisp and even," Case sang, hugging herself inside the mink coat she had won in a bet with a Toronto reporter.

This was the scene Dan dreamed of in the trenches when he realized he would not be home for Christmas after all. Horses and sleighs slid past, harnesses jingling; tree branches were iced with snowdrops; passers-by called out cheery greetings, all modern machines banished by the snow. Even Case, who loved to drive and went everywhere in top gear, left her rich aunt's car buried in the snow and skipped along in silly red leather boots like the ones Greta Garbo sported in a picture at the Bijou. When Dan asked how Case knew they were red, given that the movie had no colour, she accused him of lacking imagination. Dan had lots of imagination, and Case played a big role in his imagining, but it never seemed the time to tell her.

As they turned the corner to plunge through the drifts along Princess Street, snow beaded the lenses of Dan's glasses, making it hard to see. Case got a few steps ahead despite the slippery soles of her fancy boots. "You should've shopped earlier," Dan called, thinking of his gift for her, tucked in his coat pocket.

"Danny, I had no idea working was going to take up so much time," Case said over her shoulder. "Anyway, I didn't have a cent for Aunt Stella's present until I cornered Colonel Smiley in the business office and got advanced a month's pay."

A month's pay! Eighty dollars! For a Christmas present! Dan's gift seemed smaller now. But Case did not have annoying inconveniences like room and board and the occasional clean shirt. She lived with her aunt, the newspaper's publisher, in a big house far from the breweries and locomotive works and factories stretching across the busy Kingston harbour. The smell of tanning hides and belching engines did not wake Aunt Stella—Mrs. Matthews to Dan and the ordinary joes at the *Kingston Chronicle*—from her feather bed. Case literally breathed a different air, one that made her want to fly and gave her breath to loudly nickname the bully who ran the *Chronicle's* business office. "Colonel Smiley," as Case dubbed him, was the perfect officer: short, scheming, and charming. He had been spending an awful lot of the time lately with the widowed Aunt Stella, and Dan had not confronted him about the weekly pay packet regularly coming up a dollar light. If there was one thing Dan had learned in the trenches, it was to keep his head down.

"Charge! Into the breach!" Case shouted. Marten van Strien was putting the closed sign in the door of his jewellery store, and Case flung herself over the threshold, sending the jeweller staggering. Dan hurled himself behind Case because, well, because he couldn't help himself, and they landed in a heap on the carpeted floor. Dan's glasses fogged up as he collapsed on Case's soft mink, and he could smell her perfume—like no flower he had ever smelled, light and foreign and expensive.

Dan got to his feet, heard the door shut and the lock click, and wondered why Case had not yet made a smart remark. He pulled off mittens crusted with sharp snow and rubbed his glasses on a speck of wool that seemed dry. The lenses were streaky when he put them on, and he thought he wasn't seeing right. He took off the glasses, rubbed harder, and pushed them firmly back up his nose, but he was still staring down the barrel of a shotgun held by a woman very, very great with child.

"Kitty Beaupre!" he said.

"Dan Tuttle, still following Case Doyle like a lapdog," said Kitty. The butt of the shotgun was resting against her huge belly; clearly, she did not know about its kick. She was a tiny thing with a sharp tongue, snapping eyes, and a proud, thin face with faint pink trails of acne. Dan had always liked her, even though she was the most expert lip-curler-upper he had ever met. She sometimes filled in as a bookkeeper at the Chronicle, scrounging work she had done full-time when the men were away at war. She was as alone in the world as Dan and she was not married, as her naked ring finger proclaimed.

"I've heard of shotgun weddings," Case said, her nose out of joint from the lapdog comment. "But this is a crackerjack idea. Steal a ring, capture a bachelor like Dan, and wait for a minister to come by."

Shut up, Dan thought, wondering if he had lived through Passchendaele to be shot by a deceived woman.

"Shut up," said Kitty. Her swollen body seemed to fill the narrow shop made small by thick glass display shelves running along walls darkened by wood panelling and red velvet wallpaper. Dan felt as if he were trapped inside a leaded glass snow globe, like the one his mother had brought out every Christmas until the Spanish flu took her.

"Can't wait for Christmas morning, can you, Case?" Kitty said bitterly.

"No, I can't," said Case, getting to her feet in a wet swirl of leather and mink. "But that's not a shooting offence."

"If you are going to rob me, Kitty, get done with it," said Marten van Strien in his dry, accented voice. The tall, unbending Dutchman was a man of few words and not because he was ashamed of pronouncing his *w*'s as *v*'s and *j*'s as *y*'s. During the War, some Kingston businessmen had changed their foreign-sounding names, but van Strien stubbornly kept his—and his business, too. Everyone knew the Dutch knew diamonds, and no one wanted a bad diamond, so in the end everyone bought from van Strien because of his foreign name. Even Dan had bought a trinket from the jeweller's shop.

"Who says I'm robbing you?" asked Kitty. "I don't want your lousy jewels."

"Are you sure?" asked Case. "A nice bauble is right up there with flying lessons on today's Christmas gift list."

Enough with the flying, thought Dan. Get your feet on the ground.

"Why would I want a nice bauble?" spat Kitty. "To remind me of the heel who left me broke and in trouble while he bought another woman a flashy jewel for Christmas?"

"You have a point," said Case thoughtfully. "That's the work of a Grade A rat."

"You bet he's a rat," said Kitty. "Living it up while I hide away, trying not to starve to death. When I found out he was getting his lady-friend a Christmas bauble, I decided to give him my own two-barrelled present."

"Shooting does sound too good for the hound," said Case. "But the majority of folks will say hanging is too good for you, and that doesn't sound good at all."

Kitty smiled a grim smile and tightened her grip on the barrel. "Easy for you to say, with a big rock coming straight to your ladylike finger on Christmas morning."

"A big rock?" said Case with too much interest, and Dan felt what was left of his heart sink into his stomach. "How big?"

"The biggest," snarled Kitty. "Show her." She nodded curtly towards the jeweller, expecting to be obeyed, and Dan thought she would have made a good sergeant. Van Strien took an engraved silver casket from one of the glass displays and handed it to Case, who expertly flipped it open. Nesting haughtily on the purple velvet was the biggest ring Dan had ever seen, and his own gift for Case shrank to nothing at all.

"Diamonds and platinum on rose gold," said Case. "One wonders if this is a Christmas bauble or a serious proposition." She slipped the ring on her finger and extended her hand to see the stone sparkle.

"It's our finest engagement ring," said van Strien.

And a too-serious proposition, Dan thought miserably. Case would wear Sammy's ring and be married in June by the bishop in the cathedral. They would go on a summer honeymoon to the Continent and come home to a big house on the lake. She would never work at the *Chronicle* again, and Dan would sometimes glimpse her driving by, too fast, in a big motor car. Sammy would be his new boss, and Sammy and the colonel would be thick as thieves. Dan wondered if the *British Whig* was looking for reporters, or maybe *The Intelligencer* in Belleville.

Rap rap rap. The sharp, sudden sound sent Dan diving to the floor before he realized he was moving, slave to a reaction he thought long dead. He cursed himself when he realized it had been a knock on the door, and a sharp voice Dan despised called out, "Let me in."

"By all means, let His Nibs in," Kitty ordered. Van Strien opened the door, and Colonel Smiley strolled in, took off his expensive fedora, and shook snow from the brim onto the jeweller's carpet in front of Dan's prone body.

"Kitty Beaupre, what do you think you are doing?" barked the Colonel in his command voice.

"Wiping the smile off your mug for good," Kitty snarled, shoving the barrel of the shotgun against the little man's chest. "You two-timing louse."

"Darling Kitty," purred the Colonel, suddenly turning on a hundred-watt electric smile on his small, handsome face. "You misjudge me. You're the only girl for me."

"Lay off the soft soap," she said. "I've had enough of your 'darling Kitty's' and opening doors and driving me home as if I were sugar that might melt in the rain."

"Now, Kitty," said the Colonel, with a look of gentle rebuke Dan thought he must have practised in a mirror. "Is that any way to talk to the man who has come to buy you a special Christmas gift?"

"My gift?" Kitty said. "It's for the rich widow you've been chasing."

Kitty was talking tough, but Dan could see she wanted to believe because it must look like her problems would be over if the Colonel gave her child his name. Dan, though, figured her problems would be just beginning if she married that skunk.

"It's the season for putting things right," the Colonel pleaded. "Show me some good will, darling Kitty."

"You were dipping into the accounts," Kitty said softly. "Shaving a little off where you thought people wouldn't complain. You only made time with me when I found out about it."

"Kitty, you've got it all wrong," said the Colonel. "The money was for us, for our family."

"He's a liar and a thief," said Case quietly. "He hoped no one would believe a woman in your, er, delicate condition."

"Of course, you'd say that," snapped Kitty. "It was your money he stole and your aunt he's trifled with. It would kill the likes of you to admit he might prefer the likes of me."

"And I do, Kitty," said the Colonel, slowly opening his arms wide. "Indeed, I do."

Kitty lowered the gun and stepped into the Colonel's embrace. He hugged her, stepped back, and gently took the shotgun from her hands. Then he slapped her across the face, slamming her into the display case. Dan heard Case's sharp gasp as Kitty fell to the carpet, broken glass and engagement rings spilling about her, her huge stomach straining against her thin cloth coat.

"You ridiculous tramp," said the Colonel calmly, breaching the gun and ejecting the shells as if he had just finished a pheasant shoot. "That brat could be anyone's."

Van Strien squatted beside Kitty, Dan thought, to pick up his spilled jewellery. But the jeweller took off his jacket and folded it into a pillow for Kitty's head. Then he tenderly began to pick the broken glass from Kitty's hair, saying, "There, there." Kitty began to cry, and Dan wanted to cry, too, seeing that proud woman in tears at such a little act of kindness.

That was when Dan felt things slow down, like when he was about to scramble out of that trench. As he got to his feet, he felt his left foot travel forward in a long, falling step. His weight shifted, his half-opened left hand coming straight out from his shoulder, chin high, and his fingers began to close with a mad clutch, his knuckles lining up like soldiers, and he hit Colonel Smiley hard, square in his smooth, smug face. Smiley hit the carpet like a ton of bricks, the same bricks that seemed to have fallen from Dan's shoulders, and lay still. Dan was leaning over, ready to throttle the Colonel, when Kitty screamed an unearthly shriek and clutched her distended stomach.

"We must get to the hospital," van Strien said. "Now."

"Carry on without me," Case said, poking the still-out Colonel with a red-booted toe. "I have a Christmas present to take care of."

How selfish, Dan thought as he gathered the pregnant woman into his arms, for Case to be thinking of her own Christmas at a time like this. It made him as sad as anything he had seen in Flanders.

"Do all babies look like Queen Victoria?" Case was saying when Dan dropped by the hospital the next morning.

"My baby looks like an angel," the new mother said with her old spunk. She was sitting up in bed and putting the infant to her breast, and Dan, about to walk into the room, blushed and stepped back.

"I'm sure she's a fine specimen," Case said, "as far as babies go. In fact, I'd say your Christmas angel deserves a present."

Dan peeped through the crack between the door and the frame and saw her presenting Kitty with the envelope full of the month's pay. "Think of it as a belated wedding gift," she said.

"Very funny," Kitty sniffed.

"I am as serious as the heart attack I am wishing on the now-unemployed Colonel Smiley," Case said, handing over a newspaper. "I was going over a back issue of the Chronicle and realized I missed your wedding announcement in February. How romantic, you marrying your young pilot on Valentine's Day."

"My young pilot?" said Kitty, peering at the page in one hand, cradling the child with the other.

"It's right there in black and white, suitable for framing," said Case vaguely, and Dan wondered what strings she pulled to have the notice printed up.

"How sad to think you were married to the dashing young fly-boy in February and a widow by August," Case went on, giving Kitty another sheet of newsprint. "A young man crashing in the prime of life—see it says right here, 'the prime of life.' And while out barn-storming a living for his wife and coming child. It's heartbreaking."

"Heart-breaking," echoed Kitty, her eyes tearing across the page.

"But not as sad as the story in tomorrow's paper, about the poor widow trying to sell her engagement ring on Christmas Eve. Mr. van Strien gave such a lovely quote. 'A woman's engagement ring ought to be sacred.' Mr. van Strien is a secret romantic, the stiff old stick. That reminds me, you left your ring behind and your gold band, too." And Case handed over the little silver casket with Sammy's ring.

"But Sammy—" Kitty began.

"Won't be needing a ring," interrupted Case. "I adore the stylish way he swans about with his hands in his pockets, and he's a wonder with a martini shaker. But the future Mrs. Sammy is in for a lifetime of bridge parties and collecting china dogs and long stories about men named Binky Batson. A girl doesn't want to spend her life with the wrong fellow just because the hoi polloi demand it."

Dan had heard people say their hearts soared, but he had never understood what they meant. Now he heard trumpets sound, angels sing, and all was right in the heavens. Case had helped Kitty when no one else could, she didn't love that silly man, and she was a pretty, laughing girl who wanted to fly. Dan coughed loudly, gave Kitty time to settle the baby, and strolled into the room with his hands in his pockets.

"I brought you a present, Kitty," he said, handing over the gift he had bought for Case. Kitty unwrapped it carefully, saving the tissue paper and the little cardboard box, and drew out the tiny airplane suspended on a silver chain.

"Dan, that is the most beautiful Christmas bauble I have ever seen," breathed Case.

"A belated wedding gift," he smiled, "in memory of Kitty's pilot."

Kitty was wearing the necklace when she and her baby drifted off to sleep and the nurse came in to give Case and Dan the push.

"Why don't you come back to the old homestead for Christmas brunch?" Case said, taking Dan's hand, puffy and red from bashing the Colonel. "There are all the essentials for a jolly time: spiked punch and fruitcake and mistletoe and the like."

He could smell her French cologne as she leaned in to kiss him on the cheek, and for the first time, he knew what it felt like to be a hero.

Kingston, Ontario, writer **Therese Greenwood** *grew up on Wolfe Island, the largest of the Thousand Islands, where her family has lived since 1812. The region forms the backdrop for her historical crime fiction. She has twice been short-listed for the Arthur Ellis Award for Best Short Story – including a 2004 nod for "A Christmas Bauble." This story first appeared in* The Kingston Whig-Standard *in 2003.*

The Sun Sets in Key West

Sylvia Maultash Warsh

*A*nita loved the two expanses of blue water: the Atlantic on her left, the Gulf of Mexico on her right as the car headed south down U.S. Route 1 along the archipelago of the Florida Keys. Carol, who was driving, chattered about all the muscle-bound, tattooed bikers they'd seen riding their motorcycles along the road.

"It's a holiday," Anita said. "Even bikers take holidays."

"From what?" said Carol. "Crime?"

Anita remembered unfolding the map on her dining table, the Florida peninsula narrowing at the southern tip into a spiny finger of islands pointing away from her life. She needed a holiday, too—from the weather, from the real estate business in Toronto, from herself. Nothing moved in December anyway. She was the boss; she could give herself and Carol, her best agent, a break over Christmas. They'd been run off their feet through the fall and needed a breather before the spring crazies when everyone with a few thousand dollars in the bank wanted to make a down payment on a condo.

Her stepdaughter, Pam, didn't want her there for Christmas, now that Phil was dead. Anita had married him when she was forty-three and Phil was fifty-eight. Not a marriage made in heaven, but he'd eased her loneliness for five years. Then the heart attack. She had no luck with men.

Carol, divorced and not quite forty, had jumped at the chance for an all-expenses-paid getaway. Anita was deducting it. She had a client who wanted a condo in Key West and she would find him one if it killed her. They had flown to Miami, stayed a few days in an art deco hotel, then rented the Chrysler for the drive to the Keys.

During dinner one of their nights in Miami, Anita had confessed over her coconut-breaded shrimp that she'd spent her honeymoon in the same hotel over two decades ago.

Blood on the Holly

"Your first husband?" Carol asked tentatively.

Anita had clammed up, surprised at herself for venturing into the mine field. It was painful, even after all these years.

They passed through Key Largo, its streets decorated with Christmas wreaths and people milling around the shops. Stores became more sporadic, palms and bougainvillea more abundant, as they drove through the smaller keys, some of which were uninhabited except for pelicans and herons. The names made her smile: Conch Key, Duck Key, Crawl Key, Fat Deer Key.

They stopped in a little café for mahi-mahi sandwiches and a bathroom break, then Anita took the wheel.

"I can't believe how beautiful it is here," Carol said. "No slushy, dirty snow. No icy roads. Why don't we live here?"

Anita smiled. "We have great summers in Canada."

"Yeah. Three months of the year. Don't you have a place up north?"

"I don't go there anymore. I rent it out."

"So much for our great summers. Where is it?"

"Georgian Bay. Pretty little place."

"So why don't you go?"

Anita sighed, picturing the screened porch of the cottage in northern Ontario, the severe rocks on the shore framing the grey expanse of water, vast and deep. Christian Island loomed in the distance. The bad dreams had stopped long ago; she never thought of it anymore.

In the intimacy of the car, the air bright with Florida sun, she said, "I have bad memories. There was an accident."

"Oh?" Carol was diplomatic, asked no questions. Maybe that was why Anita went on.

"We'd been married for four years. Stan liked to go fishing. I didn't. I couldn't swim, and it made me nervous being on the water. So he ended up sitting on the lake by himself for hours, listening to his tape player. He was a musician—good guitar player, so-so voice. But you can't make a living at music, so he went to work for my dad at the company. I didn't make him do it. He just wasn't making any money with his music."

Carol was quiet, taking it in.

At Key Vaca, they crossed onto the Seven Mile Bridge, a stretch of concrete Anita couldn't see the end of. The car glided along it, water on both sides. She was mesmerized by the imminent ribbon of bridge before them like a promise. Better times ahead. What spoiled it was the rusty old railway bridge running parallel to it, maybe fifty feet off to the right, negating all promises. A reminder that everything outlived its usefulness.

"So one Sunday in August, he goes out fishing," Anita continued. "Late in the afternoon, a neighbour comes running to the cottage, yelling there'd been accident. He found Stan's boat in the water, but Stan wasn't in it. The police looked for him for days. Georgian Bay's too big to drag. Never found the body."

She had gone through a bad patch at the time—a very bad patch— blaming herself for everything. Stan wasn't a natural-born salesman: Was that *her* fault? She knew he was unhappy. More than unhappy. Down. Maybe that made him careless. Maybe worse. Maybe he'd looked at the water around him and saw an easy way out. It still pained her that the love of her life had been willing to leave her behind. She pictured him peering over the edge of the boat, catching his image in the calm water. What did he see? Probably not the slender, confident university grad she'd met at a party. She'd been charmed by the dark curly hair and blue eyes, the slight gap between his front teeth. He had her when he hoisted the guitar from the corner and began to pick out a tune.

If you're going to sing,
Sing a song of freedom,
Use your voice for justice,
If you're going to sing.

She, a community college grad in business, was impressed that he composed his own songs that espoused a world view of social ideals. When he looked in the water that day on the boat, had he recognized himself?

After the accident, she'd gone from working in her dad's office to taking some real estate courses. Then her dad had taught her the business of selling houses. People trusted her. She didn't care if they bought the house; she wasn't hungry like the men agents who were supporting families. Her dispassion made her more credible.

Her career blossomed, and the business expanded. Her father retired, which made her boss. Both parents were gone now. Her brother lived in San Francisco with his third wife. Anita was on her own and heading toward fifty. Still attractive, but wondering what it was all about.

Traffic got heavier as they crossed the bridge into Key West, the end of the line, the end of the continent. U.S. Route 1 turned into North Roosevelt Boulevard. Carol used the little inset map of the city to navigate Anita west along the island, down Palm Avenue to Eaton Street, then north on Duval. The Gulf of Mexico peeked out beyond the exclusive, heavily landscaped resorts built on the water. Anita had splurged on a suite for the two of them.

Deep pink azaleas and bougainvillea grew around the entrance where a young valet jumped out to park their car and a bellhop picked up their luggage. In the lobby stood a giant white Christmas tree strung with red ornaments and lights that winked on and off. Their rooms, airy with translucent sheers and puffy white duvets, overlooked the water facing northeast. There was marble in the bathroom, champagne in the bar fridge, and a fruit basket on the table.

Anita stood watching the waves sparkle in the sun.

"They have a shuttle that'll take us places," said Carol, reading the hotel brochure. "There's Ernest Hemingway House and Audubon House and the Little White House. And at sunset, we can walk to Mallory Square. It's a big thing here."

"What?"

"Watching the sunset. They call it a celebration."

"The sun sets every night. So what?"

"It's the furthest point west on the most southern tip of land. Oh, come on, it'll be fun."

Late in the afternoon, the shuttle took them south through streets of charming white-painted and sometimes columned wooden houses, circa 1930. The Hemingway House, surrounded by privacy hedges, was white with ochre shutters, larger than its neighbours, and made of stone. The tour guide was a youngish man with a ponytail and a sarcastic attitude.

In the dining room, he pointed out the wall of photos of Hemingway's four wives. The writer had had a lifelong habit of falling in love, but also a problem with depression. He drank hard and loved hard and then apparently felt guilty. In the end, he lived in Idaho with wife number four. His health had deteriorated and, despondent, he shot himself with a rifle. Anita imagined it would make a bloody mess. Maybe she had been lucky. Stan hadn't left anything to clean up.

They got back to the resort in time for the short walk to Mallory Square, a puzzle of shops and museums well back from the large concrete dock. A crowd had begun congregating an hour before sunset. People had already found seats on the edge of the pier facing west. Bikers sporting tattoos on their arms and the backs of their necks stood around in black T-shirts, waiting for the sunset like everyone else. They were surprisingly well groomed and unthreatening. Obviously not Hell's Angels. Buskers were setting up their acts to compete for tourist dollars, while aging hippies unravelled black cloths flecked with silver jewellery to lay out on display stands.

A nimble couple were practising an act with their two not-so-nimble dogs—one an overweight basset hound, the other a large black and white mongrel wearing a red bandana around its neck. Anita watched the woman hold a hoop for the basset hound to jump through. She had to keep lowering the hoop, but finally the dog cleared it, triggering applause from the crowd.

Carol had taken herself to a nearby stand to buy two rum-and-cokes. A deeply tanned, wiry man in shorts bicycled past Anita and stopped twenty feet from the dog act, near the end of the pier. His battery-assisted bike pulled a small dolly behind, loaded with a beat-up black box, a drum, and a worn guitar case. Anita couldn't see his face beneath the shadow of his wide-brimmed straw hat as he unloaded his equipment. The skin of his arms and legs was leathery-brown from exposure. She imagined him cycling his way through Florida to busk on all the other piers in the state. He wasn't young. What a way to make a living.

Anita was distracted by Carol handing her the drink and by the busker couple trying to keep the crowd's attention with bad jokes at the expense of the dogs. When Anita turned to look at the man in the hat, his guitar case was open on the pier, ready for handouts, and he was setting up what looked like a one-man band. His guitar was ordinary enough, but he'd placed the drum onto his back, with sinister little stuffed trolls, varnished grey, perched on top, rattling out a beat like automated drumsticks. How did he do that? She saw the trolls were connected to his elbow by cables, so that when his elbow moved, they bent down and played the drum. The other elbow controlled a cymbal. A contraption around his neck held a pan flute in front of his face on one side and a horn on the other so that he could blow into them with no hands. The cables he'd connected to the heels of his shoes regulated the drum on his back as well as a washboard behind his head and some castanets. When he stooped over, the cables stretched tight and the instruments played. Ingenious in a bizarre way. He moved in a slow circle, stepping wearily round and round while strumming the guitar, warming up.

People passed by, holding drinks, glancing at this curiosity. Some took pictures. One or two stepped forward to throw a few dollars into the guitar case. Pity money. One pretty, middle-aged woman caught sight of him and grimaced, turning away with a sneer. The man saw her and, without missing a beat, stuck out his tongue at her, murmuring some unintelligible obscenity. Despite his appearance, he played a competent guitar. The music would've been fine, Anita thought, if she didn't have to look at him. Since this was the end of the pier, most people strolled to the black grill fence, stared at the musician for a moment, then turned their backs to him to face the water, the real show: the sun slowly setting into the purple horizon.

When he began to sing, Anita was stunned. The world had turned upside down as she blinked. She could see most of his face now, the eyes beneath the hat, and the mouth above the pan flute. Blue eyes, determined and hard; a gap between his front teeth when he opened his mouth. His voice sounded like a bad imitation of Bob Dylan. She was rooted to the pier, watching him, her lunch rising into her oesophagus. Was she in some parallel universe? She blinked again, remembering how empty her heart had felt when they held the memorial service after Stan was finally declared dead some twenty years ago. The guilt of his suicide, the sudden moments of self-loathing when she caught herself in the mirror, had plagued all the years since, defeating any potential relations she might have had with other men. He had deformed her life, just as surely as if he'd cut off an arm or a leg from her body. He had made her an emotional freak. But it had cost him: He'd become a physical freak. All these years, she had blamed herself—all these years when he'd been alive, getting up each morning and playing his guitar and singing his songs… She was so angry her vision blurred.

"Are you all right?" a voice asked beside her.

She had forgotten Carol. Anita tried to nod.

"Joe has invited us for drinks," said Carol. "He has a friend he can call to join us. You want to go?"

Anita glanced at Joe, a muscular man in his forties, with bristles for hair and a tattoo of a seahorse on one arm. Tight jeans, white T-shirt. A clean-cut biker.

"You go ahead. I'm tired."

Carol gave her the look that meant: *I won't go if you don't want me to.*

Anita nodded and with great effort, said, "Go. Really. I'm okay."

Anita could do nothing but wait for the sunset. She finished her drink, the rum burning her stomach on its way down. And she waited, arms crossed against her chest, hands balled into fists. Boats sailed by, decorated with green and red lights in the shapes of dolphins and palm trees. The air darkened around the crowds swarming the edge of the pier. To Anita, numb with pain and knowledge, they were silhouettes against the orange and purple sky. Finally, the moment they'd been waiting for: Voices shouted out the seconds as the fading ball slid beneath the horizon—six, five, four, three, two, one! Hooray!

She could hear him behind her, droning in his imitation Bob Dylan voice: "Hark! the herald angels sing…" She stood staring at the finally black sky and water as the throng dispersed. Her heart was racing. It was either the beginning or the end of her life. She was so enraged she wasn't sure she cared which.

He was still singing—did he think some straggler would toss him money if he continued?—when she positioned herself in front of him with her hands on her hips, as if they were both still twenty-five and she'd just found his underwear on the living room floor.

For the first time, he looked at her. He stopped singing. His eyes registered something. Perhaps he was unsure, with the meagre light from the distant shops.

"Why did you do it?" she asked.

"You talking to me?"

"Don't play stupid. Do you have any idea what you did to me?"

"I don't know you, lady. You got me confused with someone else. I gotta go."

The same voice. He started to move toward the guitar case when she spat out, "Wait!"

Without warning, she stepped forward and pulled off his hat. No dark curly hair. Not much hair at all. But the head was the same, the brow.

"Christ, lady! Leave me alone!" He snatched back the hat.

"You bastard! You ruined my life. You don't even have the guts to admit it!"

He stopped, all his equipment still on his back, like a turtle. Only he couldn't disappear inside.

"Tell me your name isn't Stan!" she cried.

He stared at her and something shifted, but his eyes stayed hard. "George. My name is George."

"You have no idea, do you? You don't know what I went through. I thought you were dead."

He started moving away again. "Well, keep thinking that."

"You can't just walk away."

"Hey, you're not listening. I'm not who you think I am."

"Stop lying! I'd recognize you anywhere. All these years… Why did you do it?"

"Do *what*?"

"I *loved* you! I thought you loved me."

His head tilted. "Look, lady, let me be. All I want is to do my music and be left alone."

"*This* is what you want?" She stuck her palm out at his grotesque paraphernalia.

He stuck his chin out. His voice came out breathy with anger. "Something's wrong with you. You got a hearing problem or something? Or you don't *want* to hear. You know, I'm not surprised he left you. Ever stop to think why? You just don't listen."

Stan used to say that: *You don't listen.*

That was it! She jumped at him and started beating her fists against his chest. The pan flute was in the way.

"Keep off me, you crazy bitch!" He was backing away, arms up, trying to protect himself.

"I'm going to tell the police!" she shouted. "What you did was against the law."

"No cops!" he yelled back, his eyes flashing. "You have no call to—"

"Oh, you don't like that! Cops give you a hard time?"

"You leave me the hell alone."

"I'm calling the cops and they'll lock you in jail and throw away the key. You're going to rot there!"

Everything changed then. His eyes widened with purpose and he reached out to grab her. He was awkward with the drum on his back, but the long lean muscles in his arms mobilized and his hands grasped her shoulders. He started to push her toward the edge of the pier.

She had a few pounds on him and fought back. "Let go of me!"

Did he think he could throw her over a public pier? Where was everybody?

She tried to pry his hands loose from her shoulders, but it was no use. He was hauling her backwards to the black water.

"Help!" she screamed, reaching up to scratch his face.

Just when she thought she was dead, instinct took over. She moved both her arms up inside his, and with all her energy smashed her forearms outwards, dislodging his hands. She was free! She jumped sideways from the edge of the pier, at the same time shoving him away.

With the momentum of the weight behind him, he lost his footing. He howled out once, then crashed into the water, his musical baggage on top of him. He splashed for a second, but the load pulled him down and he sank, an encumbered shadow falling deeper into the dark. A few bubbles broke on the surface of the water where the straw hat floated—that was all. It was surprisingly quiet and peaceful. Like Christmas should be.

At least this time, she knew where the body was.

Sylvia Maultash Warsh was born in Germany to Holocaust survivors. She grew up in Toronto where she earned an MA in linguistics from the University of Toronto. Her mother's stories about fleeing the Nazis in Poland sparked an interest in history that has influenced Sylvia's fiction. She has had articles, short stories, and poetry published in journals and anthologies. She writes the Dr. Rebecca Temple series, set in Toronto in 1979. Her first novel, To Die in Spring *(Dundurn, 2000), was nominated for an Arthur Ellis Award.* Find Me Again *(Dundurn, 2003), won an Edgar Award and was nominated for two Anthonys. Her third novel,* Season of Iron, *was published in 2006. All three books deal with other historical eras, particularly the Second World War. Sylvia teaches creative writing to seniors. She is a founding member of the Toronto chapter of Sisters in Crime and belongs to Crime Writers of Canada.*

Christmas Bonus

Michael Hennessey

It was the week before Christmas, and there was still no snow; nor had the harbour frozen over. It was dusk, and I was sitting in my faithful old 1991 Camry in Victoria Park, contemplating the harbour waters, calm and peaceful, nothing at all like the majestic tumbling rollers of the North Shore where I wished I was right now, tucked into my cozy cottage.

After some time of thinking about my unhappy lot and my current case, I finished my fast-food supper, jammed the bag and the containers under the seat to keep company with those already there, switched on the engine and lights, and headed downtown. I drove to lower Queen Street and climbed the stairs to the second floor over an auto-parts store, to the office of Paul Lister, who advertised himself as an import–export businessman but who was very likely dealing in stolen goods. He also ran the store below and had hired me a couple of weeks ago to keep an eye on an employee, Max Klien, whom he suspected was loading up on auto parts at Lister's expense. Stealing, one might say.

"It's over," I said. "Klien's clean."

"Klien's clean?"

"What I said."

"How do you know?"

Paul Lister is a big man, but soft. He has eyes like George W, which give him a wily look as if he's always trying to get ahead of you, which in Lister's case is true. They are also too close together, which arouses suspicion in my mind. A poor reason, I know, but of such prejudices are we made. But then, as a private investigator, I'm pretty well suspicious of everybody.

"I had cameras on him all the time," I said. "Nothing."

"Damn. I was sure it was him."

"You might want to take a closer look at Herman Walker."

"Oh?"

"Yeah. He's stealing you blind."

He laughed. "You're tricky, Shirley. I'll go after him. How much do I owe you?"

I told him, and he took a wallet that would choke an alligator out of his right-hand desk drawer. As he slid the drawer out, I caught a glimpse of a handgun—a big handgun. He slammed the drawer shut when he saw me looking.

He counted out the bills and passed them to me. "Got another job for you."

"I don't want it, thanks." I had visions of sitting on Herman Walker over Christmas and I'd had enough of that. "Surveillance is too mind-numbing."

"Not that," he said. "Something else."

"What?"

"It's Donna Victor," he said.

"Am I supposed to know her?"

"I guess not. She's married to Sammy Norton."

"Slick Sammy. That's another reason to refuse."

"Make it worth your while."

"Yeah? How much?"

"Five hundred. Just to talk to her, get her over the shakes."

"I'd have the shakes, too, married to that louse."

"She needs some help. Sammy really clobbered her the last time."

"The last time? Is he making it a lifetime project, beating on her?"

"He's not a bad guy. It's his lousy temper."

I looked around his male-decorated office: pictures of himself and friends fishing, drinking beer, hunting. Good old boys hanging out. Give the little woman a tap or two if she needs it—no harm. Keep her in her place

"You're all the same," I said acidly.

"Look at that red hair of yours," he said. "Tell me you don't lose your temper now and again."

I'd been hearing all my life about my red hair and my temper.

"And it's about to happen again right now," I said, giving him my best glare.

He backed off. "I don't mean anything disrespectful, Shirley. Donna just needs someone to vent to, and I thought another woman would be better."

"She got no woman friends?"

"Not that I know of."

"What's your interest in Donna, Paul?"

"She's my cousin. Is that okay with you?"

"I just wondered."

"Now you know. How about it? You in or out?"

"Five hundred bucks?" I said. "Okay, I'll talk to her. Two-fifty in advance."

I sat there while he counted out more bills. As I left the office, he said, "An early Christmas present, Shirley. A snap job."

"Yeah," I said. "Thanks."

Maybe Paul Lister wasn't such a creep after all. No, belay that. Control yourself, girl. Don't get carried away with the Christmas spirit. He was not only a creep; he was a complete asshole.

There, that was more like the real me—if not quite seasonal.

I was admitted to Donna's apartment by another woman, a dark, slinky doll with Uma Thurman *Pulp Fiction* hair and the same in curves. She told me Donna was "indisposed."

"Look," I said. "Paul Lister sent me over to talk to her. It's all the same to me if she don't want to see me."

"Hold on a minute."

She was back in thirty seconds. "She'll see you," she said. "She ain't pretty. That bastard really hung a beating on her."

She was right. Donna wasn't pretty. She had two black eyes, a bandage over her nose, which I assumed was broken, and a swollen left cheekbone. Her teeth were wired together: the sign of a broken jaw. She was sitting in a small room off the kitchen, smoking a cigarette, a drink in front of her.

"Sorry for your troubles," I said, not sounding sorry.

"Yeah. What do you want?" Talking through wired teeth made her sound threatening, like a wise guy's moll.

I told her Paul had sent me and what for.

"My friend is here," she said, nodding towards to the kitchen. "I don't need you."

"Okay with me. I just thought you might want to talk about it."

"The time for talk is over."

"You're leaving him?"

"Wouldn't you?"

"Yes."

She stubbed out her cigarette. "So that's all there is to that."

Just then Uma stuck her head into the den. "Phone call for you, Donna."

"Excuse me a minute," Donna said, and left.

I began poking around, slid open a desk drawer, saw a gleaming Colt .22 target revolver—the kind with the long barrel—sitting there, smelling like cordite. I picked it up, broke it, sniffed it, and saw that one shot had been fired, the brass left in the chamber, five others live and ready. I shoved it back in the drawer.

Uma came back, told me that Donna was getting ready to leave on account of an emergency, and could I come back later.

"No need. My business is finished. You seem to be providing support."

I left, thinking that was the easiest two-fifty I'd ever earned. Now if I could just con Lister out of the remaining two-fifty, that would be a bonus. I got into my car and circled the block, drawing up about a hundred yards away from the house. Soon Donna hurried out wearing a hat with a veil over her face. I could understand why. She climbed into a late-model Ford Taurus and headed uptown. I followed, noting the lit-up Christmas trees on each corner and the cheerful Christmas tableaux around the Confederation Centre.

"Bah, humbug," I muttered.

She turned east on Grafton Street, south on Prince, west on Sydney, and pulled to the curb in front of the Olde Dublin Pub. She went in and I stopped back up the block, near the basement steps of Saint Dunstan's Basilica. I sat and waited.

She was in the pub for about ten minutes, then came out followed by her husband's partner, Tom Baker. Hmmmmm. Wheels within wheels. Baker was carrying a briefcase, which he tucked in behind the driver's seat as she climbed into her car. He said a few words, then reached in and patted her arm. He tapped the roof of the car and she said something to him, then pulled away. He went back into the pub.

I followed her as she turned right up Queen Street. I could hear Christmas carols from the bell tower as we passed City Hall. She pulled in beside the phone booth at the corner of Queen and Fitzroy, got out of the car, fished behind the seat for the briefcase, and placed it carefully on the street side of the phone booth after ascertaining that nobody was in sight. Then she got back in her car and left. I was parked in a slot some distance away, with my lights out but with a clear view of the phone booth. As soon as she was out of sight, I left my car and approached the booth. I retrieved the briefcase but decided to call Police Chief Duke Jackson before I examined it. Duke was a good friend, and I knew he'd want in on whatever was going down.

When he came on the line, I told him I was in the phone booth just around the corner from the police station. I asked him about Sammy Norton and Tom Baker. He said they were looking for Norton to question him about the beating. He knew nothing about Baker except that he was Norton's partner and therefore as crooked as Norton. I said, "Uh-huh," then heard a slight noise behind me and inhaled some vodka fumes. But before I could turn, I took a blow on the side of the head and the lights went out.

When I came to, Chief Jackson was there with one of his constables, ministering to me, gingerly wiping the blood off my neck, telling me we were going to the hospital for x-rays.

"I'm okay," I said, nearly passing out from the effort to stand. "Just let me get my breath."

I told Duke about the vodka fumes.

"Could be Skunk Dickens," he said. "Smells like a Russian distillery. You can always smell him before you see him. We'll pick him up."

I told him about the briefcase. "Probably a payoff of some kind," he said. "Now for some good news. I got a call on my mobile as I was coming around the corner to check out why your call ended with a groan. Norton is dead, shot by a big calibre handgun. I think he hit Donna once too often."

I went directly to Donna's place. She was back home, perched with her drink and cigarette. I told her Sammy was dead, which didn't give her the surprise I expected. "I know," she said. "I shot him. Funny though, he walked right out the door like bullets don't affect him."

I went to the desk drawer and recovered the .22. Still the same: one fired, five live.

"You couldn't kill a squirrel with this peashooter," I said. "Where did you hit him?"

"I don't know. I pointed it at him, closed my eyes, and pulled the trigger."

"When did this happen?"

"About an hour before you arrived the last time."

"Where? This room?"

She nodded yes. "He was standing right over there." She pointed to the doorway. I went across and examined the casing. There was a slug imbedded in the crosspiece over the doorway.

"Well, Donna, you didn't hit Sammy unless he's about ten feet tall," I said. I dug the slug out, dropped it in my pocket. "I better take this cannon along with me. It and the slug will clear you of the killing."

I called Duke on his mobile, told him what I knew about Donna, and said I was going back to see Paul Lister. "Send somebody to pick up Donna," I said. "She'll wait here for you. I have her piece and the slug; I'll give them to you later." I told him about the big gun in Lister's desk.

"Be careful," Duke said. "We'll be right along."

Lister was sitting in his office as if he hadn't moved since I'd last seen him.

"What was the payoff for, Paul?" I asked. "Skunk is your man, isn't he?"

He smiled. "So you made him. Sorry about the…ummm…you know."

"The hit on the head, you mean?"

"That, yeah."

"It's okay," I said. "What was the payoff for, Paul?"

"Sammy Norton was blackmailing me. This was a pretend payoff to him to get him to lay off Donna."

"Let me get this straight. It was really a payoff to get him to lay off you?"

"That's right."

"But Sammy was already dead."

He smiled. "Smart, ain't you? That's why Skunk was there. To recover the cash."

"Why have Donna make the payoff?"

"To involve her. If her and me were paying off Sammy, as we'll testify, how could we be guilty of murder?"

"How was Sammy's partner, Tom Baker, involved?"

He took his time lighting a long cigar, twirling it, blowing smoke in my direction. His eyes were small and beady. "Well, I'll tell you, but it goes no further."

I nodded impatiently. "You're still a client, Paul."

"Okay. Well, Tom and Donna were…" He made a hand gesture. "Like that… You know."

"Oh," I said. "So you wanted to involve him as well?"

"That's right. Everybody's in the pie. Then the finger can't point at me."

"It can if I go to the cops with what I know."

"What happened to client privilege?"

"This is murder, Paul. I can't sit on that."

"Really?" His right hand was creeping towards his drawer.

"Really," I said. "I've seen that cannon you've got there. It was a slug from that that killed Sammy." I was guessing, but he didn't know it.

"You got that right," he said, reaching casually into the drawer, bringing up the big gun.

"Desert Eagle," I said. "You impress me, Paul." And I lifted the .22 and shot him in the wrist. The big gun clattered to the desk.

He grabbed his wrist, blood pumping. "Christ!" he wailed "You shot me."

"Yeah, well, it seemed fair. You were going to shoot me."

About then, the pain kicked in and he groaned and moaned, fumbling a handkerchief around his wounded wrist. Don't let anybody ever tell you getting shot with a .22 in a fragile spot like the wrist doesn't hurt. The bone damage alone would immobilize him for weeks.

He glared at me across the desk. Just to be safe, I hauled the Eagle to my side, watching him all the time.

"Be reasonable," he said, fumbling his wallet out of the desk. "How much?"

"Just the two-fifty you owe me."

With his left hand, he counted out the two-fifty, then counted a thousand into a separate pile. "Can we work something out?" I pocketed the two-fifty.

"Forget it. You're going down for Sammy. The Eagle will do it. You shoulda dumped it."

"Didn't have time. It all happened too quick."

He stared at me appraisingly. "Tell me," he said. "I should at least know the name of the doll who nailed me. What's your last name? Shirley what?"

"You twit," I said. "That *is* my last name: Shirley. Anne Shirley, Private Investigator."

"Anne Shirley! Not—?"

"That's right, bozo. Some people still call me Anne of Green Gables. And a Merry Christmas to you, jerk."

Outside, a soft snow was falling. I had money for Christmas. Perfect.

Sirens moaned in the distance.

Michael Hennessey was born on Prince Edward Island and has lived there most of his life. He spent seven years in the Royal Canadian Navy and still enjoys sailing. He has published numerous short stories, two collections of short stories, and two non-fiction books. His novel, The Betrayer, was short-listed for the Maritime Publishers Award. As well, twelve of his plays have been produced.

Wreckwood

Maureen Jennings

Even though it was the day of the Nativity, only half of the congregation had braved the fierce snow-laden winds that were sweeping in from the sea. The second altar boy had not appeared, leaving young William Murdoch alone to handle the duties of page at the court of the King of Kings. He was just as happy about that, as Jerome Gallagher was sickeningly pious (destined for the priesthood, everybody said). Unlike Will. So far, all had gone well—he hadn't missed anything—but he could see his own breath on the air and his stomach rumbled, protesting the fast he had to undertake before Mass. He allowed his attention to wonder briefly to the Christmas dinner his mother had prepared for later in the day. He knew she was watching him, kindly mostly, but also critically, and for her sake, he tried to make his face express reverence. He wasn't sure he truly felt so. Last night, he had come close to fighting with his own father. Harry, always belligerent when he was drunk, had made the evening miserable for all of them, taunting each one, but especially Will's simpleton brother, Bertie, his tone and comments stinging like whip lashes, his fists ready to fly at the slightest provocation.

One more year and William would be grown enough to stand up to him. His body tensed in anticipation.

Suddenly, he became aware that Father Keegan was moving toward him. He was frowning, and Will knew he had fallen behind with his duties. Quickly, he went to the credence table for the glass cruets containing water and wine. He handed them to the priest, remembering just in time to kiss each one reverentially. As he turned to go back for the towel and basin, his foot caught in his cassock and he tripped, feeling the hem tear away as he did so. His face burned with embarrassment. His mother would be ashamed of him for his clumsiness.

Father Keegan held out his hands for the ritual cleansing, and William poured some water over them, catching it in the basin. The priest's nails were cracked and dirty, and his thumbnail was showing signs of a bruise. In this small community, Father Keegan was expected to do his own wood chopping and simple carpentry. He wasn't very good at it, and behind his back, some of the men of the congregation mocked him for his lack of skill. He was originally a town man, sent to them last year from a parish in Halifax when their old priest died. He was also lame from a badly mended leg.

Gossip had it that Father Keegan had received his call to the priesthood later in life, serving prior to that as a surgeon in the American Union army. Gossip also claimed he had been married in his secular life, but his wife and family had perished, cause unknown. Some said his crooked leg was because he had been shot by a Rebel soldier. Nobody knew for sure, and the priest was not a sociable man who would chat about his own life, even when he was being entertained in front of the fire, a glass of hot cider in his hand. The biggest complaint about him, muttered among themselves, was that he handed out heavy penances for some sins that were, after all, human nature surely, but he didn't seem to care much about the lapses in observance that had been so significant to his predecessor, Father Bernard of blessed memory.

Will was in awe of Father Keegan.

The priest finished drying his hands on the linen towel and turned back to the altar. They were approaching the most important part of the Mass—the Canon—the point from which there was no turning back. Will took up his position, kneeling on the edge of the platform.

Suddenly, the church door opened with a bang, and a man he knew from the village burst in, the wind gusting behind him as if it had carried him along. He started yelling as soon as he crossed the threshold.

"Ship's foundering down on't shore. We need to put out the boat."

Father Keegan had been on the verge of elevating the Host, and he turned in shock at this intrusion that only one not of the Faith would dare to make.

"She's a schooner been pushed onto the shoals," shouted the man. "Looks like they got into the painter, but they ain't doing too well in this wind." He glared around the church. "Who'll come to man the oars with me?'

There was a rustle and ripple through the congregation, but nobody moved. All looked toward the priest. Father Keegan spoke.

"I cannot interrupt the Mass." He glanced quickly around at his flock. "I will administer Communion as speedily as possible, but our Lord would not wish innocent souls to be lost for want of a boat. All able-bodied men are excused. Women, children, and the elderly will stay."

He turned his back on the intruder, knelt, and began to say the prayers of the Canon.

Behind him, the men shuffled out of the pews, genuflected, and hurried out down the aisle. Will seized the silver bell, ready to ring it, but he, too, was suffused with excitement. This was by no means the first ship to founder on the rocky coast, and the villagers always did everything they could to rescue those in danger. Earlier in the summer, three parishes had come together in an unlikely alliance and built a lifeboat. Will wanted to be down on the shore himself, and it took all the discipline he could muster to continue calmly with the rituals: bowing, kneeling, responding to the priest's invocations. Father Keegan went through the rest of the Mass as fast as he could, speaking so quickly his Latin became incomprehensible. All the genuflecting was hard on his crippled leg, and he had to stifle his groans. The communicants came to the altar rail, but Will thought only the most pious of the women had their minds on what they were doing. The wind rattled at the windows, reminding them of what was happening. Finally, the priest dismissed them with his blessing.

"Now then. All of you women, fetch as many blankets and dry clothes as you can spare. I will make our parish hall available for sanctuary on your behalf."

He beckoned to Will.

"Come and help me divest."

Will followed him to the sacristy. His mother, Susannah, and Bertie left, and he suspected that the longed-for Christmas feast was going to be divided among those in greater need.

He and the priest changed as quickly as they could. Will had come to the church in his best suit, which was of good thick serge, but he knew his mother would excuse him if he got dirty. A torn hem, no, but rescue operations, yes.

They left the church, the wind grabbing them, scouring their faces. Bent double, they struggled to the cliff's edge and the rough path that descended to the shore. In the dim light of the early morning, Will could just make out the shape of a small schooner. The top mast had broken and the bow was jammed on the ragged teeth of a shoal, the deck sloping toward the stern, which was being battered by the hungry, churning white caps. The crew had managed to get into the little painter, and a lantern held aloft by one of them bobbed up and down, now hidden by the waves, now riding on top of them.

"How many do you see, Will?" asked Father Keegan. "I make it six souls."

"Yes, Father. They don't seem to be making headway at all."

Neither was the lifeboat that had been launched from the shore. It, too, was being tossed about, the oars sawing at air over and over again.

"Come on."

The priest started down the steep path to the shore, William following close behind him, both slithering and sliding on the wet stones, the priest cursing with each fall. They'd hardly got half-way down when they saw a huge wave smash sideways into the painter, flipping it up and over, throwing out the people in it. Father Keegan paused and made the sign of the cross. "May the Lord have mercy."

The lifeboat was being blown away from the stricken ship, but one of the rowers lifted his lantern and the light shone on a shape in the icy grey water, someone clinging to a piece of driftwood. Two of the men leaned over, and William saw with astonishment that they were pulling aboard a woman. Almost at once, the lifeboat began to head back to shore. There was a crowd gathered on the rocks, and several men rushed forward to help haul in the boat. One of them threw out a line that was attached to a winch, and the coxswain grabbed it and secured it to the bowpin.

The priest, not able to join in the pull, took command. "Heave!" he cried. "All together—heave!"

Will had gripped the rope along with the other men, and he felt as if he were fighting the sea god himself in a deadly struggle for this fragile vessel. The rowers dug in with their oars whenever they could. More villagers, including a couple of the younger women, threw their weight into the pull, and finally they got the boat sufficiently out of the water that the men could climb out. Each was wearing his cork life-preserving belt. Will had a glimpse of a white face, thin and young, as the woman they had rescued was handed into the strong arms of a brawny fisherman and carried to a tarpaulin that had been placed at the ready. The women surrounded her at once.

"We must go back out, Father," said a rough, bearded man who had been one of the first members of the church to heed the call for help. "There are others, but the lassie is dire so we had to bring her in first."

The five men clambered back into the boat and were shoved out to sea again. If anything, the wind was fiercer than ever, and Will doubted they would be able to get out to the shoal.

Father Keegan went over to where the young woman lay and bent over her. He straightened, and Will could see him gesticulating in the direction of the cliff top. He wanted her to be moved to the parish hall at once, and Will could see the alarm and urgency in his body. He ran over to him, and Father Keegan drew him close so he could shout into his ear to be heard above the roar of the wind and the sea.

"We have to move her immediately. She is with child, and by the look of her, near her time. Go and fetch Mrs. Cameron."

It took a long time for William to bring the midwife, who was elderly and arthritic, to the parish hall. Initially, she was nervous about going into a Catholic building, but Will assured her that the hall was just that—a building—and it was the church that was sanctified. When they did get inside, the women had been busy. There was an alcove at the rear of the hall that they had curtained off for the young woman from the sea, which was how Will was starting to think about her. Ominously, several tarpaulins had been laid out on the floor to receive the dead. The air was scented with the pine branches that decorated the lintels and the hearth where a log fire was already blazing. His mother was with the other village women, putting food on a trestle table. He'd been right about the Christmas roast-chicken dinner. His stomach reminded him he hadn't eaten since last night, but this wasn't the time to appease his hunger. He was immediately called on to carry some pots of soup to the fire, and other tasks followed so he couldn't return to the shore. Every so often, he heard a cry of pain coming from behind the curtain, but it was quickly suppressed, whether by the young woman or the midwife, he didn't know.

More than an hour must have elapsed before Father Keegan entered the hall, leading a grim procession of men who were bringing in bodies from the doomed schooner. They laid them on the tarpaulins and covered each man with a blanket. There were five corpses. Clustered at the far end of the hall were the parishioners and as many of the curious from the village as could be squeezed in. Father Keegan began discreetly to make the sign of the cross over each corpse. Discreetly, because the Methodist minister and the pastor from the Baptist church were both doing their own praying. However, this was Father Keegan's hall and they stayed back.

The priest beckoned to Will. "You are an intelligent boy, William Murdoch, and your hand is a clear one. These will all have loved ones, mothers and wives who will want to claim them. We cannot allow any confusion." His eyes were shadowed with fatigue. "These are good people. They did not hesitate to put their own lives at risk. But they are also only human. It is a great temptation to take from the dead. After all, they don't need earthly things anymore: that watch, this silk handkerchief." He sighed. "We must make sure they do not succumb to that temptation. We will examine each of these bodies and we will make a careful note of their description and of such belongings as we find on their person. All goods belong to these men's families unless otherwise determined." He smiled slightly. "You are not afraid of the dead, are you, my son?"

"No, Father."

Even if he had been, Will would have died himself before admitting it.

At that moment, from behind the screen came the thin wail of a newborn, and the women stopped their work at the sound. Several of them blessed themselves, and the Methodist minister clapped his hands together and looked heavenward in prayer. Father Keegan also blessed himself.

"Go into the office and in my desk you will see a notebook and a pencil. Bring them."

Will hurried to do his bidding. When he returned, Father Keegan had erected a rope barrier around the area.

The priest removed the blanket covering the first body. "Write this down: man approximately forty-five years of age; five feet seven or eight inches tall; scrawny; brown, grey-streaked hair and full beard." He lifted one of the man's eyelids. "Brown eyes, large nose." He gently opened the mouth. "Two front teeth missing, tobacco stains. He has lost the tip of his right index finger, but it's an old injury. Clothes as follows: canvas jacket, navy jersey, waterproof trousers, and rubber boots."

Will scribbled it down as fast as he could. Father Keegan began to empty the man's pockets and spread out the contents on the floor. "Clay pipe and tobacco pouch of good tooled leather; linen handkerchief; knife in sheath; spyglass, brass." He fished inside the inner pockets of the jacket and pulled out some pieces of paper. They were surprisingly dry.

"As I thought, this good man was the captain. He has kept his bill of lading close to his heart. They were carrying fish and dried cod." He grimaced. "All now returned to the place whence they came."

The hall door banged open, and more of the weary rescuers came in. They were carrying two more bodies.

"We managed to reach the schooner, Father," said one of the men, a weather- beaten stocky fellow, a fellow Catholic.

"Good work, Saul. Put yours at that end. Richard, bring yours here," said Father Keegan.

The men lowered their burdens carefully. Saul pointed at one of the bodies: a plump man dressed only in shirt, waistcoat, and trousers. "This poor cove hadn't even made it to the painter. He was trapped below deck."

The second tarpaulin appeared to be particularly heavy, and the men put it down with groans of relief. The body that was revealed was that of a young man, his fair hair and moustache full of bits of seaweed and sea debris. He was wearing a thick wool coat trimmed with lush fur at the collar and cuffs, all sodden.

"That one there in the fancy coat had climbed onto the reef, but he must have slipped because he drowned, stuck between two rocks. He'd been better off to throw off his coat, if you ask me. I do believe that's the lot. All perished except for the woman."

He crossed himself.

"Father Keegan?"

Mrs. Cameron had emerged from the screen and was shuffling toward them. Huffing a little, she said quietly, "We have need of you, Father. At once. The girl has delivered her bairn, but I do believe she is not long for the living. Her colour's very bad."

"And the infant?"

"'Tis small, but she appears healthy enough."

"A girl-child, then?"

"Yes, Father."

The priest tapped Will on the shoulder. "Come. If you are not afraid of the dead, you can tolerate the dying, even if it is a woman. Bring my viaticum case."

Behind the curtain, there was a pallet on the floor on which the young woman was lying. She had been stripped of her clothes, and her naked arms lay outside of the blanket. The women had unpinned her hair, which was a deep auburn colour, thick and luxuriant. Her eyes were closed, and she seemed to be hardly breathing. The side of her jaw was bruised and swollen.

"I think her ribs be broken, her labour was dreadful sore," said Mrs. Cameron. "But she hardly complained, and the poor mite is barely out of childhood."

"Did she tell you her name?"

"I asked, but all she could say was her Christian name. It is Abigail." The midwife lifted up the girl's limp hand. She was wearing a wedding band richer than any Will had seen before. Rubies on a wide circlet of gold. "Whoever she is, she married well; the clothes we took off were fine indeed."

The girl was breathing in short, rasping gasps, and her skin was chalk-white. Will's heart went out to her. Even he knew she was dying.

She opened her eyes, as blue as any he had seen. She saw the priest, and her face contorted with fear.

"Father, why are you here? Am I to die then?"

"You are of the Faith, child?"

"Yes, I am."

"Then I must prepare you to meet your Maker, my daughter."

Father Keegan reached out and made the sign of the cross over her forehead.

"In nomine Patris, et Filii, et Spiritus Sancti. Do not be afraid, my child. This day, you will rest in Paradise with our Lord Jesus Christ."

A sob escaped her throat.

"Were any saved?" she whispered.

"Alas, no," Father Keegan answered. "The men just now brought in the last two. One, I believe, is your husband."

Her eyes widened. "My husband?"

"He is blond, is he not, with a full moustache? He was wearing a fur-trimmed coat."

She turned her head and was so still that Will wondered if she had already slipped away.

The priest called over the midwife. "Mrs. MaryAnn Pierce lost her own child but a week ago. She is most grieved by the loss. I want you to have her brought here. Her breasts will still have milk."

Will flinched at the words and the image, and he lowered his head.

Abigail opened her eyes again. Her voice was so weak they could hardly hear her.

"All perished, you say?"

"Alas, yes, my child. Seven souls, all told."

She stirred restlessly. "Did they all die instantly? What I mean is, were they shriven?"

"No. We had no chance to speak to any of them."

A long sigh came from her lips, and once again, Will wasn't sure if she was quick or dead. Then she said, "Will my baby live?"

"Mrs. Cameron says she is healthy. Do you want to hold her?"

She nodded, and the midwife picked up the tiny creature that was tightly wrapped in its swaddling clothes, only the little red wrinkled face visible. She placed it in the crook of the young mother's arm, and the dying woman touched the cheek tenderly.

"She has not the best entry into this vale of tears, has she?" Again she looked up at the priest. "The man in the coat…"

"Your husband?"

She kissed the infant on the forehead, soft as snow lighting on the ground. "He was a good man. He saved me. I took his place in the boat. His name is John. "

Father Keegan shifted to a more comfortable position so he could straighten his leg.

"There is money," she continued. "My husband had it sewn into the seams of his coat. I must ask you to claim it on behalf of my infant child. I heard what you said to the midwife. Please, Father, promise me the money will go to that woman who will be her wet-nurse and to the babe after."

"Surely you yourself have a family who will take her in?"

"No, I have no one."

"Your husband, then?"

"No, he neither."

"What is your name and your residence?"

She licked her lips. "I am so thirsty."

Father Keegan reached over to a table where somebody had stood a flagon of wine, and he brought it to her lips.

She sipped but coughed so violently the priest removed the flagon, and Will saw that a gush of blood had run from her mouth. He wished he had the linen towel to wipe it away for her, but he didn't even have a handkerchief. Father Keegan himself did so with a cloth that Mrs. Cameron handed to him. He had not yet made the promise, and Will wondered why he hesitated.

"Do you wish me to hear your last confession, my daughter?"

With unexpected strength, the girl caught him by the sleeve. "Father, is it true that our Lord is all-knowing? That He can see into every soul and forgive our trespasses because He understands them? Is that the truth?"

"Yes, child, that is what our Saviour Jesus Christ taught us. Even the blackest soul can be washed clean if we truly repent of our sins."

She let go. "Thank you, Father. That is a comfort to me."

These were the last words she said. Father Keegan began the sacrament of Extreme Unction, and he had hardly completed his task when she took in one deeper breath and died. The oil with which he had anointed her gleamed on her forehead in the lamplight. He got to his feet.

"Mrs. Cameron, I will leave her to you. Come, Will. We have not yet finished."

Although he felt as if his heart was in a vice, deeply affected from seeing the death of a young woman hardly older than himself, William followed the priest back into the hall. There was a subdued hum of conversation from the people at the end of the room. Will saw his mother was among the crowd. She smiled at him, and he felt proud that she would see him performing such an important job.

"We had better look for that money and make sure it's safe," said Father Keegan.

They went over to the silent mound that was the man in the fur-trimmed coat, and the priest removed the blanket that Saul had put over the body.

"Let's get the coat off him first."

Will had never touched a dead body before, and the feel of the cold clammy skin almost turned his stomach. It was probably a good thing he'd had nothing to eat.

Underneath the coat, the man was wearing a thick woollen jersey and black serge trousers. The damp sea-soaked smell filled Will's nostrils.

"He is dressed like a sailor," he said to the priest.

"Indeed he is." Father Keegan turned the man's hands palms up and ran his finger over the calluses they could see there. "He certainly has worked like one."

He felt along the hem of the coat, then quickly tore open the seam. Will held back his gasp of surprise. Gold coins flowed out onto the floor—more than he had ever seen in his life.

"No wonder he was such a heavy burden," said the priest. "And here we have something more." He removed a small purse of purple velvet. He held it out for Will to see. It was filled with diamonds. "This sailor was no rich merchant. He could never earn that much in ten lifetimes."

"Father, I don't understand. She said he saved her. You asked if the blond-haired man was her husband, and she said yes. But she is a well-born lady. How could she marry a rough fisherman?"

Father Keegan's expression was kind as he glanced at William.

"Such things do happen, my son, but in fact, she never directly answered my question. I was aware of it at the time. I thought her anxiety to know if we had had a chance to speak to anyone on board was strange. She said she was curious as to whether they had a chance to cleanse their souls, but I did not quite believe her."

Will stared at him, not entirely sure of the implications of what he said.

"If I were a wagering man," the priest continued, "I would bet that the husband to our fine lady is lying right here—the stout man with the beautifully trimmed whiskers." He made his way over to the last body at the end of the row. The body was not covered, and it was obvious the man was no fisherman. He had the soft jowls and stomach of a well-fed gentleman. Will was chagrined he had not taken note sooner.

Father Keegan leaned forward. "Look, Will, look at his shirt. What do you notice?"

They seemed to have slipped into the role of teacher and pupil, and Will liked it. Liked being able to please this sharp-tongued man.

Will moved in closer. "The cloth is of excellent quality, pure worsted."

"Yes, but more important, see he has a small tear in that excellent shirt."

The priest unbuttoned the man's waistcoat and opened the front of the shirt. He pointed to a small hole visible even amidst the matt of grizzled hair. "The sea has washed away all blood, but I would say our merchant friend here was stabbed. The wound is a narrow one." The priest lifted the man's hand and ran his fingers across the palm. "Look at these cuts on both his hands and here on the underside of his arm. He received those trying to defend himself. Unsuccessfully, as we now know."

"And it was the sailor who murdered him for his money?"

"Not perhaps for his money. See, he has a fine gold watch and chain in his waistcoat and...yes, there are coins still in his pockets." He counted them. "Twenty dollars. But let us not condemn John Sailor just yet. Go and check his boots. See if he is carrying a knife on his person. If he is, bring it to me."

Will hurried to do as he said, his heart racing. There was a leather sheath stuffed down the right boot, and he removed it and returned to the priest. Father Keegan pulled out the knife, the sort fishermen used for filleting, sharp and efficient. He held it up to the light.

"The sheath protected the blade in spite of the water. You can see it is stained almost to the hilt. Even the sea could not wash away that mark."

He brought the tip of the blade close to the cut above the dead man's heart. "I would say we have found our weapon."

William stared at him in dismay. "If the fisherman is a murderer, surely the lady was not his accomplice? She was so..."

He paused, and the priest smiled wryly at him. "Young? Beautiful? The Bible is filled with tales of women of great beauty who were black sinners. However, did you notice the old bruises yellowing on her arm? And a severe one recent to the side of her face? She did not receive them from the ship foundering. Somebody had gripped her hard on the arm a while ago, and the other mark is typical of a blow to the side of the face administered by a fist."

Will felt himself blush. He didn't know if the priest was aware of the situation at home, but he suspected he was. His mother had received such marks more than once, and Will was deeply ashamed of it.

"Look at this merchant," continued the priest. "He is old enough to be the girl's grandfather. What is he doing marrying such a child? He cannot have cared for her. If you cherish your wife, you do not bring her on a rough sea voyage when she is so close to her confinement. What business could be so pressing that she must accompany you? And on such an uncomfortable vessel as the one that foundered. A poor fishing boat. Mr. Merchant had plenty of money; if it was imperative she come with him, he could afford better. And why did he think it necessary to hide his gold and diamonds? Was he the kind of man who views all with suspicion? A jaundiced attitude that might well have included his child-wife."

"Is it possible that she wanted to be on the voyage, Father? It does seem as if her husband's murderer was one of the crew. Perhaps she was the one who insisted on coming with him. Perhaps they thought it would be easier to dispose of her husband when they were on board ship. Men fall overboard all the time."

Father Keegan chuckled. "William Murdoch, you are showing signs of a refreshing lack of sentimentality. That is certainly a possibility. And her plea to me that our Lord understands everything was most heartfelt, was it not?"

"Her words have indeed taken on a different significance, Father. On the other hand, the sailor may have held her in his thrall. Frightened her into doing his bidding."

"A woman who has been mistreated in that way would not weep as she did when she heard of his death. And he saved her by giving her the place on the boat."

"Perhaps he did that merely so he could go back to the man he had just stabbed and steal his coat. He wanted to make his escape over land. He didn't know all aboard would perish. They could have told the tale. Perhaps he didn't even know there was gold hidden in the coat."

"Then he and our lady were not accomplices."

It was William's turn to grin. "I was only trying to examine every possibility, Father, logically and objectively, as St. Thomas would have us think. We know this knife killed this man, but we do not know who wielded it. As you say, even women can be sinners."

"The reason and the heart must work together, Will. What does your heart say?"

William hesitated. "It tells me that what I have just said is nonsense. Worse than nonsense, if truth be told. Mistress Abigail was no murderer. She may have had good cause to hate the man who so mistreated her, but I don't think she would kill him.

"I am inclined to agree with you—against all logic, of course."

William was fast warming to his subject. "She insisted to us that she was alone in the world. She did not want anybody to claim her child. She may be an orphan, of course, but usually there is somebody from the old life— an aunt, a grandmother—who you would pass your child to. So I believe in her married life, she was probably isolated and despised by those around her. She thought her daughter being taken by those who would love her would have a better life than she had."

"MaryAnn Pierce will be a doting parent, I know it."

Will bit his lip. "Father, why did Mistress Abigail die?"

The priest raised his eyebrows. "Surely you do not want to embark on a discussion of the mysterious ways of our Lord at this moment?"

"No, sir. But I am puzzled. I have been capsized more than once and know of others who have, but we suffered no harm except for a bellyful of salt water. She bled from the mouth, and Mrs. Cameron said she thought she had broken her ribs. But is that likely?"

"Let's see for ourselves. Stay here."

He went over to the alcove and called to Mrs. Cameron. Will couldn't hear what he was saying, but he saw the gesticulation, the midwife's shock and reluctant concession, and the priest ducked beneath the curtain. It was several minutes before he emerged. His face was grim.

"You are a clever lad, William Murdoch. Her ribs were indeed broken, but not by hitting the boat or the water. Her entire side was bruised, and the marks of a boot were evident."

He stood looking down at the body of the man they were calling the merchant. "It was he who did it, I have no doubt. He hit her hard, and when she fell to the ground, he began to kick her even. Perhaps she screamed. John Sailor came to her rescue and stabbed her assailant. One blow was all it took, perhaps accidentally hitting the heart or where the heart would be in one not as wicked as our merchant. The ship must have foundered or been foundering already when this occurred. John helped her onto the deck and got her into the boat, sacrificing his own life. "

"Do you think they knew each other before this?"

The priest shrugged. "John was young, handsome. Perhaps he was drawn to her; she was lovely, as you have observed. Her old husband may have been consumed with jealousy. Or perhaps John was a gallant man who would not stand by if he heard a woman cry for help. There may indeed have been an illicit love, but we will never know for sure. Either way, their souls are in God's hands, and He will be their Judge." He looked up. "Ah, there is MaryAnn now."

A young woman had come into the hall, a shawl over her head, her body still soft from her pregnancy. Mrs. Cameron emerged from the alcove, the new-born in her arms, and handed it to her. Immediately, MaryAnn brought the babe close inside the shawl and her body swayed. Her face came alive with tenderness and joy.

The priest sighed. "I had feared for that woman's sanity—her grief was so large—but I do believe she will be all right now." He turned to William. "Do you have pieces of wreckwood in your house?"

Will blinked in surprise at this abrupt change of subject. "Yes, Father. My mother has a pewter plate that her mother gave to her from an Atlantic barque that went aground off Sambro Island. My father made a table from some planks he found after the Monticello foundered."

"Perhaps everybody in this village has a memento given to us by the sea. It is our way in which to honour and remember those who have died in its embrace. If we can cherish bits of wood, we can surely cherish a flesh-and-blood child." He poked at the pile of gold coins. "The girl in her innocence thought I could dispense with this treasure on my own authority, but of course, I cannot. The magistrate will have to trace her husband's family, and they will have a claim to it. I shall also inform the magistrate of our discoveries. I would not have you hold such a secret."

He picked up a couple of the gold coins. "On this day of all days, I see no reason why we should not present our new-born child with a gift. This will be sufficient to maintain Mrs. Pierce and the infant until such time as somebody comes for her. Who knows, by then, if they will decide they do not want a child of such doubtful heritage and Mrs. Pierce can keep her."

He watched the woman for a few moments, and his expression was more sorrowful than happy, remembering William knew not what.

Maureen Jennings was born in Birmingham, England, and emigrated to Canada at the age of seventeen. This left her with a deep connection to her homeland and has also no doubt contributed to her love for the Victorian period, the setting for her popular Inspector William Murdoch books. Her second series features forensic profiler Christine Morris. Maureen has a B.A. in philosophy and psychology and an M.A. in English. She taught English at Ryerson in Toronto for years, leaving in 1972 to become a psychotherapist. Nowadays, she mostly conducts creative expression groups and writes. Always passionate about dogs, she is happy to own a border collie named Jeremy-Brett and a mixed breed named Varley.

Lucky

R. G. Willems

The night after Harold died, I had the best sleep I'd had in months. I won't lie to you; I don't miss him. But I do miss his bed.

You should know that I first slept with Harold the same night he brought me to his home. Judge me if you will, I don't care. Harold found me—saved me—when I'd given up being saved. During the period when I was scraping my living off the streets, I'd heard that there were people who did this sort of thing: philanthropists who spent time and money to rehabilitate those of us who'd given up on humanity. I just never expected to meet one. I was so naïve.

But Harold's bail money set me free, and when the bars swung open to the prairie winter wind, I knew I was the luckiest girl in the world. Those left behind followed me with their hard eyes—some envious, some trying to warn me. Even had I paid attention, I wouldn't have understood that all benefactors have some kind of fee. As it turned out, Harold's was not one I was prepared to pay.

His home was like nothing I'd ever seen before. Every room overflowed with books, cushions sat plump and inviting on tweed furniture, carpet enveloped my rough feet to the ankles, and a fireplace glowed softly. I admit to being overwhelmed and a little frightened, but Harold made no demands, and when he spoke, there was kindness in his voice.

When I joined him in his candle-lit kitchen, he simply gave me a plate of food and set about eating his own meal. For the first time in my life, I knew I was safe, there would be food tomorrow and the next day, and no one would hurt me. After our meal, he scooped me, unresisting, into his strong arms and carried me upstairs, as if I weighed no more than a feather.

Blood on the Holly

It was wonderful at the beginning. Dolly, my sweet Dolly, he called me. Where have you been all my life? I could do no wrong in his eyes, nor he in mine. We played funny childish games: chasing each other through the rooms in his big house, leaping out from behind corners, tickling and wrestling. Oh, the laughter! Harold found me amusing, and I think I brought out a playfulness in him he'd forgotten he had. Often, I dozed in front of the fire while Harold read of ancient worlds, kings, and quests.

I could hardly wait for the end of each day, when we would curl up next to each other in the big warm bed. I could have stayed in bed with Harold all day long. I believe it was the same for him—that endless delight of first love—and had I been more worldly-wise, I'd have known it couldn't last. I know better now—for when the next Harold comes along. If another one ever does.

It was a perfect life, and as the days grew shorter and the nights colder, I began to imagine little ones growing up with all the happiness I'd missed in my youth. But the desire had barely stirred in me when Harold let me know, unequivocally, that there would be no thought of babies. *It's for the best, Dolly. It's for your own good.* It was the kindness in his eyes as he told me—as if I had no choice in the matter—that drove the first shard of ice into my heart. His decisiveness left no room for debate, and I realized then that ours was not an equal relationship.

I've already told you I was naïve.

I felt damaged, defective, and most of all, bewildered. Harold was so sweet and solicitous of me during that time, but I know that's when he began to look at me differently. Change, I discovered, is inevitable. Even in those we adore. Maybe I lost that lithe, youthful energy that first attracted him, became more introspective, less interested in those games that keep a relationship vital. But on a deep, visceral level, I'd been hurt, betrayed, and I didn't really care what he felt. I guess I was pretty self-absorbed.

Dolly, honestly, he said in disgust, blowing my hair out of his face when I nuzzled close to him at night. *Find something to do! You sleep all day long, and I don't feel like entertaining you when I get home.* I tried to get his attention in subtle ways, stroking his shoulder, draping my body over his in the comfortable way we used to have together. But he turned away from me in bed, hiding his face in his book, ignoring me. *I'm tired. Leave me alone.*

I'm not the type to stay hurt for long, though. As I watched him silently from the far side of the bed, anger began to simmer. Who was he to tire of me? I was still young and beautiful, with my whole life ahead of me, and he treated me like a toy he'd grown bored with. This, I realized, is what my older, more street-wise colleagues knew, back in that cold cell: There's no free lunch. The piper must be paid.

It's one thing to think, as men will, that he could find a fresher, perkier model for a stolen bit on the side without losing his accustomed comforts. But like a barren wife of old, I was expected to steps aside, to welcome her. Our home, I vowed, was not his harem.

Harold brought a small tree into the kitchen—to celebrate, he told me—and when he returned that afternoon, I understood. *This is Tiffany,* he said *pleadingly. Isn't she lovely, Dolly? Won't you think about it? For me?*

Tiffany left in a hurry, and I'm proud to say that Emma, the next one, barely escaped with her life. By then, any comfort between me and Harold was gone. He kept on talking about how I needed to be more open-minded, more willing to try new things. I didn't care. I wasn't about to share my Harold with anyone. He'd betrayed me utterly. I'd rather see him dead.

At night, he kicked his feet and flipped the covers, stretching out over the entire space. *Dolly, you snore,* he complained. *You take up too much room. You're too hot.* I took to curling up on the couch, but I did not sleep. I missed the thick duvet, his heavy warmth, and the companionable silences we used to share, breathing together side by side throughout the dark night. How had things gone so wrong? Harold, my saviour, who had once adored me, now found me a nuisance. Well, I would make him pay. I'd let him save me, but I would not let him discard me. As the candles flickered and danced their shadows over the walls that last night, I made my decision. I didn't know who she was, or where she'd come from, or when she'd appear, but it was only a matter of time until Harold insisted that I move over and let someone else take my place.

It was a simple matter in the end.

A delicate touch to one of the tapers sent flames licking over the table, leaping across to the wall, and dripping down onto the floor. When the tree crackled into life, I slipped out the door and waited until the hullabaloo was over.

There was never a question of blame, nor should there have been. Harold paid the price for his actions. Perhaps our love wasn't as deep as it seemed at first, but still…

He shouldn't have trifled with me. It wasn't right. I will miss that bed, though.

The news item read as follows:
U OF A PROF DIES IN CHRISTMAS EVE BLAZE
A late-night blaze killed 65-year-old Harold Ruskin, Professor Emeritus, History and Classics department at the University of Alberta. Fire officials say the fire started when a candle fell over in the kitchen, igniting a Christmas tree. Emergency crews were unable to reach Ruskin, who lived alone with his cat, in time to save him. Resuscitation attempts were unsuccessful, and Ruskin was pronounced dead at the scene, of smoke inhalation.

The cat escaped without injury and is currently being housed at the Edmonton SPCA, awaiting a new home. Shelter officials say Lucky, as they've named her, is spayed, vaccinated, beautiful and healthy, but dislikes other cats.

R.G. Willems has been writing professionally for nearly 20 years and is the author of eight books and more than a 150 articles. Her non-fiction work, under the name Roxanne Willems Snopek, has appeared in a wide variety of publications, from the Vancouver Sun *and* Reader's Digest *to newsletters for Duke, Cornell and Tufts universities. In 2006, her novel* Targets of Affection *was published by Cormorant Books as the first of a new mystery series dealing with the human–animal bond. The same year also saw the release of* Half in the Sun *(Ronsdale Press, Elsie K. Neufeld, ed.), an anthology of West Coast Mennonite writing, in which her short story "Two Steps Forward" appears. Roxanne and her family live in British Columbia, where she is currently at work on her next book. Visit her on the Web at www.roxannesnopek.com*

As Long As We Both Shall Live

Rick Mofina

RE: INVESTIGATION OF SPENCER DALTON
PLACE: Criminal Court Building
DATE/TIME: December 24, 2007, 11:00 a.m.
REPORTED BY: Kim Willoughby, Deputy Court Reporter
STATEMENT OF Elizabeth Dalton

APPEARANCES:
PAUL UPSHAW, Assistant State Attorney
DONNA WHITE, Attorney for the witness

ALSO PRESENT:
BILL POPE, Detective, Fuller County Sheriff's Office
SAMANTHA VINE, Detective, State
        Bureau of Criminal Investigation
MARK AYER, Detective, Hartford Police Department
CATRINA LOPEZ, Detective, Hartford Department

Elizabeth Dalton, having been first duly cautioned and
sworn to testify the truth, the whole truth, and nothing
but the truth, testified on her oath as follows:

DIRECT EXAMINATION BY MR. PAUL UPSHAW
Q. Right off, I want to acknowledge that everyone has re-arranged plans
in order to be here and we appreciate everyone's patience as we deal with
this serious matter. Now, could you please state your name for the record.
A. My name is Elizabeth Dalton.
Q. Are you known by any other name?
A. I'm known as Liz Dalton.
Q. My name is Paul Upshaw. I'm a prosecutor for the State Attorney's
Office. We are conducting an investigation into the circumstances
surrounding the death of your husband, Spencer Dalton, 993
Hickory Shade Lane, Hartford, Connecticut. For the record, we
will summarize the facts to date. Is that okay, Mrs. Dalton?
A. Yes.
Q. In your statement to Detective Bill Pope of the Fuller County
Sheriff's Office, May 17, 2007, you reported your husband,
Spencer Dalton, missing after he had left your family cabin at
Sweet Pine Lake in Fuller County. He left alone in his 18-foot
Galaxy Aqua Glider boat to go fishing, is that correct?
A. Yes.
A. You were last to see Spencer Dalton. Is that correct?
Q. Yes.
Q. Detective Bill Pope headed the investigation that involved a
number of agencies and services who participated in an extensive
search. The search for your husband yielded no results beyond
the recovery of his boat and one life jacket. Spencer Dalton is
missing and presumed to have drowned. This is reflected in
Detective Pope's sworn report in the file dated July 21, 2007.
A. Yes.
Q. For the record, Hartford detectives Ayer and Lopez located you at
approximately 8:00 a.m. today, December 24, at Bradley International
Airport during pre-boarding for SunEx Flight #1975 to Miami, Florida,
with a connection on Globo Rio Air Flight #4587 to Sao Paulo, Brazil.
A. That's correct.

Q. They indicated to you that new information of an urgent nature in the Spencer Dalton case had arisen and that we were seeking what knowledge you have pertaining to it. Upon advice of your attorney, Ms. Donna White, who is present here in this court, you volunteered to postpone your flight and cooperate. Is that correct?

A. Yes.

Q. I've gone through the file but would like to ask you to first provide a bit of biographical information. Your date and place of birth?

A. October 13, 1950, Sao Paulo, Brazil.

Q. Did you grow up in Brazil or the United States?

A. Both. My father is an American citizen from Boston. He was a diplomat, a military attaché with the embassy in Brazil, where he met my mother. I was born in Brazil. When I was twelve, my father left his post for a job here in Hartford.

Q. You have dual citizenship?

A. Yes. I consider myself an American citizen.

Q. Do you have children?

A. One. Our daughter. She's a language therapist. We have two grandsons. Our son-in-law is Professor of American Studies at the University of Lisbon. They moved to Portugal seven years ago.

Q. I notice you did not name them.

A. You did not ask for their names.

Q. Tell me, in the seven years since your daughter moved to Portugal, how often have you seen her and your grandsons?

A. Inaudible.

Q. Mrs. Dalton, how often have you seen them?

A. Twice.

Q. Twice? In seven years?

A. Inaudible (…boys were born…?)

Q. Would you like a tissue?

AFTER RECESS

Q. Okay, we're back on the record. What is your occupation, Mrs. Dalton?

A. District manager for deli items for North World Imperial Consolidated Food Group.

Q. The retail chain?

A. Yes.

Q. What is the nature of your responsibilities?

A. I ensure the meat sections of the stores are in compliance with all aspects of the company's policy: selections, meat case display, everything.

Q. And your husband? His occupation?

A. Senior sales manager for Encore Auto Restore.

Q. The national auto body repair chain?

A. Yes.

Q. How did you meet Spencer Dalton?

A. Inaudible.

Q. Mrs. Dalton, I know this is difficult. Can you answer the question, please?

A. Inaudible.

MS. DONNA WHITE: Mr. Upshaw, can we give my client a moment?

A. Certainly, Ms. White.

AFTER RECESS

Q. Okay, we're back on the record. Mrs. Dalton, how did you meet Spencer Dalton?

A. We met at County High School in our senior year. We both attended community college. After graduation, we got married and moved to the city.

Q. At the time of Spencer Dalton's death, how long had you been married?

A. Thirty-five years.

Q. Was it a happy marriage?

A. It was a good marriage.

Q. Were you happy in your marriage to Spencer?

A. I loved Spencer.

Q. Did you feel loved in return?

A. I know he loved me.

Q. How do you know Spencer loved you, Mrs. Dalton?

A. Inaudible.

Q. Mrs. Dalton?

A. He took a vow to always love me. I... (inaudible)

Q. Here's another tissue. We'll give you a minute.

AFTER RECESS
Q. Okay, we're back on the record. Mrs. Dalton, have
you ever been unfaithful to your husband?
A. Inaudible.
Q. You're shaking your head. Mrs. Dalton, I have
to request that you please remove your hands from
your face and answer for the record, please.
A. Never. I was never unfaithful to Spencer.
He's the only man I've ever loved.
Q. Do you suspect your husband was unfaithful to you?
A. No response.
Q. Mrs. Dalton, do you suspect Spencer was ever
unfaithful in your thirty-five years of marriage?
A. How could he be?
Q. Excuse me?
A. He took a vow to love me. To always love only me.
Q. Mrs. Dalton, please answer the question.
A. Inaudible.

MS. WHITE: Mr. Upshaw, I think my client
needs another moment to compose—
A. No. We'll continue, Ms White.

QUESTIONING OF WITNESS CONTINUES
Q. Mrs. Dalton, our recent investigation shows that
Spencer Dalton travelled a great deal on business, and
he travelled alone. Would you say that is correct?
A. Yes.
Q. On March 5, 6, and 7 of this year, he was registered as a guest
at the Sunrise Luxury Suites in Houston, Texas. Here are hotel
records and his plane ticket we obtained by executing warrants.
Mrs. Dalton, did you accompany your husband on this trip?
A. No, I was at my office here in Hartford.
Q. At your office? Mrs. Dalton, email traffic originated by you
indicates that you informed your assistant that some business
crises had arisen, requiring you to fly to Atlanta on March
5 and that you would make your own arrangements. Here
are copies of records we obtained through warrants.

A. I may have my dates confused.

Q. Mrs. Dalton, you did fly to Atlanta on March 5, but according to the records we obtained, you never left Atlanta Airport for the city. From Atlanta, you purchased a ticket to Houston, then checked into the Desert Arms Inn in Houston. You'll note it is across the street from the Sunrise Luxury Suites in Houston. This is confirmed by the records and photographs in the file. You will also see that you have been recorded registering at the desk by the security camera at the Desert Arms Inn where you rented room 3009 for March 5, 6, and 7.

A. Yes.

Q. Why didn't you join your husband at his hotel across the street from your hotel?

A. I... Well, he was very busy and he had a lot of business in Houston.

Q. Did you join him for dinner or anything like that?

A. I... He was very busy.

Q. Was your husband aware you were in Houston across the street from him?

A. No response.

Q. Mrs. Dalton?

A. Inaudible.

Q. Do you not think it odd that you would fly all that way and not join him?

MS. WHITE: Mr. Upshaw, perhaps a break would—

A. No. We'll continue.

QUESTIONING OF WITNESS CONTINUES

Q. Mrs. Dalton, tell me, what was your business in Houston?

A. Inaudible.

Q. Mrs. Dalton, why did you mislead your office, fly to Houston, check into the hotel across the street from where your husband was conducting business meetings, and then never join him?

A. I had to see.

Q. You had to see what?

A. Inaudible.

Q. See what, Mrs. Dalton?

MS. WHITE: Mr. Upshaw, please. Can't you see she's not in any shape to—
MR. UPSHAW: Ms. White, I would advise
your client to answer the question.

A. Inaudible.
Q. (Expletive?) All right. Two minutes.

AFTER RECESS
Q. Okay, we're back on the record. Mrs. Dalton, I'm going to
show you a photograph. Do you know who this woman is?
A. I've never met her. I've never spoken to her.
Q. That's not what I asked, Mrs. Dalton. Do you know who this woman is?
A. Melinda Cain, it says right on it.
Q. For the record, this is a copy of the Colorado state driver's license
of Melinda Jean Cain. She oversees fleet maintenance for UGL Fleet
Corporation, which manages auto rentals. Our investigation shows
Melinda Cain has been the contact for UGL's business dealings with your
husband's company for approximately three years. Have you ever met or
spoken to Melinda Cain or heard your husband speak of her, Mrs. Dalton?
A. I already told you, no. Never.
Q. You can see from her photograph she is quite striking. She is
thirty-one years old, a former regional beauty queen. At age nineteen,
she was crowned Rocky Rivers Dairy Princess. She obtained a
business degree before joining UGL. She has no children and is
recently divorced from her husband after a year of separation.
Did you know these facts about Melinda Cain, Mrs. Dalton?
A. I do now.
Q. You do now because I am telling you? Or because you
ventured on your own to learn more about Melinda Cain
after your trip to Houston in March of this year?
A. Inaudible.
Q. Mrs. Dalton, perhaps this will help you clarify your response. You'll
see in this photograph recorded by the security camera of the Sunrise
Luxury Suites that Spencer Dalton is entering the room of Melinda Cain.
You'll note the time, 10:30 p.m., March 5, and you'll note the time in the
next photograph of his exit from Ms. Cain's room, 8:30 a.m., March 6.
A. Inaudible.
Q. Fine. A brief break and more water please.

AFTER RECESS

Q. We're back on the record. Mrs. Dalton, will you confirm that on July 24, 2007, approximately two months after Spencer Dalton disappeared in Sweet Pine Lake, you sold your family vehicle, a Blue 2000 Chevrolet Blazer Trailblazer 4WD SUV, VIN #97365398748 to Old Glory Federal Truck Sales.

A. The SUV reminded me of Spencer. I could still smell his cologne inside, and it broke my heart. I had to sell it.

Q. In turn, Old Glory Federal Truck Sales sold your SUV to Kyle Lee Jeddison of Brooklyn, New York.

A. I don't know who that is.

Q. Two months after the transaction, Kyle Lee Jeddison was arrested in a joint task force drug operation run by the DEA, FBI, the NYPD, and the New York State Police. As part of the investigation, the vehicle in question was seized and processed.

A. I don't understand what that has to do with me.

Q. Forensics on the SUV yielded traces of B-positive blood, which is the type consistent with that of Spencer Dalton. Further DNA analysis of the blood shows that it matched the DNA sample you provided police from Spencer Dalton's tooth brush and razor, to use for comparison and identification in the event searchers located his body. Have you any thoughts on these facts, Mrs. Dalton?

A. I don't. Maybe Spencer may have bled a bit in the back of the SUV when he was chopping firewood and hauling it in the rear.

Q. Why did you say the blood was found in the rear of the SUV? I never mentioned the location, Mrs. Dalton?

A. I just assumed. Please. This is hard.

Q. Mrs. Dalton. Please look at these photographs. Tell me, are you're familiar with this building and its location?

A. It is a former meat-cutting facility used by my company for training. It's located near Sooback River.

Q. Have you ever had reason to enter this facility?

A. During college, for summer jobs, I trained there as a meat cutter and butcher.

Q. A review of your work history shows that you have also worked in an abattoir, is that correct?

A. Yes, during college to help pay for school.

Q. You are skilled in the operation of meat-cutting equipment, such as a band saw, and you are not distressed by the sight of blood and carcasses being butchered.

A. I see it every day as part of my job.

Q. But you are skilled yourself in meat cutting, freezing, and storage, isn't that correct, Mrs. Dalton?

A. It's part of my job qualifications.

Q. As district manager of deli items for the North-World Imperial Consolidated Food Group?

A. Yes.

Q. As district manager, do you have access to the North-World training facility at Sooback River?

A. I'm not sure. I may.

Q. We have records indicating that you have been provided keys and security codes that give you full access to the facility and the equipment.

A. As I said, it is my job. May I have more water please?

Q. Mrs. Dalton, this is a copy of the report on a forensic analysis of the Sooback River meat-cutting facility. You will see that microscopic traces of B-positive human blood were located in the facility.

A. Inaudible.

Q. DNA analysis identifies the blood and tissue as belonging to Spencer Dalton. Can you explain how this has come to be, Mrs. Dalton?

A. No response.

Q. Mrs. Dalton, is there anything you would like to tell us?

A. No response.

Q. Where is your husband, Mrs. Dalton?

A. Inaudible.

Q. Extensive searches of the Sooback River facility have not located him. The river has been dragged, grid searches have been conducted, vapour probes have been employed, cadaver dogs have searched the entire site. All in vain.

MS. WHITE: Mr. Upshaw, may my client have a brief moment?
MR. UPSHAW: No, Ms. White. We will continue. As I stated at the outset, we have obtained new information of an urgent nature and we are seeking your client's assistance.

QUESTIONING OF WITNESS CONTINUES

Q. Now, Mrs. Dalton, I'm going to show you a photocopy of a personal check dated April 6, 2007, on your account in the amount of $1000 to Matt Barrow Investigations. It was cashed April 21, 2007. Do you acknowledge your signature on the check?

A. Yes.

Q. Do you acknowledge having business dealings with Matt Barrow, a private investigator?

A. Inaudible (…have a tissue?)

Q. Mrs. Dalton?

A. Yes. I hired him.

Q. For what purpose?

A. No response.

Q. Mrs. Dalton, please answer.

A. Thirty-five years… (inaudible)

Q. Excuse me?

A. Inaudible.

Q. Mrs. Dalton, why did you contract the services of Matt Barrow?

A. To find her.

Q. To find who?

A. His whore.

Q. Are you referring to Melinda Cain?

A. No response.

Q. Did Matt Barrow locate Melinda Cain for you?

A. You know the answer to that.

Q. He provided you with her address?

A. That's right: 4446 Cold Creek Path, Denver, Colorado. I am sure you have a copy of that, too.

Q. Why are you smiling, Mrs. Dalton?

A. Inaudible.

Q. Mrs. Dalton, is Melinda Cain in any danger?

DETECTIVE SAMANTHA VINE'S CELL PHONE RINGS

Q. I'm sorry, Mr. Upshaw. Excuse me, we have to take this from Denver PD. Earlier this morning, we requested them to dispatch a car to check on the welfare of Ms. Cain.

A. Of course. Take the call. We'll break.

AFTER RECESS
Q. We're back on the record. According to Detective Vine, Denver
PD confirms the well-being of Ms. Cain at her residence. She
is awaiting delivery of a gift before planning to depart to visit
family in Boulder. Mrs. Dalton, why do you continue smiling?
A. It shouldn't take long.
Q. What shouldn't take long?
A. Do you know, Mr. Upshaw, that as a naturalized
citizen of Brazil, when I am on Brazilian soil, I cannot
be extradited to the United States from Brazil?
Q. Yes, we're aware, Mrs. Dalton. We've been
in touch with the State Department.
A. I purchased my ticket once I learned… Well, I thought I had time.
Q. Mrs. Dalton, we still have many questions and much to do—
A. Thirty-five years.

DETECTIVE SAMANTHA VINE'S CELL PHONE RINGS
Q. Excuse me, I'll take this call in the corner…

QUESTIONING OF WITNESS CONTINUES
Q. Take the call, Detective. Now, Mrs. Dalton, with respect to Ms. Cain—
A. I found their letters, Mr. Upshaw. He hid them in his workshop.
DET. VINE: (into the phone) …the responding unit? Found what?
A. Spencer carried my books in high school. He told me I
was the only girl in the world he would ever love…
DET. VINE: (into the phone) A courier? What's… What?!
A. Spencer vowed he would always love me. Thirty-five years. Then
he tells her in his letter that she—she—would always have his heart.
DET. VINE: (into the phone) Oh my God!
A. I gift-wrapped it for her.

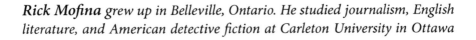

*Rick Mofina grew up in Belleville, Ontario. He studied journalism, English
literature, and American detective fiction at Carleton University in Ottawa*

where he received his Bachelor of Journalism degree. He began his writing career as a news reporter. His freelance crime stories have appeared in The New York Times, Reader's Digest, *and* Penthouse. *Rick is based in Ottawa where he lives with his wife and their two children. He is the author of several crime/suspense novels and short stories and has won two Arthur Ellis Awards, one for Best Novel in 2003 and one for Best Short Story in 2006.*

Hell Bunny

Dick Noble

The gaunt black and tan hound threw a glance over its shoulder, drool splashing its matted coat. Its wind was gone, but maybe, just maybe, it had run far enough. Slowly, the dog walked up the slope, its heaving sides sucking in fresh air, and rested on the black basalt rock at the hill's crest.

The exhausted dog surveyed the creek valley below with dim eyes and sharp ears for any sign of its tormentor. There, in the willow wands, it caught a flash of movement. It was searching for him. The dog cowered in the shadows of the rock, hoping its pursuer would pass by and not notice him.

A large grey and white shape hopped over the crest of the hill, sampled the air currents with its cute twitching nose, and pounced on the poor canine, tearing it apart like a piece of lettuce.

The bunny felt good—at the top of his game—but the dog was just a warm-up for his showdown with Fatty. The final match to determine which holiday would reign supreme. Christmas was coming…and so was the Easter Bunny.

Blood on the Holly

*Dick Noble is legally known as **Richard Bishop**, husband of the ever-patient Isabella, father of Jennifer, Gordon, and Katie, and servant to the family pet rabbit, Piggy. For the past decade or so, Richard/Dick has written many magazine articles on such topics as adoption, firearms, outdoor pursuits, and fly fishing. During the day, he masquerades as a customer advocate with the City of Calgary for folks with mobility challenges. This story is his first published venture into the world of crime fiction.*

Gifts

Peter Sellers

Back in the days when you were still allowed to celebrate Christmas, there were always high banks of snow. There was public carol singing, and the post office delivered Christmas cards in bundles to virtually every home. So many cards were delivered in those days that for the two weeks leading up to Christmas, students were hired to help the postmen on their rounds. The pay was good, the hours were short, and the work was easy. It was ideal. The jobs were coveted. Gerald had university and his rent to pay for, and he considered himself fortunate to be hired.

Each morning, Gerald went to the postal station. He was assigned to help Old Ben, who had worked the same route for twenty-four years. Ben had bad teeth, gnarled hands, and a habit of muttering to himself.

The first morning, Ben gave Gerald his only lesson about delivering mail. They went to the first house together. The letter slot was near the bottom of the front door. Ben handed Gerald a bundle of mail. "Put it through," he said.

Gerald gripped the bundle. As he bent and reached for the letter slot, he could hear Ben muttering beside him. Gerald started pushing the bundle through. Just as his fingers were about to slip into the letter slot and drop the bundle, Ben grabbed Gerald's wrist and pulled his hand back. "Don't do that."

Ben took the envelopes from Gerald. "Do this." He pushed the front edge of the bundle into the letter slot, so they were held there in place by the spring-loaded flap inside. Then he released his grip and placed his palm against the protruding end of bundle and pushed.

The envelopes had gone about half-way through the slot when there came a snarling from within the house and the bundle was wrenched inside with startling violence.

"Do it the way you were doing it and you'll lose fingers," Ben said. "I know one carrier lost two. You never know what's on the other side of the door."

"Is there anything else I need to know?" Gerald asked, now the eager student.

"Don't walk across lawns," Ben said. He never did. He would use the walkway to reach the front door, then return to the sidewalk before proceeding to the next house. Never once did Gerald see Ben take a shortcut. Gerald was careful not to do so either, unless Ben was out of sight.

Old Ben split the route in two. He took one side of each street and gave Gerald the other. Gerald quickly learned which letter slots to appreciate and which to despise. He liked the big wide ones that opened easily and let you slip even the largest stacks through with no effort. If the slots were chest-high, so much the better. He liked capacious mailboxes hung on doors and porch walls. He lifted the lids and deposited the mail with a flourish.

Best of all were the milk boxes, which were always by the side door. In those days, milk trucks still came slowly along the streets, and white-clad men with clinking bottles made house calls.

What Gerald did not like were the old-fashioned, tiny letter slots. They were cramped and mean-spirited, forcing him to fold the larger cards and send the cards through by twos and threes rather than in bundles. Magazines and catalogues were difficult, too, and he would often hear pages tearing as the flaps inside the slots tore at them. At first, he felt badly about this. Then he reasoned that if the people didn't want their mail mangled they should change the kind of letter slot or mailbox they chose to use.

It surprised Gerald to learn that people gave Christmas gifts to the postman. He realized this for the first time when he opened a large mailbox and found a package inside, wrapped in Christmas paper, with Ben's name on the tag. Gerald took the present out and brought it across the street.

Ben held the gift to his ear like a child and shook it. "Chocolates," he said. He shifted the contents of his mailbag and put the package in.

Over the two weeks, Gerald found other gifts. Often, they were bottles. Gerald discovered that Ben's preference was for rye. Gerald made a mental note to buy a mickey to give to Ben on Christmas Eve.

Other people gave Ben money. On a few occasions, Gerald discovered envelopes marked Ben or Postman in the letterbox or the milk box. When Gerald passed them on, Ben put them in his mailbag, unopened.

Lawrence hated Christmas. He hated the sound of the music. He hated the lights and decorations. He hated having to go out and buy gifts for people he didn't like. He hated the forced jollity. Most of all, he hated the fact that it was hard to find a card game, and he desperately needed one. George was badgering him for money.

These were the days long before casinos and online betting. Had he known what was coming, Lawrence would have been euphoric. But then, on a snowy December day with Christmas looming, he was broke and in debt and he needed money by Christmas Eve.

The high-stakes games of stud and draw—no one played Texas Hold 'Em then—were illegal and deeply underground. Prior to Christmas, many players were busy with other commitments and the games were fewer. Usually, when he did find one, the other players were as broke and desperate as Lawrence himself. The stakes were low, and the chances of winning as much as he needed were slim.

Since it was known that Lawrence had no money, he was not often welcome at the tables where winning would have been profitable enough to make a difference. It was a conspiracy of bastards, Lawrence knew, working together to hold him back.

Sometimes, as Gerald was about to put the mail in the letter slot, a front door would open and a woman would appear. They were always holding envelopes and they always said the same thing: "You're not Ben."

"I'm just helping him out until Christmas," Gerald would say. Then, noting the envelope, he would add, "I can take that to him, if you want."

The women always declined, some more graciously than others.

"I'll ask him to come see you," Gerald would offer then. He would cross the street and wait on the sidewalk until Ben came down the walkway. Gerald would name the house in question and Ben would trudge across the road. Gerald always waited discreetly where he was, watching as Ben and the women exchanged brief words and Ben took the envelopes and came back to continue his route.

The finance company was going to take his car. Merry fucking Christmas, Lawrence, he thought. He couldn't let that happen. He needed the car to get to the games since many of them were a long way from the subway line. He needed the vehicle for more practical purposes as well. It wasn't a good idea to take transit or walk the streets with your pockets bulging with cash. And Lawrence knew that he would win large sometime. It was a matter of patience, and if no one stood in his way and did things to hurt his chances, the time would be soon. Also, it was a bad idea to show up at a game without a car. That made you look like a loser.

He had one chance to save the vehicle. He'd been able to browbeat one of the bureaucratic idiots at the finance company into meeting him on Christmas Eve morning. "Be here at eleven," the bureaucrat had said, like a king granting an audience. Lawrence knew he could charm the jerk into leaving the car alone.

The trouble was that now he couldn't go. He'd learned of a card game that was guaranteed to attract some heavy wallets. Lawrence couldn't pass that up. He had to tell his wife that she had to go to the meeting. She had to convince the bureaucrat that Lawrence should keep his car. Lawrence wasn't happy about having to do this. If anyone could screw things up, it was his wife.

Gerald quickly learned that some people got a lot of Christmas cards and some people got few. In odd cases, there were houses that received none. This was peculiar in those days, for most neighbourhoods were not as cosmopolitan as they are now. This neighbourhood certainly wasn't. Gerald knew that you would be hard-pressed to find a Catholic family, let alone anything more exotic.

There were a small number of homes that only received bills. At least, that's what Gerald assumed from the number of windowed envelopes he put through the letter slots. He felt sorry for these people, except for one household.

Once, as he walked back along the driveway from putting more bills into the milk box, a man came out of the front door. He glared sharply at Gerald, as if knowing what had been brought and blaming Gerald for it. There was so much hate and anger in the glance that Gerald felt chilled. The man, whose name Gerald assumed was Lawrence, got into his car, slammed the door fiercely, and drove away.

If he's like that all the time, Gerald thought, no wonder no one sends him cards.

"You need to remember what Scrooge said in that movie," George pointed out.

Lawrence was irritated that George had telephoned him at home. "What are you talking about?"

"You know, that movie about Scrooge. They show it every Christmas. On Christmas Eve, when he's leaving work, this guy stops Scrooge and asks for more time to pay back his debt."

Lawrence was puzzled. What did some stupid movie have to do with him?

"Scrooge tells the guy, 'I didn't ask for more time to lend you the money. Why should you ask for more time to pay it back?' You should watch that movie, buddy. There are many lessons you could learn from it." He was thoughtful for a moment. "You have to be careful, though. There's a colourized version, but it's no good. Don't watch that. The colour looks fake, and it wrecks the atmosphere. Be sure you see it in black and white. It's much better."

Lawrence started to protest, but George cut him off. "I want that money to buy gifts for my kids. They love Christmas, and you're not going to make me let them down. Tell you what, I'll make it easy on you." George adopted an affable manner. "I'll come to your house to pick it up. That's my gift for you. I'll be there Thursday morning at eleven. If someone isn't there to give me the money, it'll go hard for you."

"Where am I going to get that much money by then?" Lawrence was shrill with anxiety.

"Six grand," George said, "on Christmas Eve. Ho ho ho!"

It took a lot of effort, but Lawrence managed to scrape together three thousand. Chiselers everywhere were giving him less than he deserved. In the bedroom, he put the bills into an envelope. He took it to his wife.

"A guy named George will be here tomorrow at eleven to pick this up." He described George to her in detail. "Don't give it to anyone else."

"Tomorrow morning?" she said. "I can't—"

"Shut up and do as you're told," he said.

"But you told me—"

"I told you to give this envelope to a guy tomorrow morning. That's all you need to know."

She knew there was no point in persisting. "Where did you get it?" she asked. The sadness in her voice angered him. It was another unfair way she had of making him always feel guilty.

"That's none of your damn business," he said, knowing that if she wanted to, she could find out soon enough what he had sold this time to raise it.

After Lawrence left with the car, his wife was troubled. She saw no way out of the dilemma, no solution that would not raise her husband's ire. She wished she could be in two places at once. She wished she could be anywhere but here. Finally, after spending a considerable time trying to decide which task was more important, she took a sheet of paper and wrote a short note.

Gerald was disappointed that this was his last day. He had come to enjoy the job. The weather appealed to him. True, it was hard on his bare hands and he understood why Ben's were so damaged. Yet he never understood Canadians who complained about the cold and the snow. It made you feel invigorated and alive. He enjoyed the biting viciousness of the wind and the way his nose, cheeks, and fingers felt when he was done for the day and was back inside and the warmth returned.

Gerald was surprised when he found the envelope in this particular milk box. He had learned that there was a correlation between how many Christmas cards a household received and whether or not they gave Ben a gift. The Lawrence house seemed to be ignored by everyone except creditors.

Yet here was a white envelope, Christmas card-sized though rather bulkier than usual. There was nothing written on the front, not even the generic Postman. Gerald picked it up. It was thick but still flimsy.

At first, Gerald thought it must be for someone else, but that didn't make sense. After all, the mail was delivered at the same time every day. And over his two weeks, Gerald had already taken more than a dozen envelopes from mail and milk boxes. Goodness knows how many Ben had found himself. What else could it be but a present left by a homeowner who didn't hold the mailman responsible for what he delivered? Gerald slipped the envelope in his bag. He'd give it to Ben at the end of the block.

Three houses further on, after picking up another envelope, this one addressed to Ben, Gerald took the blank envelope out and felt it again. The thickness puzzled him, as did the lack of a name on the front.

Since there was no addressee, Gerald felt he should be sure before giving it to Ben. Perhaps he'd find some personal item that it would be best to take back. He made a small tear in the corner but couldn't see anything. He decided to open the envelope fully. If it wasn't intended for Ben, Gerald could return it and confess to an honest mistake. No one could take umbrage with that.

Gerald tore along the flap. The contents shocked him: Gerald had never seen so much cash. He riffled the edges of the bills, and then, realizing how exposed he was, he panicked, stuffing the money back into the envelope and pushing it to the bottom of his bag. He raced through the next several houses, not wanting to fall behind.

By the time he and Ben finished the route, Gerald had lost his nerve. He handed over the other envelope and a bottle of liquor he'd collected, both with Ben's name on them. But it felt too late to give him the cash in its torn envelope. How would he explain that he hadn't handed it over right away? Why had he opened it? Why, seeing the cash, hadn't he said anything? Why hadn't he returned it? Why had he taken it in the first place? Before putting his mailbag in the trunk of Ben's car for the last time, Gerald slipped the torn envelope into his pocket.

147

Ben extended his weather-ravaged hand. "Thanks for your help," he said, "and Merry Christmas."

"Thanks, Ben. Merry Christmas to you, too." Gerald produced the mickey of rye he had bought and held it out, feeling it a feeble offering.

The card game did not go well. Lawrence was down when the game broke up early in the evening, three of the players citing Christmas and family and, in one unlikely case, church as lame excuses for leaving. He was angry that they were cheating him out of his chance to get even, let alone get ahead. This was typical. No one gave him the opportunity. Everyone took their turn, and no one gave him his.

When he arrived home, he asked, "Did you give George the money?"

"Yes," she said, but in such a way that Lawrence knew she was lying.

"What did he say?" he asked, his voice rising.

"Nothing," she whispered.

Lawrence knew that it was not like George to say nothing. "What do you mean, nothing? Didn't he even say thank you?"

"No. I don't know."

"What do you mean, 'you don't know? You handed the envelope to him. You must have heard what he said. I know you're stupid, but I didn't know you're deaf, too." She did not reply and he added, "You did hand it to him, like I told you to?"

She shook her head, almost imperceptibly.

"No? Well what did you do with it?"

"I left it in the milk box."

"You did what? I told you to put it in his hands. For Christ sake, can't you follow the simplest instruction? Now he can say he didn't get it, and there's no one, not even someone as useless as you, to contradict him."

"I couldn't hand it to him," she said, feeling the beginning of tears. "You told me I had to go to the finance company."

He had forgotten about that. "That's your problem, not mine. You should have planned your day better."

She knew there was no point saying that George must have come to get the envelope, that it was gone and there was nothing to worry about.

"Get into the kitchen," Lawrence said. "You have to learn to do what you're told."

Gerald sat at his table and counted the money again. There was three thousand dollars. It was a remarkable sum, and he thought about all he could do with that amount. He could travel, or pay for the rest of his schooling, or possibly even move out of Toronto to a town where the real estate was cheap and make a down payment on a small house.

He thought, What a wonderful gift. He wondered whom it was really for. Setting his dreams aside, he knew there was no choice. The money had to be returned.

When Lawrence was a boy, his parents would fill up a stocking for him every Christmas. It always included a book, a chocolate bar, a small toy or two, and tucked down in the toe, there was always an orange. Lawrence hated those oranges. He did not like the taste of them or the smell, and every time he upended his stocking and the orange rolled out, he felt disappointment and anger. Why did they have to give him something he didn't want? Why couldn't he find another toy down there, or more chocolate? It wasn't fair, and as he said his dutiful thank you to his mother and father, the resentment seethed.

He went into the kitchen and opened the refrigerator. In the crisper, he found those same large, thick-skinned oranges. Picking one up, he want to the storage room and found one of the old woollen socks that he and his wife had used for Christmas stockings when the children were small.

As Lawrence walked back to the kitchen, he dropped the orange into the sock. His wife, standing in the middle of the linoleum floor, looked at the stocking with the swelling in its toe like a tumour.

"Here's your Christmas gift," Lawrence said. He swung the stocking accurately, the orange pounding heavily into her lower back. She groaned and doubled over. "Stand up," he said. She straightened, and he was just about to swing the stocking again when the doorbell rang. At first, he was going to ignore it and continue. Then it occurred to him that perhaps the sound would carry through the door. He did not want anyone to interfere with what he had to do. He handed the stocking to his wife. "Hold this," he said. "Keep quiet, wait here, and think about what you have coming."

Lawrence opened the front door and was surprised to see George.

"I am very annoyed with you," George said.

"What?"

"Because of you, I have had to come out here—to a part of the city that I hate—on Christmas Eve. Not once, but twice. And there's no money. My kids are going to be so disappointed."

"What do you mean, no money? My wife left it in the milk box."

"No," George said. "There was this note on the door, but there was nothing in the milk box." Lawrence read the piece of paper George showed him. In his wife's printing it said: George, look in the milk box. "But there was no money there. There was nothing but a couple of bills. So give me my money now."

Lawrence was stunned. She was ever stupider than he'd imagined. In his rage, he said, "I don't have it, you idiot. I'm telling you, my wife was supposed to give it to you."

"Don't lie to me," George said quietly.

"I'm not lying! It's her fault!" Lawrence yelled. "She's the one who owes you!"

George shook his head sadly. "It's your debt, your responsibility." He shut the door behind him. Then he hit Lawrence in the face.

From the kitchen, Lawrence's wife heard raised voices and then scuffling. There were a few sounds of impact with which she was familiar. Then she heard something falling. Finally, the front door opened and then closed again quietly.

After a few moments, when Lawrence did not return to the kitchen, his wife went to the front door. Lawrence lay on the ground writhing. There was blood on his face and the front of his shirt. Spittle frothed at his mouth. His skin had turned an unhealthy colour. His wife noticed more blood and a bit of hair stuck to the wooden frame of the living room door. She realized that he must have swallowed his tongue after falling and that he was choking.

From a first aid course taken when the children were young, she knew that she should tip Lawrence on his side and ease the tongue free.

Instead, she sat on the bottom step, still holding the sock, and watched him patiently.

From two blocks away, Gerald saw the police cars parked in the street and knew he was too late. They had reported the theft. For an instant, he considered walking up to a policeman and turning himself in. Instead, he turned the next corner and went home.

Inside, Lawrence's widow sat on the chesterfield. A policewoman had wrapped a blanket round her shoulders. Thinking this was the best Christmas she could remember, she put her face in her hands and wept.

Peter Sellers *divides his time between Toronto and Stratford, Ontario. He writes short fiction exclusively and infrequently. Most of his stories have been published in* Ellery Queen *and* Alfred Hitchcock Mystery Magazines.

Mother Always Kept a Gun

C. J. Papoutsis

Wednesday afternoon, I was removing a black mole from Mrs. Bindorfer's chin, pixel by pixel, when the cow bell over the door rang and a tall, delicious-looking man stepped into my studio. His face reminded me why I'd taken up portrait photography and made my hands itch for a camera.

"Maxine Mandeville?" My name sounded like music when he said it.

"Yes."

"Detective Al Rossi, Victoria Police Department." He held out his badge. "Do you live at 1720 Arbordale Circle?"

"Not yet." Oh, crap! What now? My mother died last month in St. Damian's Residence for Senior Ladies where she'd lived for two years. She left me her house. I'd decided to renovate the upstairs bathroom and build an apartment in the basement for my daughter. Sylvia, at twenty-four, was again between jobs and coming off her second bad marriage. "My daughter and I are moving in on December 31."

"There's a problem over there." He slipped his badge back into his pocket. "You'll have to come to the police station."

I looked from Detective Rossi to Mrs. Bindorfer's image on my computer screen. "Oh, crap! I'm just trying to camouflage this mole in time for Christmas."

"Excuse me?"

I swung the screen around so he could see it. "Every woman wants her portrait to be beautiful—even if she's eighty years old with wrinkles, warts, and a moustache like a bull seal."

152

I caught a whiff of Alfred Sung as he leaned over to look at Mrs. Bindorfer's image on my screen. He grinned. "This one's going to be a challenge."

I swivelled the screen back and saved the file. "Did Fred Digby nail his foot to the floor again?" Fred's a carpenter who's been working on the house. According to Sylvia, who had been engaged to him briefly, he makes most of his money by suing people, and with the Christmas season bringing out his alcoholic tendency…

"No." Detective Rossi was perusing my photo display. "I'm afraid it's more serious than that. The workers found a skeleton in your basement."

"Don't you mean my closet?" I switched off my computer and shrugged into my coat. I sniffed and checked for tissue and lozenges in the pocket.

"Basement. The skull's got a .22 calibre slug in it. We're talking about murder."

"'Tis the season."

Detective Rossi's cruiser was parked behind my Volkswagen Bug. It started on the first try, and I followed him downtown to the police station. I had to wait while he found the file.

"Merry Christmas," said Martha Lane at the reception desk. We'd gone to high school together.

"Christmas sucks." I coughed and felt like a truck had parked on my chest. I'd caught a cold from shopping in the rain every night after work, buying gifts for people who didn't need anything, and now my throat was raw, my ears itched, and I was sneezing until my eyeballs popped out of my head. Colds terrify me. Childhood asthma gave me a suffocation phobia that years of therapy haven't helped.

Detective Rossi showed me to Interview Room Three. Slumped on a hard metal chair, sipping corrosive brown liquid from a Styrofoam cup, I saw my hopes for a Merry Christmas and a Happy New Year melt like a snowman in Mexico.

He explained that the workers had found the skeleton when they were laying pipes for the bathroom in Sylvia's apartment. The police had stopped work on the house until they could do a thorough search, identify the skeleton, and find out what he was doing in my mother's wine cellar. Nobody except those involved in the case were permitted access. Detective Rossi didn't think we'd be moving in any time soon. My renovation was turning into Satan's workshop. Hasn't anyone else noticed that Santa is Satan spelled inside-out?

Heading back to my apartment, I stopped at the pharmacy and selected an armload of cold remedies with enough combined strength to knock out a grizzly bear. A sneezing fit seized me as I reached the line-up at the cashier. I buried my face in an industrial-sized tissue.

"Bless you," said a cheerful woman with orange hair and grey roots, standing in front of me.

"Thanks." I'm naturally suspicious of people who are cheerful at a time when sensible creatures hibernate. Orange-hair bleated "Merry Christmas" at me, and then it was my turn.

The young cashier, with "Cam" printed on his name tag, looked at me like I was a threat to world health. I paid with my only credit card that wasn't maxed out. "Merry Christmas. I hope you live," he said, stuffing my drugs into a bag.

Smart ass. "Back at ya," I said and went into a coughing fit.

Winter in Victoria is depressing. Grey shrouds the city for weeks on end, torrential rain beats us into submission, and numbing dampness penetrates our winter coats and boots. By the time I got to my apartment, the rain was freezing on the road.

In the middle of the night, a scratchy sound woke me from my medicinally induced stupor. A light danced outside my second-storey window. I pulled back the curtains. A fool dressed like a cat burglar straight out of a sixties movie was perched in the magnolia tree peering in my window. Somebody should have told him fat Peeping Toms don't look good in spandex. I grabbed the glass of water off my night table, opened the window, and winged it at his head.

"Sheee-it!" he shouted. A branch snapped, and I heard a crackly splat as he hit the semi-frozen ground. I threw my coat over my pyjamas, groped for my slippers, and punched 911 on my cell phone on the way downstairs. By the time I got outside, he was gone, but his fall from grace had attracted several other tenants who stood around shivering in their bathrobes and parkas. A rookie cop who looked about sixteen finally arrived. My visitor had left a significant bum print in the garden under the magnolia tree, but nothing else. The cop laughed when I explained the broken water glass and herded the spectators into the lobby for questioning. I returned to my apartment, popped another twelve-hour cold capsule, and stayed awake listening to the old building creak and groan.

Next morning, light snow was falling, and I felt like I'd charged head first into a stone wall. I started off with a two shots of nasal spray, made coffee, and staggered down to the lobby for my newspaper. Miss Rendell, wearing a quilted housecoat and fuzzy slippers, had been in the group outside my window last night and was already in the lobby. She jabbed her finger at her newspaper and glared at me over her half-glasses. "Such wicked goings-on these days."

"Have a nice day," I said and took my paper from the rack. A grainy photo of Mother's house was spread across the front page. The headline read: Workers discover skeleton in basement.

Knowing Miss Rendell would be using the elevator, I sprinted up the stairs despite my fever and pounding headache, and called Sylvia to warn her about the article, although she might be spared the Mandeville infamy since she'd been using her most recent married name, Angelopoulos (which came with its own baggage, but in my opinion, baggage variety is a good thing.)

"Don't sweat it, Mom," she told me. "In a few days, something else will happen and everybody will forget about your skeleton."

I wish I had her attitude. "Our skeleton! You'll be living there, too. And do you realize we'll be spending New Year's in a motel?"

"Whatever. Don't worry, Mom, it won't be for long. I gotta run. Cam's picking me up for breakfast."

Cam? The name rattled around in my drug-fogged brain. At least, he was picking her up for breakfast. He wasn't already there. That was an improvement. I poured a giant mug of coffee and collapsed into my chair. Crap! What next?

I felt like death and stayed home to do paperwork. Detective Rossi called. We arranged to meet Saturday morning at ten. He had been doing his homework, snooping in Vital Statistics, court records, Motor Vehicles—his handsome Roman nose had been everywhere that concerned my family. He probably knew more about me than I did. The snow was still falling, and the murder investigation was gathering speed. Like an avalanche, it would crush any remaining illusions I had about my family. The phone rang three times in the next half hour, neighbours asking nosy questions about my house. I turned off the ringer. After eating a bowl of instant soup and organizing my accounts, I ended my day with a hot bath, more pills, and the old movie *Dial M for Murder*.

Friday morning, the snow had turned to rain: a steady, annoying drizzle like a leaky faucet. I turned on the news. Sylvia was right: A car accident on the Malahat Highway had replaced my skeleton.

After a day at home and with Christmas hanging over me, I needed to catch up. The phone was ringing when I arrived at my studio, and it didn't stop all day: Everyone wanted a portrait done by the woman with the skeleton in her basement. Before noon, I'd even turned down four party invitations. I was becoming a social butterfly, but I felt more like a social moth.

Lunch was two hits of nasal spray and a throat lozenge at two o'clock. Mrs. Bindorfer's mole was history. She came to pick up her portrait and promised to recommend me to her sisters. I wondered what facial disfigurements adorned the rest of her family.

At six thirty, I quit work and stopped on the way home for a burger that I couldn't taste, which was probably just as well. After a hot shower, I lined up my drugs, orange juice, and tissues on the coffee table, ready for another mindless evening of TV. The phone rang. Nobody—just dead air. Then *click*. Twenty minutes later, the same thing. Dead air. *Click*. Creepy.

I dialled the telephone company to report a nuisance call, but when a mechanical voice directed me to "Press one to report a service problem; press two for information about your account—" I hung up. Friggin' robots! The phone rang again. I waited. Twice, three times. What the hell. Nobody could hurt me over the phone. I snatched up the receiver. "Whadyawant?"

"This is Abdul. Congratulations. You have won a trip—"

Crap! "I don't want a trip." I slammed the phone down.

I wasn't going to wait around to provide amusement for phone-scammers and stalkers. The situation called for affirmative action. Since fresh air usually helped my breathing, I'd go for a drive with my window open a crack.

My mental condition had been shaky since Mom died. Having your mother's ashes in a plastic container in the closet does take getting used to, but one day I found myself in front of the open closet asking her if my butt looked too big in my new jeans. Since then, I've consulted her on major decisions as well as about what I should cook for dinner. I'd have to sprinkle her ashes somewhere, sometime, but it was still too soon. I wasn't ready to let her go yet.

I brushed my hair, pulled on black pants and my burgundy sweater. A bit of makeup made me look less like a cadaver. Feeling better, I stood in front of the closet for Mom's approval. Her pearl earrings looked good with the outfit.

I didn't plan my route, just an aimless drive to get me away from my apartment. Christmas is lonely at the best of times, but this year, my two best friends had gone away for the holidays and everyone else I knew was either shopping or busy with family. The rain bounced off my windshield as I drove along Dallas Road. Nothing says depressing like driving around alone in the rain looking at Christmas lights.

I ended up at Mother's house and saw the yellow crime scene tape flapping in the wind. Not so festive. Maybe next year.

My mother always kept a gun in her lingerie drawer: a redwood-handled Hopkins and Allen .22 calibre double-action revolver. Lots of women her age did. They drank Pink Ladies, used black rhinestone-studded cigarette holders, and wore lacy red garter belts, too. When she was young, being a woman was serious business.

Detective Rossi hadn't mentioned Mom's gun, so I guessed the police hadn't found it. Life would be much easier if they didn't. I'd pick up Mom's fur coat—it would be useful in this ugly weather—and scoop the gun, too. I parked two blocks away, and making sure nobody was around, followed the brick path at the side. The house key was on my chain, so I slipped in the back door. With all the curtains drawn, it was nearly pitch-dark. Years of memories settled around me as I groped my way to Mom's bedroom. Her things would have to be sorted and given away, but I hadn't found the time or the emotional strength to deal with it yet. I switched on my penlight and pointed it down so it wouldn't attract attention from outside. I made my way to the closet. The coat was gone.

I turned to leave and collided with a large, furry hulk. I opened my mouth to scream, but only a croak came out.

"Shut up," said a raspy voice. The hulk's breath was hot and wet on my cheek. He spun me around, twisting one arm behind me, and clamped his hand over my nose and mouth. My suffocation phobia kicked in. Panic seized me, and I chomped down on his hand.

"Bitch," he screamed, releasing me. He stumbled to the doorway to block my escape. I aimed my penlight in his face. Beady eyes glinted in the light. He was covered in brown fur. Mother's coat! With a four-inch gap over his belly, the hem dangling around his thighs, and the sleeves just clearing his elbows, he looked like a giant rat who'd outgrown his fur.

"What the fuck are you doing with that light?" he squealed. "The cops are watchin' this place."

"What the hell are you doing in my mother's coat?"

"Sleeping. It's cold in here."

I flashed the light in his face again. "You're the fat pervert who was peeping in my window!"

"I am not fat."

I stuck out my chin and snorted. "Okay, the full-figured pervert. Who the hell are you?"

"I'm your brother."

"Eeew! Bullshit! Try again, fur ball."

"You never heard of me?"

"What's to hear? Get out, or I'll make so much noise every cop in Victoria will come running."

He held up his hands like a zealous crossing guard. "I'm not gonna hurt you."

I sidestepped to the dresser and eased open Mom's lingerie drawer. I felt for the gun. Whiffs of Opium, Mom's signature scent, rose up from the lace and silk, but no gun.

"Are you looking for this?" He patted his furry pocket. "I don't think it's loaded."

Great. This overstuffed rat says he's my brother, and he's got Mother's gun. All I've got is a penlight and a red, lacy garter belt.

He smiled. "Don't worry, I don't usually kill people."

"Good." I took a deep breath. "How did you manage to break in with cops everywhere?"

"There were no cops. I got here Monday. The bones showed up Wednesday, remember? And I didn't need to break in. The key was under that stupid little statue on the patio."

Mother had always hidden a spare key under the garden gnome. I'd forgotten about that.

"So you've been pawing through Mother's things since Monday?"

"Yeah. I was hoping for money, but guns are good."

I straightened my back and looked him in the eyes. "Give me the gun. It's mine."

He did, and it shocked the hell out of me.

I held the weapon gingerly. "It's not enough to have a goddam skeleton buried in my basement, now there's a brown, furry rodent sleeping in my mother's bedroom."

He shrugged and sat down on the bed. "Some people have it all."

His attitude pissed me off. "And take off my mother's fur coat."

"Stop shining that light in my eyes." He took off the coat and threw it down on the bed, then put his hands in the pocket of his sweatshirt. This sorry creature wasn't what I'd had in mind when I'd asked Santa for a brother, but he piqued my curiosity.

"What are you doing here?"

"If you'd shut up for one stinkin' minute, I'd tell ya." He turned to face me. "I came back for my share. The bitch owes me—or I guess you do now."

Part of me just wanted to get away from this creep, but I was curious to hear his story. Still, I'd feel more comfortable hearing it in a public place with better lighting. "Listen," I said. "A crime scene isn't the best place for a family reunion. Let's go and talk somewhere else." I slipped the fur coat on over my jacket, shoved the gun in the pocket, and we headed for the Starbucks on the corner.

I ordered a tall latte and he ordered a grande Americano. We sat at a table in the back. and I watched him flick the sugar packet three times with his index finger before he ripped it open, just like Mom. What if he really was my brother?

"What's your name?"

"Vincent Vancuzzi."

"Okay, start talking." I sipped my latte. "From the beginning."

He leaned back in his chair. "Our parents were always fighting. One night when I was six, they had a real brawl and Dad took off. The next morning, the bitch's face was black and blue. I asked where Dad was; she said he'd gone out. Next day, she was digging up the dirt floor of the wine cellar. I asked her what she was doing, and she said I should shut up and mind my own business. I kept asking. She kept telling me I'd made the whole thing up. Finally, she took me to a shrink for 'behaviour problems.' When I set a fire at school, she said I was 'unmanageable' and put me up for adoption."

Was he telling the truth? I couldn't imagine Mother doing that—or could I?

"So you think she buried your father in the wine cellar?" I asked.

"*Our* father, Tony Vanccuzi."

"Excuse me. *My* father was Max Mandeville."

Vincent shook his head and took a gulp of coffee. "I was five when you were born. Your real name was Maria Vancuzzi."

I felt like I'd been kicked in the stomach by an elephant. This was like a bad B movie. "But your name's Vancuzzi and mine's Mandeville."

"Mandeville had money, but Mother couldn't marry him without digging up Tony to prove he was dead. So she changed your last name to Mandeville and your first name to Maxine. Nobody asked any questions."

"That's bizarre. How the hell do you know all this?"

"I know people and I've done a lot of time," he admitted. "Jails have computers. Staff are always willing to help out. One hand washes the other."

I was fading. I checked my watch. It was ten thirty and my cold medication was wearing off. I didn't like what this guy had told me, but what if it was true?

I checked Vincent into the Travellers' Lodge on Douglas Street, and we agreed to meet in the coffee shop at eight thirty for breakfast.

My hands were shaking so badly I could hardly get my key in the ignition and I drove past my apartment driveway twice before I found it. This day was way hell and beyond any previous weirdness, and trust me, I've had some weird days. After two more hits of nasal spray and a night-time cold pill, I fell into bed at eleven thirty.

But I couldn't sleep. My mother might be a murderer, a nut bar who peeps in windows might be my brother, and I had an unregistered, concealed weapon in my pocket. This was no way to earn points with delicious Detective Rossi. I got up and dropped the gun into a Tupperware container, then stuffed it in the freezer.

Night time is when I do my serious thinking. Eccentricity doesn't merely exist in our family—it's rampant. My daughter, Sylvia, can't hold on to a job long enough to qualify for unemployment benefits, and her marriages don't last long enough to provide divorce settlements. Mother went through two husbands, the first of which, according to Vincent, was Bony Tony in the basement. Then Max who lasted until a plane crash—not Mother—finished him off. I'd abdicated my marriage after a year because of Heidi Lefeque who ran a lingerie shop based on the theory that most people, including my husband, looked good in black lace underwear. She liked it on him.

And now Vincent. When I was a child, I begged Mom for a brother or sister, and every Christmas, I pleaded with Santa to bring me one. Mother cautioned me to be careful what I wished for. I hated to admit it, but Vincent certainly seemed loopy enough to be my brother.

At seven thirty, I woke up only mildly fogged. I found a big windbreaker that had belonged to my ex-husband and shoved it in a bag and was half-way to town when I realized I hadn't had to use my nasal spray or take a pill!

Vincent was waiting for me in the coffee shop behind a fortress of eggs, sausages, and pancakes. The waitress filled our coffee cups and took my order for a bagel.

"Hope you don't mind," said Vincent, "I already ordered."

"No problem." I fished the windbreaker out of the bag. "You might be able to use this."

"Shit. You didn't have to do that."

"You're welcome." The waitress plopped my plate in front of me. I spread cream cheese and jam on my bagel while he sliced his sausages with the side of his fork.

"Most people use a knife for that," I said.

"Never got the hang of it. They don't let us use 'em in the joint."

Right. I was having breakfast with a criminal. "What happened after Mom shipped you off?"

He continued cutting his sausages. "Nobody wanted to adopt an eight-year-old problem child, so I got passed from foster home to foster home till I quit school and took up crime."

"What was it like in the joint?"

"I really learned to hate in there." Every night before going to sleep, Vincent used to go over all the bad things that ever happened to him to keep the hate and anger alive. He vowed to come back and set things straight, but time passed, life got in the way, and now Mother was dead.

"Yeah. Sometimes life sucks." I took a slug of my coffee.

"I lived in a bunch of group homes in Vancouver," he said through a mouthful of pancakes. "Then they shipped me back here when I was ten. I used to ride my bike to the park across from your house and watch you."

My bagel tasted dry in spite of the cream cheese and jam I'd piled on it. I'd had an older brother I didn't know about, and he'd been watching me from across the street. Creepy.

"How do I know you're not lying? Do you have any ID? Something with a photo?"

Vincent put down his fork and reached for his wallet. "Here's my probation conditions, ID card, birth certificate, social insurance card." He laughed. "Never learned to drive and never needed a passport."

"I've got an appointment with Detective Rossi this morning. Would you come with me and tell him what you've told me?"

He choked on his coffee. "You mean go to a police station without being arrested?"

"Yeah. And if your story can be verified, then I'll make legal provision for you."

He held up his hands. "I don't want no legal provision. That's what always lands me in the joint."

"Will you at least tell the police what you remember and what you've found out? Then I can get the renovation crew back to work and I might not have to move to a motel."

"Some people would be happy to live in a motel."

"Not me."

"Okay, okay. What time?"

"Ten." I looked at my watch. It was nine thirty. The waitress refilled our cups. "The police station is only a few blocks away."

I paid the bill. Vincent fidgeted beside me in the car like a St. Bernard on his way to the vet. Fortunately, cheerful Martha Lane wasn't at the reception desk, so I didn't have to introduce Vincent or fend off any saccharine Christmas greetings.

Detective Rossi looked good enough to eat in a navy-blue sports jacket and grey pants. "Good morning," he said. "I'll get the file and be right with you." He pointed to Interview Room Two.

"I gotta go to the can," said Vincent. "I'll be right there."

Interview Room Two was hospital-green and had no windows. The metal light fixture was encased in a wire cage. A lone box of tissues sat on the wonky metal table. Five minutes passed; each one felt like a week. Detective Rossi came in with a file and dropped it on the table.

"Will your friend be joining us?" he asked.

"I don't think so."

Detective Rossi closed the door, sat across from me, and opened the file. "Here's what we've discovered. Regarding the skeleton, we've identified him through dental and medical records as Tony Vancuzzi. He had some unusual dental work as well as jaw, knee, and leg fractures. Tony Vancuzzi owned a strip club in Vancouver." He showed me a *Vancouver Sun* picture of Tony and four women standing in front of The Smiling Fox Cabaret.

"Here's another picture," he said. It was Tony with his arm around a young woman in a cinnamon-coloured fox costume. Mother! My chest tightened and I broke out in a cold sweat and slid off my chair. I opened my eyes and saw Detective Rossi's face inches from mine.

"You fainted," he said, lifting my head and holding a glass of water to my lips. "My apologies. I thought you knew about your family." He helped me up and back onto my chair. The room was spinning like I'd had too much wine but without the fun. "We could continue when you feel better," he said.

I groaned. "Let's get it over with." I drank some more water.

He placed a few mug shots of Tony and my mother in front of me. I looked for family resemblances. Tony and me? Nothing, thankfully. I looked like Mother. Tony and Vincent? A little, something about their mouths. Vincent and Mother? Maybe their eyes. Vincent and me? Nothing. Detective Rossi's voice guided me back to reality. "The club was raided many times during its five-year career," he continued. "After it closed, Tony put Lilly and the girls out to work the streets." At least Detective Rossi didn't use the word "hooker" when discussing my mother. "Tony had his fingers in a lot of pies and made big money selling drugs. He and Lilly moved to Victoria and he bought the house on Arbordale Circle."

"My house," I said.

"Yes. Tony invested in some legitimate businesses: several laundromats and a dry cleaning franchise that did well in the early seventies.

"And became the king of money laundering," I said caustically.

Detective Rossi smiled. "You could say that." He shuffled through more paper. A marriage certificate for Lilly and Tony, a birth certificate for Vincent and Maria. "Did you know you had a brother, Ms. Mandeville?"

"I grew up as an only child." I didn't lie; lying to the police is like lying to God. You go to hell for that.

Detective Rossi dug out more papers. "After Tony disappeared, Lilly had problems with Vincent. He was diagnosed as 'unmanageable' by several psychologists after he set fire to his school when he was six, and Lilly gave him up for adoption. About a year later, Max Mandeville moved in with Lilly, but they didn't marry." He placed certificates of change of name in front of me and used his pen as a pointer.

I grabbed the glass and chugged the rest of the water. I reached for a tissue, wiped my eyes, and blew my nose. "I thought Max Mandeville was my father?"

Detective Rossi placed everything back in the folder and closed it. His shoes squeaked when he stood up. "Thank you for coming in. I know this has been difficult for you." He walked me to the door and shook my hand. His touch was strong but gentle. "You can finish the renovations and move into the house as you planned."

"Thanks. You said Tony had been shot. Any idea by whom?"

"We didn't find a gun. We'll keep you informed."

"Thanks, and since you picked me up off the floor, you can call me Maxi."

He winked (I'm sure he did) and flashed his wonderful smile as I left.

I drove to my studio. The message light flashed in that annoying way that makes me pick up the phone before doing anything else. The first message was from Fred Digby, the litigious carpenter. "I'm gonna hafta take another job. Can't wait forever for the cops to finish with your place." Good riddance, I thought.

The next was Sylvia. "Mom? Where are you? Have you got the turkey? Can I invite Cam for Christmas dinner? His family lives in Toronto. Get back to me."

"Crap!" I longed to skip the whole turkey shtick. Christmas always starts with my hand in a yellow rubber glove up a turkey's butt.

I booted up my computer. Three portraits to touch up and print off by the end of the day. These old women all wanted to look like Ginger Rogers, but the best I could do was Miss Marple.

The phone rang. What now? It was Sylvia. "Where have you been? It's Christmas tomorrow. Did you get a turkey?"

I tried to sound cheerful. "At the police station. I've heard. No, what about Chinese?"

Sylvia still used her whiny little girl voice when she wanted something. "Pleeese, Mom. I've invited Cam. He wants to meet you."

"I bet." Another short-term Romeo. "Okay, I'm almost done here. I'll pick up a road-kill seagull on my way home."

"Thanks, Mom. I love you."

Some things never change. I finished the portraits and put them in frames. The old ladies showed up, paid, and left with a lightness of step I could only dream about.

Insanity ruled in the supermarket. Shopping carts should be registered weapons. I managed to snag a fresh turkey along with nasal spray and rubber gloves, and body-checked my way to the cashier.

I was too tired to bother cooking; I'd get enough of that tomorrow. Instead, I slipped *So I Married an Axe Murderer* into the VCR.

The intercom woke me up. It couldn't be Vincent; he'd be tapping on my window. It was Sylvia. "What brings you here so early?"

"It's not early, Mom; it's nine thirty already. We're cooking Christmas dinner, remember?"

She made the stuffing, and I gloved up and did the turkey-butt thing. I filled her in about Vincent, Tony, Mom, and Max while we prepped the veggies. She didn't even flinch. Family is family.

"Did you invite Vincent for dinner?" Sylvia asked.

"No, I never got the chance. He took off to the bathroom at the police station and never came back."

Sylvia peeled the potatoes. "Poor guy, I bet he's huddled in a bus shelter or under a bridge."

"He's not a troll. He can go to the Sally Ann." I was still mad at him, but secretly hoped he might show up.

The day passed quickly. We cleaned the apartment and took turns basting the turkey. At four o'clock, the intercom rang. Cam turned out to be the smart-ass from the pharmacy. He appeared with a bottle of wine and a huge poinsettia. I hate poinsettias. They always die. I thanked him anyway.

He looked at me and grinned. "Hey, you survived. Merry Christmas!"

I laughed. "Back at ya."

Our turkey tasted good, and I probably drank too much wine. We talked about the house renovations, and I mentioned that Fred Digby had quit. Cam put down his fork. "I know a great carpenter who's just finished a job and looking for work."

I gave Cam one of my business cards. "Wonderful. Have him call me."

Dessert was a tin of fruit cocktail with ice cream dumped over it. Nobody complained. Cam and Sylvia left around nine o'clock with much Merry Christmasing. I'd refused their offer to help with the dishes. I love the soothing feel of hot water on my hands.

At ten o'clock, Vincent called. I felt like throwing the phone at the wall. "You bastard, you took off yesterday."

"Sorry about that. I hate cop shops. It's the smell."

"If you're interested, Detective Rossi confirmed everything you told me, with copies of legal documents and newspaper clippings." Vincent didn't answer.

I waited a few seconds. "Are you still there?"

"Yeah. What about the gun?" He started coughing.

"It's in my freezer. Are you getting a cold? Why don't you come over? It's Christmas."

"Can't. I'm on the ferry. I've got pills. Might have a job on a fish boat."

"That's good. Where can I reach you about the house and everything?"

"I dunno. I'll call some time."

"Is that it?"

"Yeah. I'll think about you when I sneeze. Merry Christmas, Maxi." He had to be my brother.

As soon as I put down the phone, it rang again, and the velvet tones of Detective Rossi's voice caressed my ear. "Merry Christmas, Ms...um... Maxi. I'm calling to check up on you. Yesterday was pretty rough."

"Yeah, but I'm okay now."

"It's a strange time to call, but I was wondering if you'd like to go for coffee?"

"Sure!" Some Christmas wishes do come true.

"Not tonight."

Had I sounded too anxious, desperate maybe? Then he added, "I'm working tonight, so the family guys can have Christmas off. What about tomorrow?"

"Great."

"I'll call you when I get off work."

"Merry Christmas, Detective Rossi."

"Al. I picked you up off the floor, remember?"

What a rush! I poured more wine, marched into the bedroom, and opened the closet door.

"Well, Mom, what do you have to say for yourself?" I waited. Nothing. "Why didn't you tell me about Vincent or that Max wasn't my father? You always loved to dance, but a stripper? And about that gun. Did you kill Bony Tony and bury him in the basement? And how could you give your own son away?" I waited again. No comment. I looked up at the plastic container on the shelf and pictured Mother sitting there—legs crossed, nails painted red, cigarette in her black rhinestone-studded holder, blowing smoke in my face—saying, "Darling, we do what we must."

I raised my glass in a mock toast. "Merry Christmas, Mom! Tomorrow you're going to the beach."

I'll miss the old broad.

C.J. Papoutsis *worked for the B.C. provincial government for thirty-five years, including fifteen as a legal secretary in the Ministry of Attorney General, which gave her a taste for crime. A closet writer for most of her life, she was liberated from the public service in 2003 and took up writing seriously. Her short stories have appeared in local magazines and her personal essay "They Didn't Come With Instructions" was published in* Dropped Threads 2. *"Mother Always Kept a Gun" is her first published crime story. C. J. lives in Victoria, British Columbia, where she fishes for red herrings in Oak Bay.*

Buon Natale Johnny Toronto

Dennis Richard Murphy

Gina raised the cellophane bag of crushed almonds toward the light. Her eyesight was worse each day and her arms often hurt when she raised them above her chest. The pain in the core of her stomach had eased for the moment. Crushed almonds in a bag. Imagine. Mama would wake in her grave if she saw them, the grave in the field above Ortona.

Mama taught Gina and little Giancarlo how to gather these nuts when the mid-September air turned crisp, when dry olive leaves paved the field paths and snapped like Communion wafers under tiny feet. She beat the tree branches with a long stick, and Gina and little Giancarlo scurried to stuff rough cloth bags with the green pods that fell to the ground like dud grenades. Before the war to end wars. Before Johnny Toronto.

She was young then—fifteen, sixteen perhaps. She was old now—eighty next month. *Nonna* Gina—mother of Sophia in the family room, the grandmother of poor lost Rachel, the great grandmother of young Lisa who flirted with the boy on the deck outside the kitchen window. Even Giuseppe had come to call her *nonna* before he died.

She moved toward the sink, slowly so the pain wouldn't wake, her loose black clothes witness to Giuseppe's death, her task to persevere with tradition on this first Christmas without him. Above the sink, the kitchen window frame was strung with coloured lights—Sophia's idea, not hers. Gina's fat-leafed African violets shared their sill with herbs stuffed in pickle jars filled with cold water, hanks of fresh basil for the pasta, and sticks of rosemary for the Christmas *agnello*. Out on the deck, Lisa and the boy muttered and giggled, watching each other instead of the roast lamb turning on the spit.

He looked like Johnny Toronto. The boy had the same immature moustache. He talked out the side of his mouth like Johnny and, Santa *Matre di Di*, his top lip protruded like Johnny's to contain an excess of upper teeth. From the kitchen island, she had watched him walk hand-in-hand with Lisa across the family room, past Giuseppe's aquariums and the over-decorated Christmas tree, to the black leather La-Z-Boy where Sophia sat like a fat sycophant before the large-screen plasma television. He walked with that same slight hitch in his gait, as if he'd been injured once and healed badly. You could see it if you knew enough to look—and Gina Faricelli knew enough to look. The boy was nervous, thought Gina. Sweat on his upper lip. He stood too close to Lisa. Sixty some years ago, Johnny Toronto had saved Ortona and ruined her life. *Madonna me, tu mi capisce.* My Madonna, you understand me.

Mama had showed them how to store the fist-sized green pods in the cellar until they split. At the scarred wooden table, they pried out the nuts, cracked the pale pocked shells, and tossed the brown-hulled meat into a pot of boiling water. After a minute or two, Gina scooped them out and plunged them into a cold bath to blister the skins. Little Giancarlo, with that mischievous half-smile he had when only one corner of his mouth curved upward, pinched the skins between his fingers to squirt the nuts at Gina, chortling uncontrollably until Mama turned from the dry sink and laughed in spite of herself, shaking her head with her own childhood memories in Pescara. And now look at this. Almonds came from Dominion store at the plaza: already harvested, shelled, skinned, crushed by machines, and packaged in see-through bags. *Madonna me.*

They'd better watch the roast, those two. Barbecuing. Like Giuseppe, always barbecuing everything on his oversized deck, as if cooking meat outside was something only men should do. Everything for Giuseppe was large, as if size reflected success. Imagine. All this granite and expensive metal, not one but two ovens in the wall, and they want to cook the Christmas lamb outside on a fire. And look at Johnny Toronto. Fawning and laughing with all those teeth. Touching Lisa's soft cheek like he'd touched hers. Too close. Close enough for her to smell his heat. And she's just as bad. *Puttana.* Laughing, batting her big eyes, enjoying her power. He's too good-looking for her. Just like...

"Sophia?" Her voice cracked and her stomach screamed. She inhaled deeply, coughing, doubling over, wincing with the deep hurt. "Sophia?" she shouted, a low angry voice, annoyed at her own pain.

"Yes, Mama?" Her daughter slowly, reluctantly, lowered the volume of the television set in the family room. "Yes, Mama? What is it now?"

"Lisa's burning the *agnello* out there with what's-his-name. Tell her to be careful. It's expensive now."

"Lamb, Mama. It's called lamb, like Lamb of God. You know that, Mama. In a minute, I'll do it. I'm watching something. And his name is James, Mama. James. Use his name—he could be family soon."

"Pah. Family. Never you mind those decorating shows, Sophia." Imagine. On Christmas Day, one right after the other, all day long. She's sitting there like a pink whale in that stretchy tracksuit, pawing that oversized Christmas corsage she made of ribbon and extra Christmas decorations. Waiting to be fed like she was at some restaurant.

"See to your granddaughter, Sophia. There's nothing to decorate in this house. It's decorated. Your father saw to that." Sophia waddled petulantly to the deck door and yelled something at Lisa. Gina ducked as Lisa's olive eyes darted angrily to the kitchen window. Big black olive eyes like little Giancarlo's. Gina poured the crushed almonds into the measuring cup. The English Queen was talking on the refrigerator door television. It was getting late for making amaretti.

Mama's recipe for the cookies was a good one, and Gina made them the old way. Tradition took time. Tradition was time, and amaretti on Christmas Day was a tradition: the family Christmas treat for the eyes and the nose and the stomach since she could remember. Christmas Day was incomplete without the bitter, nutty, smell of the warm almonds in the kitchen. The door to the deck slammed, shaking the house, and a moment later, the sound on the television increased. On the deck, Lisa screamed. Gina tensed with unbidden memory of her own fear—large figures filling a doorway—but it was a young girl's shriek of pleasure, not pain: a flirting ploy followed by a coy giggle countering his deeper, pleading voice.

This kitchen was Giuseppe's idea, like everything else in this house. Gina was happy with the old kitchen. She didn't need all this stainless steel and carved wood and machines she'd never use. But Giuseppe Faricelli—everyone but Gina called him Joe—wanted a new, modern kitchen, like he wanted this too-big house and the brick arches around the porch, like he wanted giant aquariums full of bright tropical fish, like he wanted the long, curved driveway he re-blackened each spring with an old push broom and tar from a yellow pail.

These things made Giuseppe happy, and Giuseppe deserved happiness. She owed him that. It was Giuseppe Faricelli who stopped the spiteful tongues of Ortona after Sophia was born, after little Giancarlo was killed, after Mama died. It was Giuseppe Faricelli who had brought Gina and her little Sophia to Canada, who gave them a husband and a home, who never once demanded love in return. She measured one and three-quarter cups of crushed sweet almonds and poured them into the kitchen machine. Mama used some bitter almonds as well, but they were difficult to find these days.

She looked through the window, where Giuseppe's large deck stepped down to the ground, where the tips of brown grass in the yard showed through a dusting of snow. It didn't snow for Christmas here anymore. It was more like home in… She couldn't remember the name. More like home than Toronto. Ortona—that was it. More like Ortona than Toronto. The names momentarily confused her. What did it matter to an old woman? What is home anyway? Giuseppe built the deck with a roof until Gina said it darkened the kitchen and he ripped it off in an afternoon without complaint. He was a good man, Giuseppe. She could have been kinder to him.

They must be freezing out there now, the two of them, jackets undone like they didn't feel the cold, talking and touching. Lisa and the one like Johnny. Rachel had done her best, God knows, but Rachel had gone and a girl of Lisa's age needs her mother, not a fat grandmother and an old *bisnonna*. Where was Rachel when her daughter needed her guidance and advice about men? Searching for herself somewhere? Living rough and taking drugs? Or maybe not living at all. Rachel. *Madonna me*. What a name. Sophia named her daughter Rachel, another denial of her heritage. Not an Italian name. A biblical name, at least, but Jewish for all that.

She'd forgotten where she was going. She'd always made amaretti from memory, but she'd forgotten something. She shuffled across the ceramic tiles toward the refrigerator. The ache in her stomach had settled into a dull pain. Her thick nylons pinched her thighs where they were rolled above her knee. It was best that Sophia and Lisa lived here. Lisa was still in school, and Sophia, after two bad marriages, had no job, no money, and nowhere else to live. Besides, the house was far too big for Gina, too large even when Giuseppe was alive although it never seemed so big as when he died.

Anyone would tell you Joe Faricelli filled this house with his laugh and his projects and his passions. Six months now he was dead. Already six months? Her eyes filled with unbidden tears as if it was yesterday, as if she'd loved him. She shrugged. The tears were for her pain, not for Giuseppe. She missed him. It might have been yesterday. Maybe it was. She wasn't so good at time any more. She remembered it was the sugar she needed and changed direction to the set of stainless steel canisters near the stovetop.

Sophia knew nothing about Gina's cancer, nothing about Johnny Toronto or the war times, nothing about the sneers and whispers when Gina was pregnant with her and after she was born. By the time she could talk, Sophia was living in Canada and spoke English. She called Giuseppe "Papa" or sometimes "Joe." Gina had intended to tell her the truth, but there was never a right moment. Giuseppe was not consulted. Sophia was hers, not his. He had the business, the construction sites, his hobbies, and the *bocce* and cards with his friends in the evenings and weekends. She had the kitchen and her daughter, not that Sophia respected the territorial divide. She treated her mother like a kitchen slave and her father as an easily induced source of financial support.

Gina was furious when the two of them came home on Sophia's sixteenth birthday with a small car. Giuseppe had purchased it for her before she had a licence and let her drive it home in rush hour. It was a new car, small and bright blue, one Sophia had seen in a window and idly said she liked. She hadn't worked a stitch for it, hadn't saved a penny, hadn't done her chores or her homework, hadn't tried to lose weight or done anything but blink her mascara eyes at her Papa and watch him melt like soft cheese in summer. Giuseppe was confused by Gina's anger. He couldn't see a difference between providing for Gina and indulging her daughter. They'd argued: a loud, extended, bitter argument in the home dialect, two thousand years worth of Abruzzini insults as rich as dark wood, scratched with high-pitched pleas for divine intervention.

When it ended, they were spent. Shaking his head, Joe went to his club to play cards and drink liquor. Sophia called a friend to brag about her car. Gina went to her kitchen and wept. After that, none of them spoke Italian to each other in the home, as if Gina's language and heritage had been boxed and stored in the dark of a closet, as if she had been physically displaced as the centre of the family, as if Sophia's Canadian values and insensible self-interest trumped her mother's history, her legacy, her sin. How Gina had wanted to confront her with Johnny Toronto then, but it would have been invective. The time was not right and hadn't been since.

Gina pressed the button on the blender and watched the cream-coloured nuts mix with the half cup of sugar, maybe a bit more for Christmas. She couldn't complain about the kitchen machine. It hurt her forearms to crush the nuts or stir by hand. That was the osteo-something, not the cancer; her arms, not her guts. She couldn't hide her eighty years or weak bones, but no one knew about the cancer, and since Giuseppe had died, no one knew about Johnny Toronto. The sound of the television from the family room increased and women screamed, "Omigod" when they saw what their neighbours had·done to their house. Gina glanced out the window. It was getting darker. Maybe snow was coming for Christmas. Smoke rose from the barbecue. "Sophia. Tend the *agnello*. Tell Lisa. Baste the roast. The lamb is burning."

"In a minute, Mama. I'm watching something."

The two young ones were out of her sight now, to the side of the kitchen window, toying with each other like animals, except that animals knew when they were in heat. It was Sophia's fault—Sophia who strung the lights and put too many decorations on the tree. It was Sophia who told Lisa she could bring this boy for Christmas dinner. No one asked Gina. Sophia informed her as an afterthought, as if it didn't make a difference, as if it wasn't important, as if it wasn't her house. Perhaps such bad manners came from her real father, thought Gina for the fourth or fifth time that day, four or five times every day since Johnny Toronto never returned for lunch in the Ortona piazza.

She'd loved him, she supposed, if she'd ever loved anyone beyond Mama and little Giancarlo. She knew no Papa. Mama said he was from Pescara and was dead, but she never told stories about him or said she missed him. Maybe that's why Gina had never told Sophia about Giann', about Johnny. Maybe her reticence was hereditary, like language, like tradition, like Christmas cookies. Or perhaps it was the sum of Johnny's leaving and the echo of his promise to return, the solitary sorrow of Sophia's birth, and the sting of muttered abuse from a few survivors stumbling in the rubble-filled streets. Maybe that's why Sophia's rejection of her heritage hurt so much, why Rachel's whereabouts now seemed as irrelevant as her name, why Gina feared that young Lisa might be doomed to repeat the cycle of her own life, beginning with this Johnny Ortona. Toronto. James Toronto. Johnny. Giann'. She was tired. She felt old.

173

Blood on the Holly

The stomach attacks came more often now—long knives in the belly that made her gasp for breath. It hurt her wrist to hold the hand mixer in the egg whites and sugar until the peaks formed. She could ask Sophia, who would only whine and do it badly. Lisa? Lisa thought food came from microwave ovens and small windows where you ordered from your car. Mama had strong arms. Until she died, Mama had strong arms. Gina opened the small bottle of almond extract and shook the drops into the mixture. The sharp smell reminded her of Giuseppe's fish tanks, the ritual refurbishing, the day each spring he removed the fish and cleaned the giant aquariums.

"This is how they do it," he said. "This is what I read, *Nonna*." If Giuseppe Faricelli read it, then it was true. He had seen somewhere that natives in tropical waters captured these fish by sprinkling powder on the surface of the sea above the reef. The fish were stunned and harvested like nuts. The first time he'd tried the powder, many fish had died, but he simply bought more fish and used less powder the next year. Each year, his friends came to drink coffee and beer and watch him sprinkle the power in the tanks and lift out the instantly comatose fish. He'd clean and refill the aquariums, fiddle with the temperature and salt content, and return the fish to their home. He became adept; two years before, not one fish had died. Who would clean the tanks this spring?

There was noise in the family room: Sophia yelling, Lisa whining, Johnny supportively sullen in his silence. The deck door slammed, shaking the house again, and Gina saw Sophia outside in her pink tracksuit, an acid green silk scarf draped around her neck, arms folded across her large chest, pushing the ridiculous corsage up like a table centerpiece. Her face twisted as she poked at the rotating lamb with the baster and shivered in the cold. In the family room, the television went silent, replaced by a Christmas music album. Maybe Lisa wasn't so selfish, so insensitive. "All is calm, all is bright…" Gina loved the Christmas songs. The pain ripped through her stomach like a fireplace poker and she dropped the wooden spoon on the ceramic floor, holding herself barely upright with one age-spotted arm on the counter. Her weight made her shoulder scream with pain. She felt faint, and the carol became her only link to consciousness.

Inside the hymn was the memory of Casa Berardi. It was Christmas Day, but there were no bells that year. The rocks and ruins of the cathedral and bell tower filled the piazza, a German ploy to force the invading Canadians to fight in the narrow streets. The Canadians had finally taken the crossroads above the town and then the farm, Casa Berardi. Even on this day of Christ's birth, they were fighting hand-to-hand in the town, building-to-building, creeping carefully into rooms left booby-trapped by the enemy. Death was everywhere, and no one but the soldiers cared who won. Their battle was obliterating the village, a spurious prize on the way to nowhere that had become a hollow contest for which the trophy was the place they were destroying.

Many villagers had escaped north to Pescara when the fighting began, but a few, like Maria Castiglione and her children, hid in the hills close by, combing the forest and gleaning farm fields for food. On Christmas Day in 1943, Mama and Gina and little Giancarlo were searching Casa Berardi's fields. The almonds were long gone, and the fruit trees leafless, bent, and neglected. A thin layer of snow lay on the ground. When Mama heard diesel engines approaching, they hid in a small stone outbuilding at the far end of the cobbled yard from the main house. From inside the dark, dank hut, they heard trucks arrive and loud soldiers stumble into the compound. The men laughed and smoked and kicked mud from their boots on the stone sill of the farm kitchen. While their comrades battled in the town, small groups had been brought to the farm for Christmas dinner.

Inside the hut, the smells of food made their stomachs throb, but they dared not expose themselves. They crouched together, breathing shallowly, consumed only with hunger until the music began. The song came from the kitchen where the soldiers had eaten, and the deep, tired voices of men filled the courtyard. "Silent night, holy night…" In the dark shed, smelling of sheep manure and raw chemicals that made their eyes sting, Gina and little Giancarlo hugged Mama tightly and listened. Mama's tears struck their heads and ran through their fine hair and down their cheeks. The children had no tears of their own that day. Gina knew the song by different words, and she sang them in a whisper, making Mama weep harder.

"Tu che i Vati da lungi sognar, tu che angeliche voci nunziar…"

Grasping the granite countertop, Gina waited for the pain to pass. She pushed herself up with her arms, leaning over the counter, taking her weight on her elbows. She sang to "Silent Night" on the record player, rasping, still in pain: *"Luce dona alle genti, pace infondi nei cuor."*

When she opened her eyes, her tears were falling into the bowl, beading for a moment on the oily egg whites before slithering into the almond and sugar mixture. When the pain ebbed, she stood straight, wiping the sweat from her face with a paper towel, blowing her nose, sniffing the war memory of Ortona away. Her hair felt wet on her forehead; her stomach muscles ached. She picked the spoon from the floor, rinsed and dried it, and began to mix the egg whites into the almond mixture.

On the deck, Sophie petulantly slapped marinade on the lamb. There was movement in the family room. Shadows of the boy and Lisa flickered back and forth past the double doors. They were dancing. To Christmas carols? *Oh Madonna me, aiutemi tu.* Oh Mother of God, help me. Tell me these are not of my blood. She spooned the thick mixture into a pastry bag and with swollen knuckles began squeezing walnut-sized cookies onto the cookie sheets, five blobs across, seven deep.

They hid in that reeking hut for most of Christmas day, crouching, clinging, starving, listening to the diesel engines tick and gears grind on the vehicles that delivered dreary soldiers to their dinner and took the fed ones back to fight, perhaps to die. With each group, the smells of food would recur and the sad songs rise again on the winter air.

The door of the shed was ripped open with a suddenness that made Gina scream. The light from outside blinded them. Large, black, blurred silhouettes filled the doorway. Sharp knives on the ends of rifles poked at them like they were bales of rags and ordered them about in a language they did not understand. In the cobbled yard, they huddled together, so close to Mama they were one body, as soldiers talked and argued and laughed amongst themselves. The wind was cold, and Gina hurt with hunger. Her pains made her bend at the waist, and a soldier touched her ass. They laughed as she stood erect, glaring at them, defying them, shouting at them in Italian, spitting invective as Mama tried to stop her, moaning and holding her head in her hands. Cold gusts tore at Gina's thin dress and plucked at the hem where the buttons were missing, pushing her dress up, exposing her legs above the knee. She couldn't cover herself without letting go of Mama.

One of the soldiers, the one with too many teeth and the boy's moustache, waved his arms and shouted orders as men tore her from Mama and Mama from little Giancarlo. Giancarlo broke away and ran towards the fields, zigzagging like he and his schoolmates playing at war. A soldier raised his rifle, but the one with the teeth put his hand on the barrel and shook his head. Gina watched, shivering, without tears and without comprehension as the soldiers marched Mama to the farmhouse. Perhaps they'd give her food for Christmas. Only the one with too many teeth stayed behind.

The bell that said the oven temperature was ready roused her. The Christmas music played in the family room where the shadows moved more slowly now. "*Adeste Fidelis*" now: Latin, the language of the church. The two cookie sheets were full, neat rows of coarse yellow mounds equally spaced like the nut trees at Casa Berardi. Holding one arm tight against her abdomen to subdue the pain, she pulled open the eye-level oven door and slid the trays inside. The amaretti took only twelve or fifteen minutes to bake. She watched through the oven window, staring through it as if it was the window to her past.

He'd been gentle, she supposed, as gentle as an impatient man with needs and far from home could be. He didn't hold a gun to her head or hurt her on purpose. His face was rough, unshaven, and scratched her face. She'd given herself somewhat willingly, without rancour, thinking that little Giancarlo had escaped and this man deserved some thanks. He smelled of food and gravy, of stale beer and sharp nicotine. In that reeking shack where minutes before she had clung to Mama like a child, he took her as a woman. The sex hurt her and she bled profusely. When he lit a cigarette, he saw the blood on her legs and dress in the light of his match and seemed shocked—even apologetic, she thought. Guilty, perhaps. Maybe he was a good man where he came from. He became quiet then, and gentle, touching her face with one hand, smoking his cigarette with the other. His name was Johnny, he said.

"Giann'" she repeated. "*Cognome?*"

"Toronto," he said. "Toronto." He pointed west to where the hills began. He said that he had to go now and fight the Germans. Maybe he'd live and take her to a lunch of meat and wine and sweet chestnut *zuppa inglese* in the piazza. When the piazza was cleared. When the war was over.

The timer rang, and Gina opened her eyes. She felt oddly calm, numb rather than free of pain. On the outside deck, Sophia, fat breasts spilling out of her blouse, grotesque in her anger, had burned her hands trying to remove the spit from the barbecue. She yelled, foulmouthed, as the roast slipped off the rod and fell to the deck. Gina took the cookie sheets from the oven and set them to cool on the granite counter. The almond smell filled the kitchen. Tradition.

It was Giuseppe Faricelli from L'Aquila in his black uniform who knocked on the door of the ruined flat just before Sophia was born. There was still a war, but it had moved north to Roma, leaving Ortona a forgotten ruin, its streets filled with rocks and rubble, testament to irrelevant victory. Mama heaved herself to her feet, swearing, waddling to answer the door,

177

callous and slovenly since the soldiers had taken her. She wasn't Mama anymore, spitting on the ground when she saw Gina's swollen belly, joining the others who had seeped back to their bombed-out homes in calling her daughter a whore.

In his arms, Giuseppe held the bloody, bent body of little Giancarlo. The boys had been playing war in the ruined houses. A bomb had exploded. A booby trap. A "mousehole," they called it—a room wired to kill anyone who entered it. German? Canadian? Who knew? Did it matter? The war had moved on, but the death remained behind.

Within weeks, Mama had cried herself to death. Maria Castiglione was interred in a field near Casa Berardi because the village cemetery was buried under collapsed buildings. The bells of Ortona rang in the distance for the first time since the war began, not for Mama, only a coincidence of death. Gina Castiglione was left alone but for the child in her womb and a promise from Giann' Toronto.

Gina moved to the canisters. A sprinkle of fine fruit sugar would complete the amaretti. The music stopped. Gina shuffled to the door of the family room where Lisa and the boy were locked in a deep kiss, their tongues moving madly, her blouse unbuttoned, his hand on her breast.

"Lisa. Set the table, Lisa," said Gina. The words came out harshly. The couple moved apart quickly, angry, embarrassed.

"Set it yourself, *Nonna*," yelled Lisa.

"*Nonna*? What the hell is a *nonna*?" said Johnny Toronto, and the two of them fell on the hut floor, laughing, groping, consumed with the need of each other. His rough soldier's uniform would scratch her arms, his face her cheek. His breath would smell like cooked chicken and tobacco and beer. Gina's guts ached, but not so much as her heart. On the deck, Sophia struck the barbecue again and again with the metal rod, spitting and sneering and swearing loud enough to be heard down in the village where the church bells tolled Mama's death. The music began again, but the sound of Christmas carols seemed raucous, not worshipful. "*Venite adoremus, venite adoremus, venite adoremus...*"

Gina moved across the kitchen like a younger woman. She pulled the three-step stool from the broom closet. Her arms ached, but the pain seemed like someone else's. On the refrigerator television, happy families opened gifts and laughed together as a puppy played with wrapping paper. Holding her stomach with one hand, as if afraid her entrails would fall out, she climbed the steps. One step. Rest. The thick rolled nylons slipped to her ankles, and the air on her white legs felt cool. Sophia slammed the door to the deck and started shouting about the ruined meat, waving the empty spit high like a sword. Step two. Rest. Her privates ached somewhere deep in the core of her belly, the precursor of greater pain. Sophia was yelling at Lisa and Johnny, telling them to stop, poking him with the spit, tearing them apart as if they were dogs stuck together in the street. Step three. She reached high, straining her shoulder, feeling the pain come in waves as she pulled open the cupboard door and reached for Giuseppe's fish powder.

It looked like fruit sugar on the amaretti, like the light winter snow on the stubble fields of the Casa Berardi. Perhaps a more generous helping than that. For Christmas. Sophia shouted, cursing like a tramp, swearing words only Giuseppe's men knew. Giancarlo zigzagged, setting off land mines in the fields behind him as Lisa screamed and swore and scratched at her grandmother's face. Johnny Toronto smoked and smiled as Mama walked to the farmhouse, lifting her skirts and doing a foot dance that made Gina laugh and forget the blood on her dress and legs.

Nonna Gina dusted the warm amaretti with Giuseppe's snow, and carrying the warm cookie sheet before her, shuffled into the family room with a smile on her ancient face. Mama was there, and Giann' and little Giancarlo.

"Amaretti, my family. *Madonna me, tu mi capisce.* Mother of God, you understand me. Eat them before they get cold. *Buon Natale*, Johnny Toronto."

***Dennis Richard Murphy** is a film and television writer, director, producer and teacher. His documentary series appear in seventy countries in thirty-three languages on Discovery, History Television, and National Geo. He has been nominated three times for the Crime Writers of Canada Arthur Ellis Award for Best Short Story, winning the award in 2007 for "Fuzzy Wuzzy." He also won the top prize in* Storyteller *magazine two years running. His stories appear in* Ellery Queen's *and* Alfred Hitchcock's Mystery Magazines *and in several anthologies, including* The Adventure of the Missing Detective

(Carroll & Graf) and Dead in the Water *(Rendezvous) among others. He has served as a judge for the Arthur Ellis Awards and for the International Association of Crime Writers. He is a full professor of film and television at Centennial College and is completing his first novel. Dennis lives in Toronto, Ontario, with his wife, Joanna, son Adam, and aging beagle, Barkley.*

The Parrot and
Wild Mushroom Stuffing

J. C. Szasz

I stand in the glow of my blue Christmas lights and fumble through my purse for my keys. Inside the house, I hear my phone ring. *Once...twice...*

Compact, lip liner, Tylenol.

Third ring.

Cold medicine. Brush. Breath mints.

Fourth.

Pen, cheque book, hairnet.

Fifth.

Keys! I shove the house key into the lock, turn, and barge into my home.

Silence.

Crap! I slam the door and kick off my shoes, leaving a black smudge on the wall.

Today had been the worst—December twenty-third, the busiest shopping day of the holiday season. One woman yelled at me because our department ran out of Butterball turkeys. Another woman hugged me when I found her the last smoked one; she didn't care that my apron was covered in meat debris and my sleeve was splattered with teriyaki sauce. Then Dave Dubrinski, my boss and the store's meat manager, got on my case because I hadn't joined in the department's Secret Santa. All I wanted to do was drop my cold, tired body into my hot tub and forget about the holiday season.

I crawl upstairs and toss my coat on my bed. I wiggle into my one-piece bathing suit and slip on my terry-cloth robe. Back downstairs, I step outside and flick a switch. My hot tub froths with bubbles. I flick another switch and red Christmas lights illuminate the patio. Not exactly Kim Mitchell's *Patio Lanterns*, but good enough.

I duck inside, grab a cocktail glass from the kitchen cupboard, and pour a vodka/*sake* combination to the rim. After working six days straight, it's time for some relaxation. Out on the patio again, I drape my robe over a chair and place one foot into the warm water, smiling at my distorted toes. Tonight, it's all about me. Tomorrow, I'll visit Mom. As usual, she'll complain that the chef at the senior's complex doesn't use real cranberries but *canned*, and then she'll grill me as to why I don't have a boyfriend yet. I'll give her a cheese basket, which she'll hide from thieving Geraldine, and a bottle of Red Door, which she'll stash with the other bottles I've given her on previous Christmases.

I bring my glass to my lips and sip. Lovely. Relax. Let the tiny bubbles melt the tension of being a meat wrapper during the busiest time of the year. Melt it all away.

"Hey, Josey."

I jump, spilling *sake* and vodka on myself.

Dave Dubrinksi stands in his winter jacket, still dressed in the store's uniform.

"Jesus Christ, Dave. What the hell are you doing here?"

Dave looks me up and down, then clears his throat. "Your doorbell's broken."

I submerse myself to my shoulders. "What are you doing here?"

"Your mom called."

I frown. "Why would my mom call the store?"

"Because she was upset and couldn't find your number, and considering you don't pick up when people do call, a person has to resort to breaking and entering to get hold of you."

So he was my hang-upper. "Is my mom okay?"

"She wanted to give you a message. Marco died. There's going to be a service for him at your Uncle Russell's tomorrow. She wants you to drive her there."

"Oh, dear God."

"You don't seem cut-up about it, Josey. What has Marco done to tick you off?"

I step out of the hot tub and reach for my robe. "Nothing, except poop on my head."

Dave's eyes pop.

"Marco Polo," I continue, my voice laced with disgust, "is my aunt's thirty-year-old Scarlet Macaw."

Dave still looks confused.

"A parrot."

Dave stares. "No shit."

"No shit."

He shifts his weight from one foot to the other. "So I drove like a madman to give you a message about a stupid bird?"

"Yeap. Hope you didn't get a speeding ticket."

"And your mom wants to go to this bird's service?"

"When your deceased sister's beloved macaw dies"—I flip my hair out from my collar—"and you don't have much on your social calendar except the last funeral you went to,"—I yank on my terry-cloth belt—"yes."

"Bring him to the store, Josey. We can sell him as an exotic delicacy."

"That's not funny, Dave. My Aunt Corinne loved that bird. I guess Mom is still upset over her sister's death."

Dave arches an eyebrow. "Wait until the guys hear about this."

"Dave," I point to the side gate. "Go, and I don't want anyone in the meat department to know."

He shakes his head and walks toward the gate. "Yeah, okay, Josey. No one will know. Have a good Christmas. Give my regards to the deceased."

When I was fifteen and hormonal with a lollipop shape—toothpick legs with a 36D bust—my mother tolerated my low-cut shirts and skinny tight jeans, and prayed that I wouldn't come home and tell her I was pregnant. Someone must have been listening because I never did.

When I was nineteen and passed up a chance to enrol in broadcasting school because I had fallen in love with sleazy Scott in seafood, instead of greeting her jilted daughter with criticism and I-told-you-so, she stood at my door with a bottle of Baileys and a Sara Lee frozen cake.

My luck with men still hasn't improved, and once again, I'm sitting with my mom, this time in Uncle Russell's living room. A retired fitness instructor, Mom has had both knees replaced, and arthritis has attacked her ankles. Although she's stuck in a wheelchair, she mostly has a happy disposition, and in her baby-blue Afghan and matching cotton pants, she looks great.

"Your boss, David, seems nice," she says, nibbling on a gingerbread man.

"Why do you keep bringing him up? He's all you talked about on the drive over."

"He mentioned that you're not participating in the Secret Santa."

"Nope, I'm not."

"You should. It'd be fun. If you got David's name, you could buy him some kinky underwear."

"Mom, I have to work with the man."

"It's all in the name of fun, Josey. You used to be such a carefree girl. What happened to you?"

"I'm a forty-year-old meat wrapper whose previous marriage was as memorable as feminine itching. I am not participating in the Secret Santa. A ten-dollar gift is not going to restore my faith in men."

Just then, Uncle Russell, my deceased aunt's husband, places an eight-by-ten photograph of Marco Polo on the mantle between the poinsettias and bouquets of red roses. Good grief.

"Well,"—my mom crosses her lace gloved hands—"it might restore something, even if only the itch."

My mouth drops open and my head whips around.

"Sweetheart, pay attention. Your uncle is about to speak."

"Family, friends, loved ones," my uncle begins, "Lizzie and I are touched that you are here to celebrate the life of Corinne's beloved Scarlet Macaw, Marco Polo."

Where's the rum and eggnog?

I try to focus on my uncle but I'm distracted by his second wife, Lizzie, perched in the putrid-brown rocker. Her blonde hair is teased and backcombed into a flowing crest on the top of her head. Wearing a glittering rainbow-coloured sweater with matching pants, she sits, legs crossed, chest pushed out, her talon fingers curling over the chair's arms.

My uncle drones about how much joy Marco Polo brought to my deceased Aunt Corinne and how protective the Scarlet Macaw was towards her. Having learned a poker vocabulary from Aunt Corinne, Marco Polo would have made the perfect player.

My relatives laugh.

I stop myself from rolling my eyes.

Uncle Russell then introduces Lizzie, formerly Lizzie Mitchell of

Mitchell Wieners' fortune. Lizzie stammers and smiles, and preens a single lock of hair. She thanks us for welcoming her into our family. We haven't, but that's beside the point. She hopes that on this Christmas Eve, we'll enjoy the festive dinner she has prepared.

My uncle claps. I do, too, so as not to be rude, and I look at my mother, who sits arms crossed. "Mom!"

She gives me a look that only a mother can give. "She's nothing but a harlot with bright plumage," she whispers, but half the room can hear her.

"Mom!"

"A bony one, too. There isn't enough meat on her bones for broth."

"Mom," I hiss, "shhh!"

A shadow bobs in front of us and we look up.

Lizzie.

My cheeks grow warm. Had she heard us?

"Jacyln," Lizzie chirps in a sing-song voice, "thank you so much for coming." She pumps my mother's hand as if she were hoping money would fall from between her fingers. "I know this is a lot to take in all at once."

Mother fixes an alligator smile. "I can hear you, dear, no need to shout."

"Oh, good. That parrot was such a handful," Lizzie crows in the same loud voice. "Every day was a new...surprise."

"Corinne loved that bird," my mother replies.

"And so did I, when he behaved. I mean,"—Lizzie's beady eyes flick from side-to-side—"the bloody thing hated me. You see this?" She holds up her bandaged index finger. "This is not from a carving knife, but from that damn bird's beak when I tried to feed him a carrot. And *this*," she holds up her middle finger, "is when I tried to clean his cage. It screeched whenever I stepped into the room, and when I turned my back, it would swoop down onto my shoulder, batting its wings on my head. And if that wasn't enough, its feather dust aggravated my asthma, and then it'd *mimic* me breathing into my inhaler."

My mother and I are speechless. Talk about feeling rejected.

Lizzie clears her throat. "Well, excuse me." She cocks her head to the side. "I must check on the turkey." With quick steps, she bobs into the kitchen.

Mom looks at me. "Something's not right about that girl. Josey, make sure she's serving turkey and not parrot tonight."

"Trust me, I will."

"Oh, and Josey, could you get me some punch, the non-alcoholic kind. I need to take my pills."

I manoeuvre between Uncle Nick the Stick, who lives in Whisky Creek and butchers his own cows, and my cousin Sara, the realtor, who is always talking on her cell. Then there's my sad cousin Ray, who talks non-stop about all his girlfriends but always attends family functions alone.

At the far end of the living room, stockings hang from the fireplace, while a large Christmas tree obliterates the front window. Poinsettias and holly glare red and green from every bookshelf, ledge, and table, and Dean Martin croons "White Christmas" from the record player. The needle catches in a scratch, and Dean keeps repeating *Christmas...Christmas... Christmas...* Someone, please?

I make my way around the sofa and over to the dining room table, which has been converted into a buffet table and a mini-bar. I ladle non-alcoholic punch into one crystal cup.

"Hey, Josey."

I look through the chandelier's bevelled stained glass and see five images of Dave. Good God! More than I can handle. I drop the ladle, and punch splatters onto Lizzie's table cloth. "Dave. What are you doing here?"

"I'm an old friend of Lizzie's. I used to scare the kids at school who teased her."

That doesn't surprise me. The bizarre thing is that without his hairnet and green blood-splattered apron, Dave actually looks good.

"How's your mom?" he asks.

"Fine," I reply, ladling alcoholic punch into my cup.

"Not too much punch there, Josey." Dave nods at the two crystal cups in my hands. "I may not be able to help myself and have to sneak a kiss under the mistletoe."

Mistletoe? There's mistletoe? I nervously laugh and inch my way between aunts, uncles, and cousins, hoping no one will ask if I've found a man.

I make my way around a table covered with plates of gingerbread, tarts, and Nanaimo Bars, except half the bars have the green mint filling and chocolate layer eaten off, leaving behind the chocolate coconut base. A toddler barrels into the room, licking mint icing from his lips. Our pint-size Nanaimo Bar thief? I put a few edible tarts on a plate and find Mother.

"Here you go."

She takes the cup with the non-alcoholic punch and throws back her pills. "Josey, I heard the most disturbing news."

"What? Santa's not real?"

"No, silly. It's about Sara, who... Is she eyeing the blow-up snowman?"

I look over at Sara. Sure enough, she has her arm around Frosty's portly white waist. "Mom, she's working on her fifth Caesar, and Frosty looks cuter than most of her boyfriends."

"Josey! Be nice."

As if *she* can talk.

"I heard Sara tell Ray that her company is tearing down this house and putting up condos."

"Well, Mom, this house sits on prime Shale real estate. Step out back and you can look over Finlayson Arm. I'm surprised Uncle Russell didn't sell this place sooner and skip off with Lizzie to a tropical island."

"You don't understand. No one can touch the property."

I choke on a morsel of mincemeat. "Excuse me?"

"There's a clause in Corinne's will."

My mother takes pleasure in tormenting me with information bites. She never tells me the full story. "What clause?"

"Corinne had a clause that said that as long as Marco Polo lived, Russell could not sell the property. Corinne insisted that Marco Polo live in a stable environment. Parrots don't even like their cages being moved."

I dab my mouth with a napkin. "The bird's dead."

"Convenient, isn't it."

"You're saying Uncle Russell deliberately killed Marco Polo?"

"The Scarlet Macaw is part of the parrot family. Parrots have been known to live into their sixties. Marco died in middle age."

"You can't prove that."

"Yes, I can."

"How?"

"By having you search Russell's office."

"I can't do that!"

"Yes, you can. Look for feathers, bird seed, a carcass. Determine the cause of death like they do on CSI."

"Mom!"

"All Russell had to do was fry a steak in a non-stick pan and Marco Polo would have died from PCP poisoning."

"Uncle Russell's pans are coated in angel dust?"

"No. What's that stuff called? I saw it on the news."

"PTFE is used on non-stick pans."

187

"That's it. Parrots have sensitive respiratory systems. The fumes would have killed him. And don't you find it strange that Russell held a wake for his deceased wife's parrot?"

"Well, yeah, but it's…" *your family.*

"And why is Lizzie going to all this fuss when she knows we don't like her?"

"Because she's psychotic and wants our acceptance."

"Something's not right, Josey. Those two are hiding something."

A few relatives look our way.

I stand. "Here." I give Mom my cup and plate and wheel her through the living room doorway. I glance up and see something green hanging. Good grief, the mistletoe. Where's Dave? Not anywhere near, thank God. I push mother into the hallway, which is littered with shoes. "How the hell am I supposed to search his office and not get caught?"

"You snuck stash in your bra when you were seventeen. You'll think of something."

She still remembers that?

Uncle Russell steps into the living room, and trailing behind him is Dave with a beer mug in his hand. Dave sees me and holds up the mug.

Yikes!

"Dear friends and family, please come enjoy the bountiful meal my sweet Lizzie has prepared."

"Now's your chance. Go. I'm hungry." Mom wheels her chair over my toes and across the hardwood.

Thanks, Mom. I love you, too.

My relatives line both sides of a long table.

"Make room." Lizzie struts in brandishing a large silver platter. "Partridge, everyone, for those of us tired of turkey, and Russell's wild mushroom stuffing." She places the platter at the end of the table.

Mother looks at me.

I glance at the bird. Yeap, partridge. I nod and Mother takes a slice. I'm taken aback by the plethora of decorations, gifts, and food. Come on, Josey, where's your Christmas spirit? Somewhere lost between my crazy relatives and trying to prove that Marco Polo died a suspicious death.

I tiptoe down the wobbly steps, eyeing the strips of orange insulation in the unfinished basement. Petrified of spiders, I swat at my hair. This is crazy. Why did I let Mother put me up to this? Because she's Mom. I walk past the bathroom and rows of canned peaches when my eyes spot a baggie of something dark and shrivelled. What is that? I lean closer. I'd swear I'm looking at dried 'shrooms. Hmm. At least I haven't found a bird carcass. I shiver and make my way through the yeasty fog of my uncle's U-Brew beer kits. There's a thump above me and I jump. A toddler wails through the flooring. Whew! I'm safe.

Through an open door, I see a desk and bookshelves and the glow of a computer monitor. I step inside. With its green shag carpet and oak panelling, the room smells musty. I manoeuvre between a bookshelf and an armchair, then bang my hip on the corner of the desk, jiggling the monitor. I hobble around the desk and scan VISA statements, bank receipts, and Grand Cayman holiday brochures. Uncle Russell and Lizzie must be planning a vacation. I shuffle through more papers and hear a crash upstairs. I jump again.

"Don't worry, Jaclyn," Uncle Russell's voice reverberates.

Mother murmurs something.

"Where's Josey?" Uncle Russell asks.

My heart pounds.

Mother murmurs something else. I hear someone sweeping broken glass. I flip through plumbing estimates, blueprints, a surveyor's certificate, a state-of-title certificate… Hold on… I pick up the blueprints and unroll them. They're for a twenty-storey condominium to be built right where I'm standing.

"I'll be damned."

The condo includes a gym, swimming pool, and sauna. Nice. If Uncle Russell sells the house, he'll definitely be able to afford a trip to Grand Cayman. Did he do the deadly deed to Marco Polo after all? Or had Lizzie?

I roll the blueprints back up. I slide open a drawer and find a power-of-attorney how-to kit. Not to cover the bird obviously. Lizzie?

"Hold on, Lizzie, I'll get another bottle from the cellar." Footsteps thump down the stairs.

Uncle Russell.

Shit. Where do I hide? No closet. No window to escape through. Just cabinets. Damn it. I crawl under the desk, pulling in the chair, and tucking my knees to my chest. My uncle's footsteps echo on the cement, then stop.

Don't come in.

He does.

I can hear him breathe and smell his Axe deodorant. I press my lips against my sleeve.

He stops near the side. "That's strange." He closes the drawer and shuffles a few papers.

He's so close. I'm going to throw-up.

"Russell," Lizzie crows from upstairs.

"Coming, darling." He taps the desk, then his steps retreat. The door shuts.

I gasp and lean my forehead against my arm. Jesus! That was too close.

Uncle Russell thumps back up the stairs and closes the door.

I push the chair out, crawl forward, and stand, nailing my shoulder on the keyboard tray. Geez. Joints creaking, I pick up the blueprints and unroll them one more time. On the second page, I notice the street address. Mom was right. She and Auntie Corinne's home is being demolished. There's enough evidence here to confront Uncle Russell.

I roll up the blueprints and leave them where I had found them. I march over to the door and turn the knob. Locked.

No!

Frantically, I turn the knob again.

Definitely locked.

Shit! I pull on the knob, panic rising in my chest. Do I bang on the door? How do I explain myself?

"Someone…" I pound on the door. "Somebody…" I say louder, "…let me…"

"Josey?"

Who's that?

"Josey? Are you in there?"

Thank goodness, Dave likes his beer. If he hadn't been downstairs checking out my uncle's U-Brew kits, he wouldn't have heard me. He quickly finds the key—it was hanging from a nail by the back door—and lets me out. I explain my covert behaviour and the macaw's suspicious-death theory. After a few snickers and raised eyebrows, Dave eventually takes the idea seriously.

"You think the bird was poisoned?" he asks, walking up the steps.

"Mom thinks the bird died from PTFE poisoning, PTFE being the coating used in non-stick pans."

Dave shakes his head. "No. Lizzie would never use a non-stick pan. She's completely organic, that girl."

And a little weird.

We reach the top of the steps, close the door behind us, and turn down the hall. "Then how else?"

Dave steps into the living room and points. "That's how."

I follow his gaze and see Mom deadheading the yellow leaves of a poinsettia.

"My mom," Dave continues, "has a cockatoo. She can't have poinsettias in her house. They're toxic and deadly to parrots. So is holly. Where was Marco's cage?"

"Over here." I stand by the front window. There's a water stain on the ledge. I recognize the mark, having over-watered my own plants. I pull aside the vertical blinds and find a decorative vase holding sprigs of holly. A couple of pointed leaves have beak marks, and there are a few berries missing. "Look." I pick up the vase. "This is the right height for Marco to reach from his cage."

"Josey? Dave? What are you doing?"

Dave and I swing around.

Lizzie holds a plate of Christmas pudding. "What are you doing with the holly? Here, give it to me. I'll get rid of it."

"No." I hold the vase against my side. Holly leaves prick my arm.

Lizzie's eyes bulge. "What?"

"It's evidence. I'm taking it to the police. Uncle Russell poisoned Marco Polo with the holly so he could sell this place to a developer."

"That's silly, Josey. That bird was a nuisance, but Russell would never harm it. Now give me the damn vase."

"Then you killed Marco because he didn't like you."

Dave fires me a now-you've-done-it look.

Lizzie remains silent. One eye blinks, the corner of her mouth twitches, then she drops the Christmas pudding and jumps me. The vase flies from my hand. I fall back onto the Christmas tree, taking it—and Lizzie—down. Sharp needles scratch my skin, and I hear the tinkle of broken ornaments.

"Lizzie, get off," Dave shouts. "Josey…"

Lizzie screams, "I hated that damn bird! Hated it!" She smacks my nose and face.

Branches poke between my arms and legs. I try to fend off Lizzie's slaps but get tangled in glitzy red garland.

"Josey!"

Mom.

Lizzie nails me in the mouth. I swing—and a clothes-peg reindeer pings off her forehead. *A little help would be nice.* I feel Lizzie being lifted from my body. Her eyes pop and her hair is a tangled nest. Dave hauls her, kicking and screaming, over to Uncle Russell.

"Do something with her."

"That bird was possessed!" Lizzie screams. "Possessed!"

"Lizzie, this way, darling." Uncle Russell wrestles her into another room.

I put my hand down and come up with a sticky half-eaten candy cane. Lovely. My head throbs. I brush my hand across my cheek and see blood.

"Josey…" Dave slides his arm around my waist and helps me up. "You're bleeding."

"My nose."

My mother wheels over. "Josey, sweetheart, are you all right?" She holds out a kitchen towel. "You know, David, she always was a scrapper."

I press the towel to my nose. "Thanks, Mom."

Dave gives Mom his cell and asks her to call the police. He looks at me. I'm moved by the concern in his eyes. "God, Josey,"—he picks tinsel out of my hair and tries to suppress a smile—"with the way that tree was vibrating, you two looked like you were performing a bizarre mating ritual."

"Thanks, Dave. Thanks a lot."

"Are you sure you're okay? Do you need anything?"

"Home. I need to go home."

"Soon, Josey, soon. But first, we better talk to the police."

I have a fat lip and the skin around my cheekbones is tender.

Lizzie has cackled all to the police: Russell had bought the poinsettias and then the holly to kill Marco Polo because he couldn't sell the house while the parrot was still alive.

The police are questioning Uncle Russell about the hallucinogenic mushrooms in the baggie downstairs: the same mushrooms Lizzie had unknowingly put in the wild mushroom stuffing. Now my stoned mother thinks she's doing aerobics with Jane Fonda, Sara believes she's negotiating a deal with Frosty, and Sad Ray is purportedly dating Pamela Anderson. Maybe he'll have better luck than Kid Rock. Dave and I are the only ones not stoned because we were downstairs while everyone else was enjoying dinner.

I slip my arms into my coat sleeves and step into the hallway, coming face-to-face with Dave.

"Hey, Josey. How are you holding up? Are you done with the cops?"

"Yes. I gave a statement. How's Lizzie?"

"With a little counselling, she'll be okay. According to one constable, Uncle Russell was cooking the mushrooms in his homemade spaghetti sauce. He was trying to drive Lizzie crazy so he could get power-of-attorney and control her money."

"That's terrible. That's why she was acting like a bird."

"Yeap. The police may also re-examine your aunt's death to see if there was any foul play."

"I'll tell Mom when she's finished competing with Ms. Fonda. Speaking of whom,"— I look over at Mom who is doing biceps curls—"I better get the fitness diva home."

"Before you leave,"—a mischievous smile softens Dave's face—"look up."

I do and see a leafy green plant. "Dave, that's basil."

He kisses me tenderly on the cheek and steps back.

"I know nothing about produce, Josey. I cut and de-bone meat."

I smile. How the hell am I going to face him in the New Year? Not my problem now. "Merry Christmas, Dave, Merry Christmas."

*Joanna Vander Vlugt, writing as **J.C. Szasz**, resides on Vancouver Island, British Columbia. Her short mystery story "Egyptian Queen" was published in the* Dead in the Water *anthology, and her non-fiction crime story, "No Beatles Reunion" was included in* Dropped Threads 3: Beyond the Small

Circle. *When not instructing fitness classes at the University of Victoria, Joanna can usually be found in her favourite coffee shop huddled over a manuscript. Joanna dedicates "The Parrot and Wild Mushroom Stuffing" to her husband, Ed; her daughters, Ashley and Kara; and her awesome critique group: Sandi, Brianna, and Carolanne. She'd also like to thank Debbie Kinloch, www.parrotscanada.com for providing invaluable information on parrots.*

The Santa Game

Jane Burfield

"Fired! What do you mean—fired?" Joe stared at his boss, confusion in his blue eyes.

"You're not getting the job done, Joe. Your team hasn't fixed the problems with the Santa game. You've missed the launch deadline."

"We're so close, Ormond. So close. We've been working overtime on this, cancelled holidays, worked every weekend. There are some problems, sure, but we're getting close to solving them." Joe glanced out the window at the cars leaving the Don Mills parking lot early on this October Friday afternoon. None of *his* team would be among them, he thought. They were still working on the bugs. How was he going to tell them?

"Clear out your cubicle, Joe. Boxes are waiting for you downstairs."

"But why? I've even got a small team of kids testing the youth version. We're this close!"

"Close doesn't cut it." Ormond stood up. "Sorry. Executive decision. You'll get the usual benefits: pay, continued health coverage, outplacement consulting. Not quite a golden handshake—maybe a bronze one."

"I don't care about that. What about my program, Ormond. My program!" Joe leaned across the desk, his knuckles white with pressure.

Ormond backed up, but he was smiling. "You never were that swift with the business details, were you, Joe? We own the Santa game. Everything to do with it stays with the company. We'll take it from here. The company wants something back for their investment. Now. Not sometime in the future. We're done waiting."

"It's going to be worth a fortune! The early focus groups loved it. And I have profit-share rights to it, don't forget."

"Well, according to our lawyer, that's not true." Ormond rocked back on his heels, that half-smile still on his moon face. "Those rights revert to the company if you leave before it's launched."

"But that's not fair! You fired me!" He slammed his hand down on the papers Ormond was shuffling on his desk.

Ormond shrugged. "I'll send Jeannie down to help you clean out your desk. Susan can, of course, continue to work here. Leave your laptop—and don't take any hard drives or computer files."

Joe stared at Ormond, at a loss for words. Finally, he turned on his heel and walked to the door. The distance had never seemed so long before.

Joe walked into his sister's kitchen an hour later, slumped down at the Formica table from their old family home, and silently stared out the window, one hand on his trim goatee.

"What are you doing here, Joe? You never escape that place till eight or nine." Emma sat down opposite her brother and looked at his bewildered face.

"I…uh… Oh Em, I don't know what to do!"

"What happened? Is Dad okay?"

"Yes, yes. I think so. It's me. Or rather, it's work. I've been fired."

"Why? What happened?"

Joe shook his head. As he tried to explain what had happened, he saw again Ormond's moon face, that half-smile, the glint of satisfaction in his tiny eyes. They had never gotten along. Ormond was just like the bullies who used to make fun of him in the schoolyard, he realized now. Why hadn't he seen it before?

"Oh Joe. You worked so hard on that game." Em reached out and began to rub his arm soothingly.

"I know. The first time I got to lead a team in game development. After all these years pouring my creativity into other people's projects, I finally get my own. And it's good! So good! And now… All gone." He bent his head, ashamed at the tears stinging his eyes. "What did I do wrong?"

"Nothing!" Emma sprang to her feet. "We can fight this, Joe. You'll see. I'll call Uncle Brian. His law firm handles wrongful dismissal suits, I'm sure of it."

"It won't do any good," Joe said, his voice a monotone. "I'm supposed to turn in all copies and all backup data. I'll have to get Peter's copy. Oh God! It's going to be so hard to tell the kid about this." Leaning his arms on the table, Joe looked across the kitchen to the tired fridge art Peter had drawn for him several years before, just after his dad was killed in a car crash. How was Peter going to feel now? Joe had become an unexpected hero to Peter's friends at school, appearing at Career Day in place of his father to talk about game development, choosing the bright kids to test the game. They were proud of their role in the process, proud of Peter, proud of him. Nowhere else had he ever found this kind of appreciation. Susan tried, but she didn't really understand what he did, never had, never really cared. Peter, these kids… "What is he going to tell his friends? What a loser his uncle is, I bet."

"He loves you, Joe. He'll understand."

"He's eleven. How can he, when I don't? Oh Em, I don't know what I'm going to do."

"If you need money, Joe, I can lend you some."

Joe looked at his sister's old appliances, her make-do furniture, and his heart swelled with gratitude. "No, that's not a problem. At least, not yet. They're giving me a decent leaving package—*if* I turn the program copies in. I'm going to have to think about this."

"What can I do, Joe? How can I help?

Joe looked up, and a flicker of a smile lit his face for the first time all afternoon. "What about a coffee, sis?"

An hour later, Joe drove home and unloaded his boxes from Quiszle Games into the garage of his old downtown house. There was no lock on the garage door so he'd have to secure the papers and items from his office, but he didn't have the heart to find a safe place right now. He knew he'd have to face Susan when he went inside.

In the foyer, he heard stirring noises to go with the dinner smells coming from the kitchen. Dear Susan, always on time, organized, cheerful. But she craved the status quo he had just shattered. How would she react?

"Oh sweetie, I heard what happened at the office. I'm so sorry. How are you?"

Joe felt his knees give way with relief as he sat down for the second time that day at a kitchen table. "Not good, Susie. Not good."

"What happened?"

"They took the game." Joe dropped his head into his hand as Susan came around the counter and wrapped her arms around him.

"I can't believe they'd do that to you. You're creating their future."

"A future I won't be in." He described it all again, feeling again the confusion and anger and fear in that big office with the sneering Ormond, feeling again the helplessness he used to feel as a kid.

"I'm so sorry, sweetie." She hugged him. "Let me get you a beer. What are you going to do? Do you think you can sue them?"

"Em thinks so." At once, he saw his mistake, saw the hurt in her eyes that he had gone to his sister before coming home. He rushed on, "Anyway, I'm not giving them the program."

Susan brought his beer over after turning the oven off. She sat down opposite him and took his hand. "We'll get through this, Joe. We'll fight." But Joe knew Susan was not good with adversity. And how long could she support his fight against the company she continued to work for?

The next week, Joe and Emma consulted with Uncle Brian. He suggested Joe document everything he could about the development of the game idea, the program, and the testing period. Joe had kept a copy of the latest version of the game and of his suggested changes. He saved the information to DVD, and gave a copy to Emma to be kept out of harm's way and to Brian to be examined by a specialist in software development law. The hardest part is the waiting, Joe thought.

Ormond, a less-than-competent man who held his position mostly because his father had founded the company, had cheated him out of his one chance at the brass ring. But gradually as the days passed, the fire of indignation sank lower as his energy drained away and depression set in. Joe did little at home, rarely opened his laptop, stopped going out. As his spirits sank, he stopped caring about how he looked, seemingly content in dirty clothes. His preternaturally white hair yellowed with neglect and his beard started to grow straggly. Susan rarely confronted him on his growing hermit-like traits, but sisters are less tolerant. Emma came by one afternoon and found Joe still in his boxer shorts, unwashed, unbrushed, and smelling of neglect.

"For heaven's sake, Joe. You've got to start taking care of yourself." She moved over, pushed a pile of newspapers off his sofa, and jabbed the television remote button. Silence—a silence Joe was becoming increasingly afraid of—settled down on the room. "Where's Susan?"

"She went back to her mother's for a few days. She said she had to help her sort something out."

"Sure. She's probably escaping this cave of depression. Do you know that you smell? That this house smells? What is happening to you?"

"I got fired, remember! And I lost the Santa game."

"You're allowed to be unhappy, mad even, for a week or two, but this is more than a month. It's December already. Pull yourself together. What did Uncle Brian say?"

"He called last week. I haven't phoned him back yet."

"For heaven's sake, Joe, go upstairs and get showered and dressed. I'll clean up this mess. And then, little brother, we are going to talk."

Twenty minutes later, when Joe came down in more-or-less clean jeans, hair wetly pulled back behind his ears, Emma presented him with a coffee in one of the many mugs she had excavated from the debris in the kitchen and washed. "You are going to phone Uncle Brian tomorrow morning. And you're going to look for something else to do."

Joe shook his head and stared at the coffee. "I don't know what I can do. That game has consumed my time and my thoughts for more than a year now."

"That was just one game. You'll think of others. You've done it before."

"They have a non-compete clause in their contract. Quiszle locks up your work, your thoughts, everything."

"What do you want to do? What do you really care about?"

"The goddamned game, Em! The Santa game! And getting back at Ormond."

"Well, you need a different focus. What about the outplacement sessions the company arranged for you to take?" Emma started plumping up cushions on the chesterfield. "Have you called the agency? No? Tomorrow, you'll get up, shower, and after your call to Uncle Brian, you'll go over to the agency and sign up. I want to see some change here. And you'll phone Susan tomorrow night to talk."

"It's not that easy, sis. She's fed up with me."

"Nothing is easy, Joe. I know that. And what do you think Peter has been thinking about his uncle for the last few weeks? You haven't called him. You never explained, and I couldn't bear to say anything. That's your job. So the poor kid's been testing the game with his friends, and they've found a way to fix one of the big problems. He even called Quiszle Games to tell them."

"He *what*?" Joe leaned forward so suddenly his knee hit the coffee table, knocking Susan's Royal Doulton balloon lady to the rug. "What did they say? Who did he talk to?"

"I don't know." Emma picked the figurine up and checked for damage. "They told him to bring the fix over."

"Jeez, Em. He has to stay away from them. They'll know he has a copy now. Tell him to put it somewhere safe. Wait. I'll call him. What's his cell number?"

"Joe, he's in class. They don't allow cell phones in his school."

Joe sank back against the chair. "Okay. I'll come by after school and talk to him. And pick up all the game DVDs so the company can't give the kid a hard time."

As Joe got ready for bed that night, he ran things over in his mind. It was Ormond who had decided the licence would only work for six weeks, probably the only good idea the man had ever had. Limited playing time would boost demand. Not something Joe would have thought of, but typical of Ormond. For the six-week playing time the game allowed, players could download iPod and cell phone music, and they had to complete the game itself before it expired at the end of Twelfth Night, a few days after New Year's.

The game also contained a section on the darker side of Christmas. Called "Nasty Holiday," this variant for cynical adults was password-protected so kids wouldn't find it, although the smarter kids usually managed to. Initially, Joe had been unhappy with this option, but Ormond claimed it doubled the game's appeal. Focus groups proved he was right. Players loved finding the hidden key to the dark side of Christmas.

Joe reared up on one elbow and punched his pillow. For the first time in weeks, he wanted action. He flopped back, staring at the ceiling, wishing Susan was next to him. Why couldn't he explain to her why this Santa game meant so much to him? It was his own creation—his first autonomous project. His baby. Years of dreaming and working on his own time had gone into it. His very identity was wrapped between the plastic covers of that DVD. By taking it away from him, they were rubbing him out, deleting him from the database of life.

By morning, Joe had the beginnings of a plan to get back at Ormond. Christmas, either for good or bad, was central to December. And Santa was the answer. He contacted the local Santa Association with the outplacement agency's help and arranged for an interview the next day. As he hung up the phone, the thought of what Susan might say if she found out the real reason behind his bizarre new job choice almost stopped him, but not quite.

Next day, Joe was hired by the Yorkdale Mall manager, who was delighted to replace a disreputable Santa with a presentable, non-alcoholic one who had extensive knowledge of computer games and a real beard. After his first day on the job, Joe was smart enough to get some waterproof Santa pants.

Joe discovered there were side benefits to the Santa job. Elves dressed in short red outfits trimmed in white fur were easy to look at. He was building up impressive biceps, lifting wriggling kids on and off his lap. And he was learning much about the behaviour of young kids, a bonus for junior game development. Even when handed babies with dirty diapers, Joe as Santa managed a sincere-sounding *Ho Ho Ho*.

The disadvantages of the job, apart from germs from the infected, were minimal. He was out of the house and out of the cold. In a moment of excessive good cheer, he even decorated his car for Christmas.

In his time off, Joe worked at rebuilding his relationship with Susan. She felt awkward talking about Quiszle Games where she still worked, so they found new things to talk about. Together, they explored back corridors in the mall—areas only employees could use—where they could escape young eyes. They met for sandwich picnics, drank Bloody Caesars out of paper cups, and giggled like teenagers hiding from the adults. He just wished they wouldn't play "Jingle Bells" on repeat so often. There was no escaping that, even in their hideaway.

After a few days in his red-garbed persona, Joe made an interesting discovery. When Tony, the Quiszle CEO, brought his kids to the mall to see Santa, he didn't recognize Joe, even though Joe had no disguise on his face. It was confirmation for Joe that Santa really could help to liberate his game.

In mid-December, Susan told Joe the date of the company holiday party. With a little fast chat, he talked the Santa employed for the evening into changing gigs. It would be interesting to attend the party as old Saint Nick when the executives were relaxing with too much holiday cheer.

On Friday at six thirty, Joe put up his "Santa will be back tomorrow" sign and left early, hoping the mall bosses wouldn't realize he'd gone two hours before he was off duty. The party restaurant was in a corner of the mall. En route, Joe went into the washroom to freshen up and install green-coloured contacts left over from a mid-life fling. He thought they might bother him a little, but he didn't anticipate the immediate tears and growing redness of his eyes. Now his usually bright blue eyes were a decided but really watery green. After primping with a last-minute brushing of his coat and beard, he said, "Ho Ho Ho" to the grinning guys at the urinals and walked towards the restaurant.

Ho Ho Ho, indeed, he thought. His cover was good. Employees wanted to have fun at the party, and after a few drinks, were more open than usual. He had high hopes of learning about the executives' intentions and of causing some chaos tonight. Sort of like the dark side of the Santa game, he thought suddenly. The thought gave him pause—briefly. But they deserved what was coming.

Jeannie and Susan were at the door, overseeing the final preparations. Glittering metallic chains of tinsel hung from the doorway and draped over a sign welcoming the Quizzle Group, home of the Santa WireBox game. A few strands of silver had fallen onto Susan's soft green sweater, and Joe had trouble not putting his arm around her and removing it. Jeannie saw the look Santa gave Susan and, pouting, pulled him into the room.

"Hey, Santa. You're late. Our group is expected in about ten minutes."

"Sorry. Are you Miss Jenkins?"

She nodded, scarcely glancing at him. "I'll show you where you'll be working." They walked past the disc jockey who was warming up with naughty carols, past tables decorated with sweet-smelling cinnamon candles. Joe sneezed loudly, his normal reaction to the spicy smell. He didn't notice Susan glance his way.

Joe looked up at the decorated tree and red-draped chair on the stage. "Does Santa stay up there the whole time?"

"Yes. People will come up to you and tell you what they want. Think of them as big kids. Then later on, you hand out the presents."

"Will there be children here?" Joe said, as they climbed a short flight of stairs to the stage.

"No. After last year's debacle when our president got too involved with one of the elves, we decided to make this an adult-only party."

Joe was relieved. He remembered last year well. He'd been asked by Jeannie to get Tony and the green-tighted temptress off the stage. And he'd incorporated the roving eye and hand of Santa into his bad-Santa variant of his game.

"Right. I'll stay up on stage at the beginning, but I'd like to walk around after and bring a little fun to the party. Okay?"

"I guess so. One of the execs, Mr. Pike, likes to dress up as Santa and go around to each group later on. Don't interfere with him. How long are you contracted to stay?"

"Two hours, but I can stay longer if you like. When do you think the party will be over?"

"Let's play it by ear." Jeannie looked at him a little more closely. "You seem familiar somehow."

"People often say that, Miss Jenkins. Santas always seem familiar."

"Still… Oh, never mind. I want to finish getting the tables organized. Your sack of goodies is over by your chair. An elf will join you shortly. Not the one from last year," she added with a grin. "Anyway, you know the drill, I'm sure. The photographer will be nearby to get pictures for the company bulletin as people come up for their presents."

"Okay. Don't worry. It'll go well."

Joe smiled with satisfaction. If Jeannie couldn't recognize him after seeing him in and out of the CEO's office several times a week at work, others wouldn't either. He hoped Susan didn't yelp when she twigged. It helped that a cold, a gift from one of the little darlings at the mall, darkened his usual voice. And the red of his suit changed the look of his complexion, giving it a rosy glow very different from its normal programmer's pallor.

Everyone was at the party, from the top execs down to the receptionist, all with spouses or friends. They drank and flirted, gossiped, danced, got food at the buffet, and drank some more. Voices got louder; laughter, more shrill. Ormond arrived late, just before the presents were handed out, dressed in full Santa rig. Everyone groaned, and most ordered drinks to buttress themselves against the usual mess.

"Susan, come and sit on my knee, you little honey." Ormond, holding the latest of many large martinis, beckoned to her while his own wife was circulating on the other side of the room. Joe, on his throne nearby, shuddered.

"Ormond, why don't you just settle down at your table, and I'll bring you some buffet supper in a little while?" Susan winked at Jeannie and neatly eluded Ormond's wandering hand.

"I don't want to eat, but I do want to enjoy. You were always so tied up with Joe. Now it's my turn. Come over here, sweetie."

Susan backed away but was stopped by a friend for an introduction to her husband. Ormond came up and grabbed her arm, but the friend managed to get her free.

On stage, Joe seized this moment to clear his throat. In his best deep Santa voice, he asked Jeannie to start sending people up on stage for their present and kiss from Santa. He played his Christmas role well, and no one except Susan even looked at him with any sense of recognition. Susan raised an eyebrow but didn't say a thing, bless her.

Finally, the moment he had looked forward to arrived: Ormond climbed up the stairs and plumped down on his lap.

"So, Ormond, have you been a good little boy?" Joe began, switching on the mike hidden in the fur of his red coat. "Have you been kind to your staff and to your family?"

"You betcha, Santa. I'm always kind." He gave a knowing wink out at the audience, not letting on if he was startled at hearing their voices magnified.

"That's funny, Ormond. I've heard differently. I've heard you dumped a team that was developing a game so you would get the profit. I heard you fired the guy in charge and got rid of the others by reassigning them or by making their lives so miserable they quit. I heard you stole the game and plan to release a buggy version. Now why would I have heard that?"

"S'not true, Santa. The game's good. And I've been good. Just ask Jeannie. Or ask my wife!" Ormond looked out at the crowd who were now listening carefully, whispering among themselves. "Sheila, come up here and tell Santa I've been good."

Sheila looked at Ormond, turned away, and walked slowly towards the door.

"Sheila! Where'ya going? Sheila?"

"Perhaps she heard about you and Ellen in Accounting? Or Bev in Production? Are you still interested in Lesley in Sales?" There was a brief microphone squawk as Joe leaned too close to the amplifier.

"What the… Who *are* you?" Ormond squinted at the Santa face so close to his own.

"Santa, of course. I've been keeping a list and checking it twice. And each time, you go down, Ormond, for a lump of coal, or at least a lump." Grabbing the arms of the throne, Joe pushed up, jettisoning Ormond from his lap. Ormond hit the stage, rolled awkwardly off, and landed half on top of a table, spilling drinks and leftover dinner. Joe moved sideways so fast, he knocked the elf over. Startled silence settled on the room; people peered at Ormond and back at Santa. Joe knew it was time to get out of there. After righting the fallen Christmas helper, he ran off, accidentally sending the bag of presents cascading over the edge of the stage.

Joe had never felt so fleet of foot, in spite of his oversized black boots. One benefit of working at the mall was knowing the many back alleyways. Fuelled by adrenalin, he raced through the employees-only door, sped along the bare passageways, skidded around corners, and burst out into the garage. He found his red Jeep quickly thanks to the sparkle of tinsel decorating the aerial, climbed in, pulled his red hat off, and revved the engine.

"Merry Christmas, Ormond!" he yelled as he pulled out of his spot, burning rubber. In his rear-view mirror, he saw two of the sprightlier middle executives rushing towards him. He had to stop decorating his car for Christmas. He left them with a wheelie that dislodged tire slush and sent it flying. Appropriate to cover corporate sludge with road mud.

Joe knew his home would be the obvious place to look for him—if they were so inclined—so he turned east and headed out towards his sister's house instead. Now was the perfect time to help with the outdoor decorating he had promised Emma he'd do ages ago. At one point near Bayview, he thought he spotted a company car following him, but it drove by.

There was no sign of a power shortage in North Toronto. Lights twinkled everywhere. Wired trees, automaton deer, and scarily inflated snowmen beckoned from every lawn. Joe preferred his eclectic neighbourhood downtown where Christmas lights mingled with leftover Halloween decorations and Chinese lanterns. Joe parked in a dark spot around the corner from Emma's.

His sister had put up a wreath and some lawn ornaments, but the large decorations on the roof—a Santa, sleigh, and reindeer—were only partially arranged and the Christmas lights looked as if someone had thrown them there from a passing plane. Joe felt a pang of guilt. After the death of her husband, he had tried to help her out, tactfully, as often as he could, but this Christmas, he had let her down. Well, he would fix that tonight.

He unlocked the door and cursed when the wreath fell, playing a jolly carol. Taking off his Santa boots, he went into the foyer and called up the stairs. No one was home. Off at the school "holiday" night, he supposed. Well, he'd better get to work. A Santa on the roof with a sleigh was not likely to be noticed, especially this time of night. He grinned, his good spirits restored.

Joe headed upstairs to the attic, where he opened the dormer window and stepped out in his stocking feet onto the slippery down-slope of the roof. He edged down towards the gutters where the sun had melted the snow, ready to finish stringing the lights.

Joe tried gently to pull the light strings free, but they had frozen to the roof. He gave a strong tug, and one string of lights came loose, wrapping around the legs of a full-sized reindeer and dislodging it, sweeping it off the roof. It landed with a gentle thump, feet first in a pile of snow. Ah well, Joe thought, I'll just pull it back up with some rope when I've finished with the lights.

As he anchored the extension cord around the chimney, headlights swung around the corner of the street, making him duck instinctively. A black car careened towards the house and skidded over the curb, slewing to a stop on the front lawn. As Joe watched in astonishment, the driver got out and staggered up the walk.

Ormond.

Joe froze, wishing he were closer to the fake sleigh so he could blend in with the display. He struck a pose anyway, one hand flung up in a jolly wave, and hoped for the best.

What was Ormond doing here? Had he followed Joe somehow? Did he intend to get back at him for what he had done at the party? But if so, why had it taken so long to get here?

Ormond, still wearing his Santa hat from the party, was obviously feeling no pain. Joe leaned forward cautiously, watching as Ormond lurched to the front door. In the clear air, he heard the scrape of pottery on brick. The creep was looking for the extra key! How many times had he told Emma not to leave it under the large flower pot!

Joe wished he had his cell with him to phone 911, but he had left it in the car. He listened as the front door banged open, as Ormond walked about heavily inside. He must have seen my boots, Joe thought uneasily. When Ormond started up the stairs, Joe panicked. He even peered over the edge of the roof, trying to gauge if there was enough snow to cushion his jump. Then he had a flash of intuition. Ormond wasn't here to get back at Joe. He had another plan in his alcohol-soaked brain.

The bastard!

Joe slipped back inside the house, tiptoed into Peter's room, and grabbed a DVD case from a pile on the desk. Just as quietly, he retraced his steps to the attic and waited by the dormer window in his stocking feet. Then he dropped a storage box of old tools and listened. Footsteps creaked on the attic stairs. Joe stood still, just out of sight of the doorway, near the open dormer window.

As Ormond entered the dark room, Joe whispered, "Hello, boss."

"Wha…" Ormond turned towards him, startled. "What are you doing here, Joe?"

"Me? What are you doing in my sister's house is a better question, Ormond."

A slow smile spread across Ormond's oily face. "Hey, funny guy, you really got me back at the party, dintcha, eh? We can call it quits now, right? Buddies again?"

"We were never buddies."

"Ah, come on, Joe, you're a smart guy. You know what I want. Why not just give me the fix for your program, the one your nephew told us about, and I'll be out of here. No hard feelings, okay?"

"*My* program, eh, Ormond? I though that's why you came here, you sneak. I called the police. They'll soon sort this out."

"Ah, come on. Why'd ya do that?" Ormond looked anxiously out the window to the street below, but there were no distant sirens. He grinned, his face shiny with sweat and all the alcohol he had consumed. "A real kidder, eh, fella? Now, why not make this easy on both of us. I need that patch. I'm sure you don't want your family involved. Where's your nephew's computer?"

Joe moved a little closer to the window and pulled the case out of his pants pocket. "Leave my family alone. You can have what you want."

"Okay, Joe. Just hand it over and I'm outta here."

"Fine. Go get it" With a quick twist of his wrist, Joe threw the DVD out the window onto the roof. Coloured lights sparkled off the plastic case.

Ormond bellowed in frustration. "Damn, Joe, stop foolin' around! Go get that thing!"

"You want it, you get it." He could see the indecision on Ormond's face, the same indecision that marked why he had not been a good boss and never would be.

With a curse, Ormond put a booted foot over the window ledge. He found his footing, swung the other leg over, and reached for the DVD. It was just out of his grasp.

Joe held his breath, counting on Ormond's greed to win out. Sweat soaked his shoulders, dripped down his under arms. "Just a little more, boss," he whispered, both hands on the sash of the window, ready to slam it shut.

Ormond lunged for the jewel case. Both feet slipped out from under, and he fell with a grunt. Spreadeagled on the sloping roof, his big body began a slow slide. He grabbed a string of lights hanging from the chimney. Light bulbs popped as his hand raked down the string, and a jolt of electricity made him let go. He skittered down further. At the edge, he grasped the copper gutter and held on tightly with his bloodied fingers.

"Help me, for God's sake!"

"Hold on!" Joe was already out the window. He eased forward, but his feet were so cold he could hardly feel them. He started to slip. Next thing he knew, he lay sprawled on the roof, smelling asphalt from the wet shingles.

"Don't just lie there!" Ormond shrieked.

Joe blinked at him. His eyes were watering so much that Ormond's desperate face was a smear of rainbow colours from the remaining Christmas lights. The effect was grotesque. Wiping his eyes on his sleeve, Joe slowly eased himself up and spidered his way back to the window. Inside, the warmth reached out to him seductively, but he grabbed an extension cord from the tool kit, tied it around a roof joist, and climbed back out.

"Grab on when I throw it." He hurled the cord, but it landed too far to one side. "Hold on. I'll try again."

Ormond whimpered. "Hurry up, man. I can't. My hands can't hold."

Joe aimed carefully, but this time the bulky wire coil twisted too far to the other side. Ormond lunged sideways. And missed. He clutched the gutter again, sobbing. As Joe threw the cord a third time, Ormond grabbed at the air with his right hand, still grasping the gutter with his left. "I can't get it! Do something. Help me!"

"I'm trying!" But as Joe reeled the wire in again, he stopped. Why should I try? he thought suddenly. "You threatened my family," he said quietly. "You broke into my sister's house. Stole *my* game!"

"Please! I'm sorry." Ormond's desperate eyes appealed to everything in Joe's being.

But the memory of Ormond at the party, leering at Susan, stopped him again. He thought about the man's nastiness to his staff, his total inhumanity. He knew Ormond would make Susan's life hell at the office after what he had done. And he thought about how Ormond had tried to steal the Santa game program, to obliterate his best work. He drew his arm back, then watching the man's struggles, lowered it.

Ormond's eyes widened as he realized there was no help coming. As his bloodied hand lost its grip on the icy gutter, he began to slide down further. Suddenly, he plunged from the roof, landing with a sickening yelp on top of the fake reindeer's antlers. As his right foot hit the wreath, which had rolled nearby, it played "Silent Night," one of the few carols Joe still liked. Around Ormond, the snow was turning pink where he lay face down, pierced by the antler, his Santa hat a splash of blood red on a nearby drift.

Joe rushed down the stairs and outside, yelling, but no one came. He ran up beside the still body, and after hesitating briefly, felt for a pulse beneath the sticky fur collar. Nothing. Back inside, he dialled 911, but he knew it was too late. Pulling on his boots, he went outside to wait for the emergency team. He had little regret for Ormond's death, but he felt as if he had just lost another piece of his own humanity. He stamped his big Santa boots in the snow, trying to warm his feet as the sirens wailed closer. And he shivered, thinking of the game—*his* game—and of the dark side of Christmas.

Jane Burfield wrote her first short story in 2001, winning a Bony Pete award from the Bloody Words Mystery Conference. She was gobsmacked to win again at the next three conferences, and has now decided she likes the challenge of the short story form. She is a member of CWC and her recipe, To Die for Brie, in the CWC's Dishes to Die For...Again cookbook has hopefully not been used to dispatch too many dinner guests. Jane looks forward to enjoying future Christmases with her three daughters and two cats in her fourth-generation family home in Toronto.

Christmas Can Be a Killer

❦

Stephen Gaspar

I've never liked fruitcake. It is one of those seasonal treats that only comes out during the Christmas holidays, like eggnog and those overly sweet Yule logs. I remember growing up, and during the holidays, my parents would make their own fruitcake. They would lay out all the ingredients on the kitchen table: sugar, eggs and flour; cherries, pineapple, raisins, apricots, and dates; vanilla, coconut, and almonds. It was an annual event at our house. My brothers, sister, and I would sit around the table and watch in fascination as our parents combined the entire concoction, adding one item at a time. My father would stir the thick mixture together, then pour the caramel-coloured batter into three pans, which would bake in the oven until the outer crust turned a rich dark brown. The cakes would then be wrapped in wax paper and placed on the top shelf of the front hall closet inside a pot to cure. When enough time had passed, one of the cakes was taken down and sliced up as a holiday treat.

Everyone in our house enjoyed the cake—everyone but me, that is. Whereas the rest of my family thought the fruitcake was delicious, I could not stand the taste. I think it was because there were too many ingredients. I like things kept simple. Over the years, I tried other fruitcakes, both homemade and store-bought, but I never found one I liked.

But though I do not like them, it never occurred to me that a fruitcake could be deadly.

Blood on the Holly

As a police investigator, I do not look forward to the Christmas season. People tend to get downright psychotic during the holidays. Suicides increase considerably and violent domestic disputes are prevalent. For some odd reason, during the "season of peace, love, and joy," there are more violent crimes and deaths than at any other time of the year. There was the exasperated wife who was frustrated beyond endurance with her husband because he would not help her put up Christmas decorations; we found the husband in his La-Z-Boy recliner, strangled to death with a string of Christmas lights. There are also regular occurrences every year involving someone getting stabbed with a carving knife during one of those special holiday family dinners. And there was the singular incident a few years ago when a street-corner Santa was stabbed and the perp ran off with the plastic container of change and small bills—and for some unknown reason, he even stole Santa's bell.

At the police station in Windsor, it has been a longstanding tradition to bet on the first homicide of the new year. At the annual Christmas party, everyone on the force puts in ten dollars and chooses a date. Any date will do. There've been years when we've experienced zero killings, but as time goes on, Windsor has decided to join the ranks of greater cities such as Toronto or even Detroit, which lies just across the river.

I don't know if anyone chose January first this particular year, but whoever did, won the lottery.

We weren't called in until January second. Windsor had experienced an unusual amount of snowfall, but the roads were kept fairly clear by the salt trucks and snowploughs and I arrived at the scene just before noon. It was a modest home in the Riverside area. The house was neat and clean, and whoever had lived there seemed to love houseplants, for every room was full of them. Most prevalent were seasonal poinsettias. The deceased was one Henry Watkins: thirty-nine years old, divorced, and living by himself.

"He was discovered lying here on the kitchen floor, Inspector," Sergeant Carvello told me as we stood over the body. It lay on the ceramic tile floor in a natural position, save for the fact that the corpse appeared to have a grin upon his face as if the man had died laughing or someone had told him a funny story just before he expired. "Medical examiner estimates the man's been dead for a little over twelve hours."

"That would make it the first. What did you have?" I asked Sergeant Carvello.

"February nineteenth. You?"

"September fifteenth. Hope springs eternal. Who discovered the body?" I asked as the Crime Scene Unit went about their job of dusting for prints, taking photographs, and checking the room for clues.

"It was the mailman," Carvello told me. "He had a package for Watkins that had to be signed for—most likely a belated Christmas gift."

"Why February nineteenth?" I asked.

"It's my girlfriend's birthday."

"When are you going to marry her?"

"Why? What's the hurry?"

"No hurry. I just haven't been to an Italian wedding in a while," I said, then added, "I need to talk to the mailman."

"He asked if he could continue on with his route, but I have his name and address," the sergeant said. "The mailman's name is Mark Tremblay and he's been on this route for four years. Tremblay said he rang the bell a number of times because he didn't want to have to bring the package back tomorrow, so he looked in the window and spotted Watkins on the floor. Then he called us."

I turned to Shirley Havinga, the medical examiner on the scene.

"What can you tell me about the cause of death?"

"Happy New Year to you, too, Ted. Not much, I'm afraid. No discernable mark on the body. If I had to make a guess, I would have to say natural causes."

"The guy looks too young to have a heart attack."

"I was thinking it was related to his diabetes."

"He was a diabetic?"

"He's wearing a Medic Alert bracelet," she said, but seemed almost reluctant as she said it.

"What is it?" I asked.

She shook her head. "It may be too early to say, but I wouldn't rule out poisoning."

"You ever been to an Italian wedding?" I asked her.

She looked at me coyly. "Is that a proposal or a date?"

"I need to know cause of death as soon as possible, Shirley."

"You will."

I found out later that night. Shirley Havinga called me at my office.

"I should learn to trust my instincts," she uttered in a self-congratulatory manner. "He was poisoned, all right."

"Any way to know what it was that killed him?"

"It was some kind of chemical compound. Looks homemade."

"Any way to know how it entered his system?"

"He ingested it inside of something."

"Any idea what?"

"Just to be on the safe side, I took samples of everything in the kitchen. Fortunately, there wasn't that much food—you know bachelors—so I was able to isolate it fairly quickly. Guess what holiday treat the poison was in."

"Eggnog? Turkey stuffing? Cranberry sauce?"

"Nope. Fruitcake."

"You're kidding."

"I am not kidding. There is enough poison in that fruitcake to kill ten people," she said. "What was all that talk about going to an Italian wedding?"

"Some other time," I said. "Thanks, Shirley."

Early the next morning, Sergeant Carvello and I entered the home of the late Henry Watkins.

"What did you find out about Watkins?" I asked the sergeant.

"He was a drama instructor at the University of Windsor and worked with theatre groups at the U and around the city. He was also a playwright. He wrote and directed that play at the Capital Theatre—you know, *Summer Love*. It only ran for three performances."

"I heard about that," I said. "There was all kinds of hype about it, but from what I heard, it really sucked."

"The reviewer for *The Windsor Star* crucified Watkins. If I didn't know better, I would have suspected Watkins had committed suicide over it."

"The review was that bad?"

"They were saying on the news that the review was enough to keep Watkins down for years and that his reputation would never recover. I even heard a rumour that Watkins was going to sue the Star over the review."

"That poison fruitcake came from somewhere," I said. "We have to find out where."

We searched the house, paying strict attention to the garbage, much to the dismay of Carvello.

"Yuck!" he exclaimed as we sorted through Watkins's refuse that we dragged from the garage out into the snowy driveway. "What do you expect to find in all this mess?"

"This!" I exclaimed triumphantly, and held up a piece of plain brown wrapping paper.

"What's *that* supposed to be?" the sergeant asked.

"Look at the shape," I said. "It's very likely the fruitcake was wrapped inside. Notice the tape is still hanging on the paper." I held it to my nose and said, "Smells like fruitcake to me. Good, here comes the mailman."

Carvello walked across the snow and greeted the mailman.

"Mr. Tremblay, could we have a word? This is Inspector Edward Young. He's in charge of the case."

I shook hands with Tremblay and wished him a Happy New Year. He was middle-aged and fat, with a full dark beard and dressed in the winter garb of a letter carrier.

"Mr. Tremblay, do you know anything about what was wrapped in this?" I said, holding up the item.

"Why should I know anything?" he asked with attitude.

"Because it has Mr. Watkins's name and address on it as if the sender intended to mail it, but there is no return address or postage. We believe a fruitcake was inside, and if anyone were to send a fruitcake in the mail, they would send it in a box. This was delivered by hand, but not through the post office."

"So?"

"So the reason it was sent in a paper wrapping and there is no postage is because the sender may have given it to a letter carrier such as yourself to deliver it *post haste*, in a manner of speaking."

"That's against Canada Post policy," Tremblay said hesitantly.

"Yes, it is, but I'm certain you didn't mind too much, now, did you, especially if when they asked you to do it, they were giving you your Christmas bonus?"

Tremblay looked to each of us in turn, then admitted, "All right, so I delivered this package. What does that have to do with anything?"

"Did you tell Watkins who sent it?" I asked.

"I didn't think I had to," Tremblay said, with a shrug of his shoulders. "There was a card attached."

"Just tell us who asked you to deliver the package."

The name Tremblay gave us was Mrs. Janet Barkstone who lived several blocks away but still within Tremblay's mail route. It wasn't too difficult to see why Tremblay broke company policy. Janet Barkstone was about forty years of age and very attractive, with long blond hair, sky-blue eyes, and a fine figure. She answered the door with a friendly smile. Though it was the middle of the day, the lady was made up as if she were going out for the evening. We introduced ourselves and she invited us into her home, which was tastefully decorated although a bit overly feminine with sheer window treatments and a lot of pinks.

"We're looking into the death of Mr. Henry Watkins," I said delicately, so she would not suspect we suspected her. "You knew him?"

"Yes," she said, looking distressed and placing her palm against her bosom. "I just read of his death in the paper this morning. Poor man. Yes, I knew him, however not well. Can I offer you gentlemen some coffee? A plate of cookies or some fruitcake, perhaps?"

Sergeant Carvello gave me a quick sidelong glance, and I said to her, "No, I'm afraid we don't have time for that, but if you could tell me how you knew Mr. Watkins."

"My daughter is in his drama class," she said with pride and reached over and handed us a picture. "Isn't she lovely? Melissa was in Mr. Watkins's latest production, *Summer Love*. She could have played the lead, but... "

The picture was a framed eight-by-ten colour glossy, professionally taken. The young woman in the photograph was even more beautiful than the mother and made up so much they could almost be sisters.

"Melissa is only nineteen, but she has more talent than—"

"Mrs. Barkstone—"

"Janet, please."

"Janet, I am going to say this as delicately as possible, but we have it on good authority that you had little love for Mr. Watkins."

Her face showed her surprise, and her entire manner seemed overly dramatic. It was not difficult to see why she pushed her daughter into acting. "I don't know why you would say that, Inspector, or who would have given you this information."

"I'm afraid we can't reveal our sources," I said, then allowed my own gaze to grow stern and locked it upon her. "But let me assure you, our sources are reliable."

She blustered a brief moment, then said, "I may have been a trifle perturbed that Mr. Watkins did not give my daughter the lead in his production, and we might have had one or two arguments, and I shouldn't have called him on the phone as much as I did. He said I was harassing him, but still, I would never— "

"Janet, Mr. Watkins was poisoned."

"Poisoned!? And you suspect *I* poisoned him?"

"Janet, you asked your postman to deliver a package to Mr. Watkins?"

"Yes."

"It was a fruitcake?"

"Yes, we had an extra one. Actually, my daughter Melissa suggested... " Mrs. Barkstone stopped and a look of terror came over her face.

"Is your daughter home?" Carvello asked.

"You don't suspect Melissa?" she exclaimed.

"It was your daughter's idea to send the fruitcake?" I asked.

"No, no. This can't be. You say the poison was in the fruitcake?"

I nodded.

"I didn't even buy that fruitcake," she said anxiously. "We never even cut into it. It was a gift from— "

"From who?" Carvello prompted her.

"From my ex-husband."

Janet Barkstone informed us that she and her husband, Marvin, had divorced two years ago. By her own admission, their divorce was in no way amicable and had gotten quite nasty where alimony was concerned.

Marvin Barkstone owned the fourth largest tool shop in Windsor, out past Walker Road. His receptionist told us we could find him on the shop floor. Barkstone was about fifty years of age. His once-dark hair was greying and thinning, but he was still rather handsome. It was a bit difficult trying to talk above the noise of machines cutting and grinding steel. When we informed Barkstone we were investigating a murder, he suggested we speak in his office. It was a nice office, with dark wood panelling, leather chairs, and Bateman wildlife pictures on the walls. On his large mahogany desk sat a picture in a silver frame. The picture was of a beautiful redhead. Her age was somewhere between his daughter's and his ex-wife's.

"Just who was murdered, Inspector?" Barkstone asked as he sat behind his desk.

"Do you know Mr. Henry Watkins?"

"The name sounds familiar. Didn't I hear about his death on the radio?"

"Your wife or daughter mention Watkins to you?" I asked. "He was your daughter's drama coach."

"My daughter seldom calls, and my wife and I are not on speaking terms."

"She is your ex-wife, isn't she?" Carvello added.

Barkstone paused and glared at the sergeant. "That's right. We're divorced."

"Things couldn't be too strained between you," I said. "You sent her a Christmas gift."

The man thought a moment, then said with a wry grin, "Oh, the fruitcake. It was half a joke."

"Which half?"

"Look, she got plenty out of me in the divorce," he said, with more than a trace of resentment. "Sending her that cheap fruitcake was like saying, 'Screw you, Janet.'"

"Maybe you wanted to say more than that," I suggested.

"I don't get your meaning, Inspector."

"The fruitcake you sent your ex-wife was full of poison," I said bluntly.

"And you think I tried to poison her?"

"You practically admitted your feelings towards her," I said.

"Her death would take care of those heavy alimony payments," Carvello added. "Your new girlfriend looks like she's high-maintenance and expects a lot."

Barkstone stood up and faced us. "Now hold on," he said as he felt the law closing in on him. "I wouldn't poison anyone, not even my ex-wife. I didn't even buy the damned thing. It was given to me."

The sergeant and I exchanged looks.

"Who gave it to you?" I said.

"Who? It was some guy in my men's group."

"What men's group?"

"It's for divorced men. We meet every two weeks in the basement of the Lutheran church on Parent Avenue."

"Who in your group gave you the fruitcake?"

"I can't remember. We all exchange small gifts. What's-his-name gave it to me... Evans...Peter Evans."

By the time we left Barkstone's business, it was close to dinnertime, and Carvello suggested we stop for a bite to eat at Franco's on Tecumseh Road. We had a table by the window and we watched pedestrians pass by, bundled up with hats and scarves and gloves, while carefully treading the snowy sidewalk. Over our veal parmigiana, we discussed the case.

"This fruitcake is certainly making the rounds," Carvello stated.

"Personally, I never liked fruitcake. Any time I get a fruitcake, I just re-gift it to someone else. None of the people we spoke with even suspected that by re-gifting the fruitcake, it very well saved their lives," I said.

"Where do you think it started?" he asked.

"We'll find out," I said without a doubt.

"You know, any one of those people could be lying to us," Carvello said. "It could have been Mrs. Barkstone or her daughter or both of them. Mr. Barkstone might want his wife dead. Hell, even the postman could have injected poison into the package."

"Why the postman?" I asked.

"Maybe he didn't get a Christmas bonus from Watkins."

"Maybe. Or it could be this man Evans wanted Marvin Barkstone dead."

Sergeant Carvello nodded thoughtfully and said, "If you don't like fruitcake, what do you suggest I give you next Christmas?"

"Just do what everyone else does. Don't give me anything."

We traced Peter Evans to an apartment complex on Ouellette Avenue. It was a one-bedroom apartment on the tenth floor. The rooms were not unlike what one was likely to find in a bachelor's domicile. There were newspapers, magazines, and dirty dishes lying about the place. The living room was lined with filled bookcases. The apartment smelled of cigarette smoke. Evan's window offered a view of the Detroit skyline and a bit of the river.

Peter Evans was a middle-aged man, unwashed, unshaven, and unkempt. He answered the door with a drink in his hand and a cigarette dangling from his thick lips. We introduced ourselves.

"Ah, the local gendarmes," he said with a noticeable slur. "Come to arrest me, have you? I trust you will be gentle." He proffered his wrists while spilling his drink on the carpet.

"Is there something we should be arresting you for?" Carvello asked with a grin.

"I must have committed a crime somewhere, sometime. Come in and see if you can find anything. I won't even ask for a warrant."

Evans ushered us into his apartment, swaying slightly, then plopped himself into a worn, corduroy swivel rocker. Carvello and I cleared off two seats and sat in them.

"We had an interesting chat with Mr. Marvin Barkstone earlier today," I told Evans. He appeared uninterested. "You and Barkstone belong to the same men's group, isn't that so?"

Evans nodded.

"During one of your meetings, did you happen to tell Mr. Barkstone something in confidence? Something very private about yourself?"

"Whatever we spoke of in the group cannot be repeated outside the group," Evans said.

"You wouldn't repeat it," Carvello said to Evans, "but are you certain Barkstone wouldn't?"

"What did he tell you?" Evans said, his attitude becoming quite surly. "Did he tell you I molested my daughter? Is that what Evans said? If he told you that, he misinterpreted what I said, and if he told you anything, he broke the sanctity of the group. This will get him thrown out."

"Perhaps you regretted what you told Barkstone and you thought you would do something about it."

"What are you talking about?" Evans asked, confused.

"I am saying that you thought it better to silence Barkstone than to take the risk that he would repeat it."

"Just what kind of police are you?" Evans asked.

"Homicide."

"Are you saying Barkstone is dead? That someone tried to kill him?"

"Mr. Barkstone received a fruitcake from you that was filled with poison."

"And you think I poisoned the bloody fruitcake?"

The travel habits of a Christmas fruitcake were becoming abundantly clear to me, so I thought it prudent to ask, "Mr. Evans, where did you get that fruitcake?"

"I can't say."

"Are you saying you're refusing to tell us?" Carvello asked.

"I am saying I don't remember," Evans said, downing his drink. "Someone sent me the damned fruitcake in the mail. There was no card, no return address. Nothing. I don't like fruitcake so I gave it to Barkstone. Some idiot in the group suggested we exchange gifts. Is Barkstone all right?"

"Yes, he's fine," I said. "By the way, Barkstone never told us anything. He never betrayed your confidence, so there's no need to kick him out of your group."

"Do you know what you are?" he said, realizing how I had bluffed him into betraying himself.

"Yes, I know. People tell me every day," I said, unperturbed. "Now tell us about the fruitcake."

"The fruitcake! Who cares about the damned fruitcake?!"

"You said you don't know who sent it," Carvello said to Evans. "Do you still have the package it came in?"

Evans looked about the room lazily, then focussed in on the small silver Christmas tree that sat upon a table next to the television. Evans did not get up from his chair but motioned to the tree. Carvello went to the tree; beneath it were a few sad-looking gifts: a shirt, a cheap tie, and a fountain pen in a handsome case. Among the gifts lay the wrapping paper Evans had failed to throw out. Carvello picked up a box with the wrapping paper still adhering to it. The wrapping had pictures of holly on the outside.

"Did the fruitcake come in this?" the sergeant asked Evans.

"Yes, I believe so," he said.

Carvello showed me the box. Evans's name and address were printed on it. There was a return post office box number, but I suspected it was false.

"What do you do for a living, Mr. Evans?" I asked.

"I'm a writer."

I looked over the large number of books in the room and nodded. "What do you write? Anything I might have read?"

"I've written some novels," he said, then added rather reluctantly, "but I have never been published. I see myself more as a playwright."

"Would I know any of your plays?"

"I doubt it," he said. "I supplement my income as writer for *The Windsor Star.*"

"What do you write for the *Star*?"

"Entertainment section. You know, movie reviews and all-around critic."

I marvelled at life's little jests. In my line of work, I've seen my share of ironic twists and turns, such as the time a man sued his wife for custody of their two children but lost his case when a routine blood test proved he was not the father, or when a wife went to elaborate means to kill her husband for his insurance money but later confessed to the murder when she discovered her husband's beneficiary was his mistress.

But what I suspected happened to the late Henry Watkins was more ironic than either of these.

To prove my theory, Carvello and I went back to Watkins's house. We called and asked Shirley Havinga to meet us there.

Once there, I asked Shirley to look through the house to see if she could find any poison that matched the one in the fruitcake.

"Watkins was a diabetic," I said to Carvello. "See if you can locate Watkins's medical supplies."

After a few minutes, Shirley called me into the living room.

"This guy has a lot of plant food," she said. "Even without running any tests, I can tell you the poison could have been made from the plant food and common cleaning supplies. I don't get it, Ted. Did this guy poison himself?"

"In a roundabout way, he did."

"So what actually happened?" she asked, still a bit confused.

Just then Carvello came in, carrying a box. "Here is all his diabetic stuff. Test strips, cotton balls, syringes, insulin, alcohol pads. He kept most of his stuff in the bathroom off the kitchen. There is a plastic container with used syringes in the bathroom."

"Ted thinks he knows how it happened," Shirley said.

"Who was it, and what was the motive?" Carvello added.

"The motive was revenge, but by a quirky twist of fate, the killer was done in by his own scheme. It's incredible but quite simple," I stated. "Watkins sought revenge against Evans for his harsh criticism of his latest production, a criticism that Watkins felt crippled his career. With murder in his heart, Watkins planned his revenge. His plan was both diabolical and deadly—but it did have a touch of seasonal flavour.

"He could have learned how to concoct the poison from the Internet. We'll check his computer to see which Websites he visited. He brewed up the poison and injected it into the fruitcake with one of his hypodermic syringes. As a diabetic, he disposed of his syringes in a plastic container he kept in his bathroom. We'll take them all and check each one. I am certain we'll find traces of the poison in one of them.

"Watkins sent Evans a poisoned fruitcake that was passed along to Barkstone, who gave it to Mrs. Barkstone, who sent it finally back to Watkins. Watkins could not have suspected this was the exact fruitcake he sent to Evans, and with little else in the house to eat, he took a bite. It only took a moment for him to realize what had happened, but it was too late. I suspect that before Watkins died, he saw the irony in the entire affair and grinned at the irony of it all. Henry Watkins died with that grin on his face."

"Sounds reasonable to me," the sergeant stated.

"This might seem a bit premature and perhaps a bit inappropriate, but let's celebrate a successful conclusion to this one," Shirley said, bringing out a thermos and pouring its steaming contents into three Styrofoam cups.

"That smells good," Carvello said. "What is it?"

"Soup," she replied, handing us each a cup.

"What kind of soup?" I asked.

"Italian Wedding."

Stephen Gaspar was born in 1958 and is a high school teacher in Windsor, Ontario, where he lives with his wife, Susan, and teenage twin sons, Ryan and Tommy. A student of history and a fan of detective stories, he has combined these two interests to find his niche as a writer of historical mystery/detective stories.

How Silently, How Silently

Sandy Conrad

The phone calls started three weeks before Christmas. She was just starting to regain her normal telephone voice: "Hi. Merry Christmas. Diane speaking." For friends and family, it was the most positive they'd heard her since her daughter had disappeared. The old Diane seemed to be emerging from the dull-eyed woman who dreaded the sight of a police car at her door and scanned every crowd for a tiny dark-haired Goth girl with an impish smile and piercing green eyes.

Diane was sure that her daughter was the silent presence on the other end of the line.

"Ashley?"

No response.

"Is that you, Ashley?"

Nothing.

"Say something. Please let me hear your voice."

Was that a breath?

"Ashley. Why don't you speak? We've been so very, very worried. Come home. We love you."

Click.

Silence.

Diane sank to the floor and clutched both knees to her chest. Terrifying hope and a renewed sense of loss pushed through every layer of normalcy within her. The sight of the shortbread dough and green icing for the Christmas tree cookies was confusing. It didn't belong in her world of needing her daughter and living in constant fear of never seeing her again. She sobbed herself sleepy and only barely managed to convince herself not to nap on the floor.

224

Her husband returned to a dark house, an oven heated to 350 degrees, and a counter covered in unbaked cookies. His wife was asleep in their bed, and he woke her when he turned on the television. Diane sat up with a shock to a disorienting twilight world where she vaguely remembered something good had happened for a change.

"There was a phone call this afternoon. I think it was Ashley."

Joe turned from the closet where he was folding his pants over a hanger. "What are you talking about?"

"I'm sure it was her."

"Calling to wish us a Merry Christmas? After three years, she suddenly feels sentimental."

"Maybe she finally realizes how much we love her."

"Yes, and maybe she just needs money."

Diane had always been uncomfortable with Joe's callousness. Because he believed Ashley's disappearance was an act of defiance, he'd never properly mourned her absence. But three years, even between two people so angry at each other, should have taken all the rough edges and found at least one gaping wound awaiting the prodigal's return. Diane discovered, to her surprise, that she had many wounds, but Joe, even more surprisingly, seemed to have none.

Diane repeated the words she'd said so many times already. "We don't even know for sure if she ran away. The police—"

"Couldn't be bothered to chase down a spoiled slut who just happened to leave with all her skanky clothes, CDs, books, diary. Don't start, Di. The principal was on my case today about my marking policy because one parent called the school to complain. I don't need to come home to this. It's bad enough I have to fight with the ignorant and lazy all day. Do I have to fight with my wife, too?"

"Don't call her that name. I told you I can't bear it. I won't."

"It's what you called her yourself."

"In the heat of anger, when she was still here in front of me, I said a lot of things I regret now. Don't you throw that in my face." Diane rubbed the dried salt around her eyes. She was tired of crying and tired of fighting. Why couldn't he just be hopeful, too?

"One phone call doesn't mean anything. It could have been a heavy breather getting off on freaking you out."

"I'm calling the police tomorrow. I have the number. They can trace it."

Joe pulled on his track pants. "I'm going to the gym. I assume supper will be ready in an hour." He paused on his way out the door. "Maybe it was her, babe. But if she's calling out of the blue, why scare her off with the police? If she doesn't want to be found, she won't be found. Leave it. If she comes home, she's yours; if she doesn't, she never was."

"That's not funny, Joe. I don't know how you can be so flippant."

"Oh, believe me, I'm not kidding. I can see the happy little picture now: Ashley standing in our front door with some lowlife husband and a kid in her arms. And a Merry bloody Christmas we'll all have. My heart rate is climbing, just thinking about it. I'll be back in an hour. Don't let me down. And don't, for heaven's sake, call the police and embarrass yourself."

Diane washed her face, patted on moisturizer, and reapplied mascara. Spidery lines around her eyes made her sad. Nothing about her life was staying good. But surely the evening could still be salvaged. Maybe Joe would let her open a bottle of Chianti. They could treat themselves to one glass each. She would like to secretly celebrate the tenuous connection she was feeling with Ashley, for in her heart she was sure the phone call was just the first step in a Christmas homecoming.

When the second phone call came, Diane tried the silent technique, too. After a cautious hello, she waited. And waited. She thought she heard a car horn in the distance, a lighter, an inhalation of air. The person on the other end was smoking. Ashley was a smoker. She'd picked up the habit in her sixteenth year—along with a taste for black clothes, net stockings, purple hair, and smelly boys with their noses pierced. Her beautiful and radiant daughter had turned into her own permanently angry evil twin.

Diane had heard parents talk about their children becoming strangers, but until the day she'd come home to find Ashley smoking pot in their living room, playing a game of strip poker with boys, she'd never believed it would happen in her family. It seemed that Ashley had become a different person overnight. She remembered the shame her daughter brought to their name: the shoplifting, skipping classes, drinking in the school parking lot at lunch. There was a time when Diane had loved the sight of Ashley at her salon door, loved showing her off to the clients with her perfect skin and confident personality. But in that last year, Diane had felt only humiliation at Ashley's drop-in visits to ask for cash and to stare down Diane's clients and colleagues when they looked sideways at the greasy little tart at the counter.

Silence had never been Diane's strength. "Ashley, please. I'm your mom. The only one you'll ever have. What could we have done to hurt you so much? What did we do to deserve this?"

Click.

Diane checked the number on the screen. Not the same digits as last time. She'd call this number, too, although the first number had produced nothing, had rung more than twenty times with no answer and no machine. Thinking that Ashley might have been staring at the phone watching it ring, Diane tried the number over and over, hoping to catch an innocent passer-by who could give her the whereabouts of the phone, but no response had ever come. She couldn't help but wonder what the police would find if she could actually get them interested. They were so apathetic about runaways. Yet Diane could not completely deflate her expectations. This was the second call—and the most hopeful sign she'd had in three years.

Joe started answering the phone more often. He'd try to look casual in his haste, but she could see that he'd jump to be the first there. Diane always froze, waiting to see what her husband would say into the silence. Would their daughter be more likely to speak to him? They'd been so close at one time, geniuses together, playing chess and watching the History channel. There were times Diane felt jealous of the intimacy. Her husband complimented her, made love to her, treated her to expensive vacations and showy jewellery, but he never talked to her with the intensity he showed Ashley. The possessive pride he took in his daughter's brilliance was his alone, and he never shared it with his wife. Diane wanted to believe that his rush to the phone was a reflection of his own terrible need to hear Ashley's voice, to hear even her breath. Maybe he carried the same vast ache that she tried to hide from a world that wanted so badly for her to be okay. Maybe his anger was an act, and in his deepest heart, he wished her home, too. Of course, he did.

The third call came in the morning of Joe's last day of work before the holidays. Diane had sent him off with a tray of squares and homemade truffles to share with his department.

"Ashley, I know you want to come home. You'll always be welcome here, no matter what you've done."

Silence.

"I know we had problems. I said terrible things to you. I'm so sorry for everything I said."

The lighter. The inhalation.

"Please listen, Ashley. Your disappearance made me understand what a bad mother I was. I worried about all the wrong things and I hate myself for even caring what you looked like. I just didn't know better. I just didn't know what was important. But now I do. Now all I want is to see you alive. I want to make things right between us. I want you to be okay."

Silence.

"Are you okay?"

Exhalation.

"Will you come home for Christmas?"

Click.

Diane immediately called the number on the screen. No answer.

When Ashley first disappeared, it had been a luxury to feel sorry for herself, to live in a house without tension. Christmas was quiet, sad, but not without its moments of peace. There was no daughter to argue with, no all-night binges and coming home drunk, no screaming matches with Joe over her choice of companions. Diane had realized, to her sickening shame, that worrying about her daughter was easier than living with her. For a few weeks, Ashley's absence was almost a gift. As long as they could tell themselves that she had run away to be free of their grating presences and live in the company of like-minded dropouts, she and Joe could carry on with their normal lives. They could live quietly and go through the motions of worrying. They'd called the police but received little support. Seventeen-year-old runaways who disappear with clothes and other personal items were not high on their list of priorities. Friends had been questioned, but no one admitted to knowing where she was.

The calls from the school finally got Diane worrying. The guidance counsellor feared for the loss of Ashley's credits and had the nerve to ask if there'd been some trauma at home recently. Apparently, Ashley was making no effort at all to get to her classes, and none of her friends had any idea where she was. Diane explained the situation again, but her confidence that Ashley was merely AWOL was wearing off. The girl was completely incommunicado, even with people she supposedly liked—no MSN, no emails, no text messages. Nothing. Her daughter was missing, and Diane had to face the unspeakable shame that it took almost four weeks before she actually cared. What kind of a mother was she? After three years, she had come to believe that she was unworthy of her daughter and that both she and Joe did not deserve to have had a child at all. Ashley had been a bad ass for that last two years, but Diane had never once wondered why the change had occurred. What had made Ashley so angry so suddenly? Did Ashley somehow know how shallow and conditional her parents' love for her was?

By the time she'd realized that Ashley was truly gone and not trying to get attention or make a point, Diane tried to interest the police again, but the case still didn't mobilize them. Too many kids on the street. They would keep her picture on their missing persons database: that's about all they could promise. They'd need a body before their interest was piqued. And that, Diane hoped and prayed, would never happen. A private detective had had no better luck, but hiring him had caused a nasty fight between her and Joe. He called it a waste of money. It had been, but only because the man had found nothing, not one trace of Ashley. Every action had been a waste.

But the phone calls had changed everything. The possibility of a second chance was like the first glimmer of clear blue sky in years of foggy grey. Diane could be a better mother; she knew that now. She was ready for the fourth call. No tricks, no pleading. Just tell Ashley the truth—that they were shit for parents and they wanted a second chance. That they would do right by her this time: let her choose her friends, her clothes, her career. Ashley could be a tattoo artist for all Diane cared; she could take her MENSA IQ and work at Wal-Mart if she wanted to. No more lies—only truth between them. Diane was prepared to admit her own vanity and shallowness, but Ashley needed to know that despite all her faults, Diane loved her daughter more than either of them had ever suspected.

But when the fourth call came, Joe answered.

"Hello."

Silence.

Diane saw his brows knit in annoyance.

"Who's this?"

Diane signalled frantically, mouthing her message: *It's her! It's her!* Joe rolled his eyes and turned his back.

"If you have something to say, say it. I think you owe us an explanation."

Diane ran for phone in the office and pushed *Talk*. "Ashley, honey, it's me. I was a terrible mother and I'm sorry. Please forgive me, forgive us. Please give us a second chance. We can do better."

Nothing.

She'd already hung up.

"No! Please, no! Ashley!"

"Hang up that phone right now. Don't you ever pick up another line when I'm on the phone." Joe came toward her to grab the receiver.

"Don't touch it. You said the wrong thing."

"Oh, did I? And you've been so successful?"

"We were bad parents Joe. She's twenty now. We can't give her orders anymore. We just have to get her to come home."

"Don't be an idiot. She comes back on our terms."

"No…no. She comes back. That's all. I have no terms. I want my daughter."

"Have you forgotten what she was like? She made this house a hell to live in."

"It doesn't matter. She gave us fifteen wonderful years, too. We should have talked to her; we should have done things differently."

"She despised you and your business and everything you stood for. She referred to you as the 'plastic bitch' when talking to her friends. She stole money, smoked in our house, drank our liquor, and treated us like dirt under her feet. Unless she's ready to apologize and promises to change her attitude and behaviour, quite frankly, she's not welcome here."

"I don't care…I don't care. I just want her to be okay, to know I love her anyway."

"Well then, maybe this is your lucky day."

"Why?"

"Because despite your pathetic little outburst a moment ago, she did speak to me."

"What? What did she say?"

"She said, 'Make sure there's a present for me under the tree this year.' Doesn't sound like she's changed much to me."

"She's coming home for Christmas! I knew it! I've sensed it! Oh, Joe, thank you!" Diane threw her arms around him. "Let's go shopping right now. The stores are open late." Diane held both of his hands and smiled. "We are going to be a family again, honey!"

Joe pulled his hands out of her grasp, walked to his desk chair, and turned on his computer. "Honestly, babe. Haven't you liked our life these last three years? Hasn't it been easier?"

"I don't want easy anymore, Joe. I haven't felt this happy for so long."

"I thought we had it pretty good."

"Don't you have any love at all for Ashley? I don't understand how you can be so cold."

"I loved our daughter once. She ruined it. If she wants it back, she'll have to earn it. That's the way it is, Di. That's who I am."

The screen of the computer made Joe's face look blue. For a second, he didn't look like her husband at all. For a second, she hated him. She left the office and quietly picked up the phone he'd answered in the kitchen. She recorded the number on the screen, put her cell phone in her purse, and drove herself to a crowded mall.

"Hello." Somebody was answering the number. This was different.

"Hello. Ashley? It's Mom."

"Sorry, you must have the wrong number. There's no Ashley here."

"Please don't hang up. My name is Diane Rackley. I'm trying to find my daughter. She called from this number."

"Mrs. Rackley? You're married to Joe Rackley who teaches math at Leaside?"

"That's right. Did you just call our house?"

Pause. "Uh, yes. I spoke briefly to your husband. He's been tutoring my daughter Jess in calculus."

"It can't be. He said my daughter called. I haven't heard from her in three years."

"I'm so sorry, Mrs. Rackley. I can't imagine what that must be like."

Diane was flustered, not ready to give up her great joy, not ready to accept her husband's lie. "What did you want? What would make you call two days before Christmas? Doesn't he have a right to a holiday?"

"Mrs. Rackley, I'm sorry. I just wanted to be sure he understood that there would be no more private math lessons. He's been terribly persistent with Jess."

"What?"

"My daughter. He's been tutoring her. She's not great at math, but she needs it for university. Your husband has coached many weak students to an 80 percent."

"I don't understand. He gives extra help to lots of kids."

"Yes, but we've been paying him to work privately with Jess. He does charge for that, not that we mind."

"Then why are you stopping the lessons? What do you mean by him being persistent?"

"I'd rather not say. You've been through so much, Mrs. Rackley. You both have. I can understand needing to replace your daughter, but some things just aren't appropriate."

"What do you mean?"

"Please… I'm uncomfortable talking to you about this. You should be talking to your husband. I have no intention of taking this any further as long as he leaves Jess alone. Jess knows she can't call him and he can't call here anymore."

Diane's hands were shaking. The car was frigid. "Jess has been calling our house?"

"She's only seventeen. She doesn't know better. Your husband put way too much on her shoulders. She can't be responsible for his emotions."

"Why has she been calling us? I need to know."

"Mrs. Rackley, I'm a sympathetic person and your husband's a pretty special teacher. The kids love him. My daughter loves him. But, well, he told her that he needed her to help him get over the loss of your daughter, that being near Jess made him feel less lonely. I'm sorry, but that's way too much for a teenager to deal with. I don't know what all went on in those tutoring sessions, but… I picked her up once, and he was pushing her hair off her face. Jess said it was because she was crying. I don't know. I'll give him the benefit of the doubt. But I don't want them near each other again. I have to protect my baby girl."

Diane stared at a young couple loading parcels into the trunk of their Subaru.

"Mrs. Rackley? Are you there? Are you okay?"

Silence.

"I'm hanging up now. Please keep your husband away from my daughter. Good luck to you."

Click.

She didn't think of it till later that night while watching the late news and waiting for Joe to fall asleep. Did Jess smoke? Diane was sure the caller had been smoking!

Diane was up very early on Christmas morning. Every molecule of her being wanted to not be in the same building—let alone the same bed—as her husband, but the mother's intuition in her was so sure that Ashley would be there Christmas morning. She just couldn't jeopardize that moment. She wanted to come down the stairs and see a rumpled Ashley asleep on the couch, waking up groggily to hot chocolate and a hug that would never stop.

But there was just an envelope taped to the front door. Diane knew whom it would be from and who had written it—not the same person. She slit it open quietly and saw exactly what she'd expected.

Dear Mom, I'm sorry but I can't do it. I'm really happy where I am now, and I'm not quite ready to be in your lives again. I do love you. I know you did your best. It's not over. Love, Ashley.

Diane dropped the letter on the table by the front door and went to the closet. Intuition aside, she had prepared herself for this moment. She grabbed the large suitcase and a box of photo albums, and pulled on her warmest leather coat and boots. She very quietly made two trips to the car, which she had left out in the driveway the night before. Joe may or may not have been awake, but Diane was pretty sure he was waiting for her to leap into their bed with the letter, declaring herself happy and disappointed at the same time—that their daughter was alive and still loved them but was not coming home this Christmas. He would comfort her then, and they would have another quiet, dignified day of opening tasteful gifts and listening to Handel's Messiah.

Diane wondered what he had done with their daughter. Had he molested her? How long had he molested her? Was he capable of murdering his own child? She was pretty sure that something had gone very wrong, that Ashley's rage was more than justified. But had he driven her away? Was he still threatening her? She had so many questions—and only one answer. Her husband was sick and dangerous, and she was going to be his worst nightmare. There must be other students who were inappropriately dealt with, other mothers who'd felt uncomfortable taking the situation further. Well, this mother was going to the police, then she was going to the principal, then she was going to every guidance counsellor in the school. Joe's life was about to get very nasty.

Blood on the Holly

Christmas lights were coming on in streets all over Cabbagetown: moms and dads up early with kids in pyjamas asking to open just one present before breakfast. Diane loved this morning more than any other morning of the year—a day dedicated to family. In her own way, she was dedicating this day to Ashley, promising to search until either she found her or died trying. No stone would be left unturned. Other detectives would be hired. The police would be harassed day and night.

When her cell phone rang, Diane didn't answer. It would be Joe, coming downstairs and wondering why his blueberry pancakes weren't ready. That life was over, and she could not have summoned enough saliva to speak to the man for one second. No, she would not even give him the satisfaction of responding. This meant Diane didn't get the message till she stopped for gas at the first open station and pulled out the phone to call her own mother. There was a short text message, and it wasn't from Joe after all.

Hey mom. Took u long enough. I'm at the Starb's on Bloor St. I'll order u a capp, but u'r $ing. C U SOON! A.

Sandy Conrad lives on the Saugeeen River near Paisley, Ontario, with her husband, Ian, and an ever-changing menagerie of rescued dogs and cats. She teaches high school English and has written a number of plays and short stories. Her first success in the mystery genre was winning the Scene of the Crime Mystery Festival's short story contest in 2005, but her real delight has been meeting so many talented and interesting people with a passion for stories and a glass of good red wine.

Mamma's Girl

Mary Keenan

*A*lan took Eleanor's elbow and pulled her back onto the curb as a Packard lumbered around the corner.

"That was a narrow escape."

Eleanor laughed this off and leaned a little closer than Alan's grip on her arm strictly required. "I suppose he didn't see us. I should carry an electric torch if that street lamp is going to go on burning out every other week."

"I'd like to see you in a safer place," Alan told her. "Someplace where no harm could ever come to you."

"This one isn't so bad," she said.

They were across the street now and passing a newsstand that had been decorated with an amateurishly painted Christmas wreath and a sagging garland. The front page of today's paper was strapped onto a board by way of advertising, and when another car rushed along the street, its headlights revealed that the police were still baffled in the case of the East Side Strangler.

Eleanor glanced at her companion, but preoccupied with adjusting his hat to prevent its blowing off, he had obviously not seen it. She decided to say nothing. For days now, the strangling of a wealthy industrialist in an east end alley—a crime without a known motive—had pushed even the war in Europe off the top of the front page. The story was the primary topic of conversation at Denton's Department Store, where she spent her days and earned her keep. She was thoroughly sick of it.

"You'll come in for a cup of coffee?" she asked at the door of the house where she and her younger sister, Lucille, had a flat.

"Of course."

Once inside, Eleanor had a shock. Lucille was home in spite of having told her sister that she was to sleep over at a friend's house, the better to assist her in preparing for a Christmas luncheon party the next day. At least, she was still fully dressed. Eleanor didn't like to see such a young girl parading about the flat in a satin dressing gown at the best of times—with Lucille's blond curls, too, it seemed so decadent, so fast—but when Alan was there, it was quite painful. Even in her skirt and pullover, however, Lucille could make trouble. When Eleanor came back from the kitchen and her coffee-making duties, she found Lucille standing in the hallway staring at Alan, who had leaned back on the sofa and closed his eyes.

He did make a lovely picture there next to their little Christmas tree, with his hat off and his overcoat open to reveal the expensive and uniquely patterned scarf he'd bought just a few weeks ago. His suit, where exposed, suggested the finest tailors. No wonder people constantly mistook him for Cary Grant. It wasn't just the cleft in his chin or the haircut Alan cultivated to look as much like the star as possible. Though he never mimicked Mr. Grant's voice, he copied his manner of speech and his style of movement. Eleanor remembered how pleased she had been when she met Alan in the fall and how much more so when he immediately asked her out to lunch.

Checking these thoughts, Eleanor touched her sister's arm. "Lucille, you must get off to bed. It's so late, you'll be exhausted tomorrow."

Lucille wrinkled her pretty nose. "But you're up, and you have to work in the morning, too. And," she added slyly, "you know Mamma would have wanted you to have a chaperone, with a man in the house."

"Mamma would have known that I of all people don't need a chaperone. When you're twenty-eight like me, you'll thank me for sparing you a late night at eighteen."

"You still think I'm a little girl!" Lucille stormed suddenly. "Won't you be surprised when you find out just how grown up I really am!"

Eleanor, embarrassed, looked over at Alan and was relieved to see he had not moved so much as an eyelid.

"Come now, Lucille. You know we've been over this before." She ran her hand affectionately along her sister's arm, but Lucille twisted away and moved swiftly down the hall without another word. That she was still angry was amply illustrated by the sound of the lock turning in her bedroom door, a sound that gave Eleanor much more satisfaction than Lucille could have imagined.

The couple enjoyed their coffee in the sitting room at the front of the house, Alan remaining on the low sofa, Eleanor on a cushion she'd thrown on the floor beside him. After she'd taken his cup and set it beside her own on the end table, she rested her neat dark head on his chest. He had taken off his overcoat by now, but left the scarf in place. The silk was exceptionally soft under her cheek.

"This is a lovely thing," she said, feeling that since he had left it on, he was prompting her to take notice of it. She did so, tracing with her fingertip the elaborate design at the ends—long horizontal bands of gold that terminated in a single tassel, which she presumed had replaced, in the name of the latest fashion, the more commonly seen fringe. One of the two had been slightly damaged some time before, and as it had not yet been repaired, she ignored it in favour of the other. Alan placed a high value on perfection.

"It's certainly very practical."

"Yes, it must be warm."

"It has other advantages. I killed a man with it."

"What a useful skill!" Eleanor said immediately. "I must help to keep you in practice. I had a customer today who I felt very strongly deserved no better fate."

"I suppose you were tempted to strangle him with that little scarf of your own?" Alan gazed with a half-smile at the square she had wrapped around her throat to keep the wool of her sweater from scratching her skin.

"No, indeed. Can you imagine: a clerk disposing of holiday shoppers in that way? The management would have something to say about it, I'm sure."

"It's getting late," Alan said abruptly, prompting Eleanor to sit up. He rose from the sofa and collected his overcoat.

"I have an idea," he said easily. "Why don't we walk down the hall together and open the front door and then close and lock it without my going outside? Just in case Lucille is listening."

Eleanor paused; they were not on these terms. However, it seemed her agreement was not required as he slipped his hand affectionately but firmly under her elbow and propelled her down the hall.

"I'm having some trouble with my landlord, you see," he went on. "I won't be any trouble to you at all, but it would help me enormously to have another place to stay tonight. The pillow you keep on the sofa will be sufficient."

Eleanor tried to show she could take this in stride.

"We can do better than that," she told him. "You must let me throw in a blanket or two."

"No need." They were at the door now, and Alan opened and shut the door just as he had said he would. "And now you should get ready for bed, I think. I'll settle myself in for the night; no need for you to check on me again. The bathroom would be your next destination, wouldn't it? A nice long bath would be very relaxing for you after the difficult customer you had today."

She heard the dark undertone in his voice and thought it best not to argue the point. "A hot bath would be very pleasant indeed," she told him. "It's kind of you to suggest it."

As she ran the bathwater, Eleanor tried to fix her attention on the furniture that surrounded her. It was an unusually large bathroom, which, she suspected, had been a small bedroom for a servant or three before the house was divided into flats. It was a lucky chance since it had allowed her to keep some of Mamma's more awkward furniture after her death. The patio set, for example—a small, round table and two chairs intended for a garden and useless on the third floor of an apartment house—could not be affected by the damp and served perfectly for sitting to undress or for piling up a change of clothes.

The hat stand, too—so convenient for hanging up one's night things. She had come into the bathroom directly as instructed, and it was a relief to think that even her dressing gown was here waiting for her when she finished her bath. She supposed she would have to take that bath, she thought uncomfortably, watching the tub fill slowly and listening to the pipes pounding at irregular intervals. Alan would expect her to have the bath; he'd listen for her to get in and out of it, for the water to swish around in its distinctive way. And then…what? Would she be allowed to go quietly to bed? She did not fear for her virtue, but there were other things, so many other things. She was glad that, having come home unexpectedly, Lucille had at least seen fit to lock her door.

The pipes clattered to a standstill when Eleanor turned off the taps. When they were silent again, she stopped, one foot poised above the water, to listen. What had she just heard? A footstep outside the door? Someone's arm brushing along the wall of her bedroom? A branch rubbing against the window outside? Whatever it was, it was not repeated. Taking a deep breath, Eleanor stepped into the tub.

She allowed exactly five minutes for her bath, lying quietly and listening, straining to hear the least sound, until she remembered to swish the water around so that Alan, if he cared, would know she was still exactly where he'd told her to be. This duty complete, she rose and dried herself off and dressed, watching the water drain away until you couldn't drown so much as a fly in it.

It was silent in the hallway. The lights were out in the living room, but Eleanor could not pick up a hint of Alan's breathing—in sleep or otherwise. She could not possibly check to see if he was really there, she knew that. He had told her not to. All that was left was to move down the hall to her bedroom, avoiding if possible those parts of the wood flooring that squeaked. If Lucille was by any chance asleep, her sister wanted her to stay that way.

It was no good thinking, Eleanor told herself sharply as she snapped on the light in her bedroom. Either Alan would be here or he would not be here, and if he was, she could fight. She was prepared. Of course, he himself had set her on her guard, telling her about the scarf like that. Or had he been teasing her? Testing her, even? Maybe he didn't know what she knew. Or maybe he did, and he had come to a decision about it. He knew she was not the kind of woman to shield a killer, no matter how much she might have thought herself in love with him two days ago.

Only two days ago! Eleanor sank down onto the side of the bed and took off her slippers. How long ago that seemed. All the worry and the bustle—for of course, with all the news and talk of the East Side Strangler, she had realized immediately the meaning of that short strip of braided gold thread found clutched in the dead man's hand, had known what it meant. It was the only clue the police had. She could imagine in horrifying detail how it had come to be there, dangling as it must have been from the loose end of that soft, unyielding fabric as Alan pulled even tighter on the efficiently small segment that was applied to cut off all hope of air and life.

Eleanor dropped her hand from her own throat and forced herself to breathe deeply, slowly, calmly. She was perfectly safe. Perfectly safe, she repeated to herself as she surveyed the room. Her closet door was slightly ajar, but she would not investigate it any more than she would the shadowy corner behind Mamma's tall wardrobe or the space behind the curtains.

Still mouthing these two precious words, she turned down her bed, got up to turn out the light, and slipped under the blankets.

She had not locked her door. The police had told her not to, and she had followed their instructions to the letter, from getting Lucille out of the flat—though that hadn't proved successful—to obeying Alan, no matter how strange his request. And it had been strange, she told herself as she lay there in the dark. Not the request to stay overnight, of course. She had expected that. The police had told her they would make it known to Alan that his own apartment was not safe. They wanted him to spend the night with Eleanor, suspecting that something might happen to their advantage if he did. There was some complication in their case, it seemed, some reason that Alan's possession of a scarf with a string missing from its tassel might be insufficient to prosecute as they wished to do.

She was a kind of bait, she supposed, if a willing one. A willing—and definitely curious—one.

Why had he insisted she take that bath? To buy time? To reassure Lucille that everything was completely normal? To be sure, she did sometimes take a bath after a stressful day, though not if Lucille had already gone to bed. The noise of the pipes were certain, in that case, to wake the girl, and Mamma would not have been pleased, having taught each of her daughters always to consider the convenience and rights of others, no matter how small the instance. Poor Lucille had not been entirely successful in this lesson, Eleanor sometimes thought, but she put the occasional sign of selfishness or deceit—if that wasn't too strong a word—to her youth. In spite of tonight's outburst, Lucille was in many ways still a child, not much older or wiser than she had been when Mamma died so many years ago. It had been Eleanor's task to look after Lucille and protect her, if possible, from…well, the past, for want of a better expression.

Guilt crept into her bones, and Eleanor had just acknowledged how poor a job she was making of the former tonight when a small sound leapt out of the dark.

A click. The kind of click a door makes when the knob is turned and its closing mechanism is snapped back into its sheath. It couldn't be Lucille's door, she told herself desperately. The bolt she had used to lock it would roll, not click. It must be her own. She stared, willing the thin light from the window to gather itself on the doorknob. Was it turning? Was the door opening? She could not tell, but surely a creaking would be next as the hinges yielded to pressure from a determined visitor?

Several creaks did come to her ears, but they weren't long or plaintive enough to come from a set of hinges. It didn't make sense. Who was in the hallway? If neither her own door nor Lucille's had been the source of that click, what was left to cause it? Could it have been a gun? Eleanor knew so little about guns and whether or not they clicked, but surely it could not be a gun. Alan had his weapon. He had brought it with him. She willed herself to lie still in the bed, trusting the police, believing clear through from the guilt that still lay in her bones to the embroidered flowers on her nightdress that they would protect both her and Lucille from whatever terrible thing might happen next.

Another click. This time closer, so close that Eleanor scorned herself for having considered the last click to be so near as her own door. It had not been, but this one was near. It was her own doorknob; she could actually see it turning, her eyes straining as if, by reaching out of her skull, they could hold the doorknob in place and prevent the entrance of whoever might be on the other side.

And now the creaking she had expected, the familiar whine of the hinges Eleanor never remembered to oil. Eleanor lay very still, fear washing a kind of peacefulness over her body. She wondered if this was what death felt like.

"Eleanor?"

It was Lucille—Lucille's soft, familiar voice!

"Can't you sleep, dear?" Eleanor said evenly. She mustn't let on to Lucille that anything was wrong, but oh, how she wished her sister were back safely in her own room with the door locked.

That was when she caught a glimmer of the truth. Lucille's door had been locked. Why hadn't she heard the lock roll back before the click, before the creaking of the floor? The only explanation was that the door had been unlocked already, when Eleanor would not have been able to hear it. When she was running or draining her bath.

The peacefulness that had come through the fear was gone now. Eleanor had never felt more alive. Certainly, she had never felt more determined to stay that way.

"I thought perhaps you might not be able to sleep," Lucille said gently, affectionately. Had she not been so alert, her sister might have missed the menacing undertone. "After our argument. You do worry so much about crossing me, don't you, Eleanor."

"I want you to be happy," she agreed. "I am always very sorry when you see me as the cause of your unhappiness."

Lucille sat down on the side of the bed, causing the mattress to slump slightly. "It's hard on you to be my mother and my sister, too."

"I hope I don't seem to complain about it."

"No, you never complain, but I see your difficulty, however much you may think I don't appreciate it. That's why I thought…"

Eleanor waited.

"Really, it's better if we are apart now, Eleanor. I am eighteen, and though you may not know it, I've been living my own life for some time. The only problem is that you have all the money, dear. You've been so good about saving it, working at the department store to cover our expenses so that we have what Mamma left us to use for a rainy day. But I have a use for it now. I want to go away, and I have a good idea you'll tell me I shouldn't and keep the money from me. Because I want to go away with a man," Lucille said, giggling as she emphasized the last word.

"Mamma wouldn't—"

"Mamma wouldn't want me to do that. And neither will you when you know which one I mean. But we don't want to make you unhappy, Alan and I. We don't want you to fuss about us or worry. And he really can't stay here, Eleanor. Not after killing that man."

It couldn't hurt to satisfy her curiosity, not now. "Why did he kill him?"

"He insulted your sister," Alan said from the door, a trace of humour in his voice. "He gave her some jewellery and wanted it back when he found out his wife was expecting it as a Christmas present."

Eleanor turned back to her sister. "If you have the jewellery, why not just pawn it? Then you wouldn't need Mamma's money at all."

Lucille took her sister's hands in her own and laughed again. "Because, Eleanor, you can't pawn something the police are looking for. I probably won't even be able to wear it, except in private," she added coyly, flashing an all-too-sophisticated look at Alan. "Besides, we know what a fine upstanding character you have. You'd never let us go; you'd tell the police all about us. Oh, it would be hard for you, naturally. But you'd do it. Mamma would have wanted you to."

Abruptly, she pressed Eleanor's wrists into the mattress, pinning the older girl's arms. "You can ask her if that isn't so, just as soon as you see her."

Alan moved forward then, the scarf already twisted in his hands.

"No!" Eleanor cried. She had just enough time to think what a poor rejoinder this was to everything Lucille had said to her. Then she blacked out.

It wasn't for long, and she got nowhere near Mamma. When her eyes fluttered open, it was to see the overhead light glaring down and the room in disarray: curtains shoved to one side, closet door wide open. A pair of police officers held Lucille and Alan in handcuffs, while three others hovered nearby. Someone else, the detective she had met with after she first recognized Alan's scarf, was rubbing her hands and repeating her name.

"Miss Foxworth," he said, his voice breaking in its urgency, "are you all right?"

"I'm all right," Eleanor said, her attention fixed suddenly on her sister's face. It was astonishing how much, in her current snarling state, Lucille looked like Papa, that awful man who had been convicted of murder all those years ago and never regretted since. She had never understood until this moment Mamma's demand on her deathbed that Eleanor do everything in her power to keep Lucille from doing wrong. Well, a mother's insights were different from a sister's after all—she had done her best and could wash her hands of it, just as they had with Papa. She knew Mamma would say so.

"I'm all right," she repeated, turning her head and her gaze to the reassuringly sane eyes of her rescuer. "I don't have anything to trouble me now."

Mary Keenan is a writer and editor whose short stories have appeared in Storyteller magazine and the Ladies' Killing Circle anthology Fit To Die. *Her former weakness for knitting freakishly large sweaters was the subject of an essay for the original KnitLit, published by Three Rivers Press. She celebrates her new and improved procrastination techniques with a sometimes-current blog on her Website at www.marykeenan.com*

The Hounds of Winter

D. J. McIntosh

*L*ilacs lined my front walk. The bushes had grown so old they'd reached the size of small trees. I scraped a hole in the window frost and saw they looked the same—cracked and hunched over like old men—as all the other trees in the little landscape of our street. The storm was taking a heavy toll.

On Christmas Eve, the power failed and the pipes burst. No serviceman would come to my rescue. My only choice was to make the trek from old Montreal over to Grandmother's. Not a great option because, under the best conditions, I was afraid to walk alone after dark. *Keep to the safe streets. A woman can never be too careful,* Grandmother liked to remind me.

The echo of her words seemed to follow as I put on my parka with its snug red hood and packed a Christmas cake and a bottle of her favourite sherry in my little hamper. I left, taking some comfort in the knowledge that soon Grandmother would fold me under her wing and this hardship would fade away like a bad dream.

The storm fought me every step of the way. A huge willow moaned when it split down the centre, its trunk actually turning in a vain effort to ward off destruction. Telephone poles teetered like drunken soldiers on some arctic battlefield. For a few wild moments, I panicked, fearing the ice would rise up in an angry wave to claim me. Of course, that was impossible. "Calm down," I told myself. "You'll make it. You will."

Turning onto a street so narrow it seemed more like a laneway, I noticed the familiar store signs: *Boulangerie, Dépanneur.* The street was black and deserted, windows empty holes, doors frozen shut. Everyone was at home, breaking out the rum and eggnog, hugging relatives who bustled in with arms full of gifts, laughing and brushing the icy chips off their coats, kisses all around. My Christmas Eve would be more placid, although with its own quiet pleasures. I'd listen to Grandmother's gentle tones as she read the Nativity story—an annual tradition—while I drank a cup of hot apple cider and snuggled under an old down comforter.

Should I take this shortcut? Keep to the safe streets. Grandmother's words of warning seemed to hang suspended in the frozen air. But I was still weak from my recent hospital stay and bone-weary from struggling through the tempest. I decided to take it.

Looking up to get my bearings, I saw lights after all. As I approached, they grew stronger. Christmas lights. A string of bulbs—red, white, and green—circling a store window. Inside the window, a fibreglass Santa raised a mittened right hand in a wave; in his left, he grasped a bag of toys. Above this, a small neon sign flashed on and off: *Bar Café, Bar Café.*

I stumbled and slipped on the glassy sidewalk, a weak *Ho Ho Ho* emitted by the Santa when I crossed the threshold. Ashamed of how I must look—even my eyebrows were caked with ice—I stopped and registered a moment of shock. It was empty. A small place: ten or twelve tables at most, each covered with red gingham oilcloth. Oilcloth. I hadn't seen that since I was little.

Someone had made a half-hearted attempt at Christmas decorations: red and gold balloons hanging like a row of limp sausages, a string of icicle lights. A lingering scent of balsam drifted over from a small Christmas tree parked in one corner.

The screen on a TV fixed to the wall flickered as the image of the weather forecaster spoke earnestly into the camera against a backdrop of freezing rain. Normally, I wouldn't have set foot in a dump like this. Better here, though, than freezing to death on some dark street.

As my eyes became adjusted to the weak light, I did spot someone. A dim figure hunched over a table next to the rear wall at the end of the bar. His back was turned to me. Probably some loser who occupied the same chair every night for as long as anyone could remember, with beer breath and a gut the size of Niagara spilling over his trouser belt. Not even the storm could get in the way of his regular date with a Blue.

I flipped off the hood of my parka, pushed my matted wet hair back from my forehead, and wiped my face with my scarf. A rustle came from the dark hole behind the counter. Thankfully, a woman emerged. She looked in her early twenties, a real low-life with the face of a rodent. Bright beady eyes and a twitchy little mouth.

"*Vous êtes venue par l'orage.*"

I could read a little French but had never mastered the spoken word. She may as well have been speaking Mandarin.

"You came through the storm," she repeated.

No, I just flew in on the Concorde (of course, I didn't say this). The woman had the intellect to match a lab rat that failed the maze. I forced up the corners of my lips to fabricate a smile. "Thank God you're open; I couldn't have made it much further."

"Are you on your way home?"

"No, I'm going to the Plateau District, my grandmother's place on Rue Dorien."

The woman looked out the window and shook her head sympathetically. "You must be freezing. Can I get you a sweater?" She took in my dripping hair. "Or a towel?"

"Can I get some coffee, some hot food… What do you have?"

She shrugged her shoulders. "Sorry, no, we ran out and nothing's open I can get to. Booze only."

Before I beseeched her to ransack the cupboard and find something—anything—to eat, she reached behind the counter and pulled out a package of chips and some peanuts wrapped in ancient cellophane. At this point, I would take anything to staunch the ache in my stomach. In the process of ripping open the package of chips, I heard a voice float up from the end of the bar.

"A hot toddy is what's needed on a night like this. Nothing else drives away the winter spirits quite so effectively." His speech had a brittle quality, like the sound of glass breaking on ice.

I'd forgotten about the occupant of the rear table. He scraped back his chair, reached into his pocket, and tossed a five on the bar. He glanced at the mouse. "Do you know how to make one?"

Without waiting for an answer, he said, "Two ounces of liquor. I prefer rum to whisky, but double that amount on a night like this. Mix in a teaspoon of honey and the juice of a quarter lemon. You do have that at least?"

She nodded.

"Top it off with hot water and make sure the glass is good and hot before you put it in." To me, he issued a command. "You'll join me."

This was the last thing I wanted, but I didn't have the energy for an argument.

I shrugged off my parka, faked another smile, and moved over to the proffered chair. It was the one next to the wall. I would have to push past him if I wanted to leave, but I took it anyway. A pair of kid gloves was tucked into the side flap of my purse. I pulled them on to warm my hands and stave off the germs I imagined were swarming this place by the wagon-load.

An army-surplus coat was draped over the back of his chair; a glass, half empty, and a folded newspaper sat on the table. I got a better look at him and realized he was not as old as I'd initially assumed: early forties, at most. A very ordinary face. But what big eyes and ears he had! It made his entire countenance appear oddly distorted.

His hair and eyebrows were iron-grey, and his skin had a pale, almost translucent quality. He gave me the once-over, his eyes dropping to the outline of my breasts. I crossed my arms over my chest, grateful for the bulky shirt I wore over my turtleneck.

"We take the weather so for granted." He mumbled this, revealing a set of large teeth with long, prominent canines.

A noise. I jumped at the sound, but it turned out to be Mousy scurrying over with my drink. She'd wrapped a tea towel around the glass to keep it hot. She'd got that right, at least. She flashed me a quick roll of her eyes, a signal from woman to woman that said: *That guy. What a loser.* I didn't trade eyes back with her, offended she'd think we had anything in common.

I put my hands around the glass, and it was blessedly hot. I tried to think of some way to take the initiative.

"My name's Elizabeth." I didn't extend my hand.

"Henri." He nodded. "You must have been pretty desperate to go out in that storm alone."

Was this the time to launch into my life story? To explain I only had Grandmother left and she was bedridden most of the time, too weak to venture outside her home? This man was definitely not soul-mate material. I had no intention of sharing anything personal with him. I tried to think of a way to change the subject and blurted out, "You don't seem to have a hat; your ears must get awfully cold in weather like this."

My face flushed red with embarrassment over that clumsy remark, but he didn't seem to take offence. He just tugged at his ear lobe.

"Ah yes, my oversized ears," he cackled. "All the better to hear you with, my dear." Then he slammed his hand down hard on the table. "Never underestimate the fury of a storm like this. There is no criminal as savage as that ice."

I'd been sipping my drink, loving the feel of the hot liquid slipping down my throat, but I was so shocked by this abrupt mood switch I gulped the rest down, burning my mouth in the process. My gaze fell on the folded newspaper; a black and white photograph took up most of the space. A man and a woman. I leaned closer and peered at the copy.

My God, it looked like him. Younger, certainly, but him all the same. The woman was seated in the foreground, laughing, her hair in curly tendrils framing a pretty, vibrant face. She was heavily made up, with a slice of dark lipstick and charcoal liner drawn around her eyes. A cigarette dangled from her right hand, the plume of smoke trailing off in curlicues. The caption read: *Francine and Henri Loupe in happier days/Early release for beating death of wife.*

I tried to drag in a breath. I wanted to race out the door, but I knew I'd probably make it only a few feet before I felt his teeth sink into my back. The media were full of warnings about cases like this: inmates released prematurely, only to repeat their crimes.

He watched me get up, walked over, and gripped my hand. Just as abruptly, he let go. "I'm sorry," he said. "It must hurt from the cold."

I looked at my hand and noticed his long nails had left red marks on my palm.

Spotting my empty glass, he yelled for the woman. "Elizabeth," he said, drawing out every syllable of my name, "needs another drink."

In truth, I was desperate for another one but didn't want to be obliged to him, so I reached into my handbag, pulled out my VISA, and waved it at her. She picked up the card and disappeared into the back.

A million red-hot needles punched into my hands, driving the numbness away: a sign my circulation was returning. Tears flooded my eyes, whether due to anxiety or pain

I did not know. I sank back in my chair and groped in my bag for my medication. Call me old-fashioned, but I preferred Valium to the newer drugs. It didn't make me as drowsy, and that was important because I seemed to need it more and more often. I swallowed two and topped them off with a couple of extra-strength Tylenol. Along with the alcohol, this would turn me into a zombie, but it was worth the risk.

While he waited at the bar, I listened to the ice thrash against the window glass and the wind groan like a wounded animal. How I hated this time of year.

"The hounds of winter pursue us again," I whispered. "If you listen closely, you can hear them howl. Before they are finished, they will have shaken and torn this city to shreds."

The mouse finally emerged with my drink and dumped it on the bar along with my card and Visa slip. Henri set them in front of me, then resumed his seat, pushing his lips into a grin that came out more like a leer. "There's no need to be afraid, you know."

He glanced down at the newspaper and then up at me. "Let me tell you about that couple." He pointed to the newspaper photo. "Those two were sleepwalkers moving through each day in a daze as if precious time stretched out before them with no limit. As it turned out, they were wrong to take life so for granted. The whole neighbourhood adored Francine. Sure, she liked a drink a little too often, and it was rumoured she took the occasional lover, although no one had ever actually witnessed her with another man. But she was forgiven for this. Living with Henri, they said, would drive anyone to it. Henri rose at the same time every morning, ate the same breakfast. Day in, day out, he left the house at precisely eight. At noon, he would walk over to the mall across the street from his office, pull out his *La Presse,* read and eat lunch for exactly one hour, then go home at six."

The one valuable I brought with me was my Cartier. Had he noticed it? I slid my hand onto my lap, undid the strap, and dropped the watch into my purse. My drinking "buddy" droned on.

"Henri despised winter. All he needed to hear was a weather report predicting snow and he'd be out with his bag of chunky rock salt, dumping the stuff everywhere. As soon as the first flakes began to fall, he'd work like a fury, removing every square inch off the drive, the walk, even the house."

He cleared his throat and reached for his glass.

This was my chance. I could make some excuse, pretend to go to the washroom, and leave quietly out the back way. The prospect of facing the storm again was almost welcome compared to spending another minute there.

He saw me begin to get up and shifted his chair to block my way. "I'm not used to having anyone to talk to. Please wait. It won't take much longer."

I was not taken in by this new gentler edge to his voice, but decided not to test his patience and sat down again. I tore strips off the Christmas paper napkin the mouse had provided: a tawdry looking thing with a design of red poinsettias along its border. I shredded the strips as he talked; they floated onto the tabletop like tiny flakes of grungy snow.

"One morning after a wicked storm, Henri had risen at five to begin the work of clearing the snow and ice. He left as usual at eight. Later that afternoon, a neighbour woman noticed Henri's car parked in the laneway behind his house and a broken window on the second floor. She found the back door open, a small drift of snow piled up on the kitchen floor. She climbed the stairs, passed the open bathroom door, and stopped, hardly able to believe her eyes. Francine's nude body lay submerged in the tub."

That was enough. I threw my bag into my hamper, grabbed my parka, and bolted out of the chair. I flew out the door without even pulling the zipper up. As I rushed down the street, I heard my name being called but did not dare look back.

A block or two away, I fell and turned to get up. Was that a shadow slipping in between two buildings? Could he actually be following me? Once, I thought I could hear footsteps scrape on the icy walkway behind me.

When I spotted the three tall oaks perched on the front lawn of Grandmother's house, I gasped in relief. The plastic wreath in the front window, with its three old-fashioned candles and tapered light bulbs for flames, felt like a beacon of hope.

I reached for the latch on the front door to Grandmother's flat, then drew back in surprise. The door was already open. I walked inside. The stillness of the living room was punctuated by the steady *tick tock* of the antique mantle clock. As if to announce my entry, the chimes sounded, ten in all, to ring in the new hour.

"Grandmother, are you there? It's Elizabeth."

There was no answer.

I took off my coat, peeked through her bedroom doorway. The bed had been stripped bare. There was no sign of her. Would Mrs. Corrigan have invited her to come upstairs so she didn't have to spend Christmas Eve alone? No. I remembered she'd gone to her son's for Christmas.

I went to the little alcove that served as a kitchen, thinking Grandmother may have left me a note, but there was nothing.

I heard the front door creak open. Henri Loupe stood in the doorway.

Suddenly, I understood. This was not the first time he'd been here.

"What have you done to my grandmother?" I cried.

"What are you talking about?" He grinned and held up my VISA card.

"You forgot this. I just wanted to bring it to you."

A convenient ruse. It didn't fool me.

He approached me with his hand held out. His fingernails appeared to lengthen and curve into claws; his teeth glistened. Was that a growl I heard coming from deep within his throat?

Blood sang in my ears. I reached behind me for one of the kitchen knives sitting in the wooden block holder on the counter. Despite the fear, a tiny corner of my brain was still capable of operating rationally. I refused to become another one of his victims.

I rushed toward him, holding the knife in front of me, and struck out with all my strength. A scream began to form; my vision seemed to fade. Then I blacked out.

I woke up prone on the floor. How long had I been unconscious? My right leg killed me, but I got up anyway. A trail of blood led to the front entrance. Grandmother would be horrified to see that mess. Using a tea towel—rinsing it in the kitchen sink and wringing it out over and over again—I managed to wipe the blood off the floor.

Now that the danger was over, I knew Grandmother would come back. I cut the fruitcake into precise little squares and got two cut-glass tumblers from the cupboard for the sherry. I put these on a tray along with folded linen napkins, not the paper serviettes she always said looked so cheap. A sprig of cedar from the shrubs outside added a festive air. When I finished, I folded the comforter around me, sat in the armchair and waited for her to return.

Montreal Gazette, December 27, 1997

BODY IDENTIFIED

The body of a man identified as Henri Charles Loupe was found Christmas Day in the laneway behind the house he once owned on Rue de Pin. The coroner has determined Loupe died from a knife wound to the abdomen. In a bizarre twist of fate, Loupe had recently been released from prison when a new forensic investigation cleared him of any responsibility for the death of his wife, Francine Loupe.

Elizabeth Anne Hill has been charged with second-degree murder and destruction of evidence in the course of committing a crime. Since childhood, Ms. Hill has been known to suffer from psychotic episodes dating back to Christmas Day 1972 when she was skating with her parents on Lac des Iles.

In this region, hunters bring hounds with them to flush out deer. The dogs are often abandoned when hunting season ends. Most die, but the survivors interbreed with wolves. Just such a pack emerged that Christmas Day from the brush along the shore of the lake, charging toward Ms. Hill's parents and driving them further out onto the lake where the ice was thinner. The girl watched in terror as her mother and father slipped through the ice and drowned.

Ms. Hill's most recent psychotic episode, requiring her to be hospitalized, was brought on by the death of her grandmother last month.

D.J. McIntosh, a former co-editor of Fingerprints, *the Crime Writers of Canada one-time newsletter, is a Toronto-based writer of short mystery fiction and is putting the final touches on her first novel* The Witch of Babylon, *which was short-listed for the Crime Writers Association's (U.K.) Debut Dagger Award in 2007. Her story, "A View to Die For," a runner-up for the Bloody Words Mystery Conference's Bony Pete Award, was subsequently published in* Bloody Words: The Anthology *in 2003.*

A Bigfoot Christmas

James Powell

Winters were a quiet time for Acting Sergeant Maynard Bullock of the Royal Canadian Mounted Police. The flowerbeds he patrolled on Parliament Hill, posing for tourists' cameras, lay frozen now, and his sidekick, Winnie-the-Peg—the bear with the wooden leg, scarlet tunic, and Stetson, with whom he often appeared on television supporting one good cause or another—had gone into hibernation. So come mid-December, Bullock put in for some well-deserved leave. Yesterday, he washed down the kitchen cabinets. Today, he would paint them as a surprise for good old Mavis, his wife who was away in Toronto visiting her mother.

Now as he sat over coffee and his morning stack of toast, Bullock opened the newspaper to find this headline: *FREAK ACCIDENT KILLS SANTA. John "Connie" Constable, a Santa at the Bay department store,* he read in astonishment, *was killed yesterday during the installation of a giant papier mâché shoe for the "There Was an Old Woman Who Lived in a Shoe" exhibit in Santa's Throne Room. A winch cable broke, sending the toe end of the shoe down onto Constable. It then swung back and forth in a small arc, snuffing out his life like a cigarette butt.* How ironic, thought Bullock, his old friend killed by a giant shoe.

He and Connie had started at the Mountie Academy together over twenty-five years ago. But in the middle of their first year, the top brass realized that when he graduated, Connie would be Constable Constable, which might make the Force the object of mirth. So Connie had been dismissed.

Soon after, Bullock's friend passed the civil service exam. Waiting for his first posting with External Affairs, he'd worked as a department store Santa. From then on, no matter where in the world he was, Connie always managed to get two weeks vacation at Christmas time and returned to his Santa job. He claimed that seeing the kids' eyes light up when he ho-ho-hoed was vacation enough. But Bullock suspected the scarlet tunic was the real draw.

He thought of their last get-together a mere three days before, when Connie had taken him to the Butterfly and Wheel, an Ottawa bar in the English-pub style. Outside, the snow was falling. In a corner near a side door, two codgers in rocking chairs played cribbage by the crackling fireplace. The bar was freshly decorated for Christmas. So was Constable who wore the full Santa regalia except for the beard and moustache, which, for ease in beer drinking, he had pulled down under his chin, giving him the appearance of an overdressed billy goat.

Bullock had just called attention to the scene outside the window. Winter had turned the Rideau Canal, which slanted through the heart of the city's downtown, into an ice rink fifteen kilometres long, crowded with skaters of all ages in bright winter gear. "A frozen cameo of Canada," said Bullock proudly. "We laugh in the face of winter."

But patriotic rhetoric wasn't going to distract Connie. He repeated what he had just said, his beard trembling earnestly. "Christmas, Bullock, Christmas. What better time for a surprise attack? One, they'd catch us off our guard. Two, it's a holiday they've never much cared for, them not being able to hang their stockings from the mantle-piece."

Bullock rolled his eyes heavenward. Once Connie got on the Bigfoot, you could never get him off. His first posting abroad had been Ulan Bator in Mongolia. This may have sparked his interest in the Bigfoot and their ilk: the Yeti and the Abominable Snowman—who, some say, were the famous Lost Tribes of Canada, members of the Sasquash nation after whom the province of Saskatchewan is named—who had migrated across the Siberian land bridge to Asia and into Europe thousands of years ago. (Once from Canberra, Australia, he sent Bullock a handbill advertising the Billabong Brothers' Circus with one act circled in red: Joey-Joey, the Kangaroo-Footed Boy. Another time, from Rome, it was a postcard with a picture of Donatello's bust of Pope Paul II, who, according to the printed information on the back, had issued a papal bull in 1469 banishing from Christendom those whose feet were so long they could not kneel to pray. Connie's message: "Having a wonderful time. Wish they were here.") Finally, Connie's Bigfoot paranoia became so marked that it earned him early medical retirement, and he returned to Ottawa to live with his sister.

"You're telling me the Bigfoot are here?" asked Bullock impatiently. "You mean Ottawa?"

"Oh, we've always had the native Bigfoot. But now they're converging on us from all around the world."

"Then, hell's bells, Connie, tell me this: Why haven't I seen any?" demanded Bullock.

"Maybe it's all this drive-in this and drive-in that," said Connie. "And all the cell phones in cars. Believe you me, you've got to keep your eyes peeled. Last October, out for a stroll, I saw one and he didn't see me. He was standing with a rake in the middle of a big pile of leaves and looking around with a gloat in his eye, like someday all this will be his. Suddenly, he raised this immense six-foot-long foot out of the leaves and gave himself a real good scratch behind the ear with it."

Bullock's snort of disbelief didn't deter Connie. "I've been nosing around," he added. "Got enough stuff to blow the whistle on them. I brought you here because it's one of their hangouts."

Before Bullock could snort again, Connie explained, "The wall-to-wall carpet's the give-away. They call it On-the-Town Brown."

An erect man with a trim moustache, bushy eyebrows, and a green and white wool cap with a Toronto Maple Leafs logo had entered by the side door and joined the cribbage players. Before he sat down. he gave Bullock and Connie a careful once-over.

"That's a Bigfoot bigwig," whispered Connie, who had quickly slipped his Santa beard back in place. "Watch this," he added. "Keep an eye on the cribbage players." He went over to the jukebox and punched in a selection. After a solemn drum roll. a military band struck up "Oh My Darling Clementine."

The two card players jumped to attention and stood with their hands over their hearts. The new arrival spoke to them sharply before shooing the pair ahead of him toward the side door. All three milled about for a minute before going outside. (Were they putting on their galoshes? wondered Bullock, who couldn't see because of the tables.)

With the record still playing, Connie came back, sat down, and pulled his beard down under his chin again. "Light she was and like a fairy, and her shoes were number nine. Herring boxes without topses, sandals were for Clementine."

"I know the words," said Bullock. "You and I sang them enough times around the bonfire at the Academy. So Clementine has big feet. So what?"

"So she's Queen of the Bigfoot, that's what. They thought she was lost and gone forever and they were dreadful sorry about that. Now she's come back to lead them in battle."

"But what the heck's this got to do with Canada? It's about the California Gold Rush in 1849."

Connie shook his head. "I think not. Try southern Saskatchewan. On the border. She was born near the forty-ninth parallel. Her father was excavating a mine there in Cavern Canyon."

"And is there such a place?" demanded Bullock. He must have hit a weak link in Connie's theory, for his friend looked away. Bullock pressed his advantage. "Look, Connie, remember how she drove her ducklings to the water every morning just at nine?"

"Sure," said his friend. "That's where she hit her foot on a splinter and fell into the river."

Bullock wagged a scolding finger. "'Into the foaming brine,'" he quoted. "Salt water. And that puts us right back on the California coast." Connie looked so crestfallen Bullock gave him a consoling slap on the arm. "Hey, you can't win them all," he said. "Well, time to make tracks."

As they left the Butterfly and Wheel, Bullock glanced over to where the cribbage players had been sitting. There were no rockers, just a table and a cribbage board. Connie saw his puzzled look. "The Bigfoot find it relaxing to arch their feet and rock back and forth on them," he explained.

Bullock snorted.

Outside, as they went their separate ways, Bullock noticed the guy in the Maple Leafs cap across the street watching them from behind a knee-high rampart of snow.

When Bullock called Connie's sister to offer condolences, she told him the funeral would be the next afternoon. He promised to be there. Then he got back to painting the kitchen. Good old Mavis had been fond of Connie and would regret missing the funeral. But he didn't expect her back until Christmas Eve, the day after tomorrow. She never missed the Debutantes' Ball, Ottawa's winter social season opener when all the young women entering society were presented to Her Excellency, Mrs. Bowes-Bouchard, Canada's first Governor General of part American Indian, part Asian Indian extraction.

This year, the Ice Palace where the Debutantes' Ball would be held was in the oriental style of Brighton's Royal Pavilion. The Mountie Academy cadets who built it with their chainsaws had interspersed the blocks of river ice with artificial ones, coloured bright reds, golds, and blues. Lit from inside, the Ice Palace shone so brightly that a Talking Head on CBC-TV declared it more suited to Aladdin's Cave than to a scene of homespun Canadian simplicity.

The Ice Palace would decorate the canal all winter and serve as the centrepiece of February's Winterlude festivities when the frozen canal hosted sulky, dogsled, and speed skating races, and all-round good clean outdoor fun.

The Debutantes' Ball was for the ladies, God bless them. But when Bullock dropped good old Mavis off, he would head further down the frozen canal for the annual curling match where the Prime Minister and his cabinet took on the Leader of the Opposition and his shadow cabinet. As a special treat this year, the match would be preceded by a visit from the band of the I Trampoli, the Italian regiment that marches in double time on stilts, harkening back to its early years clearing the Pontine marshes near Rome of *banditti*. There would also be a display of synchronized dogsled manoeuvres by one of Canada's most famous regiments, the Queen's Own Sledded Foot.

As Bullock stirred the paint pot, he reflected on the changes he'd seen on the Force over the years. Yes, the Mounties were out of sled work now. The Queen's Own Sledded Foot guarded the vast Canadian northland from enemy attack. Bullock smiled, remembering a game the Mounties used to play, crowded around an open fire on the trail or smoking their pipes on the porch of some lonely outpost. Overhead swung the constellation Orion with the dribble of stars down his pant leg. In the game, he became Sergeant O'Ryan of the RCMP and the six brightest stars strung out ahead of him were his dog team. Mounties vied to name the perfect team. Bullock remembered how fancy-dan the lead dog names could get, like Snow-

Strider, Wind Runner, Load Star, Master of the Storm, and Tundra Momma. In his heart, Bullock had named his lead dog Little Trotty Tugwell, but he never told the others, knowing it would get a big horselaugh.

A slanting snow was falling the afternoon of the graveside service. Bullock stood at the curb in front of his house in boots and breeks, short winter-issue coyote-fur jacket, and Stetson, for he believed his friend's heart had remained with the Mounties. Connie's sister had offered to pick him up in the undertaker's limousine on the way to the cemetery. She always seemed to him to be a level-headed type. Small, with short grey hair and a smoky voice, she had risen from the Ministry of Justice secretarial pool to a minor official capacity from which she was now retired.

Getting into the limousine with her, Bullock discovered a large cardboard box on the seat between them. "Here's Connie's Bigfoot stuff," she explained. "I'd like you to have it. Like a memento. I get the heebie-jeebies just having it in the house. I loved my brother. But on that subject, he was crazy as a bedbug."

She shook her head and gave a sad laugh. "A few years back, I told him flat out I didn't believe in the Bigfoot. Well, he smiled and said, 'Dollars to donuts you're working alongside one right now. You know, the eager beaver who's already at his desk when you get there in the morning and never takes a coffee break or hangs around the water cooler, the one who's still there plugging away when you and the others head for home.'"

She dabbed her eyes with a handkerchief wrapped in her fingers. "Well, he had me there," she said, "about the eager beavers, I mean. Back then, every office had a couple. But it never got them anywhere, promotion-wise. The civil service is big on conviviality, how you handle yourself at the water cooler or over drinks." She cocked her head. "Funny how the eager beavers went out about the same time the wall-to-wall came in."

Bullock knew what she meant. Some ten years before, a member of parliament from Saskatchewan accused the Prime Minister of sweeping scandals under the rug. To prevent a recurrence, he proposed installing wall-to-wall carpet in Parliament and the adjacent government office buildings. And so it was ruled.

For Bullock, Parliament, the Governor General (who represented the Queen, God bless her), and the civil service (that fine bureaucracy whose convivial competence kept the government humming like a well-oiled machine) were the three pillars on which Canada rested. Knock out any two of these pillars and the country would still stand: true, north, strong, and free.

The cemetery was a vast white landscape studded with snow-covered tombstones and monuments, Connie's grave a black gash in the ground surrounded by sections of artificial grass. The memorial service was windswept and mercifully brief. At the end, Bullock gave his old friend one of his snappiest salutes.

Then as he turned to get back into the limousine, he noted, several plots over, an excavation vehicle had broken the frozen earth to dig another grave. A bareheaded workman was standing in the hole up to his neck. Apparently he had been clearing out the broken clods of frozen earth but had stopped out of respect for the dead when the funeral cortege arrived. Now he pulled on a Maple Leafs cap and turned his head to match Bullock's stare, stroking his moustache thoughtfully.

When Bullock got back home, he took the cardboard box up to his office—as he now called the guest room where someday he hoped to write his autobiography, *That Man in Scarlet: The Reminiscences of Commissioner Maynard Bullock, RCMP (Ret.)*—and set it down on the card table, meaning to change out of his uniform and get back to painting. But curiosity made him look inside. The first thing he came to was a book from the Ottawa Public Library, titled *Canada and the Bigfoot Agenda*. Connie had used a Billabong Circus flyer to mark a place and had underlined the following passage in pencil:

> *Some say the Bigfoot has become extinct like the dodo. I say he may still prowl in Abyssinian forests, range still over Asiatic steppes, and lope the Arctic tundra far from the eyes of man. We may not see him. But he is watching us. How it must rot his immense socks to see what we have done to the land we have taken from him. Please God, may he never find a way to walk among us. If he ever does, Canada could well get a giant kick in the slats that might well prove our undoing. Then we would find ourselves the ones who are on the outside looking in.*

Bullock turned to the back of the book and discovered it had already been three days overdue the day Connie died. He thought for a moment before shaking his head. No, librarians wouldn't kill a man for that.

The phone rang. Connie's sister had arrived home to find her house broken into. Every dresser drawer in her brother's second-floor bedroom had been dumped out onto the floor and the mattress on the bed turned over. "The police just left," she said. "Can you come over? I've got something to show you, something I just couldn't show them."

When he got there, Connie's sister led Bullock around to the side of the house, pointing out the marks of the intruder's skis and ski poles coming and going across the lawn. Then she stopped under her brother's window. "The police couldn't figure how he could get in without a ladder. Here's what I wanted to show you." She pointed out two partial footprints on the first-floor window ledge. "My late-departed brother always insisted a full-grown Bigfoot standing on tiptoe on a first-floor window ledge could look through a second-floor window."

Before Bullock could snort, she added, "Oh, by the way, leaving for work the day he was killed, my brother asked me to remind him to call you when he got home. Something about Salt Springs, Saskatchewan."

The snow ended and evening brought a new weather front with thunder and the dim pulse of sheet lightning. Still wearing his scarlet tunic and boots, Bullock sat deep in thought at the guest-room card table, a half-eaten cheese sandwich curling at his elbow. Before him on the table was his atlas and the magnifying glass he'd used to follow the forty-ninth parallel across Saskatchewan until he came to Salt Springs at the juncture of the Big Moccasin and Little Moccasin rivers.

Then he'd gone through the rest of Connie's box, piling its contents on the table. First came a glossy stock prospectus for a company called Saskatoon Carpet and Sleeve. The name rang a bell. Hadn't they won the contract to wall-to-wall the Parliament buildings with their Civil Service Beige, as elegant a beige as you could find anywhere? Subsequently, the literature boasted, the same carpet had been introduced onto all Air Canada passenger flights, foreign and domestic. The prospectus also showed the company's other carpets: Snow White, Pavement Gray, Red Carpet Red, Grassy Green, and On-the-Town Brown.

This was followed by a newspaper clipping describing the tragic event of three years before when Canada's senior civil servants on their annual holiday outing to Niagara Falls had vanished during a trip on the *Maid of the Mist*. The ferry had entered the fog beneath the Canadian Falls, and when it reappeared an hour later, all the passengers, the crew, and the military band on board to provide music for the occasion had disappeared without a trace. By Godfrey, mused Bullock, what a giant step forward that must have been for the middle ranks of the Canadian civil service.

Were the senior civil servants dead, as some said, or had they moved to the States, lured by Washington's high salaries for seasoned bureaucrats? This last would certainly explain all the plastic raincoats with *Maid of the Mist* printed on the back that pop up on rainy days around the Capitol.

But by far the most puzzling things Bullock found were at the bottom of the box: two six-foot-long tubes of Civil Service Beige closed at one end and open and bound with elastic at the other. He looked inside each in turn. Nothing. He held the openings to his nose. They smelled of foot. Bullock sat staring thoughtfully ahead, trying to put the pieces of this complicated puzzle together. At last, he slipped the tubes on the ends of his boots and wagged them in the air.

As he did, a flash of sheet lightning illuminated a face in the window. In an instant, the window was dark again, but Bullock would never forget the malice of those eyes glaring in at him from beneath the Maple Leafs cap. When the lightning came again, the window was empty.

Bullock ripped off the carpet tubes and pounded down the stairs, grabbed his fur jacket and Stetson, and was out the door. He followed the marks of a cross-country skier across the lawn and out into the street. The lightning flashed again, just in time to illuminate his man as he disappeared around a far corner. Bullock set out after him though he knew his chances of catching up with a man on skis were slim.

He followed the tracks down a ramp to the snow-covered surface of the Rideau Canal where they blended in with many other ski tracks. Had his man headed downtown or out toward the suburbs? As Bullock stood there indecisively, a familiar sound came to him across the ice: the bells of the old horse-drawn sleigh used by the Mountie glee club, the Stout-Hearted Men, for their tunesome entry in the Winterlude festivities. The sleigh was heading back to the RCMP stables downtown after a glee club rehearsal. Bullock flagged it down with his Stetson.

No, said the driver; no skier in a Maple Leafs cap had passed him heading out of town.

Pleased with his luck, Bullock swung up onto the sleigh and told the man to pick up the pace. Soon Bullock's quarry came in view. When the man herringboned up an off-ramp, Bullock jumped down and followed close behind. After several snowy blocks, the man turned off into a narrow alley and disappeared, skis and all, through a back door illuminated by a bare light bulb on a gooseneck mounting.

Bullock tried the door, but it was locked. As he stared up at the building, several dogs started barking nearby. Turning back the way he'd come, Bullock stumbled over something under the snow. Then he stumbled again and would have lost his balance if someone hadn't reached out and grabbed two fistfuls of fur lapels to steady him. "G'die, mate," came an Australian voice. "What you sniffing around for?"

Bullock, struggling unsuccessfully to shake himself loose, decided to take the man down a peg. "I'm Acting Sergeant Maynard Bullock of the Royal Canadian Mounted Police," he said.

"Hell if you ain't, mate," said the man, shifting his weight to one foot. As he did, an accomplice sneaked up behind Bullock and hit him across the side of the head with something very hard and cold.

Bullock regained consciousness, sitting on a floor with a pillowcase over his head, his back against a wall, tied by his wrists to a small radiator. Deciding he was alone, he leaned against the radiator and worked the pillowcase up so he could get his teeth at the knots. Square knots and tightly made. Your bad guy never used grannies, depend on that. Under cover of the pillowcase, Bullock began to chew. The trick was to chew off small pieces and spit them out. Otherwise, warned the Mountie Academy escape-techniques instructor in his only joke for the course, you'll get bound up. Bullock chewed until he heard voices coming. Then he pretended he was still unconscious.

"Maybe I should've tied him in a chair, sir," said the Australian. "Handier for slapping him around to find out what he knows."

Another voice laughed. "We know exactly what he knows, Joey-Joey. He knows everything. He's gone through the box. He'd have to be a bloody fool not to put two and two together."

Bullock wondered if the man was talking about the same box.

"Then should I kill him, sir?"

"What's the hurry? After tomorrow, we'll be the law of the land and can execute any Teensy-Toes we want. Now go alert our security people. I'll keep an eye on Bullock here. Then you and I will go over to his place, get the box, and we'll be home free."

Joey-Joey left the room. His superior remained there, whistling tunelessly and turning the pages of a magazine until a telephone rang in another room and he went to answer it.

Bullock ripped the shredded rope apart and tore off the pillowcase. He paused to get the lay of the land. He was in a small anteroom furnished with wooden armchairs and a coffee table strewn with issues of *Mega-Savate* magazine, whatever that was. Through a partially opened door, he saw the man in the Maple Leafs cap standing behind a desk shouting into the phone.

Bullock dashed into the hall and down a wide staircase leading to the first floor. At the bottom, he didn't know which way to go. Then he heard the dogs barking again. He ran down the hallway toward the sound. He saw a door, turned the knob, and was out in the snow again under the gooseneck light fixture. A voice inside his head said, *Run like the wind, Bullock.*

⁕⁕

Bullock left his house with Connie's box, got into the waiting taxi, and drove to Mountie headquarters to see Inspector Marcel Nickerson of the Mountie Lunatic Fringe desk, who was Christmas duty officer that year. Bullock had a bit of a reputation as a teller of tall tales, and only Nickerson would give him a fair listen. Maybe the man could make some sense out of the contents of the box.

But as luck would have it, the inspector was over at the Ice Palace. CSIS, the Canadian Special Intelligence Service, suspected a glass bomb filled with transparent explosives had been placed somewhere among the blocks of ice. (As a cynical Talking Head on CBC-TV had recently remarked, "George Orwell had Big Brother. Canada's got Big CSIS.") Nickerson wasn't expected back for an hour.

Something told Bullock Canada was in danger. But he wished he had a better handle on it than that. To get his thoughts together before he saw Nickerson, Bullock went across the street to the coffee shop. He sat at the counter with the box on the stool next to him. Waiting for his coffee, he flipped absently through the selections in the little jukebox menu at his place. There was "Oh My Darling Clementine" again. And hey, look at this, played by the band of the Queen's Own Sledded Foot! Cocking a thoughtful eyebrow, Bullock dug out the *Maid of the Mist* clipping. Yes, it was the same band that vanished with the senior civil servants. Maybe that fine old military unit would have a few of the missing pieces to help him put the puzzle together. Bullock paid for his coffee and took up the box. The regimental association's headquarters was not far away.

Pleased with himself, Bullock mounted the steps to the building two at a time and rang the doorbell. As he did, dogs began to bark. "G'die again, mate," said Joey-Joey, opening the door and grabbing Bullock by both lapels. The next thing Bullock knew, the man's damned accomplice sneaked up from behind and clubbed him alongside the head again.

When Bullock came to, he was tied securely to a wooden armchair, his legs to its front legs, his arms to its arms. And the pillowcase was back over his head. Been here, done this, got the T-shirt, he told himself. No, it wasn't the first time he'd been in this predicament.

"We've got man and box now, Joey-Joey," said the voice of the man in the Maple Leafs cap. "Tomorrow is Teensy-Toes Armageddon day."

"Yes, sir," said Joey-Joey.

The other voice changed to a gentle scolding tone. "And, hey, didn't I tell you to call me Abe?"

"I can't call you that, sir. You've never been abominable to me."

"Yes, abominable's a hard label, isn't it? Oh, I'll admit I can get a bit testy and don't suffer fools gladly. But if the Teensy-Toeses want abominable, I'll give it to them."

"And if anything goes wrong, sir, there's always Plan B," said Joey-Joey.

"I wish the hell there wasn't," growled Abe. "This is my country. Our kind were here first. Let the Teensy-Toeses go back where they came from. And good riddance. But come on, we've got a lot to do. We can leave him here. You sure know your knots. I'd like to see him get out of that."

When they were gone, Bullock quickly grabbed a large mouthful of pillowcase in his teeth and pulled down until it fell to the floor. Bullock had been tied to so many chairs he always entered the six-legged race, come Mountie field days. Racers were of two minds: the clumpers who held to slow-but-sure and chugged around the oval and through the obstacle course in small jumps, and the pivoters who sprinted ahead first on one front leg and then on the other. Then in the back stretch came the great equalizer: Dead Man's Corner, a breakneck flight of wooden steps down to a sand pit beyond which stood the finish line.

Bullock needed a quick start. He sprint-pivoted out of the room and down the empty hallway toward the back stairs. When he reached the staircase, he swallowed hard. Half-way down was a landing and another flight of stairs. Landings were hell, with a bounce that was anybody's guess. Bullock heard someone shouting behind him. He thought of Canada, good old Mavis, and his friend Connie. Then he pitched himself forward, reaching the bottom dazed and in a jumble of loose rope, kindling, and aching bones. He staggered to his feet. This time he knew which way to run.

Bullock found Inspector Nickerson standing in front of the Ice Palace, waiting for the men of the bomb squad to finish their search. Starting at the very beginning, Bullock told Nickerson about his friend Connie Constable's ideas concerning the Bigfoot and about Connie's death in a freak accident. He described the contents of Connie's box all the way down to the strange six-foot tubes of Civil Servant Beige carpet. He told of the face in his window and his two escapes from the headquarters of the Queen's Own Sledded Foot regimental association.

Inspector Nickerson's expression changed from puzzlement to alarm and finally, when Bullock had finished his story, to a kind of relief. "My God, man," he said admiringly, "you've explained it all—all the strange stories crossing my desk at Lunatic Fringe, little things that I've been catching a glimpse of out of the corner of my eye in the halls on Parliament Hill. And what about that funny walk the new crop of senior civil servants have? I was afraid I was losing my mind. But you've made sense out of it all. We have to nip this vast conspiracy in the bud."

Nickerson began pacing up and down, struggling to formulate the correct plan, shaking his head of this one and rejecting that out of hand. Once he stopped and said, "Of course, we'll have to swear everyone to secrecy." Then he went back to his pacing.

Bullock waited there on the ice, his feet getting colder by the minute. Finally he said, "Sir, if you don't have anything more for me here, I'll head home. Maybe I'll see you tomorrow at the curling after I drop my wife off at the Debutantes' Ball."

Nickerson looked at him vaguely, deep in thought. Then he blinked. "The Debutantes' Ball? The curling? Brilliant, Bullock, you sly fox! Brilliant! Yes, indeed, you most certainly will see me tomorrow night."

Bullock escorted Mavis as far as the red-carpeted steps of the Ice Palace. Then he hurried off to the floodlit curling rinks. Inspector Nickerson had wrangled him the best seat in the house on the Stout-Hearted Men's horse-drawn sleigh parked at the edge of the canal next to the six sleek RCMP Zamboni ice-cleaning machines. The ice was decorated with roses, fleurs-de-lis, thistles, and maple leaves disappearing off into the distance, for it is, Bullock knew, in the nature of stencillers to go too far.

The members of parliament stood in the middle of the canal with their curling stones, waiting for the contest to begin. Now here they came, the I Trampoli band—in lofty, stilted magnificence in their long green, red, and white striped trousers—their kettledrums setting a rapid pace. They formed up next to the Stout-Hearted Men to open the ceremony by playing "O Canada" in the quick winter version before their spit-valves froze up. But after a long drum-roll introduction, the band struck up "Oh My Darling Clementine" instead. Surprised, the Stout-Hearted Men switched to that popular favourite without missing a beat.

At the end of the song, the Queen's Own Sledded Foot emerged from the darkness of the upper canal, coming in single file for their demonstration of precision dogsledding. The regiment began by making a large, fast-moving circle around the curling teams, each soldier grace itself and one with his sled. Now the circle tightened and tightened again until the Prime Minister and the others had to crowd together to protect their toes from the sled runners. The spectators laughed at this bit of good-natured high jinks.

Suddenly, the colonel of the regiment reached out and grabbed the Prime Minister and threw him across his sled. Simultaneously, the other members of the regiment scooped up the cabinet and the loyal opposition. Then the Queen's Own Sledded Foot sped off in single file back into the darkness from which they'd come, the pitiful shouts and cries of the parliamentary leadership vanishing with them. Bullock stood dumbfounded on the sleigh.

The second pillar on which the Dominion stood had just been kicked out from under it before his very eyes.

Suddenly, the Stout-Hearted Men were cheering. From the direction of the Ice Palace came Canada's gilded sleigh of state carrying the Governor General (God bless her), with Inspector Nickerson at the reins. On the bench beside him was a debutante with a black eye and the cap of a Mountie of the female persuasion. Inside, Bullock could see Her Excellency with three other debutantes in Mountie caps, holding service revolvers to her head. By Godfrey, had the world gone mad?

Bullock jumped down and ran over to the sleigh of state as it came to a halt. The Governor General called to him. "You there, Mountie," she commanded, "arrest these people. They want to depose me because I am part American Indian and part Asian Indian."

Nickerson was at Bullock's side. "Here's the final piece of our puzzle," he said. "I checked it out. Her Excellency here was born Omaha Darjeeling Clementine Snow. She's the daughter of Colonel Abe Snow of the Queen's Own Sledded Foot."

The Governor General leaned out the carriage window and shouted up at the I Trampoli, "Bandsmen, defend your queen!"

The stilted musicians dropped their instruments to draw their weapons. But suddenly, with a roar of machinery, the Mountie Academy cadets, armed with chainsaws, stepped from the darkness and surrounded the band. Meanwhile, the Zambonis had moved into position behind the sleigh of state, blocking the canal.

Now in the distance came another roar of engines, which Bullock recognized at once: snowmobiles—stinkpots as he called them contemptuously in his own dogsledding days. The sound grew louder. Now the Queen's Own Sledded Foot reappeared in unmilitary confusion, milling about the sleigh of state, prevented by the Zambonis from going any farther. Behind them came the snowmobiles of the Mountie crack machine gun unit, closing the trap.

Inspector Nickerson approached Colonel Snow's sled and pointed back at the man's daughter, the Governor General, with guns to her head. Bullock could not hear what he said or what Snow said back. But after a moment, Snow tipped the Prime Minister off his sled and held up his hands. His men and the I Trampoli band followed suit. The Stout-Hearted Men disarmed the band and the dogsled regiment. Then the Mountie snowmobiles escorted the Queen's Own Sledded Foot away, dogs and all.

That Christmas Eve out there on the Rideau ice, the Prime Minister signed the document to implement the War Measures Act. Later that night, Mounties raided Snow's regimental association headquarters, confiscating a list of its friends and sympathizers.

On Christmas Day all across the country, Mounties and provincial policemen were knocking on doors. By Boxing Day, crowded RCAF transport helicopters were converging on Salt Springs, Saskatchewan. Nearby, in the heart of Cavern Canyon, a broad mineshaft led southward, an eerie tunnel where hot springs and winter cold combined to create a thick, grey, waist-high fog.

Every ten feet, a Mountie stood at attention beneath a dim light bulb caged in the ceiling. Bullock had been given the place of honour beside the broad yellow stripe on the wall marking the border between Canada and the United States. Yes, the Cavern Canyon mineshaft had figured in Colonel Snow's Plan B. If the attempt to kidnap the parliamentary leadership failed, he and his followers would use the mine to escape to the United States.

And here they came, striding four abreast through the fog: Snow and his regiment, all dressed in civilian clothes and straight as ramrods, marching with the distance of a dogsled between each rank. Bullock couldn't see through the dense fog, but he thought perhaps they had been provided handcarts to carry their possessions.

Snow's face was impassive, his stride military. But as he came to the stripe, Bullock saw the man's chin tremble and tears start down his cheeks. Then he threw back his shoulders and, as he had sworn to do, led his men past the stripe and into snowy Montana.

The I Trampoli, all cut down to size and no doubt pushing their musical instruments on handcarts, followed after them. Friends, sympathizers, and senior civil servants came next, all spaced for handcarts, too. The stripe on the wall had a sobering effect. Even the CBC-TV's Talking Heads shut up when they saw it.

As Joey-Joey passed, bringing up the rear, he offered a menacing "G'bye mate," making the Mountie start and look around for the man's club-wielding accomplice.

When the cavalcade had disappeared southward, the demolition people came and wired everything up and cleared the mineshaft. Someone cried,

"Fire in the hole!" and depressed the plunger. With a large explosion, the Cavern Canyon mineshaft vanished from the face of the earth.

Only then did a sealed step-van carry the Governor General and her ladies-in-waiting across over the Peace Bridge to Niagara Falls, New York. The newspapers would later report she had resigned her position to move to the United States, just as they would tell the tragic story of the Queen's Own Sledded Foot perishing to a man on winter manoeuvres when unseasonably thin ice, no doubt due to global warming, gave way beneath their sleds.

Later, Bullock heard about the Debutantes' Ball from good old Mavis. At the end of "Oh My Darling Clementine," the Governor-General interrupted the proceedings to read a proclamation from the red-carpeted dais. But before she could speak, four debutantes pulled Mountie caps and pistols from their bodices and shouted she was under arrest. The Governor-General's ladies-in-waiting rushed forward to her defence, and there was a scuffle that ended only when Inspector Nickerson came up from behind and put a pistol to the Governor-General's head. Mavis swore she saw a lady-in-waiting grab a Mountie debutante by the front of her dress, and then, all of a sudden, a six-foot length of red carpeting rose up and whacked the Mountie alongside her head.

Bullock chuckled with warm condescension. Et tu, Mavis? he asked himself. But he couldn't really blame her. Since Christmas Eve, Bigfoot stories had been coming thick and fast. Poor old Connie would have loved it. At first, Bullock butted in when the young Mounties in the locker room started in on the Bigfoot. "Come to your senses, men," he would snort. "Are you telling me the Queen's Own Sledded Foot didn't have sleds, just runners on their immense feet?" Or he'd scoff and ask, "Are you saying the I Trampoli band weren't on stilts but were Bigfoot walking around on tippy-toe?"

But after he laughed to scorn someone's suggestion that the new regulation requiring all visitors to Canada to place their shoes in trays of disinfectant had nothing to do with preventing the spread of hoof-and-mouth disease but was meant to keep the Bigfoot from getting back into the country, he noticed the young Mounties were starting to drift away when they saw him coming. So Bullock stopped mocking their Bigfoot stories. He didn't want to alienate them. He knew it was important they felt free to come to him for advice whenever they wanted.

Bullock's only regret was not investing in Saskatoon Carpet and Sleeve, which had just won contracts to carpet the Mother of All Malls in New Jersey, several state legislatures, and the very Senate of the United States. Yes, Saskatoon's carpet looms were humming, and the quick fingers of Canada's youth were plucking their way to prosperity.

There was talk of the Mounties getting back into sled work to fill the northern void the Queen's Own Sledded Foot had left behind. Bullock thought of volunteering, but when he tried to float the idea by good old Mavis, she described in graphic detail exactly how thick hell would have to freeze over before she'd return to the far north.

Bullock never brought the subject up again. But sometimes at night when he turned in for some well-deserved sleep, he would close his eyes and let Little Trotty Tugwell pull him into the land of dreams.

James Powell was born in Toronto, Ontario, in 1932. He has published more than 120 short stories. The readers of Ellery Queen Mystery Magazine *voted his "A Dirge for Clowntown" their favourite story of 1989. His story collection,* A Murder Coming, *was published in Canada in 1990. In 1992, he was a co-recipient of the Crime Writers of Canada's Derrick Murdoch Award "for making a long Canadian story short." In 2003, he won the Arthur Ellis Award for Best Short Story for "Bottom Walker." In 2006, the Scene of the Crime Mystery Festival (held annually on Wolfe Island, Ontario) presented him with their lifetime achievement Grant Allen Award. A Canadian citizen, Powell lives in Marietta, Pennsylvania, with his American wife.*

About the Editor

Caro Soles is the founder of Bloody Words, Canada's biggest annual mystery convention. Her work has been published in many anthologies and gay magazines. Her latest mystery, *Drag Queen in the Court of Death,* appeared in 2007, as did the SF espionage thriller staring the dancing hermaphrodites of Merculian, *The Danger Dance.* She has also published *The Tangled Boy* (mystery) and *The Abulon Dance* (science fiction) as well as two short story collections , six novels and four anthologies under a nom de plume. In 2002 Caro received the CWC's Derrick Murdoch Award for contribution to the mystery community. Caro teaches writing at George Brown College in Toronto and spends a lot of quality time with her dachshunds Archie VanBuran III and Princess Ruby.

Printed in the United States
208303BV00002B/241/A

3   1119   01141   7392

9 780968 677674